'Til GRITS DO US Part

Jennifer Rogers Spinola

BARBOUR
PUBLISHING

Print ISBN 978-1-61626-366-9

eBook Editions:
Adobe Digital Edition (.epub) 978-1-62029-558-8
Kindle and MobiPocket Edition (.prc) 978-1-62029-557-1

Published by Barbour Publishing, Inc., P.O. Box 719, Uhrichsville, Ohio 44683, www.barbourbooks.com

Our mission is to publish and distribute inspirational products offering exceptional value and biblical encouragement to the masses.

 Member of the
Evangelical Christian
Publishers Association

Printed in the United States of America.

Dedication

To Lessa Goens, AKA "Grace": a cousin, friend, and partner in fun.
Most of this book is yours. You're the best pal a girl could have!

Acknowledgments

It's a bit of a mystery how a book is written. One holds the contract, but a hundred others rightfully deserve their names on the cover.

For starters, none of this would have been possible without the help and encouragement of Roger and Kathleen Bruner, who read my earliest work and taught me about publishing. Roger, congratulations on your awards, and thanks for this amazing journey. I never could have done it without you.

Lessa, you gave the initial idea with your legal background and spent countless hours (probably hundreds!) on the phone with me going over details. Thank you for your patience and perseverance!

To my critique group—the "Yay-Sayers"—you have been incredible. Thanks so much to Jennifer Fromke, Christy Truitt, Shelly Dippel, and Karen Schravemade. Your spur-of-the-moment solutions and ideas held this book together. I owe you everything.

To the Barbour team, especially Rebecca Germany, April Frazier, and Laura Young, you are wonderful! Thanks for making this book—and all the others—possible. I am so grateful for the opportunity to work with you.

To all of those who gave me grace and patience through the last crazy months of writing and editing—like Lila Donato, my husband, Athos, and my son, Ethan—thank you! I can hardly believe it's done.

Thank you, Lord, for making one of my life's greatest dreams come true!

Chapter 1

Are you crazy?" I put my hands on the seat back of the pickup truck and swiveled my head from Tim to his wife Becky. "I'm not doing this, whatever it is!"

Tim's white Chevy lurched across a gravel driveway that bordered a dark field, and he cut the lights. Tim shifted into NEUTRAL and glided us to a smooth stop right in front of the pasture fence. A ridiculous grin crinkled his eyes in the rearview mirror.

"Why not? It's loads a fun!" Becky poked her blond head around to see me in the backseat, where Tim's camping stuff and fishing poles poked me in the knees. At least hunting season had ended; tents and inflatable mattresses were a lot softer than his crossbows and ammo boxes.

Tim turned off the ignition, and the lilting mandolin plinks and tinny voice abruptly died in his tape player.

"Good. No more country music." I smirked to myself, peering out the window at a spread of shadowy grass. Christie, my German shepherd puppy, put two paws up on the glass and whacked her tail in my face.

"You crazy, woman? That ain't country music."

Oops. He heard me.

"That's bluegrass." Tim scowled.

"Country, bluegrass, whatever." I pushed Christie off my lap. "It's all the same to me."

Becky inhaled with an audible gasp, and Tim froze in his seat, hand still halfway to the ignition to grab his keys. "Oh no you don't." He turned around and raised a warning finger at me. "Don't touch the bluegrass. It's sacred."

He pressed a closed fist to his chest like I'd pained him. "Bluegrass is old-time fiddlin'. It's Gospel and longin' fer heaven and laments of Appalachia. It's pure soul poured out in strings, Shiloh. Don't ya ever forget it."

For Pete's sake. Tonight I wasn't in a mood for speeches about redneck music—especially when I had no idea what Tim and Becky had planned, and I had three unfinished news articles to finish on my laptop. I tried to move my legs, muscles still stiff from a five-miler before daybreak, and pulled a battered volume from under my thigh. I held it up to the dim overhead light as Becky tugged open her door.

"Shakespeare. You read Shakespeare." I tossed *Julius Caesar* on top of Tim's fishing tackle box. Which already groaned with Hank Williams and Brooks and Dunn tapes piled on top. Yes, tapes.

Tim put a finger to his lips and peeked over his shoulder at the darkened ribbon of road behind us then reached for his door handle. "Good stuff, that *Julius Caesar* book," he said, nodding in its direction. "That Mark Antony guy says it jest right in his funeral oration—lotta things about honor and power that's still true today. Y'oughtta read it, Shiloh. I'm sure Jerry'll lend it to ya when we're done."

"Jerry? The same Jerry who used to sign my paychecks with a pen he swiped from Taco Bell?"

"Don't sound so surprised! He's an extremely literary man. Yesiree." Tim shot me an indignant look. "People ain't always what ya think, Shiloh. Ol' Jer got me hooked on the classics. I'm jest itchin' to read *War 'n' Peace*." He waved at me. "C'mon, Yankee! Yer stallin'! Hurry up an' get out."

Hmmph. Literary my foot.

I shoved away a Styrofoam cooler and reached for the squeaky door handle, feeling a headache come on.

"Well, I doubt Jerry would be too keen on our little outing tonight. Especially when Tim keeps peeking over at the road like he's nervous." I crossed my arms. "I bet whatever we're doing's illegal, isn't it?"

"It ain't illegal. And Faye's farmer friend don't care." Tim scooted out his open door, shifting his toothpick to the other side of his mouth before leaning over to kiss Becky on the cheek. " 'You are my true and honorable wife,' " he said in his distinctive country twang. " 'As dear to me as are the ruddy drops that visit my sad heart.' "

"Great. Now you're quoting Shakespeare." I rubbed my forehead wearily with the heel of my hand. As if bluegrass wasn't bad enough.

Becky grabbed her jacket. "Aw, come on!" She reached back to punch my shoulder affectionately. "We do all kinds a fun stuff here in the South, and we're jest givin' ya a li'l peek at it. Seein' as how you're gonna be livin' here a while longer." She bobbed her eyebrows at me.

"Fun?" I reluctantly unclipped my seat belt and threw my black leather jacket to the side. "You call this fun?" I waved a hand at the dark fields.

"Well, sometimes we sit 'n' watch bugs sizzle on them blue lanterns. Or shoot tin cans out at the gun range, or birds 'n' stuff like that. Shucks, Shiloh!" Becky drawled out my name in her own distinctive way, which sounded more like *Shah-loh*. Two long, lazy, syllables. "We invented fun! Now hush and get outta the truck."

She hopped out and yanked my door open, letting Christie jump down with a clatter of toenails.

"Speakin' of fun," whispered Tim, shoving aside a camping tarp so I could swing my feet around and drop into the cool grass. Scents of damp cornfields and distant honeysuckle tickled my nose. "If yer gonna play hide-'n'-seek, don't hide in the bathroom! Why, one time I hid in the shower, and my big ol' two-hunnerd-pound uncle come in there, not knowin' a thing, and—"

"Stop!" I hollered, clawing for the truck door. "Take me home right now!"

They burst into guffaws and high-fived each other.

"Now shush, Yankee! You'll wake up the neighbors!" Tim clicked the truck locked and pushed me away from it. "And make sure that dog a yers don't run off. Here. Give 'er ta me." He clipped on the leash and pulled her away from a patch of orange daylilies.

"I'm not a total Yankee, you know," I muttered, crossing my arms. "I know how to say 'Staunton.' "

That ought to chalk up some points. After one year in this small Virginia town—pronounced STAN-ton by the locals, not STAWN-ton, thank you very much—I could even make biscuits and sweet tea. Not that I'd admit that publicly.

"Say 'bought.' " Becky put her hands on her hips.

"What?"

"Just say it."

I mumbled it under my breath.

"Told ya." She winked. "You still got that funny New York accent. But yer gittin' there, my friend. Maybe in another year or two you'll git ya some redneck blood and learn how ta talk like me!"

In my cranky state, I decided to keep my comments to myself. "So what are we doing, anyway? I'm busy." I tried to see my watch in the moonlight.

"Well, since you're one a us now, ya gotta act like one."

"If you think I'm going to start eating squirrels or something, forget it."

Becky cackled. "Wouldn't do ya more harm than that nasty raw-fish sushi you're always talkin' about. You eat grits, don't ya? Adam said so."

"Grits?" I screwed up my nose. "Gross. I ate grits once, okay? Because I had no food left in the house. And I didn't say I liked them."

"You will soon enough. Now git over here an' let me put this on ya so you can be formally initiated."

"Initiated into what?" I yelped.

"The South." Becky dug in her pocket and pulled out a bandana. "G'won! Close yer eyes."

And before I could dash off, she grabbed me by the arm while Tim tied the bandana around my eyes. Tight. I stumbled around and hollered, groping for the bed of the truck. Then I boosted myself up onto the bumper, stomach bent over the tailgate.

"Hey! Come back here!" Becky tried to pull me by the waist, but I wiggled free and plopped into the hard metal truck bed, rubbing my banged knees and elbows.

"Forget it! I'm not going." I wrestled with the knot at the back of my head, which had swallowed several tender strands of hair.

"You're really gonna stay in the truck?" Tim leaned over and peeled my blindfold off, his mustache and shaggy brown mullet grinning back at me from under his battered NASCAR cap. "With that killer on the loose? The one that knocked off that Amanda gal a few years back?"

"Cut it out!" I tried to smooth my hair back in place, suddenly feeling chilly in the night breeze that blew in from across the deserted fields. "You watch too much *CSI*. There's no way her killer could be back—if someone actually murdered her. It's been what, eleven years? Twelve?" I rubbed my arms. "Forget it. It's just a bunch of kids pulling pranks. Leaving notes. Silly stuff."

"Hey, you're the crime reporter." Tim shrugged, taking a few steps back as Christie pulled at the leash. "Not me."

"I'm not doing that story. It's a hoax anyway." I peeked over my shoulder at the desolate country road, winding into a blue-black distance, figuring the lunatics I knew were better than the ones I didn't.

Nobody did much in Staunton but smash mailboxes and spin tires, but Tim's stupid "killer-on-the-loose" business creeped me out.

"Fine. I'll do whatever you guys planned. But no blindfold. And you've got to tell me what we're doing."

"And then you'll come?" Becky put her hands on her hips.

I sighed and nodded. "So what is it?"

"Cow tipping."

—⚉—

Hands down, this topped the list of the most ridiculous things I'd ever done. The night glowed with moonlight, still and soft, and a velvet breeze swelled up from cornfields and pastures that teemed with the hum of crickets. We slipped across Faye's yard, past the grassy spot where we'd set up her wedding arch and decorated it with flowering redbud and dogwood branches, and up to the barbed-wire fence that separated her yard from her neighbor's cow pasture.

Whew! I could smell the cows already.

"Okay, now quiet, y'all," whispered Tim. "Grab yer dog while I hold the wire for ya."

He stuck one cowboy-booted leg on the barbed wire and pulled it open, leaving a space for us to squeeze through. Becky shimmied between the rusty strands with a practiced air, not catching her jean jacket on the barbs. (A *nice* jean jacket, thanks to me, the so-called Fashion Nazi who saved her from rumpled overalls and too-big NASCAR T-shirts). She gestured for me to follow.

Crickets chimed in low throbs across the darkened hills, and I thought of Amanda's case files sprawled across the mess of my desk. The way she'd supposedly vanished without a trace twelve years ago, from right here in town, and the recent rash of spray-painted messages and letters the police thought might be related to her.

Please. This was Staunton, Virginia, not New York. From the little I'd heard about the case, nobody could prove anything—including foul play. Amanda probably skipped town and moved to a place where rednecks didn't shoot the deer in the public park.

And if you asked me, the vandals were probably one of Tim's sixteen first cousins out on parole with spray paint and nothing to do.

"I'm a *crime* reporter!" I whispered as Becky helped Christie under the fence. "If we get caught cow tipping, what's everybody going to say?"

"Aw, quit being a baby! Nobody's gonna find out," fussed Becky, tugging on Christie's leash. "Who knows? If ya did get arrested, might

Jennifer Rogers Spinola

be Deputy Shane Pendergrass again an' ask ya out on another hot date. He sent ya roses a couple times, didn't he?"

"It wasn't a date! I've told you that a hundred times. And I'm engaged anyway." My silver ring glinted in the moonlight, stoneless. The best Adam could afford in our current financial famine, but good enough for me.

"So. . .where's that gorgeous child of yours? Who's got Macy?" I blurted, doing my friend Kyoko's famous split-second subject change on Becky. "You guys are supposed to be responsible parents now."

"Mama's keepin' her. She's awful hooked on that little gal." Becky shook a finger at me. "And if Macy'd come tonight, I guarantee she wouldn't whine half as much as you, an' not even a year old. Shucks, woman! You'd think you was scared of some li'l ol' cows or somethin'."

"I'm not scared! But this is just. . .just. . ." I threw my arms up. "I don't even see any cows!"

" 'Course not! They're over yonder. Now git!" Tim shoved the barbed wire open in frustration. "I ain't holdin' this all night!"

I sighed and rubbed my face. As long as nobody found out, maybe I could do this. Just this once.

I stuck one leg through the wire.

———

Tim's flashlight bobbed a weak beam along the ground. "Watch yer step!" he whispered as we hurried through the grass. "Ain't much fun washin' that stuff off yer shoes!"

"Exactly!" I minced carefully around a brown cow pile, wondering if Kyoko back in Japan had the right idea. I'd lived here too long, and I was turning half nuts like practically everybody else. What, was I supposed to start craving those pale, soupy grits Becky kept harping about or spit in a cup or something?

I fell in step nervously behind Becky, scrutinizing every suspicious spot.

"So how's yer weddin' plans comin'?"

"Huh?" I lurched to a stop just inches from a brown pile.

"Your weddin' plans! You are gettin' hitched in August, ain't ya? Or did ya call that one off, too?" She tittered.

"What do you mean, 'too'?" I scowled, slapping aside some ticklish weeds.

Becky tugged Christie away from something stinky. "Well, ain't this your second time to plan a weddin'?"

I froze in midstep, trying to wrap my mind around the fact that (1) Becky Donaldson was talking about my upcoming wedding while we ran through a cow pasture and (2) she'd brought up my ex-fiancé.

"That's it!" I turned and stomped back toward the truck. "I'm going home!"

"Aw, I'm just kiddin' ya." Becky grabbed my arm between laughs and pulled me back, Christie's leash wrapping around my legs and nearly knocking me over. "Don't be mad, Shiloh! Yer jest awful uptight lately." She put her arm around my shoulder and steered me around a muddy low spot. "I'm only tryin' to make ya laugh."

I untangled my left foot from the leash. "Well, talking about Carlos sure isn't the way to put me in a good mood."

Especially now that I'd found Adam. I twisted my ring back and forth on my left hand, missing him. He was working late tonight at UPS, and after that, helping take care of his older brother, Rick, a double amputee.

And even if he wasn't busy, I guarantee he wouldn't be tramping through cow pies. Although he did drive a pickup truck. And. . .he owned an alarming number of plaid shirts.

Maybe I should do more walking and less thinking.

"So what time is it now?" My eyes puffed, bloodshot, from two all-night story write-ups and a court hearing, taking Christie for her shots, plus wasting hours vacuuming and Pine-Sol-ing Mom's house for a prospective buyer who "decided to go in a different real-estate direction."

I'd like to show her another real-estate direction, all right. One right under the local train tracks.

"Time for you to start gettin' yer weddin' together, woman! Yer family comin'?"

"Family? You mean Dad and Ashley?" I made a face. "I don't think so. Dad wouldn't come if his life depended on it, and Ashley will be sure to come and make herself the star of the show. Bossing me around. No thanks."

"Aw, come on. You're invitin' 'em, ain't ya?"

"I don't know." I shrugged. "Why should I? They never change. Dad doesn't care one bit what I do now that he's got a new family. An apology for leaving me and Mom all those years ago? Fat chance. I know how he is."

Becky pursed her lips. "Well, ya never know. Might be like Jerry and all his highbrow books and surprise ya." She winked. "People ain't always what ya think. And life ain't neither."

"Right. And I'm Garth Brooks."

Becky tittered. "Well, how's the weddin' plannin' comin', anyhow?"

"Planning? You think I know anything about planning a wedding?"

"Tell me about it! When Tim asked me to marry him, my mama carried around a satchel full a magazine clippin's like I was Princess Diana or somethin'. It's all she could talk about right up to the honeymoon. Shucks, I didn't have to do a doggone thing 'cept sample cake an' try on weddin' gowns!"

I stumbled slightly, feeling my stomach contract as I reached down to rub my leg. "Well, it's not like I have a mom to help. So if I'm a little slow in the wedding department, you'll have to excuse me."

I didn't mean for my voice to turn bitter, but it did. Everywhere I looked I saw reminders of Mom's death—her gaping absence, like a hollow in a cow field filled with nothing but muddy water.

Becky clapped a hand over her mouth. "Aw, Shah-loh. I'm sorry. I didn't mean nothin'. But you ain't gotta worry—we'll he'p ya! Ya got what, two months or so left?"

"That sounds right. Adam starts classes in August, so we picked the fourth. No. The third. I forget." I rubbed my bleary eyes. "I've got it written down somewhere. Besides, it's not like we have money for a wedding anyway."

"What about your book you wrote? Ain't you gettin' some cash for that?"

"Enough to pay for Adam's first year of college, since he sold his business to pay my back taxes." I fingered my ring. "And that's all it'll pay for. It's a small publisher." I shrugged. "Who knows? Maybe I'll pick up some royalties when it goes to print at the end of the year, but not in time for August third."

"Well, you could always have your weddin' at the gun range. I reckon they'd let ya have it for free for the afternoon."

I tripped on a rock, laughing. A sound that felt good in my ears. "Right. And Jerry can play the banjo for the reception."

"Tim does fiddle. How 'bout it?"

We chuckled together a few minutes, and then I looked over at her, night wind blowing strands of pale hair across her face. "Do you think I can do this, Becky?"

"Do what? Git Jerry to play at your weddin'?"

"No! Live here in Staunton. Without family. Without. . .well, anything but you guys." I rubbed my arms, shivering not just because of the cold. "A city the size of a MoonPie. Nothing ever happens here."

"You crazy? You just said there's a killer on the loose!"

"I didn't say that. Tim did." I rolled my eyes. "I promise you, nothing big happens in Staunton. Nothing."

"What do ya mean nothin' happens? We go squirrel huntin' sometimes. That's pretty excitin'." Becky stifled a smile.

"Don't start." I glared. "The most that happens out where I live is people squealing their jacked-up trucks and that petty theft I had to write up a while back. People stealing lawn ornaments, Becky! There's no theater here. No subways. No. . .anything. Please don't be offended. It's just a lot different from Tokyo, where the city whirls all night long."

My fingers tightened in an almost palpable ache at the memory of steaming noodle shops and street crossings jammed with fashionable urbanites chirping into high-tech cell phones. Cities crisscrossed with whirring subways and sleek JR trains, all going somewhere. Pushing higher. Reaching into a future gleaming with concrete and glass— while I tromped through cow-bitten grass.

"Shoot, we got theater! Ol' Clive Clevenger gets drunker than a skunk every Friday night, shore as sunrise. We can git ya a front-row seat! Why, sometimes he shoots at ol' hubcaps, thinkin' they're space aliens."

I hopped an unexpected cow pie, righting myself with difficulty. "That's exactly what I'm talking about. It's just the same old boring life here, day after day. I've never lived in a small town like this, and all these memories of Mom. . . . Her town. Her house. Her car. Her. . ." I kicked a grass clump, unable to form the word *grave*. "I love Adam, but sometimes I think I'm crazy to stay here."

"Aw, you'd be crazy anywhere ya went, Yankee."

"Yeah. Maybe." I laughed, feeling an unexpected rush of affection at Becky's slightly bucktoothed smile. Her harebrained ideas. Even her silly nicknames, which should be offensive but somehow weren't.

"Well, anyways, family ain't just blood, Shah-loh. Macy proved that to us. We're your family now." She patted my shoulder. "Don't ya forget it."

Becky untwisted the leash as Christie wrapped around her leg and trotted away, bending her over sideways. "Doggone it, Christie! Quit pullin'! Your gonna. . ." She let out a shriek. "Hey! Hey! Git back here!"

She sprinted off, waving her arms. "She got loose, y'all! Tim! Help!"

"Don't let her go!" I hollered, taking off after them. "I told you this was a bad idea!"

"You outta train your dog better!" Becky flailed an arm at me.

"It's your fault! You gave her to me!"

"Christie, you ol' hound!" Tim lunged for her leash, and I watched in horror as the slippery soles of his cowboy boots slid on the grass, sending him careening between two cow pies like a skater on ice. He turned sideways, whooping, and missed them both—then leaped and tumbled after her leash with outstretched arms. Catching the loop between two fingers.

Just as she dashed off again, happily licking Tim's face.

Tim and Becky bounded after her, flashlight bobbing—leaving me in a dome of starlit darkness. And utterly alone.

I stood there for a moment, motionless, and then waited for the moonlight to illuminate slight dips, hills, and spades of silvery grass around my feet. A misty cloud bank had come up over the hills, damp and cool, and the sound of my own breath startled me. Weeds crunched softly under my tennis shoes. An owl hooted from the edge of the forest, a desolate sound. I took a few hesitant steps back, wondering if I could find my way back to the truck in the dark without soiling my shoes with cow manure.

Something snorted behind me, thumping the ground.

I spun around and found myself staring into the nostrils of the biggest cow I'd ever seen—close enough for a blast of its hot, stinky-sweet breath to puff my sideswept bangs off my forehead.

I screamed and leaped back, flinging my arms up. "Shoo! Get out of here!"

The cow jumped, rearing her head, and lurched a few steps backward on the grass, moonlight glimmering in her enormous eyes. She stood there staring, chewing her cud like a Tastee Freez waitress jawing watermelon bubble gum.

Then she inched forward with another snort and sniffed my hair. The audacity!

"Go on!" I squirmed away and hollered for Tim and Becky, but all I heard was Christie's distant barks.

Two more cows loped over, curious, and I put my hands on my hips, angry breath flaring. What was this, some kind of small-town circus? I needed to get home and finish my articles. Southern initiation bah-humbug. Becky could say all she wanted about fun in the South, but I drew the line at cud-scented cow breath.

Wait. Didn't Tim say cows slept at night? Maybe they were sleepwalking. I craned my neck to see their bulging eyes in the darkness.

I twisted around to see across the rest of the moonlit field, but no sign of Tim and Becky. Just cows. And a few more loping over, shadow-like, their hooves making a soft swishing sound in the grass.

Maybe I could just. . .touch one. Really fast. And see if it tipped over like Tim told me.

And then I could get my tail out of the cow pasture and reward myself back home with a hot bath and an even hotter cup of my favorite Japanese green tea.

I wiped sweaty palms on my jeans and inched forward.

"Shah-loh?" Becky called from across the pasture. "We got yer knothead dog. She ran after some ugly ol' possum. Shoulda seen him!"

"Shh!" I waved her away in a loud whisper, reaching out a trembling index finger. "You'll break my concentration."

"Shah-loh?"

I found cow fur and pushed, hiding my face with my free arm.

Nothing. The cow just stood there munching. I uncovered my face and blinked in surprise then pushed against her warm, fuzzy side with two hands.

Nope. She didn't budge.

I leaned against her with all my weight, grunting with the effort. "What's the matter with you?" I complained through gritted teeth. "Aren't you supposed to tip over?"

A flashbulb and a snicker startled me, and the cow jumped back with a snort. A low chorus of moos filtered up from the field, and my bovine friends grunted and stamped in irritation.

"Becky Donaldson? Tell me you didn't." I backed away, horrified, as Becky's shadowy figure held out something like a cell phone. "If a picture like that gets out, I'm sunk."

Silence.

"Becky?" I whirled around. "Where are you?"

"Shush!" she whispered fiercely, dropping down on the grass as dark clouds covered the moon, like a bad omen. "He'll see ya!"

"Who'll see me?"

"That big bull over there! He don't like no one messin' with his cows. I thought Ron had him penned up."

"What bull? I didn't see a bull."

As soon as I said it, I heard him. He gave a low, angry bellow, and suddenly the thud of heavy hooves pounded on the ground. Louder and louder, rising to a low thunder as the cows scattered in all directions.

"They're gonna stampede!" Becky screamed, jumping up and jerking me by the arm. "Ruuuuun!"

Chapter 2

Becky Donaldson!" I hollered, sprinting across the field so fast I knocked into Becky, nearly bumping her to the ground. "You're in so much trouble!"

"I don't care, so long as we get outta here alive!" Becky pushed me ahead, yelling for Tim to open the gate. "What on earth got into ya?"

I screamed and swerved around a cow pie, hearing a furious snort not far behind me—and a loud pounding of hooves. Dust rose up from the grass, making us cough.

"You're the one who told me they tip over!" I lunged for the gate as raindrops began to spatter, making the grass slick. I slipped and slid, muddying my jeans as I fell and scrambled back up. "It was your idea in the first place!"

"You gotta be kiddin'! Cow tippin' ain't nothin' but a joke." Becky gasped, out of breath. "We weren't really gonna let ya do it!"

"Are you crazy?" I whirled around, furious. "I can't see a thing! It's too dark!"

"Watch out!" Becky shoved me through the open gate and tried to shove it closed behind her. Tim hollered from the other side and then jumped away as the cows stormed right through the gate, snapping it in pieces like rotten cardboard. Two cows barreled past me at full speed, so fast my hair and clothes flapped. The ground shook, rumbled. Leaves rained down from the black walnut and sugar maple trees as dark shadows fled, en masse, through the trampled gate. Too many to count.

"They're everywhere!" Tim shouted, pulling Christie out of the way. "They're gonna make a big mess outta Faye's yard and ev'rything

17

else. Quick! Call Ron!"

"I can't find my cell phone!" Becky patted all her pockets. "It musta fell out."

"What?" I shrieked. "With *my* picture on it?"

"Great day in the mornin'. Here comes the bull." Becky grabbed me by the arm as the smell of rain wafted over the damp grass. "Quick! Git in the truck!"

Good thing I was a runner, or I wouldn't have made it.

Tim jerked up Christie and sprinted, throwing open the driver's side truck door. Becky sailed inside with Tim close on her heels, and I lunged for the back door handle. The moon's reflection in the glass shook as the bull charged, roaring.

"Good gravy! Git in the truck, Shah-loh!" Tim squawked, reaching out the open window. "He's gonna pound us all!"

"It's stuck again!" I tore at the metal handle, banging and yelling. "Let me in!"

Becky screamed. Christie barked, scratching at the glass. I clawed my way up into the bed of the truck in raw panic, gasping for breath, and pounded on the top of the cab. "Go! Go!"

Tim stepped on the gas and squealed out of the yard, making deep tracks in the dirt and throwing up clumps of grass. He careened into the street at top speed while I hung on to the cab for dear life, hugging it with filthy arms and legs. My jeans stained and one knee torn, and a shoelace hanging limp.

The truck sailed around the curve, past a cornfield, and down a side street lined with fragrant oaks, my hair flying out behind me as the rain picked up.

Just in time to see blue lights flash against the back glass.

"Not again," I moaned, my teeth rattling as Tim eased over to the side of the road, his tires bumping over gravel. I covered my head as rain spattered down, moistening the dusty asphalt. Wasn't it enough that somebody called the police on me last year for eavesdropping outside my own house?

Some small town this was. Nobody can catch the vandals spray painting Amanda Cummings's name and stuffing fake flowers in mailboxes, but law-abiding Shiloh P. Jacobs gets two visits from the cops.

At least he hadn't caught me driving on the left side of the road, an old tic I occasionally carried over from my Japan days.

The police car stopped behind Tim's truck, blinding me with his headlights and flashlight. I heard the squad car door squeak open and shut, and footsteps crunched across the gravel.

"Well, well, well." He shined his light on my face, revealing a blondish buzz cut on the other side of the rain-pricked light. "Shiloh P. Jacobs. We meet again. What on earth are you doin'?"

I raised my head, humiliated. "Ask Tim and Becky, okay? It's not my fault."

Light rain spattered down, turning my windblown hair into damp strings. I hugged myself, shivering.

Tim rolled down the window and stuck his head out, hastily turning down the bluegrass on the stereo, but Shane ignored him. "Naw. This is too good. Lemme guess." He shined his light on my dirty jeans and manure-stained tennis shoes, raindrops swiping through the beam. "Snipe hunting?"

"Cut it out."

Becky handed me my black leather jacket through the window, and I reached for it, slipping in the wet truck bed. I shrugged on my jacket and plopped down on the side of the truck, fuming.

"Fishin' outta the Gypsy Hill Park duck pond?" Shane winked and reached over the side of the truck to rub a smear of something—hopefully dirt—off my cheek with his thumb. "You can git fined for that, ya know."

I hate this town. I brushed Shane's hand away, squinting miserably as headlights from a passing Chevette swept over us in a slow swipe of brilliance. Some rubbernecker gawked out the window.

"Hold up." Shane pulled out his vibrating cell phone from his uniform shirt pocket and clicked through it, shielding it from the rain with his hand. "Is this you, Shiloh?" He jerked his head up, chewing on a toothpick. "Are you cow tippin'?"

"Is what me?" I swiped for his cell phone, furious.

"This pitcher! I jest got a pitcher from Becky." He leaned inside the cab and tipped his head toward her. "Beckers? You send me a pitcher of Shiloh here pushing over a cow?"

Oh please. No. NO.

My new cell phone—Adam's surprise gift to me after I'd borrowed his old one for more than a year—rested in my jeans pocket, and I reached for it with sweaty hands. "That's impossible. Becky dropped her phone back at Faye's."

I flipped it open and turned it on. New message from Becky

DONALDSON, read the text above the envelope icon. I clicked. And there I stood—in all my cow-tipping glory. Both hands pushing against her furry side.

"Becky!" I hollered, scrambling to my feet in the bed of the truck.

"One of them cows musta stepped on it!" she called from inside of the truck, her voice frantic. "I swear I don't have my phone on me. I dropped it back in the field somewhere. Ya think it sent yer pitcher to ev'rybody on my list?"

"Becky!" I bellowed again, barely noticing the rubbernecking Chevette pull over to the side of the road, engine still running.

Shane hooted, slapping his knee. "So that's what this is all about. Good one, Donaldson!" He reached up to the window and fist-bumped Tim's hand. "Jest tell her to stay down in the bed of the truck on a public road next time, ya hear?" He glanced up. "And git outta the rain. For pity's sake."

"Oh, I'll tell her. But it ain't like she'll listen anyhow." Tim stuck his head out the window and twisted around to grin at me. "Hey, Shane, ya got any idea how we can git Ron's cows back in the pen?" He waved Shane over to the window. "They sorta busted down the fence. Know where I can get a hay bale?"

"Yep. A hay bale will do it. Works every time." Shane pointed over a tree-lined ridge as the rain let up. "My brother-in-law's got a couple. Hold on. I'll see if he's home." And he picked up his cell phone, still snickering.

I was pacing back and forth in the bed of the truck, livid and fuming under my breath, when somebody jumped out of the parked Chevette and rushed up to the truck.

Ahem. *Meg West's* Chevette.

"Shiloh?" Meg, photographer at Staunton's *News Leader* newspaper where I worked, gawked up at me, shielding her eyes from the police lights. "Shiloh Jacobs? What on earth are you doing?" She wrinkled her freckled nose. "You're filthy!"

"I can explain." I put my hands up. "It's all a misunderstanding."

Meg raised an eyebrow and put her palms up. "You know what? I don't even want to know. But I've been paging you for forty-five minutes, and nada."

"What?" I yelped, patting the top of my mud-spattered jeans for my pager. "My pager's gone! It must have fallen off."

"Well, get in the car! What are you waiting for?" Meg tugged on my arm, her long hair tied back with an Indian-print headband. "I'm driving! We're late."

"Now? Like this?" I tugged on my dirty Japanese *kanji*-print T-shirt, horrified. "Look at me! I can't interview anybody looking like I crawled out of a sewer."

"Too bad. You're the only writer left. Kevin will have both of our heads if we're not there in ten minutes." She checked her cell phone. "Make that five minutes. Now hurry up!"

I really, really hate this town.

I gripped the dirty tailgate, searching for a foothold, while Shane guffawed over his shoulder at me.

Meg stood there strangely silent, clicking through her cell phone. "Shiloh?" she looked up.

I stepped over the tailgate and onto the bumper. "What?"

"I just got a picture from your friend Becky. Is that you with a. . .cow?"

Meg drove at the speed limit until Shane's squad car disappeared around a bend, and then she stepped on the gas—flattening me against the passenger's seat with both arms outstretched.

"I didn't know a Chevette could go seventy miles an hour," I chattered as she bumped over some bad paving. I tugged vainly at the passenger's seat belt, which hung limp and stained with something that stunk of herbs.

"Oh, it can go a lot faster than that." Meg swiped a peace sign dangling from her rearview mirror out of her way as she roared around a wet curve, tires squealing. "My boyfriend, Cooter, swears he's had it up to a hundred and twenty on some funky fuel mix he concocted." She glanced over. "Oh, and that seat belt doesn't work. Sorry."

A Dalai-Lama bobblehead grinned at me from her dusty dashboard, its head whapping back and forth.

"So what's the big deal about this story?" I hung onto the armrest as Meg punched the accelerator harder.

"The big deal?" Meg took one hand off the wheel to turn and shake a finger at me, and my stomach lurched. "Some drunk ran his SUV through a guy's bedroom window. It stopped about six inches over the guy's bed."

"Yikes." I winced.

"Nobody hurt."

"Huh?" I spun my head around. "How's that even possible?"

"I know, right?" Meg chuckled and jerked to a screeching stop at a STOP sign, turn signal clacking, and then squealed around the corner. Streetlights, some lit and some dark, glimmered like a broken necklace past quiet houses and porch lights. "We've gotta get there before the clean-up crews put everything back together, or I won't get a single good photo. And trust me, this one'll run front-page spread if I do it right."

The Chevette swept under a streetlight, and a giant turquoise ring sparkled on Meg's index finger. "But there's something even bigger about this story."

"What could be bigger than an SUV through somebody's bedroom?" I shook out my damp hair.

"Ray Floyd." She reached a patchouli-reeking arm in my face and fiddled with the dash. "Get it?"

"Who?" I tried again to click the seat belt into the lock as she swerved around a very dead squirrel. "Never heard of him."

"The guy who nearly got creamed by an SUV is Ray Floyd." Meg glanced over at me. "Ray Floyd, Jacobs! Doesn't his name ring a bell?"

"No!" I grabbed the bobblehead as it toppled sideways, sliding across the dash. "I have no idea who he is."

Meg lowered her voice to a mysterious near-whisper. "Amanda's former fiancé."

"Amanda? Amanda who?"

As soon as I said her name, a ripple of something eerie flashed through my stomach. "Amanda Cummings?" I asked, sticking the bobblehead back in its stand. "The girl who disappeared?"

"That's her." Meg slowed a bit as we came into city limits, her Chevette flashing past a darkened Food Lion and Dollar General— their signs still glowing blue and red into the night sky. Country music blasted from a pool hall next to a lighted Shell station, clogged with jacked-up pickup trucks in various states of mud splatters.

"Amanda's that woman who turned up missing twelve years ago, Shiloh." Meg jerked in the other lane around a slow-moving minivan. "Remember? 'You were my first'? That's what they found spray painted in red outside her old mailbox, in some weird loopy handwriting with funky *A*'s. Probably written by a lefty."

She jerked to a stop at a red light then looked both ways and ran it.

Ohhhh, God. . . . If a bull from Ron's pasture doesn't cream me tonight, an oncoming turkey truck might.

"Plus flowers and letters and a bunch of weird ranting gibberish." Meg waved an arm. "Whoever's doing this is nuts. I'm telling you."

"So. . .why is this a big deal?" I raised an eyebrow, trying to understand. "So what if Ray is Amanda's former fiancé? I guess he still lives here, right? From what I understand, they cleared his name years ago." I crossed my arms stubbornly. "But I'm not doing this story anyway. I've already told you that."

"You might not do the story, but you've gotta know why it's so important." Meg slowed again and turned down a rain-shiny side street near Gypsy Hill Park. "I've got a hunch Amanda's killer really might be back."

"What? Come on." I made a face. "That's what they said when this same stuff happened five years ago, and nothing came of it."

"Oh, it's way bigger this time." Meg glanced up at me. "And this time he's after Ray."

She craned her head in the dim streetlights to read house numbers, checking them with the directions she'd scrawled on the back of a napkin from Thai Diner in Charlottesville.

"You're not making sense, Meg. Nobody left Ray flowers or letters or spray painted his mailbox." I leaned sideways to see past a long crack in Meg's windshield. The crash site must not have been far because caution cones and flares already lined the street. Floodlights glimmered up ahead, and I glimpsed two red fire trucks through the spreading oak trees. "Spell out your theory for me."

"First, somebody who might be Amanda's killer seems to be resurfacing, leaving all those creepy messages and threats related to her. And then somebody narrowly misses flattening her former fiancé by six inches and a piece of wallboard. What if somebody actually meant to kill him?" Meg looked over at me, a glow of police lights illuminating her pert, turned-up nose.

She pressed on the brake, slowing as another police car zipped past us toward the fray. "I dunno, but it makes sense to me. And it makes me wonder something else."

"Wonder what?" I untangled the lifeless seat belt and stuffed it behind the passenger's seat, feeling my hands grow cold despite myself.

Meg jerked the car over to the side of the road and threw it in Park. "Who's next?"

Chapter 3

"So, do you dig my theory?" Meg shook whatever so-called herbal brew she'd concocted, tipping her stinky mug dangerously close to my cubicle desk. Even under the glow of fluorescent lights in *The News Leader* office, she looked exactly the same as she did last night—down to her spacy expression and the same old stinky sweater with the hole under the arm.

I, on the other hand, had wasted an hour and a half of precious sleep time scrubbing manure off my tennis shoes and showering several times with antibacterial soap. And then ironing my best silk pantsuit that the dry cleaners had left, wrinkled, in a Kroger's paper bag with my name scrawled on the side in pen.

If the Japanese laundry tag didn't stump them, the kimono-style top with cute side-tied bows probably did. Because they looked like a bunch of Boy Scout knots when I opened the bag.

Note to self: buy one of those at-home dry-cleaning kits.

"It's an interesting theory, Meg, but I don't know if somebody's really trying to knock off Ray Floyd." I stuck *The News Leader* labels on press packets while we talked. "That drunk seemed like a pretty random guy. He didn't even know his name—much less whose house he hit." I pressed on a label and smoothed it with my palm. "I guess I'll see what the intern does with my interview notes when he writes up the Amanda bit."

"Right. As if you can actually get Matt to do work."

"Tell me about it. His idea of work is rearranging his Facebook icons and making up excuses for why he can't help me." If Kevin ever decided to hire Matt Tellerman full-time, so help me, I'd make his life a living nightmare.

"Well, anyway, I have a hunch this Amanda thing is gonna be big." She nodded toward the blue folder on my desk labeled *Amanda Angela Cummings*. "If I were you, I'd go through that folder and start calling people."

"I've looked at it. Thanks. But I don't want that story."

"Chicken."

"If I have time between trying on wedding dresses and showing my house, I'll think about it. I'm getting married in August, remember?" I shook my index finger at her, a label waving from the end of it. "Which doesn't give me time to chase dead-end stories like this one."

"I'll say. Why don't you just elope?"

"Don't think I haven't considered it." I slapped the label on the envelope then rolled up my sleeve and twisted around to see my elbow, swollen with two red dots. "You know what's really bothering me now? These horrible bug bites." I scratched at them in frustration. "I must have gotten them last night."

"Chiggers." Meg nodded firmly. "They'll getcha every time. And if you were really out there tipping cows, I bet you're full of them."

"Shhh." I put my finger fiercely to my lips. "Keep quiet about the cow stuff, okay? So what did you call those bugs?"

"Chiggers. They love old logs and rotting wood. During the larval stage they burrow into human flesh and—"

"Ugh. Stop!" I clapped my hands over my ears. "Just tell me how to get rid of them."

"Bathe in bleach water." Meg sipped her tea as if she dispensed chigger advice every day. "That'll kill the critters. And it's about the only thing."

"Bleach? Like the kind we clean toilets with?"

"Yep. Welcome to the country."

I groaned, scratching at my elbow and another welt that had since risen on my knee.

"You better check for ticks, too, if you were really out in a cow pasture," Meg added. "They carry Lyme disease, you know."

"Let's talk about something else," I said, feeling crawly all over. "Today's my birthday. Did you know that? I'm going home early. And my next-door neighbor Stella made this amazing sushi cake and left it on my front porch. She—"

"Wait, wait, wait." Meg put her hands up. "You can't mean what you just said."

"About my birthday?"

"The sushi cake. Please tell me that's a figure of speech."

"Oh, that." I resisted the urge to scratch my bug bites and peeled off another label. "No, I mean coconut cake in the shape of a sushi roll, with a carved slice of watermelon for the raw fish. A green band around the whole thing and chopsticks on the side. You should have seen it."

"No thanks." Meg the Vegan looked suddenly pallid. "I'll stick with my tofu and bean sprouts."

I stuck the last label on the stack of envelopes and pushed them aside. "So do you have the proof sheet from last night?" I held out my hand. "I need to write the captions before I leave."

"The what?"

"The proof sheet. The photos from last night." I raised an eyebrow. "That's why you came over here. Remember?"

Meg looked blank then jerked a shiny page from under her arm and gave it to me with a sheepish look. "Oh, these. I forgot. Sorry."

Meg, Meg. I hid a smile. I sometimes wondered how she stayed employed, living as she did in a virtual utopia of "everybody's-happy-don't-rush-me." Which is why our editor Kevin kept a bottle of Maalox in his desk.

I studied Meg's sheet of photos: Ray Floyd's smashed wooden siding, neat boxwood hedges ripped in half, and the gaping hole crisscrossed with yellow police tape. Broken glass and uprooted clumps of sod. A shiny new Jeep Cherokee protruding from the mess of broken plaster and drywall, and the drunk driver being led away in handcuffs.

"That SUV stopped two feet over Ray's bed." Meg quit spinning my little Japanese lantern hanging in the corner of my cubicle and tilted the photo sheet toward the light. "Did you see the big piece of wallboard that could have skewered him like a bug?"

"Gross." I tried not to think of it. "He's a nice guy, you know? He gave me coffee, too—some of the best I've had in years." I perked up slightly, remembering steam curling up from the white porcelain mug. "A really good Colombian roast, if I were to guess."

I pulled my crisp navy-blue jacket tighter in the over-air-conditioned office. "What I wouldn't give for another cup of that right now."

"Coffee? He didn't give me coffee!"

"You don't sit in cushy chairs and do interviews."

"Right. I squat in broken hedges and get rained on while you drink coffee. Thanks for bringing that up, Jacobs." She rolled her eyes. Meg squinted at me a second as if trying to remember something. "What am I forgetting?"

"Something related to the crash story?"

"No. Something else."

I flung out my arms. "How am I supposed to know?"

I wondered if maybe Meg should get herself tested for ADD. When I needed her for a story, I usually had to hunt all over the building—eventually finding out that she'd gone across town to buy a new lens and come back instead with a mushroom farm.

"Oh, I remember. Hold on a second." Before I could comment, Meg had ducked around the corner to her cubicle. I heard shuffling, a drawer opening, and then she headed back to my desk. Her baggy, bell-bottom-style pants dragged on the carpet. "Happy birthday. I almost forgot."

She dropped a pile of brown carob chips and a plastic spider ring in my inbox.

"Don't," I said, separating the two and picturing cow patties. "If you put them together, that looks. . . Just don't."

"What? Carob's good for you. And it's not carcinogenic."

"You think dryer lint's carcinogenic."

Meg didn't answer, even to rib me back. She still stood there. Staring at something. I looked up and followed her eyes.

"That's Mom." I took the faded photo down off the cubicle wall and handed it to her. "Her high school graduation picture."

Meg froze. Mug at her lips. I saw her eyes slip down from Mom's picture to the blue Amanda Cummings folder splayed partially open on my desk—Amanda's high school senior picture sticking out, her wheat-colored hair glowing.

And Meg promptly choked on her tea, spattering it all over the carpet.

—⁂—

"Oh my word!" Meg fumbled for the tissue box, and I jumped up to help her sponge the mess. "I just. . .wow. They look alike. Your mom and...Amanda."

I kept my eyes down, mopping up chunky bits from the tea-soaked carpet. I sniffed. "What is this? Garlic?" I drew back, holding my squashed tissue a good distance away.

"Of course. I used like eleven or twelve cloves this time," she replied proudly. "I smash them with a spoon, add some ginger, and just enough alcohol to clean out the old ticker. Whatever's in the cabinet."

Her long strings of beads jingled as she bent over to wipe something off the back of my chair. "Once my maple syrup fermented, and it made some pretty good stuff. I mean, I didn't know maple syrup could ferment, Shiloh, but when I took the top off, *boof*! It hit the ceiling."

My hand holding the tissue halted partway to the trash can. "You mean you drink. . ." I dropped my voice to a horrified whisper. "At work? Are you crazy?"

Meg jiggled the grayish liquid. "What? I've got enough antioxidants in here to fertilize an entire cornfield. Want some? I never get sick."

Sickness sounded strangely welcome compared to whatever brew Meg had in that mug. I scooted back a few more inches and pointed to my Japanese teacup. "No thanks. I've got my antioxidants covered right here."

"Well, the next time you get the flu, don't come crying to me."

"Believe me, I won't." I shook the folder and photos to make sure they were tea-free. "Sorry." Meg sponged the side of her mug. "I just didn't expect. . . I mean, they look like sisters. I can see why you might not want this story, huh?"

"Yeah." I smoothed the corner of Mom's photo on the cubicle wall. "It's silly, but the resemblance is a little overwhelming."

"I don't blame you. They're not related, are they?" She held the two photos side by side.

"No way. Mom only had a younger brother—and died at age forty-nine. Amanda was what, twenty when she disappeared?"

"I think so. Maybe twenty-one."

"Besides, Amanda disappeared five years before Mom even moved here." I swiveled back and forth in my chair. "There's no correlation. Period."

"Does your mom have relatives around here? Cousins? Something?"

"Don't even." I put my hand on my hip. "No relative of mine has ever been south of the Mason-Dixon line. I'm descended from a bunch of drunk French trappers who got permanently stuck in New York."

"So your family tree forks." Meg snickered.

"In all directions. I'll never be a Southerner, no matter what Becky says."

Meg flipped open the top of the blue folder and thumbed through some pages. "What about Amanda then? Where's she from?"

"Deerfield, from what I read." I glanced uneasily at the folder. "There's not much else about her, and absolutely nothing in common with my mom. Amanda was a die-hard vegetarian though." I poked her. "You're not Amanda, are you?"

"You never know." Meg bobbed her eyebrows.

"She worked at a place in town called The Red Barn when she disappeared." I flipped a page in the folder. "Ever heard of it?"

"Nope."

Like I said. Nothing in common. Except our birthdays—Amanda's and mine. Both June twelfth. I tipped her bio sheet toward me, raising my eyebrows.

"So Amanda grew up in Deerfield," Meg repeated, tipping her head thoughtfully. "That little place south of. . ." She bent over my cubicle wall and hunted on the Augusta County map. "It's around here somewhere. Just a double-wide trailer or two away from Craigsville."

I stuck Amanda's bio sheet back in the folder and pushed it away. "That's the place."

"Do they have enough jacked-up trucks in Deerfield to constitute an actual town?"

"So says City Hall." My smirk faded, and I rubbed my arms as if cold. "Anyway, it just feels funny to do a story on a missing woman— who reminds me of another woman who. . . Well, you get it."

"Creepy." Meg's voice came out soft and mournful. "But you know, Shiloh, it's probably our eyes playing tricks on us. Look. Amanda's got glasses and too much eyeliner. Yikes." She leaned closer. "Blond hair, too. Maybe the look-alike thing is only our impression."

Meg cradled Mom's picture in her hands, not making a joke or snarky comment. "Ellen Jacobs," she read off the back. "She's really pretty, Shiloh. You look like her a little." She squinted at me. "Not a whole lot, but. . .something. I can't figure out what it is. Your hair color?"

"Not really. My hair's just plain dark brown, not reddish like hers." I ran a hand through my sleek just-below-the-shoulder cut, a little longer than I used to wear it back in Japan. "But our eyes look pretty similar."

Mine were multicolored hazel like Mom's, but brighter, with very clear bursts of green and gold. I never knew how to answer "eye color" on forms.

I looked down at the proof sheet in my lap. "And our eyes are the *only* thing we had in common. Exactly like in life."

"I'm really sorry to hear about her. . .uh. . .passing." Meg's voice fell surprisingly sober. "How long has it been now?"

The office congealed like ice, everyone moving in slow motion. A repetitive beep of the department phone. Secretary Chastity's preppy-sounding, "*News Leader?*" echoing through the office. The shuffle of the copier.

"A year." I dropped my stack of press kits in my outbox as if it didn't bother me. "To the month."

"Wow. Sorry."

I cleared my throat, fumbling for words. "I think Stella made my sushi birthday cake for that reason, too. To give me something good to remember instead. Her brother, Jerry, my old restaurant boss, put her up to it."

"That's really sweet."

"Yeah." I gazed at Mom's slight smile, as if she held a secret. In fact, she did. I'd just stumbled on it a few years late.

Meg pursed her lips as if unsure whether or not to continue. "Was she. . .sick?"

"Nope. Brain aneurysm. Virtually instant." I could still see myself standing there in my minimalist Tokyo apartment, phone in hand. The shock of unexpected news ringing in my ears.

My voice must have come out a bit snappish because Meg raised her hands and backed away. "Sorry. Didn't mean to upset you."

"Me? I'm not upset." My hands shook as I put Mom's photo back on my cubicle wall. "I mean, I never knew Mom when she was. . . normal. We didn't have a good past. We weren't even speaking when she died."

I reached for the mouse and opened up a new page on my computer to write the captions, trying to blot out memories of my seven-year-old self standing in front of the locked apartment door, begging Mom to open. Hoping she hadn't overdosed on her medication.

The way I'd stood in front of her casket, knowing it was too late to save her.

"But there are things I wish I could tell her." I hesitated, hand still on the mouse. "It would take too long to explain though."

Meg stayed quiet. "Karma," she finally said, playing with my spider ring. "Maybe you can."

"Can what?"

"Have another chance." She shook the ring for emphasis.

"As a spider?" I yelped.

Meg's mouth gaped in horror. "I didn't mean that." She dropped the ring. "I meant reincarnation. To tell her what you wish you could."

"Ha." I shook my head. "I heard enough about reincarnation from Mom's slew of gurus. And I believe a little differently now." I glanced up at the Bible verse I'd pegged on my cubicle wall, adorned with a simple cross. "No, a *lot* differently."

"Bible-thumper." Meg smirked and poked me in the shoulder blades, and it tickled. I laughed.

"Hippie." I tried to poke her back with my pen, but she moved faster. "And don't you dare spill any more of that stuff in your mug. My carpet will reek for months."

"I don't know why I put up with you, Jacobs." Meg sighed, making a pained face and gazing upward. "You're all right though, I guess. So long as you don't go offering me Gideon Bibles."

Pretty funny coming from Meg, née Mary Margaret—whose staunch Irish-Catholic parents intended her for the church.

I pretended to think about her Gideon Bible comment, tapping my chin. "I think I've got an extra one in my car."

Meg ignored me. "Or those horrible Japanese snacks you stash in your drawer. Jellyfish or something?"

"You mean my dried squid?" I pulled my drawer open. "I love that stuff! Kyoko just sent me a fresh bag."

"Keep that up and I'll take back all my compliments."

"One bite and you'd recant your vegan ways."

Meg snorted into her mug. "I doubt it. Offer some to Chastity though." I shuffled through my stack of press kits, chuckling. "I'd pay to see that."

"Chastity." I rolled my eyes. "That girl gets more flowers than the queen of the Rose Parade."

Meg dropped her voice to a smug whisper. "Too bad they're not from Amanda's killer. Then Chastity would be next." She snickered into her hand.

"Meg." I smacked her arm. "I don't like Chastity any more than you do, but I wouldn't wish her dead. Come on." I stacked my press kits up in a neat pile. "Or stalked either. Some crazy guy in New York stalked me for months when I was sixteen, convinced I was a Norse queen from his former life."

She studied me, sipping in silence. "You sure you're not?"

I rolled my eyes. "Anyway, Chastity's got to be better than that hateful old receptionist. Good riddance."

"Lee Ann?" Meg smiled. "Yep. She retired." She leaned her head close to my ear. "If you ask me, she whacked off Amanda. The old bat. Rumor has it she's hiding a boatload of secrets that most of us will probably never know."

"Right. She and Clarence Toyer, the mail guy," I whispered, peeking over my shoulder. "They'd make a good couple, wouldn't they?"

Meg smirked. "Maybe you're right, Jacobs." She checked her watch and drained the rest of her tea. "Well, anyway, so long as you don't start getting weird flowers and messages, or spray paint outside your house, I guess you're safe."

—— ⁓ ——

I smelled something. Something sweet and inexplicably familiar. I turned around in my chair, trying to follow the scent. The floral fragrance wafted through the newsroom, over the sharp scent of toner from the copier, the faint whiff of coffee, and Clarence's musty old cologne—so strong I turned my head in its direction.

I'd just turned back to my keyboard when Chastity nearly bowled me over, whirling around the corner with her arms full of roses. "Shiloh! You got flowers for your birthday. Check these out!"

"Flowers? For me?" My jaw dropped, speechless.

"Gorgeous, aren't they? From Rask." Chastity preened, fluffing the flowers. Normally I could smell her coming; nobody else at *The Leader* applied Chanel No. 5 like lipstick, approximately fifteen times a day. But I only caught the heavy perfume from the bouquet.

"Who's Rask?" I sucked in my breath in awe as she turned the full bouquet around.

"The florist." Chastity gave me a funny look, smoothing a strand of super-bleached-blond hair back into its smooth ponytail. "That downtown place on the corner that's been around forever. Don't you know it?"

"No. Why should I? I don't have money for flowers and neither does Adam. He must've saved up." A throb of tenderness flickered in my heart as I pictured Adam in his brown UPS uniform, hauling packages and loading trucks so I could pay my back taxes last March and keep Mom's house. *My* house, rather, as she'd designated it in her will—and as soon as it sold, the much-needed income would provide Adam and me a place of our own come August.

The very weight of the vase surprised me as I lifted it toward the desk—heavy not from glass, but cut and polished crystal, clear as a Blue Ridge Mountain stream.

"Wow." I stood back, temporarily breathless, to survey the load of intensely perfumed, deep red spirals. Each one perfect. Blooms so thick and full they nearly blotted out the green leaves, allowing a little lacy sprinkle of white baby's breath to shine through.

"Adam, what have you done?" I clapped a hand over my mouth. "They're beautiful!"

"They sure are." Chastity's voice dripped with envy. "And you don't even like cut flowers."

I tipped my head up from her dress-code-defying black stilettos to her cleavage-baring pink suit then quickly averted my eyes. I never knew exactly where to look when speaking to Chastity.

"Who said I don't like cut flowers?"

Chastity, whose outfits tended to cast some doubt on her name, rolled her eyes. She flicked one of my ferns, also from Adam. "You always have plants with. . .I don't know. . .roots and stuff. Why? What's wrong with cut flowers?"

"I like potted things, okay? They remind me of Adam's former business. That's where I met him, mulching trees and planting shrubs." I buried my nose in the fragrant roses. "And besides, cut flowers just die. What's the use in that?"

Chastity raised a slim eyebrow (which Meg had informed me was permanent makeup) and sniffed in disdain, as if I didn't deserve such an expensive arrangement. "You're just weird, Shiloh. I love roses. Lucky you. And there's a card."

I wanted to open it privately, but she just stood there, looming. "Aren't you going to read it?" she chided, hands on her hips. Even Clarence paused on his mail rounds, cart in hand, and waited.

I reluctantly opened the envelope. "*To my angel,*" Adam had typed in a crisp font, with matching red ink. "*My love and my joy. I can't wait to share my life with you only, no matter what.*"

"Hmm." Chastity flicked an eyebrow. "Not bad, I guess. Even if it is a little canned."

"Well, well, well. From Adam?" Meg appeared by the side of my cubicle with her trusty Cannon slung over her shoulder, interrupting the advice I'd like to have given Chastity about what she could do with her "canned" comment.

"Cool." Meg bobbed her head in admiration then bent down to see better. "Wait a sec. Is that real crystal?"

A party at my cubicle. Who'd believe it? Most of the time we avoided each other like a bad virus, hoping our editor, Kevin-the-Stickler Lopez, didn't catch us yakking and give us more work. But when the proverbial cat's away at a journalism conference, well. . . the mice stand around jabbering about who the cops picked up on Greenville Avenue or what Kristen Stewart wore to the Oscars.

Or flowers. Whatever it takes.

"I can't believe Adam sent me roses!" I played with the little ferny chartreuse things that matched my green tea. Crinkly, iridescent red paper. A fat satin ribbon pooled in a flourish of scarlet on my desk.

"Especially on a budget." Chastity's mouth turned up in a slight smile. "Aren't these a little expensive for Adam? He's got some kind of blue-collar job, doesn't he? Lawn mowing. . . ? I forgot." She wrinkled her nose.

"No." I spun around to face her, raising my voice a touch. "Not lawn mowing. And if he hadn't sold his business for me, he'd still be his own boss."

"He gave up a college scholarship, too, didn't he?" Meg tipped her head as if trying to remember. "For his amputee brother or something?"

"Well, I only let Jeff give me medium-red roses," breezed Chastity as if she hadn't heard us, examining a velvety bloom with perfect fingers. "He owns Furniture Gallery. Did I tell you that? He just bought a boat and a Jet Ski."

"Yeah. You've mentioned it." Meg wrinkled her brow in Chastity's direction and crossed her arms, making the hole in her sweater arm stretch.

"Oh, have I? Sorry." Chastity's lips curved into a sweet pink smile, obviously forgetting that her money talk had little effect on Meg, who'd lived out of a VW Bus for three years. "Well, anyway, I only accept roses that are lipstick red. Long-stemmed, and not too open. But these are cute, too, Shiloh. Enjoy. Even if they are hacked. Doomed. Whatever you call it."

Chastity patted me on the head like an ungrateful puppy. "Oh, and I loved the cow picture. Thank your friend Becky for me."

She retreated to her desk in a cloud of perfume.

Oh, please trip. Just once. I shot her a sour look, fiery color shooting up my neck. If I ever got my hands on Becky Donaldson and her dumb camera, so help me, I'd make her eat it for breakfast with her grits.

Meg watched Chastity go, obviously trying to suppress a smile. "Lipstick red, huh?" She flicked one of my blooms. "Good luck making lipstick out of this color."

"My friend Kyoko back in Japan would," I replied, sitting back down at my desk and trying to calm my temper. "She's into all this goth and punk-rock stuff. Or no, New Wave. Whatever she calls it. I don't know what she's talking about most of the time."

"Is she the one that sends you all those shrimp-seaweed rice cracker things?" Meg's brow peaked in worry. "And those dried. . . Don't say it. . ."

"Squid?"

"I told you not to say it."

"My offer still stands." I hovered my hand over the drawer. "Am I tempting you?"

"Not exactly." Meg scrunched her nose. "But listen, Shiloh." She tipped her head closer. "Don't let Chastity get to you. I think she's harmless. She's just. . .bored."

"Who wouldn't be in a town where kids get excused school absences for hunting?"

"I rest my case." Meg laughed. "She's bored. . .and, well, an idiot— to spare your newly sainted ears the appropriate word. Anyway. Enjoy your roses. And if the cow photo bothers you, just let me know. I can Photoshop it into a unicorn or something." She shouldered her camera and started off, raising her stinky mug in "cheers."

I liked Meg. In a weird way she even reminded me of Kyoko—but with a lot less angst. On the contrary. Meg was the type who'd fold a thousand (recycled) paper cranes according to the hope-filled Japanese tradition, and Kyoko would grind them all through a paper shredder with unnerving satisfaction.

Adam. I need to call Adam. I dialed his number from the desk phone, holding the receiver under my chin while I turned the vase around, curling the satin ribbon around my finger as he picked up.

"I got them! You can't imagine how special this is."

"Shiloh?" His familiar voice, touched with the faintest hint of Southern drawl, came across patchy from bad reception. "I can hardly hear you out here. Happy birthday!"

"Thanks, Adam. They're so beautiful." I gave a misty smile,

35

thinking of all the sacrifices Adam had made for me already. Knowing him, he'd probably gone without lunch who-knows-how-many-days just to save up. "I can't believe you sent me roses."

"Sorry?" Static crackled again. "Sent what?"

"The roses. I love them."

More static, and I pressed the phone closer to my ear. "Hello? Adam? Where in the world are you?"

"Verona. What did you say before that?"

"The roses. Chastity brought them over to my desk a few minutes ago."

Silence filled the line. "Roses? Sorry, Shiloh. I must not be hearing you right."

My fingers froze on the ribbon. "Didn't you send me roses?"

"Roses? No! Why, somebody gave you a bouquet?"

I jerked my hand off the flowers, whose perfume suddenly smelled sickly sweet in my nostrils. Something dreadful welling up in my stomach, squeezing the air out of my lungs.

"You didn't write this card?"

"What card? No. I'm sorry. I've got a potted arrangement for you at home. Since you like them better anyway." He paused. "By the way, Becky sent me some weird photo of you and a cow. Have you seen it?"

"Huh?" I reeled, scooting my chair back. Adam's words barely registered.

"So who's the bouquet from?"

I picked up the card again, feeling that sick feeling slither from my stomach to my throat.

"Shiloh?"

Chapter 4

can't believe this." I slumped in my chair—a gray Office Max special that squeaked when I turned to the left—and tipped my head back, not wanting to open my eyes and see the sparkling crystal vase. It gleamed like Carlos's perfect white teeth when he came from Japan last year, trying to find my house—and a free green card—in his rented Prius. *The snake.*

"Shiloh?" Adam's phone line snapped and popped. "I'm losing you. Do you know who sent them?"

"I've got a good guess." My eyes narrowed. "And I'll tell him to bug off."

"Who?" Adam's voice came loud in a sudden burst of clarity.

"Carlos, probably. The big bouquets are his style."

"Have you told him we're engaged?" Adam's voice heated slightly, and I heard the dying groan of the UPS truck engine. "I'm pulling over. Hold on."

"No, I haven't told him anything—because we haven't talked since he showed up here last year." *Showed up* is an understatement. Among other things, he'd tried to sweet-talk me into marrying him for a green card so he could jump-start his new modeling career on American runways.

I could see the headline: HOTSHOT MODEL USES BANKRUPT EX-FIANCÉE TO CATAPULT HIMSELF TO FASHION FAME. Personally, I had a lot more respect for Carlos when he was a rich, arrogant stockbroker.

I dug through my supple leather purse for my wallet and pulled out a glossy international calling card. "I'll call him right now."

"Good, because if you don't, I will. It's probably close to midnight in Tokyo, though, you know."

"Too bad for Carlos." I closed my purse. "So, I'll see you after work Friday then?"

"Looking forward to it." Adam paused, sounding not quite ready to hang up. "Listen, I'm so sorry I can't meet you tonight, Shiloh, on your birthday. I hate that you have to wait. But I'm a trainee, so I can't choose my own hours like I used to."

"Don't worry. Friday's fine." I winced, remembering when Adam had hired his own contractors and signed their paychecks. "We can meet at the park if it's not raining."

"Sounds great. I'll bring your flowers."

I leaned back in the chair, not quite ready to say good-bye either. "Okay. And thanks for the arrangement you bought me."

"Oh, I didn't buy this one. I made it. With some of my leftover bulbs and things. I hope you like it."

"I'll love it." My throat tightened a little as I thought of him there in his hulking delivery truck, hauling boxes instead of kneeling over green saplings, his fingers dirty with fragrant Virginia soil. "Do you miss being a landscaper, Adam?"

The line weighed silent a moment, and I heard a car whiz by Adam's truck. "A little," he said finally, the line crackling around the edges. "But not as much as I like being able to marry you."

I told Adam good-bye, put my head down on the cool desk, and scrunched my eyes closed. Because it was, after all, my fault he'd sold his business. My fault he now wore brown polyester and stacked packages instead of setting his own hours.

But now wasn't the time for sentiment. I had a dragon to vanquish. A dragon with a Spanish accent.

"Let's see what you've got to say, eh, Carlos?" I dialed and held the receiver a little away from my ear, as if his gorgeous Argentinian good looks and sultry voice might zap me into hypnosis even over the phone line. Not that he could pull me away from Adam. But Carlos's brilliant, beautiful smile reeled in women the way Tim reeled in trout—by the bucket load.

At least I'd managed to unhook myself from his line before it was too late.

The phone clicked as someone picked up. "Hi, Carlos?" I said.

"Hi?" demanded a female voice in a decidedly suspicious tone. "Who's calling?"

I ignored her challenge and raised my voice. "Could I speak to Carlos, please?"

Silence. "Hold on." And then again, defensive and demanding: "Who is this?"

"Look, should I call back later?" I tapped my pen. "I'm kind of busy here, and Carlos definitely needs to hear what I have to say. So please put him on the line."

I heard muted words, the staticky sound of the muffled receiver, and Carlos's angry voice came crisp and clear: *Moshi moshi?* Hello? Who's calling?"

"This is Shiloh." I tapped my fingers on the desk, trying to sort out my words. "Sorry to bother whatever you're. . .uh. . .doing." I smirked. "But we need to talk. Who's that, by the way? Mia Robinson again? Wow, so soon after coming here and flashing your ring at me. I should be surprised, but I'm not."

"Why are you calling me?" he growled. Not bothering to cap his sentence with the customary *amor*'s and *princesa*'s I knew so well from our brief engagement.

"Because I'm getting married in August. And if these flowers are from you, no thanks."

"Why would I send you flowers, Shiloh? You mean nothing to me."

The last words hit me with a punch I didn't expect, but I righted myself like a stumbling tango dancer, a thorny rose between my teeth. "That's not what you said a few months ago," I muttered, jabbing him with the stem. "But the feeling is mutual, Carlos." His words suddenly registered. "Wait—you didn't send me a bouquet?"

"Of course not. I have nothing to say to you."

"Right. After I refused to let you freeload off me. I know how you work." I kept my tone icy and detached. "Well, let's just say it's a good thing you didn't send these. Because whoever did is going to be in big trouble. And not just with me. *Comprendes?*"

I paused. "And don't you dare say a word about me and the stupid cow. Got it?"

And I hung up on the longest, most profound silence I'd ever heard from Carlos Torres Castro.

———

So Carlos hadn't sent them after all.

I stared at the offending roses a few minutes, thinking, the quiet office swirling around me. Then I reached for the phone book and paged through until I found Rask Florist.

"This is Brandy," said the woman who picked up. "Can I help ya?"

"I need to know who sent me this rose bouquet." I told her my name and information then turned the vase around, hunting for the card. "Did the card come typed already, or did someone at your store type it?"

"I don't know nothin', hon. Sorry."

"Nothing? You can't tell me anything at all?" I tapped my pen on my desk in frustration. "Don't you have any records? Receipts?"

"I reckon, but I don't know where they are. I'll leave a message for Tammy to call ya. She's the manager."

"When will she be in?"

"Uh. . .I dunno. This afternoon, maybe? Sorry."

I threw down my pen. For crying out loud. Even calling Carlos had been more profitable than Brandy at Rask. Sheesh.

I dropped the phone in its cradle and pushed my chair back then strode through the cubicles and plopped the vase on Chastity's desk. "There's a mistake. These must be for you. Jeff's always sending you flowers."

"What? These?" She looked up in surprise from her computer screen, which she'd plastered with photos of Jeff in heart-shaped frames. "No way. I never let Jeff get me roses this dark."

"But they're not from Adam."

Chastity squinted up at me. "Isn't your name on the card?"

"Yes, but nobody else would send me a love message like that. It's got to be a mistake." I shrugged. "Anyway, I can't keep them, Chastity. It's weird."

Chastity reached out a perfumed arm, adorned by a gold charm bracelet, and turned the arrangement around. "I only accept roses from one shop in town." Her nose turned up. "And it's not Rask."

I put my hands on my hips. "Well, don't you think Jeff might have. . .I don't know, gotten you something different?"

She turned frosty eyes to me like I'd suggested she wear Uncle Herb's overalls to work. "Something. . .different. No."

───※───

I dumped the roses on a side table, which was still littered with the remains of Priyasha the marketing woman's birthday cake, and tossed the card in the trash.

"To my angel. I can't wait to share my life with you only, no matter what."

The words stuck in my head like a bad '80s song: the singer's long, puffy hair shivering on the last note. Not that I'd say that to Kyoko, who glorified everything '80s. Especially if it came clad in black or pounding an angry British guitar.

It felt. . .weird. Just a little bit. I dug the note out of the trash and tossed it in my desk drawer—just to be safe.

The mail cart squeaked by, laden with FedEx packages, and I glanced up at Clarence. His frazzled white-and-gray head looked like he'd just stood in front of a high-speed fan and hair-sprayed the result.

"You're sure you don't know who sent the flowers, Clarence? You usually bring in the mail."

"Don't look at me. Chastity took the delivery. I swear I had nothin' to do with it." He grinned and stroked his grizzled chin with a wrinkled, ink-stained finger. "But I did get a pitcher of you on my cell phone with some cow. What were you trying to do, push it over? If so, you were doin' it all wrong."

I gripped my face in both hands.

"It's more in the arms and upper body. Less wrists." Clarence flexed his forearms. "And you need more leverage—like maybe brace your leg against a fence or something."

"Go!" I pushed Clarence's mail cart away before I did or said anything that got me fired. "Just go. I'm sorry I asked, okay?"

⁂

Clarence Toyer. I shut down my computer for the day and pushed open the exit door, wondering who on earth would ever hire a guy as weird as Clarence. He'd been at *The Leader* forever, so I heard, and spouted all these ridiculous conspiracy theories about Marilyn Monroe and the JFK shooting. He and his rumor-spreading ways creeped me out. As well as his rather robust appreciation of female beauty.

Lucky for me, Clarence had settled on my eyes. Singing songs about "Bette Davis Eyes" and quoting wacko poetry about "thine orbs of spring."

Perhaps that's why Japanese employees smoked so much—so they could get away from annoying coworkers like Clarence.

I clopped down the stairs in my trendy Manolo Blahnik heels—an old leftover from my days in high-fashion, urban Japan when I actually had money. Back before I got fired and ignominiously booted out of my cushy job at the Associated Press. I opened the door to the street, dodging splattery raindrops, and unlocked my (formerly Mom's) white

Honda and headed toward home. Out of the narrow city streets and into meandering country roads painted silver with rainy mist.

Mom had lived outside Staunton, in the rural reaches of a little hamlet of Churchville—a.k.a "the middle of nowhere," as Adam had labeled it once in a crude, hand-drawn map. Sapphire curves of the Blue Ridge Mountains appeared over the rain-wet pines, dusky with heavy-hanging sky.

And then I heard it: the telltale rev of the engine under the hood as I pressed the gas and my speed refused to budge. The distinctive burning odor of transmission fluid wafting from under the hood.

Great. Great. Great. I banged my head back against the spongy headrest, dreading another car-repair bill. Another chunk of my cash forked over forever, leaving me counting dimes and clipping more coupons. As a matter of fact, I hadn't even found a wedding dress yet! At this rate, for my wedding I'd wind up with tacky blue silk carnations from Wal-Mart and Twinkies on a paper plate.

Hold on a second. I pressed the heel of my hand to my forehead, trying to remember what the last repair guy had said about Mom's transmission. Something about it being pretty new and to hang on to the warranty.

Right. As if I should know where a late parent I hadn't seen in years had stored her transmission warranty.

The engine revved again as I turned down the rural country road toward home. I slowed my speed then gently pushed the accelerator until the revving stopped—careful not to tax the transmission. If I found Mom's warranty, maybe, just maybe, Adam wouldn't have to spend his last pennies replacing another car part of mine. Or hot-water heater. Or whatever he chipped in last to have fixed.

"Come on, house," I murmured under my breath, turning down the short, winding road that led to my little redneck subdivision of Crawford Manor. "Just sell. Please. And then we'll have all the money we need and then some."

I followed a dilapidated Chevy down the wet lane, turning left at an iconic green CRAWFORD DRIVE street sign. Trying hard not to gawk at the double-wide parked over in the lot to the right. A horse inside a gnarled pasture fence gnawed on something suspiciously like an old toilet plunger.

Small, blocky country homes built just like mine lined the puddled streets—each with a different colored vinyl or wooden siding in various stages of wear and tear. Wooden shutters. Satellite dishes. Screen doors and birdbaths and narrow front porches supported by decorative pillars.

I turned before my TITANIC FARM AND REAL ESTATE sign into Mom's neat gravel driveway, which thankfully sported nothing more than trimmed forsythia shrubs, tastefully arranged geraniums, frosty-green juniper bushes, and bright summer marigolds (thanks to Adam). An American flag fluttered from the front porch, and roses cascaded in a colorful froth from her flower beds. Brown country shutters. Fresh creamy-tan siding and brown-shingled roof.

And No. Country. Music.

Or bluegrass. Whatever Tim called it.

I parked and headed up the deck steps at the side of the house, pausing to touch a fistful of Mom's white blooms that poked through the wooden railing. Roses that should have reminded me of yesterday. Of redemption. Of all the changes in Mom's life, and in mine, blooming fresh and clean and astonishing.

But now they just made me think of the weird bouquet back at work.

"Christie?" I unlocked the door and poked my head into the laundry room, keys jingling over the sound of her happy barks.

She barreled into me, licking my face, as I struggled to keep my grip on my purse, keys, folders, and laptop case. Becky had thrust Christie at me in a cardboard box last fall—all glistening eyes and trembling whiskers and wet puppy nose—and sucker that I am, I took her in. And, yes, even named her after a NASCAR driver, per the current trend among my Staunton-ite friends.

Pets are a death knell for three things: (1) immaculate furniture, (2) spontaneous weekend getaways, and (3) selling real estate. But seeing as none of those ever happened to me anyway, I'd decided to take my chances with Christie.

I squatted there in my snazzy heels and work pants, laughing as Christie covered my arms and chin with kisses, practically knocking me onto the off-white linoleum on my back.

What could I say? After years of silent Japanese apartments, it felt nice to be missed.

"Come on, Christie." I nuzzled her head as I stood and brushed off my pants, stepping over my discarded running shoes. Then I slipped out of my heels and into soft Japanese house slippers. "Let's see if we can find that warranty in Mom's stuff and save us a couple of bucks."

First things first though. A hot cup of green tea. I dropped my purse and laptop on the table and reached for my black Japanese teapot, a carryover from my time as a college exchange student, homestay participant, and two glorious years as one of the top reporters at the Associated Press's Tokyo bureau. All of it gone now, lost in the rumble of jacked-up trucks.

I poured water and set the pot on the stove, preparing my bitter *matcha* green tea powder, spoon, and favorite teacup by rote. And then I shoofed my way into Mom's bedroom in my slippers, Christie at my heels.

"Oh, Mom," I sighed, pushing open her bedroom door and taking it all in: the simple wooden dresser and mirror that had been hers. Butter-yellow curtains and flowered bedspread. The closet that once held her pantsuits for work as a special-ed teacher at the Virginia School for the Deaf and Blind, and Indian-style blouses in wild colors for off days. The antique trunk at the foot of her bed that still cradled her secrets.

"Where would you keep your transmission warranty, Mom?" I spoke out loud, causing Christie to poke her head out from under the bed and smile at me, a stray clump of dust on her nose.

Yep. Dust. How many months since I'd vacuumed under that bed? Too many, obviously. Not surprising since almost all my spare time went to (1) work, (2) driving the long, winding roads to and from town, and (3) standing in line at Food Lion hoping I had enough cash to buy boxed macaroni and cheese.

And now here I sat, preparing to dig through journals and tax returns and students' papers all layered in Mom's trunk like archaeological strata. Cross sections showing the final years of her life—a life I'd brusquely ignored on my heady march up the corporate ladder. Without a backward glance or second thought.

And perhaps, too, in part to numb the pain of my long-ago past—bitter nights of beatings, loneliness, and hunger of the stomach as well as the soul.

I slipped to my knees and sorted through the stacks of papers and files, lifting off tax documents, income statements, and W-2 copies. Boring safety manuals from work. Social Security statements and school meeting notes. Everything crisp, professional, unemotional.

Christie poked a curious nose over the edge of the trunk as I piled more papers on the floor, trying not to soil my white, tailored dress shirt with newsprint and the grime of years. "Recipes," I said, dropping another handful of stuff. "And birthday cards. Lots of them."

None from me though. Not after Mom spoiled my growing-up years with her cult chasing, psychedelic tea drinking, and nervous breakdowns. Weeks in and out of mental asylums and leaving me— just a nervous, skinny slip of a kid—rooting through empty cabinets in search of crumbs.

I put the cards away and tried not to think of the terse phone conversations I'd had with Mom after I moved to Japan. The nervous tremor in her voice when she said, "I'm sorry," and the cold steel in my heart as I hung up the phone, telling her not to call.

The memories stung now, making a painful well in the hollow of my heart.

Especially when I reached into the trunk again and pulled out a thick stack of letters—stamped letters, postmarked and mail battered— bearing my various addresses. Cornell to Nara to Osaka to Tokyo. Tied with a blue ribbon into a tight brick.

And every single one of them stamped RETURN TO SENDER.

I opened one of the envelopes, mailed a few months before Mom's death, and held the letter a little away from my body as if to buffer myself against the pain. Circling Christie with my arm. And I skimmed the lines with pinched breath, afraid of what I might read.

Her tomatoes were growing. . .roses blooming. . .

That. . .that's it? I snatched the paper closer in surprise. No more sob stories? No guilt trips?

Stella's blue-ribbon lemon pie at the county fair. . .a bald guy. . . somebody's broken wrist in a cast. . .a blind student who got a job as a computer programmer. . .

I released my breath in relief at such innocuous topics. Perhaps I was wrong. Perhaps Mom's desperate attempts at reuniting were a thing of the past, and by the time she'd mailed me this letter, she'd accepted our differences—our unreconciled lives—and moved on.

"How do I say it?" she had written on the first page, her letters large and flourished. *"How do I tell you I'm sorry for the past, all of it? The lost moments and lost days? The words I wish I could take back like a rash promise, made hastily and then regretted?"*

My stomach fell in a sick drop, like when I stood at the top of Tokyo Tower. Looking down over a thousand lights below and gripping the rail with white fingers.

Jennifer Rogers Spinola

Please come to Virginia. I've found a new life here, in a hundred different ways that I can't explain on silent, one-sided paper, and I'd like to share it with you. To ask your forgiveness and start again, perhaps, as new people. New people who share by some mystery, under the skin of our many differences and years apart, the same blood.

Christie whined and climbed into my lap, her toenails slipping on the smooth fabric of my dark gray dress pants, and nuzzled my chin. She lapped at my cheek with her wet tongue, and I hugged her back—my arms barely fitting around her big-puppy body. Her fuzzy chest rose and fell against mine.

I shifted Christie slightly so her cold nose and snout wouldn't stain my shirtsleeve then straightened the paper.

I must tell you I'm not feeling so well these days, Shiloh. I'm worried. Not only about my headaches and dizziness, which I can't seem to get rid of, but about you. We haven't talked in a long time, and there are some things I must tell you, even if you don't want to speak to me. Things you need to know because. . .

I couldn't read anymore. Instead I folded up the letter and tucked it inside the envelope, as if laying my old bitterness to rest. Wrapped in a silent paper coffin.

I chewed on my lip as I leafed through the rest of the envelope, finding an eclectic mix of stuff, so like Mom: a gospel tract about success coming from God, a snapshot of Mom and Faye both clad in jeans and holding up a gigantic fish, and a penciled recipe for jalapeno-cheese grits.

Grits. Of all things—at a moment like this. When an unexpected foreboding lurked in the dim corners of my brain. Making my breath pinch faster and faster in a worried muddle.

Headaches. Dizziness.

I pressed cold fingers to my lips, remembering our old arguments. Shouts. *"You'll be the death of me!"* she'd mumbled, twisting off the top of her medicine bottle. Blood-pressure medicine, that is. A new dosage.

She'd never needed it before.

Before I could close the trunk, my eyes fell on a stack of stapled white sheets. And I drew back in shock at the black type: AUGUSTA COUNTY MEDICAL CENTER.

Mom's medical records.

—◦◦◦—

I couldn't think. Couldn't see the medical reports, which showed her spiking blood pressure the last year of her life. Right when I'd started returning all her letters.

I jammed it all back into the trunk and latched the lid, picking up Christie and marching out the side door to the deck. Cell phone and Mom's medical records under one arm.

Rose blooms shivered around me in a riot of white and red. The sprinkler swished water in silvery sheets, like my pent-up tears. And as I stared down into a whorl of scarlet petals, an odd correlation began to form in my mind.

I'm mistaken. There's no way that's possible. I rested a shaky elbow on the deck railing as I glanced over the sheaf of medical documents again, barely feeling the hot sun as I dialed Meg on my cell phone.

"Hey, why are you calling the office on your afternoon off, Jacobs?" she blurted into my ear. "Go do something. Relax."

"I will, but. . .I have a question first." The wind rustled the rose bushes, and a sprinkle of red petals sifted to the mulched flower bed. "What's the name of Amanda's doctor?"

"Which Amanda?" She paused. "The one who disappeared? I thought you weren't doing that case."

My mouth turned dry. "Just. . .can you find it in the file? I think I remember seeing his name."

I heard the rustling of papers as Meg leafed through the folder then a crackle of static as she came back on the line. "Paul Geissler," she said. "But why's it so important?"

I gripped the side of the railing, feeling shaky. "He was Mom's doctor, too."

Chapter 5

"Christieeee!" I cupped my hands around my mouth and hollered, making two women on the park bench turn and frown.

"I told you not to use that leash!" Adam ran his hand through his short, sandy hair in frustration, pushing aside some wet bushes and poking underneath. "It always comes loose."

"Well, what do you expect me to do? Buy a new one? With what money?" I looped the empty leash around my wrist and stalked across the sidewalk by Gypsy Hill Park's duck pond. Two swans glided away from me, orange beaks turned up in silent mockery.

"I gave you money to buy a leash!" Adam called back, letting the bushes go and flinging droplets.

"And I had to use it to pay the light bill! I told you that."

"Then you shouldn't have brought her here this afternoon."

"And leave her stuffed in my laundry room the rest of the day?"

"Of course not! Drop her off at Faye and Earl's—or at our place, even. Todd loves to take care of her. But you can't keep letting her run off like this!" Adam let out an angry sigh.

"I'm not letting her. She just takes off!" I put my hands on my hips, feeling anything but belated birthday joy as anger heated my cheeks. "And don't start on the roses again. I have no idea who sent them."

"What?" Adam spun around, his normally calm and sober blue eyes flashing.

"This is what this whole thing is about, isn't it?" I faced him. "You're upset over nothing. It's a florist's mistake."

He crossed his arms stiffly then turned and looked out over the

48

pond. Shredded willow fronds floated on the surface, broken by the rain.

I waited until an elderly couple shuffled by, tossing duck feed to some fluffy goslings. Then I stalked over to Adam's side. He didn't look up.

I attempted to temper my voice, thinking of those old letters in Mom's trunk and so many words I shouldn't have spoken. "The flower thing's not my fault, okay?"

"Is that what you think?" Adam turned to face me, his jaw set angrily. "That I'm blaming you? And overreacting about some flowers? I'm not." He shook his head and looked away. "It's just. . .weird, okay?"

"Well, how do you think I feel? In case you were wondering, I—"

"Hold on." Adam grabbed my arm and pushed past me. "I think I saw. . . There's Christie! Over there! I'll get her." He scrambled off the concrete sidewalk that skirted the duck pond and then leaped across the little stream that twisted through too-green grass. The rain had splintered into golden afternoon sun, glistening moist on thick leaves and turning the neatly mown grounds to ruddy sparkles. Adam jumped over three indignant mallards and scooted up the shallow embankment then took off through the dogwoods.

"Great. Now everything's my fault," I crabbed, trotting after him in my strappy shoes. One heel punched into the soft earth and came up covered with mud. "Everywhere I go Christie runs off, and I'm supposed to fix her. Fix my life. Fix everything." I fumed silently a minute, wishing I could throttle whoever sent me that stupid bouquet. Please. Couldn't everybody give me one moment of peace?

Even Adam. I scrubbed my muddy heel, wondering why things always had to be complicated. I mean, not always. Just. . .more often than I'd like.

He could be weird and stuffy, and super stubborn. Just last week we'd had a big argument over our honeymoon spot, of all things! I'd found the perfect hotel package online—if we signed up during the discount period—for a reduced-rate week in Virginia Beach. "Morning Sun," they called it. The photos looked great, and the prices were even better.

But Adam shot it down. Told me the deal sounded suspicious, and I didn't know Virginia Beach well enough.

I told him he didn't know *me* well enough. Or how to move fast on a bargain.

I leaned my head back against the tree, remembering the way he'd looked at me when he asked me to marry him. Fishing pole in his lap and eyes holding back tears.

And I, a sucker for his sacrificial heart and against-the-grain simplicity (which drove me nuts sometimes, and not in a good way) could only sob out a yes. Even though he drove a pickup truck and hauled mulch. Even though he lived in rundown, redneck Staunton, Virginia. And even though he proposed while *fishing*.

Good thing Kyoko back in Japan hadn't seen Adam's romantic setup or the orange-feathered lure sticking out of his tackle box when he popped the question. She regularly voiced worries that, after veering so far off my big-city journalism course, I'd turn into double-wide-trailer material.

And now that same worry churned inside me again like one of those ducks on the mirror-smooth pond, head under the surface and feet paddling in vain circles: *Maybe she's right. Maybe I moved too fast, and Adam and I are too different. Too. . .*

Wait a second. I leaned forward, straining at something by a picnic table. Did I see. . . ?

"Christie?" I pushed off the tree as her smoky snout turned toward me, tail wagging at the sound of my voice. "What are you doing over there? Adam went after you that way." I looked over my shoulder in the direction he'd gone, and seeing no one, threw up my hands in frustration and sprinted after her through the beaded grass.

"Christie! Get back here!" I dodged maple and beech trees as she sprinted off again, her still-fuzzy puppy mouth laughing in open-mouthed joy. "This isn't funny! If you think I'm—"

I didn't finish my sentence because someone stepped around the side of a towering oak, making me blurt out a scream of surprise. I swerved. My heel snagged on a root and down I went. Elbows first, sliding to a stop on the wet lawn. Smearing dirt all down my chic, red-flowered dress. Soggy grass and stray bark particles stuck to my stomach like one of Tim's shaggy, leaf-covered hunting coats.

I tried to get to my feet and slipped again then clawed my way up by the tree trunk and practically bowled over one very horrified Ray Floyd. Who rushed to help me up.

"Mr. Floyd?" I gasped, wiping my palms on my soiled dress. I stuck one hand out in an awkward handshake, reaching down to pat Ginger on the end of her leash. She blinked blond eyelashes up at me in a friendly smile.

"Sorry," I coughed, knees still smarting. "I didn't mean to run over you." Hello? *SUV?* What was I thinking? "I mean, I didn't see you," I covered quickly, straightening my red ribbon headband that had slid askew.

"Are you okay? Are you hurt?"

Ray reached out to steady my arm, but I'd already righted myself. "Yeah. I'm fine, thanks." I rubbed my sore elbow and stuck my foot back in my shoe, which had flung itself across the grass. So much for playing the cool journalist now. "But my dog. . ." I strained over my shoulder to see. "Forget it. She's gone again. At least yours stays put. Right, Ginger?" I reached down to pat her silky-smooth back.

Ray tipped his curly brown head. "Sorry. I'm trying to remember. . . . You're that reporter, aren't you?"

"Shiloh Jacobs." I flicked a leaf off my dress. "I interviewed you the night that SUV came through your bedroom wall."

"Oh." Ray closed his eyes. "I remember now. Jacobs." He put his hands in his baggy pants pockets and rocked back on his heels, giving a wry laugh. "Wow. Talk about bad timing on that one. I should have stayed up and finished my movie rather than going to bed, huh?"

"On the contrary. I'd say you had pretty good timing. You're still alive." I started to remind him of what might have happened if he'd raised his head another six inches then thought better of it. "So what are you doing here?"

"Here at the park? I live right over there. Remember?" Ray gestured through the trees toward his green-slatted house with its cozy, wreath-trimmed front door. Wooden shutters. Burgundy Volvo in the driveway. He squinted at me through artsy, retro-style glasses. "You sure you're okay?"

"I'm fine. Sorry." I attempted a laugh. "It's just been a long day."

Shouts mingled from across the grass, then voices, a dog's cheerful bark, and Adam's long laugh. I relaxed, resting my arm against the tree in relief. "Whew. He got her." I shielded my eyes against orange rays of sun. "You don't want another dog by any chance, do you?" I joked.

Ray chuckled as Adam strode across the park toward us, Christie triumphantly wrapped in his arms. Her pink tongue licking his cheek in ridiculous enthusiasm. She was big now, and leggy.

I shot Adam a grateful smile then turned back to Ray. "Anyway, it's good we met because I've been thinking since the interview, and I wanted to ask you one more question. If you don't mind."

"Sure. Shoot." He unclipped Ginger's leash and—wonder of wonders—left her there as she obediently sniffed under some leaves and wagged her tail. No frantic races across the park. No chewed leashes or punctured shoes.

Maybe I should trade Christie for a schnauzer.

I scrubbed some leaves off the bottom of my shoe, feeling silly for bringing it up. "You haven't had any other unusual incidents, have you? Like maybe. . .phone calls? Packages? From someone you don't know?"

Ray thought a moment, pressing his index finger to his lips.

"Phone calls? Well, maybe a couple. Hang ups, mainly. Probably telemarketers. Why?"

I sucked in my breath, warning myself not to jump to conclusions. "Anything else?"

Ray narrowed his eyes behind his rectangular glasses. "There is one thing. A letter. I got a letter the other day that makes no sense."

"What did it say? Do you still have it?"

My questions must have poured out a little too quickly because Ray paused, one eyebrow raised. "What's the big deal about a strange letter? It's probably just a reference to some old joke I'd forgotten about. I threw it away. From one of my piano students, probably. Doesn't everybody get unusual messages from time to time?"

The roses. I tensed, brushing leaves off my sleeve and avoiding his eyes. "It happens, I guess. But. . .not normally. No."

I looked over at Adam, who was striding under a thicket of lush elms, their emerald leaves shimmering against a blue-gray sky. Tiny gossamer insects hovered in a patch of glowing sun.

"Can you tell me what the letter said?" I shielded my eyes again as I faced Ray.

But Ray had paled. He sucked in his breath and took a weak step backward.

"Are you okay?" I reached out a timid hand.

"I'm fine. Just. . .yeah. Fine." He managed a smile as Adam caught up with us, out of breath.

"Adam. Thanks." I squeezed his arm briefly then took wiggly Christie and held her warm body against my chest, regretting—for a split second—that I'd offered her to Ray. "This is my fiancé, Adam Carter. Adam, Ray Floyd. You probably saw his house in the paper this week."

Ray murmured a polite "how-do-you-do" and shook Adam's hand, but his face remained clammy white. When he reached up to straighten his glasses, his fingers shook.

"What's wrong?" I exchanged glances with Adam. "Did I ask something too personal?"

"No. Sorry." Ray ran a hand over his sweaty forehead. "It's just that the letter had. . .never mind. It's silly."

"What did it say, Ray?" Despite the frost that had previously chilled our words, I felt Adam move a step closer to me.

"Well, something odd like, 'You're next.' But I can't figure out what it means." Before I could even move or gasp, Ray had opened his mouth to speak again. "But that's not the weirdest part. I saw his picture in the letter."

"Whose picture?"

"His." And Ray gestured with his head toward Adam Carter.

Chapter 6

I drew back in surprise, banging into a thick maple limb. Christie took advantage of the pause to attempt a freedom dive, legs scrambling. But Adam caught her and anchored his fingers around her collar.

"Excuse me—you saw my *what* in the letter?" Adam turned his face to avoid Christie's exuberant tongue.

"Your picture. Drawing. In. . . I don't know. Charcoal or something. What's your name again?"

"Adam," he stammered. "Adam Carter. I used to be a landscaper around here, but I don't remember. . ." He stepped back and tilted his head at Ray as if trying to recall the face, then drawing a blank.

"Charcoal?" I yelped, swiveling my head between the two of them as I untangled Christie's teeth from Adam's polo shirt.

"Maybe not charcoal. It had color, so it must be those. . .what do you call them? Pastels? Kind of smeary-grainy stuff like artists use."

"It sounds like pastels, I guess, but how could somebody have possibly drawn Adam's face? Do you still have the letter?"

"No. I threw it away. Maybe it's a weird coincidence, but it looked exactly like him. The way his hair's cut, and. . ." He gestured and then passed a shaky hand over his forehead. "It's strange, I'll admit. I'm sure one of my students decided to play a prank or something. Maybe somebody who. . .knows you?" He glanced up at Adam. "No. That doesn't make sense. And neither does 'you're next.' "

Adam drew in a shallow breath. "It's a threat, Ray. What else could it be?" He squinted in the sun as Ray digested this nugget of sickly information. "Did you give one of your students a bad grade or something?"

"No. I don't really do grades. Just extra practice sheets. Lots of them." Ray smiled faintly.

Adam shifted Christie in his arms. "I don't know what I'm supposed to do with any of it though. I've. . .never met you."

"Same here. Beats me."

"Ray." I found my voice, heart pulsing as I put together the latest threats from Amanda's purported killer and "you're next." Neither of which boded well for Ray Floyd—or possibly for Adam. "Don't you realize a strange message like that could mean something serious? That you could be in danger, especially after losing. . .uh, your fiancée in an unsolved crime case? If you'll excuse me saying so?"

Ray's eyes lost their carefree smile and seemed to darken in sadness. "I'm sorry, but do you really think that stuff is real? Flowers in mailboxes? Spray paint?"

I took a breath, trying to clear my thoughts. "I don't know. But let me ask you—exactly how was that 'you're next' thing written? Like, above the drawing that supposedly looks like Adam or. . . ?"

"No. On his T-shirt."

I turned to Adam, and he scrunched his brow in confusion.

"Do you know any artists? Anybody who paints or uses pastels?"

Ray thought a while, staring into the sunny distance. "Not really. My girlfriend, maybe. She's really good at art."

"So you have a girlfriend then." My words blurted out before I could stop them, in a sort of relief. Especially after Ray had lost Amanda so many years before.

"Sure. I haven't known her for very long, but she's the one. I'm certain of it." A distant smile danced through Ray's eyes as he reached down and patted Ginger, clicking her leash back on. "She's amazing."

He straightened up and put his hands in his pockets, nodding toward Adam. "It's definitely his face I saw though. The eye color, everything. That little scar." He pointed to a tiny line on Adam's chin—from a bike accident years ago, he'd told me once. Ray thought a moment in silence and scrubbed his fingers through his thick hair. "But what could he possibly have to do with Amanda?" He nodded at Adam. "You must have been a kid when she. . .uh, disappeared."

"Eleven or twelve. Yeah."

"Exactly. I don't get it."

I shot Adam a helpless glance, and he scratched his hair uncomfortably. "How about if we all sit down and talk a bit and see if we can make sense of this?" He shifted Christie to his other arm as she strained to sniff Ginger. "That picnic table is free. And it doesn't look so wet." He surveyed my dirt-stained dress. "Not that it'll make that much difference for you, Shiloh," he added with a smile.

"Hey. Becky calls me the Fashion Nazi." I held up a muddy sandal. "What can I say?"

Ray chuckled, a sound that made my heart dip in relief. "Fashion Nazi, hey? Uh-oh." He pointed to his shirt—a horrible geometric print in ugly olive green and neon yellow, with touches of pink throughout. Like a deranged Brazilian soccer player slammed into a cheerleader. Truly, one of the most heinous patterns I'd ever seen. "So am I under arrest?"

"You deserve to be." I lifted an eyebrow as we started toward the picnic table. Keeping my voice light. "That shirt's definitely a crime against fashion and probably society as well."

"What? I love green and yellow."

"Maybe you shouldn't."

—⁓—

"Well, looky here! The birthday girl herself!" Jerry Farmer held open the glass door to The Green Tree restaurant while cars rumbled behind us on the narrow historic street. All of us encased by faded brick false-front style buildings and long rows of shops. None of which had changed much in the last hundred years of Staunton's history as a Confederate supply base, farming community, and apple producer. Like I said. Small-town yawns, for the most part. If I shielded my eyes from the sinking sun, I could make out the Amtrak station in the distance.

Adam and I paused for two passing antique enthusiasts hauling colored glass vases, and we stepped off the sidewalk and into the cool interior of The Green Tree. New, golden-brown laminate flooring, the color of straw, gleamed under soft overhead lights and mimicked hardwood exactly.

"You took the carpet up!" I looked around in surprise as the door fell closed behind us. "It's gorgeous!"

"Best thing I ever did to this place, even if it did cost me an arm and a leg." My old boss Jerry Farmer flashed a smile that seemed, for a quick instant, a little forced.

I couldn't help but stare. "Jerry. Your hair. What did you do to it?"

"It's bad, ain't it?" He ran a hand sheepishly over his hair, which sported gaping patches cut so close they nearly showed his scalp. "Tryin' to save a buck and cut it myself. Bad idea, huh?"

"Wow." I refrained from further comments.

Jerry turned back to the new flooring. "Well, anyway, carpet's just a haven for bacteria, dust, and ketchup stains. You shoulda seen it! But this baby here?" He squeaked a shoe across a shiny section of flooring. "Built to last, I tell ya. It's tough stuff. And don't it make the restr'ant look like one a them fancy places in Tokyo you're always talkin' about?"

"Maybe if you had sushi," I teased.

"Ha. I need the budget a one of them fancy Tokyo places for that." Jerry grinned through round-rimmed glasses, but his voice fell a bit flat. "Have a seat over there, folks, by the plants." He gestured, patting my arm. "I saved ya a table. Trinity'll be by in a minute."

"Trinity's working tonight?"

"She is after she heard you were comin' in. Says once you quit working here and started cow tippin', you ain't got time for old friends."

"Funny, Jerry. You got the picture, too, didn't you?"

He put his hands on his hips and chuckled, looking absurdly out of place in such a fancy dining room with his mustache and botched redneck bowl cut. But Jerry knew business, and he knew it well. Probably half the restaurant owners in town were scratching their heads, trying to figure out how a simple country fellow like him could get three years of foodie awards in a row. Jerry Farmer, who once stole the lighted deer off somebody's front yard at Christmas and hung it from a tree, skinning-and-gutting style.

"Well, how's my favorite bride-to-be, anyway?" He winked.

"I'd feel a bit more bride-y if I had a wedding dress." Adam and I exchanged glances. "Adam's helping me plan out the ceremony and price invitations and things, but we still have a long way to go."

Voices echoed faintly from the kitchen, and Jerry turned, poking his head over tables to see. "G'won, y'all." He held up a hand. "I'll come talk to ya in a sec."

He disappeared through the double swinging kitchen doors, leaving me staring at a couple cutting into The Green Tree's famous spicy samosas, dipping sauce on the side. *Yum.* My mouth watered.

I smoothed my clean white skirt and grass-green top—for which we'd driven all the way to my house, post-mudbath—and followed Adam. We headed toward the corner table and dying fern that Jerry had indicated, passing similar glass-topped tables covered with white linens. Servers poured iced tea and sparkling water into shimmering wine glasses, and white Christmas lights twinkled from the top of the walls like starry nightfall.

"Here?" I paused in front of the side table Jerry had indicated, its napkins rumpled and silverware askew. A vase with a wilted white freesia sat next to an oil stain on the white tablecloth. "Are you serious? Is this the seat Jerry saved us?"

"I thought so," Adam replied. "He said by the plants, didn't he? Here's the fern and all those hydrangeas on the wall." I could smell the dusty scent of their blooms from glass vases on staggered wooden boards.

"Maybe we should check the napkins and make sure they don't have your face drawn on them." I shot him a wry smile, trying to cut the strain of too-heavy topics.

"Funny. Under the plates, perhaps?"

"You never know." I pretended to look through my purse. "Let me get out my pastels, and I'll draw one for you."

Adam glanced back over his shoulder for Jerry, but he hadn't reappeared. A noisy crowd filed over to a nearby table, laughing and pulling out chairs, blocking the rest of the restaurant.

"That's what he said. I think he meant here." I took my purse off my shoulder. "Maybe the busboy's just a little sloppy." My wine glass wore streaks, but it glistened back, dry and empty.

"Sloppy isn't the word for it." Adam brushed the crumbs off my sleek wooden chair before politely holding it out for me. Something no man, in all my twenty-five years, had ever done. "Here. I'll just borrow that water pitcher over there and fill up our glasses."

I thanked him and sat, pushing a rumpled napkin out of the way.

"So did you guys ever get the cows back in Ron's pasture?" Adam asked with a smirk, sitting down across from me with two fresh glasses of ice water.

I choked a laugh into a cough. "Come on. What makes you think I had anything to do with that?"

"Um. . .nothing." Adam feigned ignorance, covering a grin with his hand. "Nothing at all. Except Tim hauled a hay bale over to Ron's pasture late Tuesday night. Kind of an odd time to feed the cows, don't you think?"

"Hmm." I didn't answer, pretending to study the menu.

"Faye swears she saw him fixing that pasture fence when the sun came up Wednesday morning." Adam leaned forward, the corners of his mouth twitching. "And. . .there's one other thing." He started to reach for his cell phone.

"Don't do it!" I threw the menu down and pushed his phone back in his pocket. "Becky must have sent that silly photo to everybody in Staunton."

"Staunton? Becky has a bigger contact list than you think." Adam bobbed his eyebrows. "I hear it's already showed up in West Virginia and Tennessee."

"Stop it." I covered my face with my hands.

"Sorry." Adam chuckled. "This is a small town, you know."

"Don't remind me."

I brushed crumbs off my elbow where I'd been leaning. Adam helped me, shaking his head. "Sorry, Shiloh. I wanted dinner to be nice. But there's a reason I brought you here tonight to celebrate your birthday."

"So I can be suddenly thankful I'm employed as a reporter now instead of a Green Tree waitress?" I smiled, recalling weary days of waiting tables and scrubbing booths. Carrying trays and ferrying orders. Stuffing the few dollar bills from between leek-and-cheese-encrusted forks into my soiled apron pocket.

"Or because of the bread?" I tipped the bread basket toward me, revealing several tender, crusty slices and a small ceramic bowl of whipped butter. "I'm starving. The bread looks cold, but. . .oh well." I wiped the smudged knife on a cloth napkin then swirled it in the creamy butter.

"You sure looked cute in that apron though." Adam's eyes softened in a smile. "Sure you don't want your old job back?"

"Me? No." I snorted, flicking some crumbs from under the plate onto the floor. "Don't tell Jerry that."

"I think he knows." Adam smiled, waiting until I'd put the knife down to trace the contours of my fingers with his rough hands. "But he said if we were going out tonight to bring you by here because he wanted to ask if— Shiloh?" He tipped his head at me. "You listening?"

"Yeah. Sorry. I thought I heard my phone." I gestured toward my purse. "I figured it was your younger brother calling to tell me Christie ate the sofa or something."

I tipped my purse to check. "But it's fine. Nobody called."

I flicked a piece of lettuce off the chic bamboo placemat. Yes, real bamboo. Jerry believed clients wouldn't mind shelling out bigger bucks if the ambiance felt exotic, like they've gone on a trip. In other words, far away from Staunton.

"The sofa in the den's pretty old, so nobody'll care if Christie chews it up. If it's that new one my mom just bought for the living room, though, she'll have a coronary."

She'll have a coronary. From stress. The words flew into my already crowded brain like unexpected barn swallows, chirping and flailing wings. And my half sister's voice: *"It's probably your fault, anyway. You drove her to her death."*

I frowned, rubbing at a small sticky spot on the plate and thinking about Mom's stack of returned letters, all stamped and postmarked. Her words about headaches and dizziness.

I shook ice water in my glass, the dim lights and my troubled face smearing into a swirl of color. My green-gold hazel eyes staring back at me, for one frozen instant, so much like Mom's.

"What did you say just a minute ago?" I looked up.

"About Becky's huge phone and e-mail list? You know she has like four hundred contacts, right?"

I pretended to smack him. "I asked what you said about your mom." I set my glass down and avoided his eyes, buttering a slice of bread and then setting the knife on the edge of my plate. "Having a. . . what you said."

"Having a coronary? Because of the new sofa? I told you—I was kidding."

"No, I mean the way you said it. That stress could actually give somebody a heart attack."

"Sure. It happens all the time."

I dropped my bread and sank back in my chair, suddenly not hungry.

"Hey, you okay?" Adam tipped his head at me. "What's wrong?"

"It's nothing. Just. . ." I peered up at him, not sure how to put the whole mess into words. "That coronary thing you said reminded me. Ashley told me a while ago that she thought Mom might've developed high blood pressure, too. Before she. . .you know. Passed away."

"Your mom?" Adam dropped his tone a notch.

"Yes." I pressed my lips together and met his eyes, hoping he'd understand. But their bluish-gray depths echoed back only pain and sympathy—and the same confused expression that flitted through them when Ray made his "charcoal drawing" speech.

"High blood pressure can cause brain aneurysms." I straightened the placemat and avoided his gaze. "Ashley said Mom never had high blood pressure until she and I started to. . .um, not get along so well, to put it nicely. A few years back. Before I moved here."

Adam started to speak, but I stopped him. "And then last year it got worse. After I told her to stop writing and calling me."

"Shiloh, there's no comparison between what I said and your mom. Everybody has trouble with parents." He reached for my hand. "I mean, Mom always told Rick he'd be the death of her. And look at them now—as close as butter on grits."

Oh. My. Word. The color drained from my face like a tablecloth slipping onto the floor.

"The death of her. She said that?"

"Sure. Rick was a big prankster for a while and kind of hotheaded. Now that he's recovering from his amputations, he's been a lot more. . . What?"

"My mom. She used to say that exact thing—that I'd be the death of her."

Medical reports. Green Hill Cemetery. Dr. Paul Geissler. Amanda. Red paint. Death, death, death.

The room spun, and I held on to the table.

Adam's eyes popped, wide and incredulous. "And because your half sister made up come crazy story about you causing your mom's blood pressure to go up—"

"She's right." I closed my eyes.

"Now wait a minute. If you think for one second that—"

"She's right," I interrupted again, louder, until Adam fell into silence. "I checked."

Adam did a double take. "You did what?"

"I looked through Mom's medical records. Ashley's right."

—∞—

"Shiloh." Adam scraped his chair back and came to sit next to me. He put his arm around me, and I rested my head against his shoulder. Breathing in his familiar fragrance of musty truck scent and aftershave, now mainly covered by doggie smell since he'd carried Christie. Mud on his tennis shoes where he'd hopped the creek at Gypsy Hill Park to run and catch her.

"She started taking blood pressure medication seven years ago—

when I was eighteen. The first time we had such a big fight I didn't speak to her for months."

"Shiloh, that's ridiculous."

"Even when Dad and Ashley bailed, Mom didn't need blood pressure medication. But she increased it three years ago when I left for Japan without saying good-bye. Last year she doubled it."

Adam twisted a strand of hair behind my ear. "You can't go down that road. It's not healthy. Not for you, not for anybody."

"They call high blood pressure the silent killer," I whispered, tears filling my eyes.

"The what?" Adam turned his head to hear me better.

"Hold on. Here comes Trinity." I sat up and wiped my face as Trinity Jackson came through the double kitchen doors, an apologetic look on her face.

"So sorry to keep you waiting, guys," she said, out of breath, smoothing her black curly hair back in place. "The sanitizer hose broke again, and Jerry's back there on his hands and knees. Water everywhere." She leaned over to hug us both.

"Believe me, I remember. That used to happen all the time." I turned my wine glass in the light, wishing I'd brought some aspirin to dull the ache behind my eyes. Maybe cold water would help. I lifted the glass, and my stomach grumbled at the sight of my poor little buttered bread slice lying untouched on the edge of my plate. "Why doesn't Jerry just replace that hose?"

"He has. Twice." Trinity glanced back at the kitchen, her impeccable dark eyeliner revealing her years as a model. "He's really mad at the guy who installed it. Says if he comes in here again he'll—" She broke off, turning back to the far wall with a confused grimace. "Hey, why are you guys sitting over here? Jerry set up that booth over there for you."

She glanced down at our plates, and her eyes bugged out. "This table hasn't been cleaned yet! What are you guys doing?"

"What?" I jerked the wine glass away from my lips.

"Gross! You didn't drink out of that, did you?" She snatched it out of my hand and smacked me with the menu. "Are you out of your mind, Shiloh? Get out of here! *There*." She pointed. "See? Jerry put you right next to the new fountain."

For the first time I registered the steady tinkle of water over laughter and clinking glasses and the soft Enya music piped over the speaker system. "But he said next to the plants."

"The tree with Christmas lights." Trinity swept her arm toward an alcove behind a large table. "And all the orchids. Plants, Shiloh. Not that old fern."

"Oh, *those* plants." I stood up sheepishly after Adam and shook the crumbs off my skirt then slid into the table she indicated. Gleaming clean. Glistening, untouched china and crystal. A bottle of sparkling apple juice chilled in a bucket of ice. "Wow. Now this is great."

"You like it?" Trinity gestured to the bamboo-and-stone semicircle in a little alcove, shrouded by ferns and potted apple-green orchids. A fake topiary-style ficus tree with a braided trunk glimmered with white lights. "Yeah, everybody loves the fountain. Except Flash in the kitchen, who says it sounds like a urinal."

"Nice." Adam chuckled, unfolding the sumptuous cloth napkin. "I'll try not to think about that while we eat."

"The fountain's amazing. The table. Everything." I leaned on my chin and listened to the soothing ripple of water dripping from a bamboo spout, swirling around the rocks. Calming my frazzled nerves.

"And candles." Trinity gestured to the silver candlesticks. "Romantic, don't you think? I'll be right back with a match."

She lowered her head to Adam's and whispered in his ear, and I barely made out the words "on the house."

"What? He didn't. I told him not to." Adam lifted his head.

"Well?" Trinity shrugged and put her palms up. "What's done is done." She grinned, showing dimples.

"Jerry. Let me guess." I shook my head.

Adam's mouth turned up in a wistful smile. "He's a good guy. I hope one day I can run a business the way he does."

"I know. People love this place." I brushed my finger along the sleek, square lines of the plate, everything beautifully dim in the soft light. "Check this out. Japanese style."

"Jerry says he had 'inspiration' on the Japanese setup." Trinity bobbed a slender eyebrow as she turned toward the kitchen for the matches. "Whatever that's supposed to mean."

"It's nice." Adam held up a shiny fork. Then he put it back next to his plate and reached across to take my hands. "But listen, Shiloh. We need to finish our conversation about your mom."

"I was talking about the silent killer." My words came out in a whisper. At exactly the same moment my eyes lit on the sleek shine of

Jennifer Rogers Spinola

something tall and flute-shaped in a shadowy corner of the table, right next to the pepper grinder. A bottle of olive oil? A flask of balsamic vinegar?

I carefully slid it between our plates. And found myself staring not at a white freesia bloom, but a vase topped with a full, fragrant, dark red rose.

Chapter 7

"Who put this here?" I shoved the crystal vase away from me, practically knocking Adam's plate in his lap.

"Why, what's the problem?"

"It's the same color rose."

"Same color as what?" Adam paled. "You mean like the bouquet that came on your birthday?"

"Definitely." The beautiful square plates and white tablecloth blurred into a shadowy mess of lines, punctuated by a dark red splotch. "Jerry wouldn't have ordered this, would he? He hates roses. Says the smell makes his allergies flare up—hence the practically odorless freesias and orchids and things." I waved toward the other tables. "And not only that, it's a red rose."

"Red?"

"Jerry's color blind. Red flowers all look brown to him. He never buys anything red on purpose."

"Okay, but think with me here. He did it for you, Shiloh. It's your birthday." Adam diplomatically placed the vase back over to the side, against the wall. "I asked Jerry to set up a table for us, and he did. I'm sure it's not what you're thinking."

Before I could reply, Trinity appeared with the match, lighting the pair of slender white candles into flickering pulses of golden flame. I waited, all my theories about roses still on my tongue, as Trinity shook the match—and I stared into the twin glimmers of flame. So fragile. So easily extinguished. Like a life, suspended between two worlds.

I breathed, and the candle on my right sputtered and went out, leaving a faint trail of smoke. And a hole of darkness, pricked with a single fading ember where the light had been.

"Thirsty? It's been hot lately." I looked up at the sound of Trinity's voice. Her gold rings glistened in the candlelight as she struck another match, her slender, coffee-brown fingers moving as if in slow motion.

"Sure." I pushed my glass forward. Glowing spots still hung behind my eyes like memories, draining slowly into darkness.

"So when are you going to Grandma's again? She's been asking about you. Says you haven't been to dinner in a month, and she wants to help with your wedding plans. Whatever you need." Trinity opened the bottle of sparkling apple juice, a wisp of mist trailed up like smoke.

Before I could answer Trinity's question, she winked. "Nice touch, Adam. I didn't know you had such good taste in flowers."

"What?" Adam and I both jumped at the same time.

"The rose. It's pretty." Trinity's nail polish sparkled as she passed a finger over the spicy-scented petals. "So fess up. Where'd you put my chrysanthemums?"

"Huh?" I spun around in my chair to face Trinity. "What chrysanthemums? I didn't see any."

"Jerry asked me to set up the table." She waved a hand in the direction of the kitchen. " 'A bouquet of chrysanthemums, even if the allergies kill me,' he said. Where'd they go? I put them right in the middle of the table."

"Chrysanthemums. I get it. This gorgeous Japanese setup." I smoothed the bamboo placemat.

"Exactly. I think he wanted to make you feel at home. Japan-home." Trinity turned and looked around the restaurant then shrugged. "Beats me where they went though. I'll ask Jerry. Maybe he. . . Nah. Forget it." She waved it away.

"Forget what?"

Trinity sighed. "I don't know, Shiloh. He's just been. . .different lately."

Adam squinted up in the candlelight, reflections dancing in his eyes. "Different how?"

She dropped her voice. "Nervous. Stressed. I don't know. His head in the clouds."

"Don't say stressed." I closed my eyes, trying not to think of Mom and her pile of unopened letters. "But why's Jerry on edge? Because the sanitizer hose keeps breaking?"

"Not exactly. He keeps changing things around, trying to cut costs.

Cheaper flowers. Lower-quality cheese. Slashing stuff off the menu that people love because he says it's too expensive. That sort of thing."

"He can't be too hard up, can he? He must've shelled out big bucks for this new flooring." I looked across at the polished wood grain, shining dimly in the yellow-white overhead light.

"Exactly. Because the dirty carpet cost too much to shampoo, and people were complaining. He had a relative lay the flooring and sold his car to pay for everything."

"His car?" I jerked my head back, stunned.

"Yep. He's borrowing a car from your next-door neighbor until he can buy a cheaper one."

"Stella? His sister?"

"Yep. She dropped him off today, and they went in the back and talked a while. And she didn't look happy when she left. I don't know, Shiloh. But something tells me all Jerry's little changes to the restaurant are last-ditch efforts."

Adam leaned forward. "You mean like. . .he might have to close the restaurant?"

"I'm not sure." Trinity's full lips formed a line. "He hasn't let anybody go yet, but I've seen him going over numbers for hours, glued to his accounting books."

The bad haircut. "To save a buck," he'd said.

I ran my hands over the thick tablecloth and brown wicker charger, light dancing in pale ribbons across its surface. "But it's all so beautiful."

"Well. Everything ends sometime."

The bright candle flames bobbed in a current of air.

Trinity lowered her voice to a whisper. "I'm looking for another job just in case." She shrugged. "Anyway. You can ask him about the rose while I go get your appetizer."

We all turned at the sound of Jerry's voice from across the tables, unusually tight as he called something over his shoulder. I sized him up as he strode between the tables toward us, a no-nonsense leather folder under his arm and a weary look in his eyes.

Trinity shook her head. "Poor guy. Wait to bring up the rose until he's talked to you about what's on his mind first. Otherwise he might keel over. Stress and all that."

—⁓—

"So I'm offering you a proposal," said Jerry, leaning forward on the chair he'd swiped from a neighboring table. "A business proposal. I need your help, and you need moola. For that weddin' of yours." He grinned. But when he settled back in the chair, the tired lines crossing his forehead spoke louder than his smile. For the first time I noticed some gray edging his chopped sideburns.

"You want us to help you give The Green Tree a face-lift," I summarized.

"Yep. That's what it boils down to." Jerry sighed and set his glasses on the edge of our table, wiping the sweat from beneath his eyes. "We need a new direction. A new. . .something."

"But I don't understand. The place is gorgeous." I pointed to the bamboo placemat. "You nailed the Japanese theme. If this is your new direction, it's perfect."

"It does look nice, don't it?" Jerry's tight face relaxed a bit. "I had some special help with that one. But I'll be blunt. We ain't doin' so well."

"But people are packing in here!" I gestured at the crowded tables.

Well. Maybe not crowded, exactly. Now that I looked, I could see a few empty tables here and there, lonely chairs—but wasn't that normal?

"Not exactly." Jerry sighed and reached for his leather folder. "Take a look at this." And he tossed a magazine on the table.

" 'The Green Tree offers plain vanilla,' " Adam read out loud then looked up at Jerry in surprise. " 'Upscale veggie-heavy joint serves up more of the same tired dishes and flavorless design.' "

"Flavorless design?" I yelped, snatching the magazine closer. "Who said that?"

"I'm afraid there's more." Jerry pulled out a folded newspaper. "This ain't much better."

" 'The Green Tree's steady slide from alluring to abysmal just goes to show that farmers should stick with fried eggs and pork shanks.' " I gaped at the blocky type. " 'Farmers'? They're making fun of your last name, aren't they?"

"That ain't the half of it. We've had a thirty-eight percent decrease in customers since these things ran." He shook the newspaper. "The lowest I've seen in nine years of business. Today we had half the usual number of lunch customers. I'm at my wit's end."

The numbers fell hard on the table like a dropped spoon, shattering our thoughts.

Jerry sighed, slumping back in his chair. "I jest don't get it. I work hard. I break my back. I treat my folks right and give my customers the best. And doggone if it don't come back and bite me in the leg." He pointed a finger at the newspaper. "This stuff's death for restaurants, folks. One-and-a-half stars? You think people are going to shell out cash for me to buy fresh organic spinach and Jarlsberg cheese with a rating of one-and-a-half stars?"

Jerry looked haggard. "Maybe they're right. Maybe I'm washed up or my time as a restaurant owner is done. I dunno." He put his hands up. "I gotta do somethin' though, or. . .who knows what'll happen."

"Jerry, no." I shook my head. "You can't fold. Staunton needs at least one place that doesn't sell fried chicken and ham biscuits. Please."

Jerry's cheek crinkled into a wry grin. "Don't ya think I've been up night after sleepless night thinkin' about that? And what about Stel? She'll take a hard cut."

Jerry's sister Stella. My Marlboro-smoking, school-bus-driving, big-haired next-door neighbor who looked out for me with a tender fierceness. Stella made her heavenly caramel-chocolate brownies and cherry cheesecakes for Jerry, who then sold them at The Green Tree. Giving her a good-sized amount of the proceeds.

I could imagine her now, bent over her stacks of bills and gripping her hair-sprayed 'do in a posture of desperation.

"And how's Mama gonna get along without the checks I send her? She don't got nothin' else. Pop left me all this seed money for a business, and I shore as anything don't wanna let him down. God rest him." The Adam's apple in his throat bobbed as he swallowed. "That's why I'm askin' for your help. I'll pay ya. Shiloh, you got a good head for logos and stuff. Make me a good one. Help me come up with some new layout design for the room or colors or something."

He raised his palms. "I'll do whatever it takes to keep this place goin'. I'll take out a loan. Mortgage the house. Whatever. It means a lot to me."

I lifted my head briefly to catch Adam's gaze, recalling his former landscaping business cards and flyers we'd worked so hard to design and print. His brand-new catchy logo, now slapped on the side of somebody else's truck.

"Adam. You're the plant guy."

"I was the plant guy." Adam gave a half smile.

"Naw. You *are* the plant guy. Gabe Castle's great, that fella who bought your business, but you're the brains behind it all. See, here's where I need ya. We're supposed to be The Green Tree, but I don't see much green in here except a couple a ugly ferns and a fake tree. Can you help me without breaking my bank?"

"I'm on it." Adam nodded firmly.

"Recipes. I need new dishes. Catchy dishes. Appetizers and entrées that'll draw people in and won't bankrupt me." He tapped his chin. "Maybe Asian. Noodles and rice are cheap. If you get my drift."

"And light on the meat. Gotcha."

"Atta girl. You're definitely my gal for Asian stuff, Shiloh." He crossed his arms. "You and that sushi of yours."

"Me? I can't cook worth anything, Jerry. All I can do is eat."

I turned my frosted wine glass around, remembering the burned biscuits and half-cooked deviled eggs from my first attempts at cooking Southern food.

"Well, you've been to all these snazzy places I ain't set foot in." Jerry closed his folder. "Tell me their secrets. And by next month, because that's when *Fine Dining* is coming to do a review, and what they say'll make or break us." He lowered his voice. "If it ain't good, and I mean real good, you might be kissin' The Green Tree good-bye."

The image of an empty storefront lot flitted through my mind. A SOLD sign pasted over the door, and a LEROY'S GUNS & AMMO placard in its place.

Oh. My.

"Jerry. I'm not a professional." I let go of my wine glass. "As much as I'd like to help, you'd probably be better off with somebody who knows what she's doing. I'm just a Yankee in the wrong place."

"Oh no. You're in the right place." Jerry's smile finally reached all the way to the crinkled corners of his eyes. "And I don't want a professional. I like your work, Shiloh. I've seen it. And I'm willing to pay. It might not be much, but it'll help with those weddin' bills, won't it?" Jerry slapped Adam's shoulder.

I gazed into the candle flame again, thinking.

Thinking about second chances. Chances to do now, here, on this earth, what I wished I could have done with Mom. While my heart still beat. While time still trickled, grain after measured grain, into the hourglass.

Only now it was too late for Mom. Too late for me to take back the hateful words I'd flung at her or to swallow my wounded pride and take her hand, forming a bridge even our cold and painful past couldn't shake.

But maybe it wasn't too late to help Jerry.

I leaned forward and shook my head. "No, Jerry. I'm sorry."

Jerry's face fell, but he smiled anyway. "That's fine. I know you're busy."

"I mean, no, not as a paid consultant," I heard myself say, raising my eyes to Adam's blue ones, which gleamed back at me across the honey-dim table. "I'll do it as a friend."

"What? Of course we're friends, Shiloh." Jerry squinted in confusion.

"I mean for free." I had to close my eyes when I said the words, feeling the sting of pain that flashed briefly. I *needed* money. Needed more income. Bills screamed at me one after another—water bills and car-repair bills and electric bills. And how on earth were Adam and I supposed to pay for anything remotely resembling a wedding? Unless we had it at the local Tastee Freez and threw fries at the reception?

And now I'd just given myself one more crazy thing to do on top of everything else—selling the house, figuring out where that crazy rose bouquet came from, and sorting through Mom's medical stuff.

But when I opened my eyes again, Adam smiled back proudly, reaching across the table to squeeze my hand. Nodding in agreement.

Even the candle seemed to bob its golden head, bright and cheerful. An incandescent *yes.*

"Aw, no." Jerry leaned back in his chair and shook his head. "That ain't what I meant."

"I know, but let me do this. You were a good boss to me. The best I've ever had."

The words struck him blank, as if I'd thrown my glass of sparkling cider in his face. "Me? Sorry, what'd ya say?"

"You were the best boss I've ever had." My face fell sober, imagining the line of men and women who'd hired me over the years for—admittedly—more upscale jobs than waiting tables.

"Shiloh. You worked for the *New York Times.*"

"And my boss was the Wicked Witch of the West. Or North, I should say. We put salt in her coffee." I leaned forward. "Jerry, you gave Trinity money when she needed it, and you sent me home and worked my shifts yourself when I needed sleep. Trinity already told us you've put tonight's meal on the house, and you're paying for our wedding rehearsal dinner here at The Green Tree. No. This time I'll do something for you."

And I know you live in a broken-down house with no car, so don't argue with me.

"Wait a second." I shook my finger at him. "On the other hand, you posted that ridiculous cow picture of me back there by the register. I saw it. Maybe I'll reconsider."

"Oh, you saw that?" He chuckled. "Well, ya oughtta reconsider." Jerry's eyes had misted behind his round wire glasses, making him look less redneck restaurant owner and more tenderhearted poet.

"It's done. When do you want us to come over and start going over ideas?"

"I'll. . .uh. . .just go get my Day-Timer." He stumbled off the chair as if in shock.

"Wait. Just one thing." I pointed to the vase, about to ask.

But Jerry's brain apparently moved faster than my mouth. "Hey, wait a second." He leaned over the table, face creased in bewilderment. "Where'd my chrysanthemums go? Did Trinity put 'em somewhere?"

———

"I really don't know what to make of it." Adam shook his head as we cut into appetizer sweet potato fries with our forks, crisp and piping hot. "If Jerry didn't put the rose there, who did? Somebody in the back maybe?" He aimed an accusatory look toward the double doors.

"Like Flash the cook?" I imagined him there at the deep fryer, laughing and showing his missing tooth. An apron wrapped around his stick-skinny middle. "I don't think so. He always treated me respectfully. A perfect gentleman."

I reached for the creamy, spicy dipping sauce. "And I don't know the dishwashers anymore. It's a restaurant, Adam. Anybody could come in here right off the street, and nobody would notice."

I'd stuck the rose vase on an empty table, and it grinned at me among the scraped plates and disheveled napkins. "But I don't want to talk about roses anymore." I turned my chair away from the vase. "And I don't want to talk about Mom either. Let's enjoy tonight, for five minutes. Please."

Adam laced his fingers through mine, eyes bright from across the white tablecloth. "You did the right thing with Jerry, Shiloh. I'm proud of you. And that's why I wanted to bring you here to The Green Tree."

"Because the restaurant's in trouble?"

"No, I didn't know that. Jerry just said he wanted to talk to us about something." Adam took a sip of his cider. "But I know you have a lot of memories here, and I wanted to give you some good news."

"Really?" I speared a crunchy orange wedge of sweet potato fry with my fork and swirled it in the sauce. "Tell me. I could use some."

Adam seemed to be holding back a smile, reaching across the table to brush a strand of my hair behind my ear.

"What's the good news? You shot a deer?" I grinned in jest and shook the sauce off my fry, sorting through slightly more realistic possibilities. A raise? A new job offer? Something about the college engineering course he'd start in the fall?

"It's not deer season yet, Shiloh." Adam chuckled. "No. Better than that."

"What then?"

When he told me, I let go of my fork and sweet potato fry, dropping it all coated with sauce right down the front of my shirt.

Chapter 8

Ro-chan! I've been trying to call you for days! Where've you been?" Kyoko Morikoshi hollered into the Bluetooth as my Honda swished past sunny fields, headed to work at *The Leader* office.

A bit later than usual, I might add, because Kevin kept me up all night writing up a house fire.

"Where've I been? Cow tipping," I replied, accelerating over a gentle rise in the narrow two-lane road. Frilly tufts of creamy white Queen Anne's Lace rippled in the summer breeze as I mentally sifted through my shopping schedule with Becky: price wedding dresses and cakes, choose colors for the bridesmaids' dresses, and, oh, look for wedding flowers. Even though the mere thought of fragrant petals turned me off.

All of this while returning pointless calls from Rask Florist, where nobody could tell me anything. Brandy finally told me she'd mixed up the dates and Tammy wouldn't be back for another week.

Argh.

"You've been cow tipping? Very funny." Kyoko snorted. "And that picture I got from Becky better be a joke, hear me?"

I'm toast. I'm really and truly toast. "Actually I've discovered cows don't really sleep standing up," I managed, attempting bright nonchalance. And pointedly avoiding her question. "Tim says it's an urban myth, and I'd have to agree."

I heard Kyoko suck in her breath and decide if I was joking. "You're making this up," she snapped, but I could tell I'd worried her. "Aren't you?"

I laughed, and Kyoko relaxed.

74

"Partially."

Her sigh of relief stopped abruptly. "Ro," she moaned. "What am I going to do with you? You're becoming a hayseed the longer you stay there in Virginia! I can feel it!"

I didn't know which was funnier—Kyoko's nickname for me, made from the first syllable of my name butchered in Japanese plus the honorific -*chan* that declared me honorable—or her contempt for all things redneck and backward.

Well, not *all* things, technically. I think last year's visit to my house changed her mind a bit, although she'd never admit it now.

"I still don't do grits, pig's feet, or squirrel," I reminded her. "Some things never change."

"Yeah, well, they'd better not." Kyoko sounded grumpy. I could imagine her black-lined eyes glaring as she held her glittery cell phone. Shoulder-length, shiny, mushroom-shaped black hair, dyed a burgundy-reddish shade (if her most recent Facebook and Azuki photos told the truth) with some new pink streaks. Eyebrow piercing and nose ring glinting in the light. Black suit jacket to cover her tattoos, or at least make dress code for the Associated Press office.

"You working now, Kyoko?"

"Are you crazy? It's 10 p.m. here. I never take work home. I've been in Okinawa doing a few last stories before I go."

"Go?"

"You know. Leave Japan."

Yep. She was really leaving. For Japanese-American Kyoko, all the bowing and mouth-covering and incessant apologies went against her. . .well, crabby grain. Angry music pounded in the background, as if in agreement.

"I left you a ton of happy-birthday messages though," said Kyoko, thankfully turning down the music. "Did you get them?"

"I did. Thanks." I smiled, wishing Kyoko would move close by so we could eat *tonkatsu* fried pork with chopsticks again. Me giving her a hard time about her smoking and horrible music, and Kyoko ranting about cowboy hats and gun racks. "And your birthday's coming up soon, isn't it?"

"Two weeks after yours, babe. The same day as Kaine here at the office. Statistically, the odds are greater that two people will actually share the same birthday than not. Know why? Because. . ."

And she launched into her birthday-statistics speech. Goodness knows I'd heard it enough times. At least she hadn't started talking about the '80s. When she started, then we were usually up all night.

Amanda. We shared the same birthday. Different years, of course, but both June twelfth. Goose bumps tingled on my arm.

"I've got some black sugar from Okinawa to mail you, too," Kyoko said, interrupting my thoughts. "It was either that or raw goat soup, but I figured US customs might not be so happy with that one."

"Wonder if Jerry'd like that soup recipe for The Green Tree?" I joked, but my mind had already slipped back into "Amanda" territory. I pressed my lips together, trying to carefully phrase my next question. "You didn't leave any messages on Adam's phone, did you, Kyoko? Maybe. . .for my birthday?"

"Me? No. What would I have to ask him about, shipping rates? Seeing how he's at UPS now?" She paused. "Why do you ask?"

"He's been getting a bunch of. . .um. . .weird calls. Somebody asking for him and wanting to know when he'll be home. Hang ups. That sort of thing."

"Eliza Harrison?"

I flinched at the name of a girl Adam had grown up with. And whom his parents had, many years before, hoped he'd marry.

"No. A man. Not sounding too friendly."

"Then why did you ask me if I called him, Ro?" Kyoko bellowed. "I might be chunky and scary and chop my hair off, but I'm not a guy."

"I didn't mean that! And stop calling yourself chunky. You look great." I drove over a very dead road-killed possum, trying not to look. "I sort of hoped you were the one calling him. A joke or something, since you have so many. . .shall we say. . .'unusual' skills. Computer hacking and so forth."

"Well, I didn't call him. Although I can start, if you like. I've got this great new voice on my computer that does Marvin the Martian in Japanese."

I chuckled. "Well, thanks for the birthday messages anyway. My birthday would have been better though without Clarence's dumb rumors."

"Who?"

"Clarence. The weirdo mail guy at work that Meg swears used to be a CIA agent or something. Nobody knows much about him, except he loves to stir up stories about everybody. This time he made all these insinuations about my car being parked in *The Leader* parking lot last

Friday until late, since Adam drove me to dinner."

"Oh, *that* Clarence. The one who convinced the whole staff you were pregnant a while back."

"That's him. The creep." I pushed the accelerator harder, feeling the transmission complain again.

"You're not, are you?"

"Not what?"

"Pregnant."

"What kind of stupid question is that?" I roared, angrily flipping the visor out of the way. "Of course not! If you think for one second I—"

I broke off, hot-faced and furious, at Kyoko's loud guffaws.

"I'm kidding, Ro! That farmer of yours seems pretty straightlaced to me. He probably hasn't even kissed you yet."

"Shut up." I'd never, ever said that to Kyoko. But she deserved it. Especially since he actually. . .hadn't.

I fidgeted with my seat belt, suddenly uneasy. Remembering how near Adam and I had come to kissing so many times, his eyes dark and brilliant and his breath warm on my cheek. But every time his lips came too close to mine, he pulled away.

Cautious, yes. Respectful, definitely.

And. . .*odd*. Just a little. Frustrating, too.

I asked him once, albeit indirectly, and he fumbled with his truck keys, nearly dropping them down a storm drain—and promptly changed the subject. But not before I saw his face flush ever so slightly, uncomfortable red next to sandy-blond hair.

Kyoko snickered. "Chill, babe. This is payback for all those nasty pork rinds you sent me last year."

"Oh. Yeah." A corner of my mouth quirked up in a guilty smile. "I remember that."

"They make nice packing peanuts. Wait till you get your next care package, bucko."

Kyoko'd probably left her apartment window open because I heard the cawing of a crow. A Japanese crow—I'd seen Virginia turkeys on display in the grocer's case smaller than the crows in Tokyo—and its haunting sound made me suck in my breath. Remembering.

"Kyoko, you're lucky you still live in Japan. I wish I did. Most of the time." I rolled up the car window so I could hear better, blotting out fragrant morning scents of verdant earth and wild daisies, sun-warmed grass and damp leaves. And then I heard it low and soft through my Bluetooth: a wisp of summery cicada chants coming from Kyoko's end of the line, tapering off for the night. Different from the Southern whispers in the trees. Musical. Metallic. Distinctive.

"Well, you'd still be here in Japan if you hadn't gotten caught copying that dumb story."

"I know." I sighed. "But I also wouldn't have Adam."

"Good point. He's a keeper, I guess, even if he does drive a pickup truck." Kyoko yawned, a dead giveaway that she was about to pounce again. "So how old is he again? Sixteen? Seventeen? I forget."

Flaming color clawed its way up my neck. "He's twenty-three, Kyoko. Almost twenty-four." I pressed on the gas. "Hey, you're the one who said age didn't really matter."

"It doesn't." She chuckled. "I might be practically twenty-seven, but yesterday I met this little fresh-scrubbed Marine recruit from the base, and if things were different, I'd—"

"Stop it!" I shrieked, turning up the radio as loud as it would go. "I am NOT hearing this!"

"Don't worry. He had a girlfriend already." Kyoko sighed, and I slowly turned down the volume. Some goofy advertising for pickup truck KC lights, which I hoped she didn't hear. "Anyway, that farmer of yours is all right. I met him, remember? At least he doesn't crochet clothes for his *anime* comic dolls like one of my last dates."

I forgot my next sentence.

"It's true. Well, I'm leaving Japan soon anyway." Kyoko's voice came harsh and strident in my ears, as if she'd dumped a bowl of hot ramen noodle soup in my lap. "Although honorably, unlike you. I bought my tickets yesterday."

I silenced, remembering our strolls through Tokyo sidewalks, golden ginkgo leaves falling in a yellow shower all around us. And soon Kyoko would leave Japan, severing my last link to the country I loved.

No more postcards. No more stinky packages of seaweed rice crackers and dried fish.

And once Kyoko moved off to her next post, no more of the Japan-Kyoko memories I held so close to my heart.

"You're really leaving?" I managed, biting my lip.

"Yep. I've done my time here, and I'm ready to move on." Kyoko paused. "Don't cry or anything, okay? I told you months ago."

She didn't get my new and unexpected displays of emotion. After all, I hadn't cried since I was seven, the day my dad walked out the door. Until Virginia. Until last year.

"Won't you miss Japan, Kyoko?"

"No, I love separating my trash into six different piles, hanging up my milk cartons to dry with little clips, and memorizing which day of the week burnables, nonburnables, cans, glass, and bottles go out," she retorted, a sarcastic bite in her voice. "I may be environmentally conscious, Ro, but I swear even Greenpeace would go nuts if they spent three years here. They'd start screaming and chucking stuff out windows. Dumping Styrofoam in Tokyo Bay."

I laughed, but it faded quickly. "But the subways! Mount Fuji, and noodle shops, and—"

"I can't wait to buy clothes in normal sizes either," Kyoko blabbered on, not appearing to hear me. "Not little dainty things my two-year-old niece could wear. I have to buy clothes in the 'jumbo' section here!"

"Come on. There must be something you'll miss from Japan."

"Let me think. . .the traffic jams? Driving on the left? Oh, sorry. That would be *you*."

"It takes a while once you come back to the States," I shot back. "Don't think you're going to do any better."

"Please. They wouldn't even notice it in San Fran, the way everybody drives on the freeway. I once saw a guy going backward at seventy miles per hour—and he passed me, too!"

"Well, I love Japan. I always will, I guess." I clicked on my turn signal at an empty intersection. "Come visit me during hunting season when people skin deer carcasses in their backyards, and pacifist Japan might start looking pretty good. You'll beg Dave for a transfer back."

"Whoa. Deer carcasses? Do you have any pictures?"

"Huh?"

"For my redneck collection. I could make a great screen saver out of that. Maybe hack it into somebody's computer at the office." She sucked in an excited breath. "Hey, can you get me a mounted deer head? What a great conversation starter on life and death! Or no—just death." Kyoko snickered.

"Ugh. Please." I waved my hand. "No death talk." Not after I'd spent another hour sorting through Amanda's file, trying to understand this case that wouldn't leave me alone.

"Listen," I began, tapping my fingers on the steering wheel as I rounded a smooth curve, sloped lines of the mountains appearing through a thicket of oaks and pines. "Do you think there's any chance a woman who disappeared twelve years ago could still be alive?"

"Twelve years? That's a stretch. Why?"

"I'm just curious about a local crime story. She just vanished. No trace."

"Did she get anonymous flowers beforehand?"

I jerked the steering wheel, swerving so much my tire bumped against the grassy shoulder, jarring my teeth.

"I just read a novel where the serial killer starts by sending the women flowers—you know, funeral flowers. Lilies and stuff. And then when he sends the ribboned wreath, it's time to—"

"Cut it out!" I screeched, sorry I'd asked. I guided the car back onto the asphalt with a soft bump. Fingers shaking on the steering wheel. "Forget it. Let's talk about something else. Like Adam's good news."

Kyoko chuckled. "Why do you think I called, Ro?"

"To congratulate me?" A muddy truck passed me, going too fast, and I waited for the whine of the engine to fade. "Adam found a buyer for my house, Kyoko! His uncle's going to buy it. It's a miracle." I exhaled, watching the green pastures and ribbon of asphalt spin past me, reviving my Japan-sad spirits. "By the end of July—just in time for our wedding in August. He got a job transfer with a company here in Staunton and wants to move in right away."

"I heard. That's fantastic, Ro. Really."

"And he's paying the full asking price! Do you know how rare that is? That's way more than that last offer."

"You deserve it." Her voice turned tender. "I'll even miss that silly screen door on your front porch."

"Yeah, and all those marigolds Adam planted in my flower bed. Mom's stuff all over the house." My throat contracted. "The kitchen table where she used to sit and write before I knew her."

"Before you. . .what?"

"I mean, before I really knew who she was. She'd changed, you know. I just arrived too late to see it." My fingers tightened on the steering wheel.

For one irrational second I didn't know which I'd miss more—Japan or Mom's house.

"So," I said, shaking the memories out of my head, "after more than a year of gathering dust on the real-estate market, Mom's house is finally going to sell. We'll rent an apartment somewhere in town so Adam can drive to college, and. . ."

Kyoko waited. "And?"

"Llama!" I screeched. Jamming on the brakes and swerving out of the way, gravel spinning under my tires. I fishtailed against a grassy shoulder, barely managing to miss a lone white pine tree before screeching to a stop.

Just inches from, yes, a real, live llama. In the middle of the road.

—⁊⁊—

"I can't believe this," I fumed to Kyoko, slamming the car door behind me with shaking fingers. "Don't people fix their fences around here?" I encountered groundhogs on my daily runs along country roads, and once somebody's overfriendly hound, but never a llama.

And I was sick of too-close encounters with livestock.

"Ro-chan—are you there?" Kyoko shouted into the Bluetooth. "What's going on? I could swear I heard you say something about a llama."

"Yes. A big one." I peered past it as it backed up a step, knobby knees bending on legs like skinny drinking straws. "Make that two. There's a baby back there in the pines."

Kyoko silenced. "You're joking, right? Like. . .the cow-tipping thing?"

"Nope. But now that you mention it, there are cows out, too. A whole section of the fence is down. Great. Do I look like I have a hay bale in my car?"

"A—a what?"

"Now I'll never get to work!" I threw my hands up in the air, shooing the llama out of the road and into the grassy shoulder. "How in the world am I supposed to explain this to Kevin? He won't believe me for a second."

The llama reared back its head and glared at me, showing thick rectangular teeth. Baby trotted behind, ears up like two inward-curving apostrophes.

"I can definitely see why Kevin wouldn't believe you. You'd better take pictures."

"With what? Adam's cell phone doesn't have a camera."

"Well then you'd better borrow somebody else's. I'm just saying."

"Don't llamas spit?"

"Like the dickens. I think they bite, too. You had your rabies shots? Diphtheria? Anthrax? You know how I feel about animals."

"Thanks, Kyoko. Some help you are," I huffed, stepping around

81

my car and marching up the long gravel driveway toward a large, blocky white farmhouse surrounded by sugar maples. "Hold on. I'm going to get help."

"You're not gonna turn around and drive to work another way?"

"And let all the animals get run over?"

"I did ask you for a mounted deer head. Llama would be fine though, too."

"You're sick, Kyoko." I clopped up stone steps. "The Brewers' house is right over here. Fred Brewer bought a llama a year or two ago. Everybody knows that. But she's an escape artist, and his fences aren't strong enough. If he's going to have a llama, he needs to use high-tensile wire, not this old rusty stuff. Something like Red Brand."

I paused at the front door just long enough to hear Kyoko gasp. "Ro-chan. Please tell me you did not just say that."

"About the llama?"

"Girl." I could almost see her shaking her head. "If you know that much about pasture fencing, you need to move. Pronto."

―᠁―

I knocked until my knuckles hurt then rang the doorbell. I finally gave up and strode through the field, past a more secure line of fencing, chickens scattering around my feet. And when I came to the neat little brick rancher up on a slight hill, I thanked God to see a car in the driveway.

"Hello?" I knocked on the screen door. Two cats snaked around my ankles, purring, and I reached down to pat one.

"Can I help you?" a woman called from inside. I shielded my eyes to see through the screen a floral sofa, walls splashed with paintings, and a brick mantel that cradled a photo of a blond preteen girl. A girl that looked like. . .like. . .somebody I felt I should know. But I couldn't put my finger on whom.

Footsteps pattered on carpet, and I jerked my eyes away from the photo.

"Hi. Sorry." I wiped cat fur off my hand as she opened the door. "It's the llama."

"She got out again?" The elderly woman, with a strikingly pretty Asian face and smooth gray-black hair pulled back in a ponytail, shook her head.

"The fence is down over there." I squinted through the sun and pointed.

"Liv, you old rascal. What's Fred gonna do with you?" She chuckled. "She didn't bite or charge you, did she?"

"No. Why, does she bite?"

"Only people she doesn't like. So she must have liked you." The woman winked. "Liv's a smart judge of character, you know. And she can smell your intentions a mile away. She never forgets a face."

The woman stepped out on the porch and bent to see through the trees. "The cows are out, too, I guess?"

"Yes. A couple of them," I replied, my "llama info quota" filling up for the day. "Are the Brewers around?"

"They're out of town. But I'll give their son a call. He lives just over the way. Sorry about that, *ne?*"

"No problem. They're not your cows." I smiled then whipped around in her direction. Ne? Japanese people tacked that onto the ends of their sentences as a customary sort of "right?" or "isn't it?" Like the French *n'est-ce pas?*

Asking sounded tacky, so I politely stuck out a hand, hoping to divine a clue from her name. "Thank you, Mrs. . . ?"

"Kate. Just call me Kate."

Oh. Okay. I patted the cats and scooted down the steps, glancing over at her mailbox. Which greeted me with a boring, American-sounding "Townshend."

So much for that. But when I looked back over my shoulder to wave good-bye, she bobbed her head toward me in a slight bow. Chin dipping down, eyes briefly closing. Arms straight and graceful. Just as I remembered from my years in Japan.

I resisted the urge to march back up Kate's front steps and scream for joy that she had to be Japanese, and what was she doing in Staunton, Virginia, surrounded by livestock? Then I'd throw my arms around her, ignoring all nontouching Japanese etiquette, and hug her until she couldn't breathe.

But I contained myself with difficulty. I stepped my way back through the grass, part of which was fouled in large sections by scattered corn and chicken droppings, and headed toward the road. Still racking my brain to remember whom that photo on Kate Townshend's mantel looked like.

That's it—Amanda Cummings. A few years peeled back, maybe— chubbier cheeks, but that same golden-blond hair? I stopped short as the realization whammed me like a flying hubcap.

Surely not. All those news articles and police reports scattered in Amanda's blue folder whirled into my brain, and an uneasy tremor rippled through me. I hesitated in the shade of a giant sugar maple tree and dialed *The Leader*—wondering if I was obsessed or if everybody in this freaky town ended up looking like Amanda Cummings.

"Sorry to bother you, Meg," I said in low tones, glancing back up at the Townshend house. "Can you help me a second? I need some information from Amanda's file."

"For somebody who's not interested in that case, you sure do ask a lot of questions," Meg replied smugly.

I chewed my bottom lip, watching the two cats curl up in a patch of sun on Kate's porch, blinking lazy eyes. "Just help me out, okay? I need to know if a Kate Townshend ever had any dealings with Amanda Cummings."

"Well, I'd look her up for you, but I'm out on a photo shoot. A livestock sale."

"Funny. So you don't want to help me?"

Meg paused. "I'm serious, Jacobs. It's out at Augusta Expo. Cattle Battle. Ever heard of it? They have milk-drinking contests and stuff. But I'll go through the files with you tomorrow and see what we can find."

⁓

"Are you back?" Kyoko's voice chirped impatiently into my Bluetooth.

"Yep. And I hear a four-wheeler coming. Hold on." I paused, hand on the car door. "That must be Mr. Brewer's son." I stood on tiptoe. "Good. He's getting a couple of the cows back in."

"You gonna wait for him to clear the road?"

"No. I'll just turn around and go to work another way. But I've done my good deed, anyway. Not that she cares." I waved at the llama, who bristled and made burping sounds in my direction. "You can thank me later, Liv."

As soon as I pulled open the door handle, I saw it: a glimpse of something white sticking out from under the door to the gas tank.

"What's this?" I leaned closer, flipping open the square metal flap and pulling out a wrinkled slip of folded paper.

"What's what?"

"This thing in my car."

"Ro. If you tell me you've got a llama in your car, I swear I'll get

84

on the next plane to Virginia and—"

"No. Right under the flap covering my gas cap. . . ?" I frowned, flipping the metal door shut and unfolding the paper.

"Okay. That's it. When you're seeing South American pack animals in your gas tank, you need help."

"No! A note." I smoothed it out, shaking my head. "But it doesn't make any sense. Listen: 'My triumph has begun with you, my angel.'"

"Triumph? You mean like the British race car? Or maybe the motorbike?"

"I have no idea."

"Well, it can't be for you then. Since you're anything but angelic."

"Hmph. Thanks for the vote of confidence."

I turned the paper over and jumped, staring down at a shockingly realistic painting of an eye. *My* eye. The brightly colored flecks of emerald-green and gold and that distinctive starburst around the iris I'd never seen on anyone else.

I scraped at the painting with my fingernail. "An eye painted in acrylics, it looks like." My blood pumped faster, and I looked up, scanning the hillside.

Kyoko paused. "You don't have any weird admirers around the office, do you?"

"Only Clarence, and he admires every woman. He does comment a lot on my eyes though." I frowned, turning it back over to the "triumph" side. "But the message is all wrong. Cars and motorcycles don't begin, they start."

"Well, technically they do begin, back in a factory somewhere. But yeah, I agree. Doesn't make sense. It must be referencing something else."

I looked around me at the cow-spotted hills, a slight summer breeze shaking the pines at the side of the road. A stalk of black-eyed Susans nodded along the edge of the pasture fence.

I smoothed my hair back nervously, trying to remember when I'd last stopped for gas. "I have no idea when the note showed up. It could have been yesterday or five minutes ago."

"Do you recognize the handwriting?"

I smoothed out the note and studied it carefully. "No. It's just plain old red ink pen. And it looks like the writer used a letter stencil. The letters are perfect." And also untraceable.

"Ro. That's weird."

I felt a shudder in my stomach, working its way up to my dry mouth. Strange notes. Strange letters to Ray Floyd. Strange roses. I put my hand on the car door, feeling dizzy.

I started to open my mouth and tell Kyoko about the roses then decided against it. After being mugged at a Confederate battle reenactment and months later chased through the woods by Trinity's abusive ex-boyfriend and cohorts, Kyoko'd already determined what sanity I had left—particularly when it came to my choice of locale—hung by a thread.

"Forget it. It's probably Clarence, the creepy mail guy at work. He made a big deal about me leaving my car here on Friday for my birthday. Adam took me out, remember?"

"But you don't know Clarence did it."

"No. But I'd bet money he did."

"For somebody who's a magnet for trouble like you, this worries me. What's next, anonymous gifts delivered to your office? A masked murderer at that city council meeting you're supposed to cover? Hmm?"

"Stop it! You shouldn't say things like that." My fingers chilled on the paper. "The council meeting's in Waynesboro, for Pete's sake—which is even smaller than Staunton."

"Hey. You never know. You're the one who's been in and out of the emergency room more times than I can count, and don't ask me how—in a cow haven like western Virginia. But noooo. Nobody listens to me, do they?" Kyoko grumbled. "Looks like I'll have to take matters in my own hands if you don't shape up and quit flirting with death."

"I told you already. Don't talk about death." I gritted my teeth.

"Then stay out of trouble."

I started to ball up the note and toss it in my car trash bag, but something stopped me. An odd bile in my throat at the sight of unfamiliar ink on paper, like the scent of roses. And instead I opened my purse and stuffed it inside, checking over my shoulder before I got in the car and locked the door.

Chapter 9

I was pounding out a story on the new speed-limit laws and mulling over options for bridesmaids' dresses when Clarence's mail cart squeaked to a stop by my cubicle. Nearly running into the thick stack of bridal magazines donated by Priyasha the marketing director—plus *Epicurious* and *Bon Appétit* for Green Tree recipe ideas.

"Hey, Sheila." Clarence's voice came out low and raspy.

"Shiloh." I looked up, still stumped as to how on earth I was supposed to dress both Kyoko and Becky for the wedding. I couldn't picture Becky in some horrid black number that looked like it had crawled out of one of Kyoko's vampire movies, and Kyoko would probably rather be shot than carry a bouquet of daisies.

"Right. Shiloh." Clarence nodded, and I caught a whiff of mothballs from his sweater vest. "You're lookin' good today. 'Specially them eyes, with all those fancy colors. What are they, hazel?"

I thought of the note inside my gas tank flap. "Go away, Clarence," I said through clenched teeth. "Leave me alone, you hear me?"

"You're doin' the story on that Cummings gal, ain't ya?" Clarence asked, undeterred. "The one who disappeared twelve years ago?"

I jumped, banging my knee on the underside of the desk, and swiveled to face him. "Why do you ask?" I rubbed the spot where it stung.

"I remember it."

"Remember what?"

"When Amanda disappeared."

My breath caught slightly. I eased my chair in Clarence's direction, narrowing my eyes at him. Trying to guess if he was telling the truth.

Jennifer Rogers Spinola

No one knew Clarence's age, but he swore he'd had secret dealings with Richard Nixon, his hero. He kept a photo of himself with Nixon on the mail-room fridge, next to all the crossword puzzles he finished and then highlighted to make weird messages.

On a dare, Matt the intern had run a check on the photo with some of his DC friends, and to our surprise, it was indeed the real thing. It spooked us all, especially when he joked that the second gunman on JFK's grassy knoll was Marilyn Monroe.

"Marilyn Monroe died the year before!" I'd argued. "We've been over this before. It's impossible."

"Oh no. They *said* she died. Suicide. Very suspicious. I know for a fact they faked it."

"Like the moon landing?" I scoffed.

"Nope. That was real. But they covered up the sightings of life on Mars."

After that I just tried to stay away from Clarence. And wished he'd stay away from me.

But here he loomed again, both arms leaning on his mail cart. And for the first time in recent memory, not a trace of a smile on his wrinkled cheeks.

"Amanda was a good kid, but troubled. Hung out with the wrong crowd, ya know." Clarence's eyes looked faraway. "Grew up in some trailer park in Deerfield, but she got good grades. A real smart gal, 'til she got in with kids and on that vegetarian kick." He shook his head. "She worked at that fancy Ingleside hotel. And after that, The Red Barn restaurant."

"So it's a restaurant? I can't find it anywhere."

"It ain't around now." Clarence waved his hand. "But I think she was working there when she turned up missing."

"You lived here twelve years ago?" I crossed my legs, intertwining my fingers over my lap.

"Lands, a lot longer than that. I've lived all over. California, New Mexico." Clarence rubbed a hand over his nose and grizzled mouth. "But the year she turned up missing still stands out in my mind. I'll never forget it."

"Why's that?" I tipped my head.

"Well, for starters, the Planters Bank in town got robbed. Cleaned the poor suckers outta millions—first time it ever happened around here."

"That's my bank!" I uncrossed my legs in surprise.

"Yep. Mine, too. And right after the bank robbery, it snowed in July—a freak storm."

I scowled. "You're making this up, Clarence. It can't snow in July."

"It happened! I swear! Ask the locals. Right during the Independence Day parade through town, an' a storm blows up, and poof! Snow an' hail fallin' everywhere."

Right. Like I was going to believe that.

Clarence, unfazed by my skepticism, ticked things off on his fingers. "Governor had a heart attack in office. North River flooded. Apple crop almost went under. And a little no-name guy from Verona won the three-million dollar lotto jackpot. I think they had some race-car game back then." He rolled his cart back and forth, lost in thought. "Yep. A weird year."

Clarence pointed at me. "Tell you what. I'd phone tap that so-called drunk that smashed through that Floyd kid's window if I were you. I smell conspiracy. This whole thing's got somethin' to do with Amanda, I swear."

"Even the police can't do phone taps, Clarence. That's against the law."

"So's what Marilyn Monroe did."

I started to turn back to my desk, rolling my eyes, but Clarence scooted his mail cart closer. "There's more." He tapped the metal rail on his cart for emphasis. "So then Amanda went on vacation just before her wedding with that Floyd fella and never came back. Never found her, and it turned into a cold case pretty quick. Just disappeared. No evidence whatsoever. Broke that Floyd guy's heart."

"Clarence." I cleared my throat. "This is going to sound awfully heartless, but was Ray ever a suspect?"

"Ray Floyd? Yeah, briefly. Just because they were engaged and all. Nobody actually thought he'd do somethin' like that. He loved her too much." Clarence stroked his chin. "But they got proof he didn't do nothin'. He was in Seattle when she disappeared. Even got a parking ticket there on the day they found her empty car and was just as surprised as the rest of us." His eyes turned distant. "I think he spent some time in a clinic there to deal with his grief before he come back to Virginia to try and find her. Suicidal thoughts and all that. But he's okay now, I hear."

You were my first. The words jumped into my head with startling force as I recalled the spray-painted message.

"She wasn't his first fiancée, was she?" I asked cautiously, searching Clarence's leathery face. "Or first girlfriend?"

"Nope. They done investigated all that stuff. He'd been engaged before, and both of 'em had other beaus in the past. Why do you ask?"

I didn't respond to his question but twirled my chair as I thought, listening to it squeak on the left side. "Is there any way to find out whose first she was?"

"Hmmph. Easy. I can tell ya that."

My mouth went dry, and I stopped rocking the chair. "Why do you know so much about Amanda, Clarence?" I asked, feeling the tips of my fingers turn cold.

He gave me a sidelong look, and I held his gaze, not sure if he was testing or teasing me. "Small town. Everybody knows everything." He didn't break my gaze, letting his pause drag out into an uncomfortable silence. "So ya wanna know or not?"

"Tell me."

"Jim Bob Townshend."

The name rocked through me with palpable force. Townshend? I glanced at the blue folder on my desk, recalling the Japanese-looking woman near Fred Brewer's farm.

"Is he by any chance related to a Kate Townshend?" I squinted, trying to put all the crazy pieces of this cockamamy story together in my head. "After all, this is Staunton, right? How many Townshends can there be?"

"Kate? I know her. She lives down by the Brewer's place, don't she? The one with the llama?"

"That's her."

"Yep. She's Jim Bob's great-aunt or somethin'. I forget now."

I inhaled sharply, remembering the photo of an Amanda-looking girl on her brick mantel. "Is Kate Japanese?"

" 'Course. You didn't know that?" Clarence shot me a comic look of disdain. "Married to some military guy off the Yokotsuka base years ago. Been here ever since."

"Wow." I rolled my chair back a few inches, tipping my head up to stare at the white-speckled ceiling tiles. "There's a lot I don't know about this town."

"Ha. You ain't heard the half of it." Clarence stuck his hands in his pockets, rocking back and forth on his heels. That ridiculous orange-plaid bow tie of his clashed horribly with his green-and-navy striped shirt. Between Clarence Toyer and Ray Floyd, I didn't know which one deserved Worst Dresser of the Year.

"Wait'll I get started on the Jester brothers who live in your neighborhood." Clarence grinned. "I got stories that'd curl your hair."

"No thanks. I don't do perms." I scrunched up my nose. "So Amanda was engaged to Jim Bob Townshend before Ray." I toyed with the corner of the blue folder. "So. . .is it possible Jim Bob might have resented Ray at all?"

"Resented him? I heard he wanted to kill him. 'Course that was years ago, and since Amanda's been gone, nobody's heard much from him. He shows up ev'ry now and then, I hear, but he don't stick around."

Clarence looked away, wagging his head. "Jim Bob Townshend. Always a big troublemaker as a kid. Gettin' in fights and whatnot. Why, I had to call the cops on him once for tryin' to steal my car, right here in *The Leader* parking lot!" He scratched his shoulder. "But? I reckon all that's in the past."

"Why? What do you mean?"

"Shucks, the guy's been gone for years. He'd been livin' in West Virginia last we heard, a good year before Amanda turned up missing. Got a family and kids now, I hear. Makes good money. Turned out to be a real salt-of-the-earth guy." He ran his hand through his wild hair. "Goes to show that people ain't always what ya think, Shelly. Like I always tell ya."

"Shiloh."

"Right. Just keepin' ya on your toes." He crossed his arms, looking out the window at the summer haze. "Although it's funny. Some folks said they saw him in town these days, sorta keepin' to himself. Didn't talk to nobody. And his car's parked up at his pop's house. I drove by outta curiosity and saw it myself, plain as day. Same ol' Ford his mama used to drive, an' after she passed, he won't sell it."

"A Ford, huh?"

"Taurus. Graphite-silver. Nice car. His mama won it in a Pepsi giveaway. I swear. She mailed in the winning entry form, and they let her choose the color an' everything. Me? I done spent a fortune on them mail-in prize contests, and all I ever got was a pack of sunflower seeds. Go figure."

Clarence stretched and patted the cart. "Anyway. I hope you find who sent you them flowers."

He leaned closer and winked, showing his yellowish teeth in a grin that chilled my spine. "Angel."

My distaste for Clarence had diminished slightly, but it flared back up with a vengeance. I scowled as he pushed his creaky cart around the corner. Nearly flattening Meg, who jumped out of the way with a string of words I was glad I couldn't hear.

"Shiloh! I almost forgot." Meg rushed to my desk and leaned over it, one hand on the back of my chair. "Kate Townshend. You asked about her yesterday."

"Jim Bob's great-aunt or something. Clarence told me. But thanks for checking."

"Jim Bob? Who's Jim Bob?" Meg wrinkled a freckled nose.

I glanced up in surprise. "Isn't that what you were going to tell me?"

"No! But you're right. The girl in that photo you saw yesterday in Kate's house probably *was* Amanda."

I jerked my chair back.

"Kate is Amanda's grandmother."

—⁓—

I slumped over my desk, staring into the distance beyond my computer screen and Amanda's blue folder. Barely hearing Meg as she rattled on about how the relation was probably by marriage because Kate's Japanese and so forth. Blah, blah, blah.

"So I guess Amanda and Jim Bob were related then, too?" I warily turned to Meg, not really wanting her to answer.

"Jim Bob again. Who is this guy?"

"Her ex before Ray."

"Oh. Well, yeah. I guess they were related." Meg grinned, cocking an eyebrow. "This *is* the South, you know. And with a name like Jim Bob, well, what can you expect?" She put her palms up.

"Don't get me started." I groaned and rubbed my face. "You know what? I need a Tylenol."

"That bad?"

"No. I mean, it's strange, but my mind's already full. This is all too much." I sighed and played with the mouse. "There's so many other things going on in my life that I don't have time for kissing cousins and kooky old love triangles. You wanna see what came for me this morning?" I dug in my purse and pulled out a folded sheet of paper then plopped it in her hand. "Read it."

Meg took the paper and read, brow creasing in confusion. " 'Commonwealth vs. Jed Tucker.' Who's Jed Tucker?"

Before I could reply, Meg's eyes popped. "It's a court summons."

"Yes."

"To Winchester."

"Yes."

She tapped the paper thoughtfully. "Is this about that thing that happened before you started working here? Where you got jumped by rednecks at a Confederate battle reenactment, or something equally silly?" She put her finger on the name. "Jed Tucker. Yup. Definitely a redneck."

"And he's a skinhead, too. He's the one who kicked me in the side while they harassed me for being a Yankee—after they discovered I didn't have any money on me."

I fiddled with my desk drawer, not relishing the memories. "I dealt with the other three guys in court in February—and they got jail time, all of them. But this Tucker guy is a slippery one. Looks like they finally got him. Now I'll have to go back to court and testify against him."

I reached into a drawer and pulled out some silvery dried fish Kyoko had mailed me. Nice and crunchy. Their familiar briny flavor made me feel slightly better, but not much.

"So when's the trial?"

"October third, just after my wedding. The prosecutor's asking for jail time and damages. Good ol' Jed did send me to the emergency room with bruised ribs."

"You're paying a lawyer?" Meg glanced at my dried fish, probably figuring all I could afford was care-package food. To be fair, she wasn't so far off.

"No. He's the prosecutor assigned to my case. Don't worry. I don't have to pay for anything since it's in the interest of public safety."

"Yikes. You do have a penchant for trouble."

"That's what Kyoko says," I muttered to myself, taking the summons and folding it up.

Meg crossed her arms and eyed me with a pitying look, turning up her lip at the sight of my fish. "That's the pits."

"Tell me about it. I'm supposed to go wedding shopping with Becky tonight, but now all I can think of is this stupid summons." I shook my head in disgust. "I knew Jed would turn up sooner or later, but I didn't expect it to be now. When everything else in my life is going nuts."

"The flowers. Right." She shot me a sympathetic look.

"That's not even the worst part, Meg. Adam's been getting weird phone calls ever since Ray saw his face on that drawing."

Meg opened and closed her mouth in shock. "Shiloh Jacobs." She put her hands on her hips. "You'd better watch out. Both of you. Has he talked to the police?"

"He and his dad filed a complaint this morning. Adam's worried about putting everybody else—his two brothers, his parents—in danger if the calls don't stop. But there's not much the police can do, unfortunately." I shook my head and dug in the bag for another fish. "And then there's Ray Floyd. I've called him a couple of times to ask questions about the case, but he turns kind of cold every time I mention Adam."

"Well, I'd be scared, too, if a drawing of some stranger's face showed up in my mailbox with a threat."

"Exactly. I just hope he doesn't file a complaint to the police about Adam." I tapped the summons paper on the edge of the desk. "I mean, Adam clearly has nothing to do with this. The only connection we can find is that his dad taught Amanda geometry in high school years ago. But even he doesn't remember much about her.

"You know what? I promised to help Jerry give the restaurant a makeover." I flailed my arm in the direction of the bridal magazines. "And I'm supposed to be planning a wedding, Meg! Less than two months until I walk down the aisle, and do you think I can manage a normal existence where I actually get to think about things like wedding cake and dresses?"

I shook the summons in defiance and stuffed it in my purse. "But I'm going wedding shopping with Becky tonight no matter what. Hear me?"

Meg gave a wry smile, her dark eyes blinking sympathy. "I'm really sorry about everything." She shoved her stinky mug into my hands. "Here. Trust me. You need this more than I do."

I glanced down into the grainy, gray-brown depths, which smelled like horseradish and cheap vodka. "What. . .on earth. . .is this?"

"Brewer's yeast. A great way to get your chromium. And the dregs of that fermented maple syrup. It's pretty potent stuff."

I felt my shoulders shake in an unexpected laugh. "No, really. It's okay." I pushed the mug back at her. "I'll stick with my fish. And maybe make some *miso* soup since I missed breakfast."

"Jacobs. You know how unhealthy it is to skip breakfast."

"Believe me, I do. Sumo wrestlers don't eat breakfast." I reached for my desk drawer. "I couldn't help it though. I got stuck on the side of the road with a bad transmission. But"—I raised a finger—"I found Mom's transmission warranty last night, so I won't have to pay for a new one."

"Good for you. I told you karma would sort things out."

"Well, if repercussions and rewards are based on my actions, past and present, I'm in a heap of trouble. Let's call it instead God's pity on a penniless writer. How's that sound?" I tipped my head in a smile. "And I discovered something, too."

"That you're a closet Buddhist?"

"No way. Mom played the guitar."

I pulled a plastic packet of brownish stuff from my drawer, Japanese kanji characters for instant miso splattered across its glossy surface.

"I found the guitar up in her attic while I was hunting for her transmission warranty. Funny, huh, the things you can still learn about someone who's been gone more than a year?" My smile turned wistful. "She had a practice sheet in the guitar case. Untitled. Just the notes." I hummed a few bars. "Do you recognize it?"

"Nope. But I couldn't carry a tune if my life depended on it."

"Me either. But I wish I could figure out what song it was."

I snipped the corner of the miso packet with scissors, lost in thought.

"Ah. Miso. Now there's one place we see eye to eye." Meg patted me proudly on the shoulder. "Vegan in the making."

"Don't get your hopes up." I snipped the corner of the packet and squeezed it all out into an old Cornell mug, like gooey brown toothpaste. The Japanese are masters at instant everything—like instant noodles out of a machine. I reached under my desk and produced a thermos then pumped in a few squirts of hot water. Stirring with my spoon until it reached a thin, soupy consistency. I tasted and shook off my spoon, wishing somebody in Japan would invent an instant "solve-everything-in-your-life" packet.

Maybe then I wouldn't be getting married in my bathrobe.

Clarence pushed his mail cart down the aisle and across a few of my bridal magazines, and I turned and scowled.

"Don't worry, Jacobs." Meg looked up as I stomped over to the stack of magazines and snatched them out of the way. Smoothing the covers. "Cooter's got a jumpsuit you can get married in. He uses it for skinning deer and changing car oil, but you can get the stains out with bleach or something. Recycle everything, I always say."

I plopped the magazines under my desk. "I'll stick with something a little more capitalistic and wasteful this time, if you don't mind." I reached out to grab Meg's arm. Lowering my voice to a whisper. "And listen. About Clarence." I peeked around the corner to make sure he'd gone. "Do you think there's any chance he's the guy who won the lottery twelve years ago?"

"What?" Meg screwed up her face. "Don't be ridiculous."

"No, really! He used to live in Verona. He told me so once. And I know he plays lotto. I've seen him at the Shell station scratching off those dumb tickets."

"Shiloh Jacobs." Meg put a hand on her hip. "If Clarence had won a million bucks, would he still be buying lotto tickets? Hmm? Or driving that clunker of a car?" She met my gaze. "Or working *here*?"

"I guess you're right." I let Meg's arm go, embarrassed. "He just seems like he's hiding something. And"—I leaned over to whisper in her ear—"he's left-handed. I purposely asked him to sign for an order yesterday, and he used his left hand. Just like whoever's been leaving all those Amanda notes."

"Oh, I'm sure that fella's hiding a lot more than lotto tickets. Please." She rolled her eyes. "But I don't think Clarence killed Amanda. Do me a favor and call the good doc your mom and Amanda both used, will you? Maybe he can help you, too. You're cracking up."

She rolled her knuckles lightly on my head before turning back to her cubicle.

—⁓—

Meg hadn't even rounded the corner when I smelled them. *Roses*. A heavy, cloying perfume, like the strange bouquet that had enjoyed its remaining moments in the company trash can.

"Do you smell that?" I turned toward the scent.

"What?" Meg inhaled. Then sniffed at the armpits of her tunic and shrugged. "Nope. Unless you're talking about my tea."

"No. This was a good smell." I wrinkled my lip and inhaled again, but the floral odor had vanished. "Forget it. My overactive imagination, I guess."

But as soon as I turned back to the keyboard, I distinctly caught the scent of roses. Even Meg froze in place, nostrils huffing. Footsteps thumped on the carpet just around the corner of my cubicle.

"That better not be. . ." I half-stood in my chair, hands clenching into fists.

"Roses," said Clarence with a grin. Appearing like a horrible vision, holding out a fat bouquet of dark red blooms.

Chapter 10

My jaw clenched in anger. "I don't think so, Clarence. That's not funny. Chastity's desk is over there." I pointed in the direction of her desk.

"Ain't fer Chastity," grinned Clarence. "They got your name on 'em."

This time even Meg gasped. I still didn't move to receive the vase. It just seemed too creepy with Clarence holding them, like another of his jokes. They'd probably squirt water on me or something.

" 'Shiloh Jacobs,' " he recited, pointing to the card. "You gonna take 'em, or do I hafta sit 'em on the floor?"

I stared at him then quickly made a space on the desk between Amanda's file and my keyboard. An identical vase wrapped in red paper. Twelve deep red roses, same as before. Only bigger, if that were possible. The same crystal vase and glossy red ribbon. And a little white envelope from Rask Florist.

"Roses again?" I threw my arms up. "Who on earth are these from?"

Clarence flexed his eyebrows. "You're the one who stays out 'til all hours a the night," he leered. "Leavin' yer car in the parkin' lot mighty late. Who knows what a fella might think?"

I slammed both hands on the back of my chair, shoving it out of the way, and marched over to face him. "You," I said, feeling angry color creep up my neck. "What was that note you left on my car supposed to mean? And if you're playing some kind of sick joke by sending me flowers, cut it out. It's not funny."

"Hey, Tiger Eyes. Simmer down. I didn't send nothin'." Clarence put his palms up and backed away, his face contorted like he was trying hard to smother a smile. "You stressed today or somethin'?" He lowered his voice. "That time of the month?"

Meg snickered. I flung a hateful look at Clarence then stalked back to my desk and looked uneasily at the flowers.

"Call the florist." Meg swooshed a pen through the blooms, ruffling their petals. "You'd better read the card first though," she added, flicking the envelope onto the table with the tip of the pen. "It might be important."

I reluctantly dug out the little white florist's card with a tissue in case of fingerprints and tore it open.

"YOU ARE MINE, MINE, MINE, ANGEL DIVINE," began the message in block letters. *"I've been waiting for you all this time, and I won't share you with anyone. No matter what."*

Everything in clear, dark red ink.

—∞—

"Not Brandy again! Why, why did it have to be Brandy?" I slammed the phone down and buried my face in my hands.

"What's wrong with brandy? Cooter gets this really good kind from— Jacobs? You okay?"

I raised my head to see Meg peering at me worriedly, her favorite Cannon slung over her shoulder. "The florist didn't tell you anything?"

"No. It's that Brandy woman again who doesn't know anything." I rolled my head from side to side, letting my tense muscles loosen. "She says if I think it's a mistake, it probably is. That things do get goofed up from time to time."

"What kind of lame answer is that?" Meg threw her hands up. "You just got a threat, Jacobs." She pointed to the card. "A creepy threat. What does he mean he won't 'share you' with anyone?"

"I know. Brandy didn't take the order and doesn't know who did." I fingered my keys. "I'm thinking of going to Rask myself and then maybe. . ."

"The police station?"

"You guessed it."

"Good move. Just to be safe." Meg adjusted the camera strap and dropped an extra battery pack in the pocket, Velcro-ing it shut. "I'm heading out to a photo shoot. Want some company?"

"Definitely. If you can spare a few extra minutes." I shoved the bouquet in her direction. "And here—take these stupid roses before we go. Please. Get them out of my sight."

"Cool!" Meg hefted the large vase, turning it in the light. "Cooter'll love this. He's crazy about flowers."

"Cooter. Crazy about flowers."

"Yeah. You should see the lily arrangements he makes. I get him a bouquet about once a month, and he's happy."

Meg's hip brushed the corner of Amanda's blue folder, nearly knocking it onto the floor, and I reached out to grab it.

"You know," she said finally, hefting the vase into one arm and stroking her chin. "Have you ever thought that maybe. . ."

Her eyes darted from the folder to me, and I sat up straight. "Don't say it, Meg."

Meg ignored me. "Since all these weird events are transpiring around the same time as Amanda's purported. . .uh. . .killer is leaving messages, maybe the perp thinks you and Amanda are related somehow, or. . . ?" Her voice trailed off, and she shook her head. "You don't look alike. Your mom does, but not you. I don't get it."

"I don't either. Amanda disappeared years before I ever came here. Before Mom came here, even."

I put Amanda's picture back in the folder and leaned back in my chair. "The handwriting on the note in my car or on the florist's cards hasn't been distinctive. Nice and neat. No weird *A*'s or loops like the 'You-were-my-first' messages."

"Well, that's all opinion, you know. But I agree. I think you'd notice handwriting that unusual."

Meg put one arm up, combing her fingers through her long, wispy hair as she searched for words. Making the scarlet petals quiver. "Do you and Amanda have anything in common? Hobbies? The kind of car you drive? The Japan connection, no matter how loose it might be?" She shrugged. "Sorry. I'm just throwing things out there."

"Besides. . .sharing the same birthday?" I glanced up at Meg with a pounding heart, feeling inexplicably guilty.

"What?" she squawked. "You didn't tell me that!"

"Well, no, because what's it supposed to mean?" I threw my arms out. "We were born in different decades. It's not that weird to share a birthday, is it?"

Meg frowned, thinking. Then finally shook her head. "I guess not."

"Besides, who knows my birthday anyway? It's not like I go around with it displayed on my forehead."

"True." She sighed. "Well, can you think of anything else? Try hard, Jacobs."

"That's just it! We don't have much in common. Amanda was a country girl from Deerfield, Meg! I don't have a Japanese grandmother, by marriage or otherwise. I'm not vegetarian or an artist. I don't collect stamps. And I wouldn't get engaged to my cousin in a million years, got it?"

Meg smirked. "Just checking. You never know."

I ignored her joke, not in the mood for jesting. "I'll talk to the police, but without any clues, this whole thing is just one big, faceless game."

"But it's a threatening game, Miss Bride-to-Be, if said admirer is meaning that he won't share you with Adam." She glanced down at the florist's card. "Hence the stalker-ish phone calls he's been getting. The drawing of his face on Ray's letter."

"But why Ray and Adam? What do they have to do with any of this?"

Meg shrugged slowly, shifting her weight to the other sandal. "I don't know—unless the perp views them both as competitors. Ray with Amanda, and you with Adam. And if he's targeting you like he targeted Amanda, then. . . ?"

I covered my face with my hands.

Meg pressed her lips together, playing with a big wooden dream-catcher earring with her free hand. The Native American kind that looked like a woven spiderweb, a long beige feather trailing from it.

"What?" My voice came out louder and crabbier than I intended.

"I don't trust the police, personally. They're the establishment. Are you with me?"

"But you just said a few minutes ago I should tell them!"

"Sure you should. So you can prove you reported it. But I didn't say to *trust* them. Deputy Shane Pendergrass is sitting on his duff eating Krispy Kremes while somebody's sending you roses with mysterious messages and harassing your fiancé, right as Amanda's alleged killer is spray painting roads and threatening people."

She lowered her voice. "And if by some chance Clarence really didn't put that note on your car, maybe Amanda's killer did. Which means he knows your car."

My head started to pulse right behind my eyes, and I grabbed my keys, throwing my purse strap over my shoulder.

"You go talk to Kevin. I'll pack up." Meg gestured toward her cubicle. "But let me say one last thing first. I don't trust big ol' Shane down at the police station further than I can throw him."

"No?"

"Not that he's evil. Just. . .a little too ignorant. And a serial flirt." She grinned. "Although he is kinda cute. A little thin on top. He's gonna be bald as a cue ball one day—not that that's a bad thing. Hey, you know who I saw him with the other day? Down at the Depot restaurant? Well, he's been on and off dating this Misty gal, and. . ."

I waved my hand in front of her face. "Focus, Meg! You were talking about Shane not being trustworthy. I could care less who he's dating."

"Huh? Oh yeah." She shook her head as if to clear it. "Well, what I meant is this: I wouldn't walk away and leave this bouquet business completely up to somebody like Shane. Use your own noggin. Stay safe, but go after whatever you can yourself."

Meg gazed down at the roses a long time, rearranging a few stray petals. "You can't think of anything you might have in common with Amanda? Or your mom, perhaps? As goofy as that sounds."

"Mom." My stomach roiled. "I knew she'd come up sooner or later." I cupped my hand around my mug of miso soup, which had turned cold.

"There is one thing."

Meg eyed me. "What, something else you have in common with Amanda?"

"No. My mom. They shared the same doctor."

Meg puckered out her lips, not moving. A strand of her reddish hair quivered slightly in the air-conditioning current. "Well. If that's all you've got, then you'd best get on it. Stat."

"I know. I've been thinking about it. Trying to get up the courage." I twisted my fingers together, remembering Mom's letters. Her grief. As if I wanted to learn how acutely I'd caused her suffering.

"Waiting for courage? Jacobs, if you don't call him right away— now—I'll personally throttle you." She smacked a palm with her fist. "And not bother to send you roses first."

⸺⸺

The phone bleeped into my ear as I pulled up a search on Dr. Geissler on the Internet. A simple website showed a photo of a white-haired man in a suit. Kind eyes. That'd make you want to pull up a chair and spill all your problems.

Which, for me right now, would take several hours.

"Dr. Geissler's office," bleated the receptionist.

I barely registered the greeting. My eyes had jumped to the caption beneath Dr. Geissler's photo.

"Hello?" the voice repeated.

"Hi. Sorry." I shook my head rapidly, still reading off the website. "So. . .Dr. Geissler's a psychiatrist? Not a general practitioner?"

"Yes, ma'am." The receptionist sounded slightly bemused. "Do you. . .have an appointment with us?"

"Me? No. I just expected a regular medical doctor." I pulled out my bottom drawer and withdrew Mom's medical forms, flipping through the pages. A psychiatrist surprised me. But then again, not so much.

I bit my lips, remembering Mom's bouts with depression during my growing-up years, and even something like a nervous breakdown. She'd stay in bed for days, weeping, and then scramble pills down her throat with shaking hands.

"Do you have any records for Ellen Amelia Jacobs?" I asked, my mouth feeling cottony from nerves. "She was my mom. And she passed away a year ago."

"I'll see if the doctor can talk to you." The receptionist, who identified herself as Melina, dropped her voice to a hush. "But if you want to meet with him, I'd recommend you do it quickly."

"Why? Is he terribly busy?"

Melina hesitated, as if wondering how much she could trust me. "Have you met Dr. Geissler, ma'am?"

"No, but my mom apparently has." I shuffled through her medical notes. "Until her death."

"He's not well, I'm afraid." Melina sighed. "I've worked with him nearly all my life. He's a good man. Retired, actually, but continues to practice. But I feel like I should advise you of his limitations beforehand so you're not surprised."

"Sorry. I don't understand." I shifted in my chair, feeling tension tighten in my neck.

"He seems to have the beginnings of. . .well, some memory problems. Possibly Alzheimer's." She paused. "He's quite aware of it. But since he's no longer practicing medicine now, mostly clinical psychology, he's stayed on a little longer. People love him. But factually, I don't know how much longer he'll be able to practice."

Fantastic. Just what I needed. Another clue about to sink into oblivion, and here I sat, completely helpless. I felt like banging my head repeatedly on my desk. Instead I leaned back in my chair and took in a long, deep breath to steady myself.

"I'm so sorry to hear that," I said finally. "So he won't remember anything about my mom, I guess. I'd really hoped he could. . .well, clear up some things."

"Oh, no. His memory regarding his patients is incredible. He hasn't lost that at all—and if you schedule with him quickly, you'll see that." She chuckled lightly. "I just have to remind him frequently what day it is. For now. But I can't guarantee how long that'll last."

"When's the soonest you have?"

"July."

I groaned out loud.

I hung up my phone and scratched down the appointment date, listening for the rattle of Meg's camera and car keys. Nothing. Just the low, rhythmic clacking of keyboards. I put down my pen and peeked over the cubicles, looking for her.

Great. She'd probably wandered off to the lobby and started posting PETA flyers or something.

A plink of new mail made me glance down at my screen, and I frowned at the unfamiliar return address.

Hate mail, probably. Now that I wrote for the crime section, I sometimes got feedback. Usually bad. People hated seeing their Uncle Willy written up for stealing tractors.

I clicked through two older e-mails, both calling me all sorts of names, and then clicked on the newest one. An e-mail address I didn't recognize.

And as I skimmed it, the cursor just sat there, blinking, as if in as much shock as me.

"Hello, my angel," the e-mail read. *"You can't fool me. I see through your phony engagement scheme a mile away. But it won't work, my love, because three was always meant to be with me."*

Chapter 11

He'd signed the e-mail "Odysseus."

"What?" I shrieked, knocking into my mug and spilling brown miso soup down the front of my shirt and all over the desk. "Who is this?"

I clicked to the second one:

> *The third is mine, my angel! Mine, mine, mine! Because you came back to the auto shop—and three is yours forever. Let's make it four. Because three times four is always twelve.*

I made such a commotion that both Priyasha and Phil stumbled over to my desk. Even Matt jerked his head away from his Facebook page to stare.

"Everything okay?" Priyasha, our marketing woman, poked a dark head down to mine, her voice carrying a slight lilt of Sri Lankan warmth.

"No! Look at this!" I pointed to the offending e-mails. "Who on earth would send me something like this? What is this Odysseus guy, a math teacher or something?" I put my hand on my hips. "And how does he know my wedding's on August third? Or what auto shop I go to?"

Phil, our sports writer, lifted some soup-soaked papers away from the keyboard and read, and then pulled back his head in surprise. "Whoa."

I furiously wiped soup from the front of my brown dress. Good thing I'd worn a matching color; I single-handedly kept stain-remover and dry-cleaning companies in business.

"You get hate mail all the time, so what's one or two on the other side?" Phil squinted at the e-mail. "You don't know anybody who calls himself by Greek nicknames?"

"No. Should I?"

"I dunno." Phil shrugged, looking irritated. As he so often did. "I guess it's a Greek god or somethin'. Most fellas think they are, anyway." He nudged Priyasha, who snickered behind her palm.

"Just you, Phil," she joked, slapping him on the arm.

I reread the e-mail in frustration, wishing somebody—anybody—felt as horrible about the whole mess as I did. "There's no way to track e-mails, is there?" I coldly ignored their banter.

"Don't think so." Phil crossed his arms. "You don't recognize the address?"

"Ody803," I repeated out loud. "Nope. But it's our wedding date—August third. But shiro.com?" I played with the mouse, brow pursed. "*Shiro* means 'white' in Japanese, but it doesn't ring any bells."

"You can create any domain name you want, which is why they're so impossible to trace. Hence the explosion of spam."

At exactly that moment, my work inbox lit up again. Priyasha and I both looked at each other.

"Surely not," I said, hovering the mouse over the unread message. Ody803 again. I blinked in disbelief.

Our special day is coming soon, my angel, for you have thawed and revived my frozen heart. And then we can finally finish what we started. Three's your number, but not two. So lose the man and the vows, and say them only with me—or prepare to be lost yourself. P.S.: the roses should remind you.

I jerked my hand back from the mouse. "It's the creep who's sending me roses! That's another threat, isn't it?"

"Wait a second." Phil grabbed the mouse and clicked back up to the second line. "That 'revive my frozen heart' part. Isn't that from. . . from. . . ? Hold on." And he commandeered my keyboard, clicking into the Google search engine. "Yep. Just as I thought. *The Brothers Karamazov.*"

"You knew that?" Priyasha screwed up her face.

"Lit major." Phil scowled. "So I like poetry. Sue me."

He pointed to the computer screen. "That's the first of what Mitya

105

says to Alyosha when he visits him in prison. Here's the second half: 'One may bring forth an angel, create a hero!' " Phil struck a pose, arm outstretched. The blue-white overhead fluorescent light gleamed down on the angular lines of his perpetually crabby face.

Angel. The angel thing again. I reached for the mouse.

"Yeah. I hated that book." Phil dropped the orator's pose. "All except for my favorite line: 'I may be wicked, but I gave an onion.' That pretty much sums me up."

Priyasha rolled her eyes. "So our secret admirer is a literary, huh?" She poked Phil. "Is it you?"

"No. And don't bother asking me for onions. I've already done my good deed." Phil snorted. "So you don't have any idea who this Odysseus guy is, Shiloh? Or why he thinks three and four is significant?" He counted. "He did send you three e-mails."

"But two bouquets."

"So far."

"Oh, I'll find out who he is." I was already clicking away on Google. Scanning lines about Greek legends and love stories at top speed. Something Homer had written about two lovers waiting years to be together, giving up hundreds of suitors and eternal youth.

"Or be lost yourself." I pressed my eyes closed, feeling ill. *Lost like Amanda Cummings?*

A shiver passed through me as I clicked out of the window and back to the e-mails, reading through them again. Recalling the strange hang ups at the Carter house.

"This weirdo. . .he's *jealous.* He wants me to get rid of Adam?" I pressed shaking fingers to my cheek. "And cancel our wedding?"

" 'Our special day,' " Priyasha read aloud, mystified. "The third. Do you think he's talking about your wedding day? Or something else? You don't have some. . .I don't know. . .upcoming rendezvous with someone from your past?"

In an odd flash I recalled the dusky evening shadows and rednecks' raspy laughter. Trying frantically to free myself as they dragged me farther into the woods.

My mouth went dry. I could see the skinhead's crazy eyes, like pale blue ice, and the glint of the knife.

"I'll show you what we do to Yankee scum who defile our land!" he sneered, just before the period replica Civil War musket whacked him in the forehead.

"And then we can finally finish what we started."

The summons to trial. October third.

"Shiloh? You okay? Sorry I'm late. I decided to make a hanging planter out of this two-liter bottle some idiot threw away. Do you know how long it takes plastic to decompose?" I vaguely heard Meg from around the corner of the cubicle. "Hey, why's everybody over at your desk? What's going on?"

There were four rednecks involved in the assault. I'd already met three in court.

Jed Tucker made number four.

Skinhead. White supremacist. White = shiro. "Shiro.com."

And suddenly my shaking hands were punching in the number for Commonwealth Attorney Clyde Argenbright faster than I could think.

Chapter 12

"Talk about a royal waste of time." I paced in the Starbucks, letting the icy froth of a caramel Frappuccino clear my head as I complained to Kyoko and waited for Becky's old green Chevy Impala to pull up outside. "Nothing useful from anybody."

I sucked angrily on my straw. "I should name them all Brandy."

"Brandy? What are you saying, Ro? Have you lost your mind?" Kyoko, still on yell-mode after I'd spilled the news to her about the roses, was hollering again.

"If Rask doesn't fire that temp and get some real help, they'll be out of business within days. If I don't call the Better Business Bureau, that is." I shook the cubes of ice that had settled in the bottom of my cup. "She threw the order notes in the trash yesterday. The order ticket laid around on the counter until last night, and Brandy thinks she rang it up but can't remember. She said she did so many of them."

Kyoko seethed through her teeth. "Imbeciles. Did the trash go already?"

"This morning. They could have given me some evidence if they'd just called me first or saved the order. As it is now, we don't know if the order was faxed in, called in, or what."

Kyoko muttered under her breath. "If you'd told me about this earlier, I could have helped you," she said, her tone like ice.

"I know. I should have told you. I'm really and truly sorry." I hung my head. "But I was afraid you'd flip out. Which, actually, you kind of did." I suppose a forty-five-minute screaming rant, punctuated by various curse words (which Kyoko rarely used), justified my wording.

"Flip out?" Kyoko flared up. "You get anonymous roses with

creepy messages while there's a killer on the loose and don't tell me? And then accuse me of flipping out?"

Oh great. Here she goes again. I fumbled with my cell phone as she blasted me with another angry barrage about redneck lunatics and the FBI.

"You don't have to shout, Kyoko! At least I told you. Work with me here, will you?" I pleaded, feeling unexpected tears burn. "We've got to figure out who's doing this, and you're super good at solving stuff. I need your help." I sniffled. "And I've got to pull a wedding together in less than two months also, if you don't mind."

Kyoko grumbled a while, still mad at me. "So what did the police say?"

"Not much." I scrubbed the straw up and down inside the plastic top, trying to reach the rest of the whipped cream. "Just like we figured. That Rask should keep an eye on any orders for me, and they'll increase patrols around Mom's house and Adam's."

I sucked up a blob of sweet whipped cream laced with caramel. "Shane came out to ask me if I'd really made up my mind about marrying Adam. He spent most of the time giving Adam backhanded compliments and implying that I'm choosing low on the totem pole." Anger burned in my cheeks. "Shane's such a jerk. I hope I never have to talk to him again."

"Yeah, me, too, but for different reasons. I hope the perp straps himself to a moving train or something so you never have to turn in another police report."

A car turned in front of the Starbucks, its headlights cutting a swath across the dusky twilight. I looked out over the barren asphalt and far-off mountains, wondering how I, Shiloh P. Jacobs, had wound up in a town of barely twenty thousand, slurping coffee in a Starbucks that shared a parking lot with (1) a grain elevator and (2) a butcher's shop with regular cattle deliveries.

But thanks to amber-colored accessories and padded armchairs, plus soft jazz over the roar of milk foamers and the sharp scent of espresso, I could close my eyes and forget I was in Staunton.

Almost.

"Forget about all this stalker stuff, Kyoko. Please. Becky's taking me wedding shopping, and I want to be in a good mood when she gets here." I picked up a napkin and wiped the ring of condensation my cup had left on the table. "Did you look at the website I sent you and

Becky for bridesmaid's dresses?"

"Oh yeah. I saw it. I'll wear whatever you want, of course, but I'd be grateful if you didn't try to shove my thick waist in some lacy yellow thing."

"Your waist isn't thick. And I wasn't thinking of yellow." I punched my straw through the plastic lid. "So what did you like?"

I cringed, afraid to hear her answer. After all, I'd never seen Kyoko in a dress of any kind. When we went to cocktail parties in Japan, she wore a dark suit. Very acceptably Japanese. But a dark suit in my wedding would make her look like a bouncer—or worse, a groomsman.

"Hold on. Let me pull up the site, and I'll tell you my favorites." She clicked away. "Know what? Once I saw a picture of a wedding party where everyone dressed in camouflage—including the bridesmaids. It was kinda hard to find the groom."

"Tim would love it." I raised my eyes to the ceiling.

"Or hey, I can dig up some of my aunt's wedding pictures from 1982. Her bridesmaids wore shiny metallic gold. With puffed sleeves and great big bouffant hair. I might be able to—"

"You'd better help me, or I'll let Becky pick," I threatened. "And for your information, all her favorites are pastels like lavender and sea-foam green. You'll be one big, frilly Easter Peep." I caught myself. "Not that I'm calling you big."

"Okay, I found one," said Kyoko quickly, not hearing anything after *sea-foam green*. "That really dark red one on page three. Wow, what a cool haircut!"

I remembered that one. Of course she liked it—it looked like Dracula's Bride.

"Or how about that black dress on page four?" Kyoko chirped. "Now there's a color I like!"

I clapped my hands over my face, overturning my cup.

Kyoko must have heard my reaction because she rushed to assure me. "But don't worry, Ro. I'll wear whatever you want. Taffeta? I'm there. Suspenders? Just say the word."

"Good because Becky's here." I saw her car through my fingers. "I'll tell her you want taffeta."

"As long as you pay attention and make sure you're not being followed, I don't care what you tell her," Kyoko snapped, the smile dropping from her voice. "Does Becky carry a Taser? And for that matter, do you?"

"I have a dog. Does that count?"

Becky's sedan pulled up outside, bathed in light from the green-and-white Starbucks sign. She waved, and I gathered up my purse and empty cup.

"You're not still running every day, are you, Ro? Do you know how many joggers disappear compared to the average population?"

"Thanks for making me feel better, Kyoko," I crabbed. "And yes, I'm still running. I want to live, you know? Running's good for you. You should try it." I bit my lip. "Although I'm sticking to daytime now and just around the block."

"Well, STOP. Your heart's fine without all those silly calisthenics. Join a gym or something. I'll wire you money."

I smiled at her generosity, not bothering to make a wisecrack. "But I'm super careful. Adam went by Rask and chewed them out today, and we've talked the whole thing to death. Tried to cover every angle."

"There's always one everybody overlooks, Ro. I'm telling you."

"Kyoko." I let out a sigh. "Adam's meeting Becky and me as soon as he gets off work tonight, and he'll follow me straight home. Okay?"

"I'm not sure I like you going home. Maybe you should bunk with somebody else for a while. But who would you move in with, anyway? Adam?" she teased. "Normal people live together all the time, you know. They say it builds self-assurance before tying the knot."

"I don't need self-assurance." I dumped my cup in the trash. "I need innocence. Which is in far shorter supply among couples today."

I pushed open the door. "And besides, I never said I was normal."

Kyoko chuckled. "You took the words right out of my mouth."

Chapter 13

"We've got to stop meeting like this," I joked as Adam opened his pickup truck door and stuck his head out. His eyes looked weary from a long day at work, and the front of his hair stuck to his forehead from sweat.

"On the contrary," he said, a smile lighting his face as he grabbed his keys and got out of the truck. The porch light from the Donaldsons' cozy, brick, ranch-style house glowed down on green grass and hydrangea shrubs, and moths circled vigorously around the bulb. "I think we should meet like this more often."

Becky grinned. "Reckon I should leave you two lovebirds alone?" She clasped her hands, fluttering her eyelashes. " 'That great vow, which did incorporate and make us one.' "

Oh great. I groaned to myself. More Shakespeare.

Adam crossed his arms and bit back a laugh, leaning back against the door of his truck. "It's a little too early for the vows at this point, although I wouldn't mind." He raised an eyebrow at me. His eyes gleamed like dark water, deep and luminous across the shadowy driveway. The yard fragrant with pinecones and petunias.

"After all our weddin' plannin'?" Becky's eyes popped. "Shucks, fella. You can wait another month and a half."

She pointed to me. "And you, Yankee, listen up." She shook her wedding-planning agenda. "You might be his now, but you're mine Tuesday night. Got it? We're plannin' an invitation party to put mailing labels on all your invitations. Not that ya have many." She gave a long-suffering sigh. "And you gotta decide about them dresses right away. And what you're gonna do about Ashley."

"Why, what's going on with Ashley?" Adam reached out for my hand, the porch light giving him a blondish halo.

"There's always something," I grumbled. "I told you it'd be like this."

"Like what?"

"Well, she called tonight, and I made the mistake of telling her about the dresses we found Kyoko and Becky. A gorgeous cherry red, which will look great on both of them. They're amazing."

Becky gave a silly bow, twirling her finger from her nose.

"Now Ashley wants to be a bridesmaid. She says she can get those same dresses from the factory outlet in Chicago at half the price. Because they are kind of pricey." I smoothed my bangs to the side. "But I don't trust her. She'll forget or buy something in hot pink and then tell me it's close enough to red. Or maybe she'll just buy something she wants and forget everything we agreed on."

I put my free hand up. "What am I supposed to do now?"

Adam didn't answer, scraping the gravel with his tennis shoe. "I don't know, Shiloh. I guess you'll have to make that decision."

For some reason his response made me feel like whining. "What if I don't want to? I'd rather leave it up to you all and go to sleep."

Becky's head came up. "Did you jest say 'y'all'?"

"What? No way. I said 'you all.' Two words." I nudged Adam, indignant. "Back me up here. You heard me!"

He hesitated. "Well, it really depends on the pause between the two words. I'm not sure yours was long enough."

"What?" I whirled around to see him suppressing a smile.

Becky high-fived him triumphantly. "See, Yankee? You're more Southern than ya thought!"

"You're both wacko. I've never said 'y'all' in my life."

"Right." Becky made a smirky face. "Anyway, about Ashley—it ain't gonna be easy either way. If ya say no, she'll be mad. If ya say yes, she's gonna interfere. Life's full a choices, and sometimes there ain't no good answer. Pray."

"What if you talked to your dad?" Adam squeezed my hand. "He knows Ashley better than you do."

"Dad? Please." I snorted. "He didn't even reply to my e-mail about getting engaged."

"No, and he didn't say much either when I e-mailed him asking his permission to marry you. I figure 'I don't care, whatever she wants' means a yes." Adam smiled. "At least that's the way I'm choosing to read it."

I closed my eyes and groaned. "That sounds like Dad. No opinion. Nothing to say. Well, good because he's not entitled to much of one anyway, after deserting Mom and me all those years ago."

Just like I did when I left for Japan, not even bothering to tell her good-bye.

"Well." Adam ran his fingers through my hair. "We asked, anyway. That's the most important thing. And to be honest, Shiloh, I don't really care what our wedding is like as long as we both make it."

"Amen," Becky muttered. "In one doggone piece."

She pushed me toward my car. "Now go on, y'all. Take her home! She's worn out, and I gotta get back to my li'l gal inside. Macy's teethin' now and in some kinda mood. Poor thing."

I'd just pulled out my keys when Becky suddenly grabbed my arm. "Wait jest a cotton-pickin' minute! I got an idea!"

"An idea for what? How to catch this Odysseus guy?"

"No—for your weddin'!"

OH. NO. I could just picture it: The church decorated in Confederate flags, and Tim carrying our rings on an old toilet lid instead of a pillow. Cheetos and Tang at the reception. A bouquet of dandelions ripped out of Stella's yard. Adam and I would walk out to an old Willy Nelson tune, past beat-up radios tuned to the latest NASCAR race.

"What's. . .your idea?"

"Asian!" Becky whacked me. "Why didn't you think a that, woman? It'd be real cute. And if ya did them red dresses right, they'd fit the theme, too."

"Well, yeah, I guess that could work." I scratched my head.

" 'Course it could work! It's you all the way." Becky crossed her arms and sized me up, grinning. "Asian with a li'l Southern twist."

"Oh, I'm not Southern," I warned. "Don't get any ideas."

"Don't matter. Ya done said 'y'all.' And once ya git that far, the deal's done. You won't get us outta your blood!"

—∞—

Adam followed me home and played with Christie on the porch while I changed into shorts and sandals, pulled my hair back in a ponytail, and poured chilled *mugicha* barley tea into two glasses over ice.

Then I let the screen door squeak closed behind me as I settled next to Adam on the back steps of Mom's wooden deck. Or Adam's uncle's wooden deck, that is, by the end of July.

Night had fallen dark and still. Christie, surprisingly quiet, stretched out next to us, her fuzzy snout pressed into Adam's lap as he scratched behind her ears.

"What did you do to Christie, Shiloh?" Adam wrinkled his forehead at me. "She's not running around in circles and tearing up the neighbors' yards like she usually does."

"Easy. A hamster ball." I patted her furry side. "Kyoko sent it to me. It's got a remote with a timer, and I set it to go off at random intervals all day long. Drove her bats, in a good way."

"Well." Adam jutted his head back in surprise. "That ought to keep her busy for a while, huh? Maybe you can get some rest now."

"Don't get your hopes up. She chewed it in half already and ripped out the toy hamster." Stars glittered overhead in sparkling profusion, and a fragrant breath of dewy coolness swelled up from the moist grass, bringing with it faraway smells: verdant locust trees teeming with cicadas, wild mint, and the water-swirled hollows of nearby Dry Branch River.

When the wind changed a bit, I detected a hint of poultry stench from local farms, too. Ugh. I pinched my nose closed.

"Thanks for following me home," I said, my shoulder brushing Adam's as I leaned back against the deck railing. Keeping a (small) space in between us for propriety's sake. Heaven knows Stella would have a field day if she waltzed over and found us making out. Not that Adam, heaven forbid, would dream of such a thing. "It's nice to see you a little more often. Even if it does have to be on account of trouble."

"Perks, I guess." Adam, still clad in that itchy brown UPS polyester, rested an arm on my shoulder. "But that doesn't mean I'm not worried. Did the prosecutor call you back?"

"This evening. And. . .no. Jed Tucker's not in jail."

"He's not?" Adam whipped his head around.

"Nope. He managed to post bond." I sipped my tea, its crisp taste reminding me of Japan. "With a house, specifically. That's all he could use since he skipped trial last time. So he's free until the next trial, although—amazingly—the prosecutor thinks he's clean."

Adam tipped his head back in frustration and groaned. "Shiloh. This is terrible! What if that guy comes here and tries to. . ." He broke off, rubbing a hand roughly across his face. "He's not left-handed, is he? Like whoever's been leaving those spray-painted notes about Amanda?"

"The prosecutor didn't know. He said he'd write up a complaint for the guy's file if we can get any bit of evidence that it's him. But nobody has any."

"Exactly. Which is why I hate this whole mess." Adam's voice sounded loud and testy in the quiet of my yard.

"Well, just to play devil's advocate, what if Odysseus is a joke and we're getting all worked up about nothing?"

Adam stayed silent a while, shuffling his shoes on the porch. "I've thought about that, too. Like some kid's pulling a prank. But we can't take any chances." Adam rested his forehead in his hand. "Dad said he's seen a car come by our house a couple of times, really slow, like he was looking for somebody."

"You're kidding." I sucked in my breath. "Did he get the plate number or a description of the driver?"

"No. It's always late at night, so he can't see much. A dull-colored car though—gray or dark green or something. A sedan. But it's easy to get turned around on our road, so it's hard to tell if it's a random driver or somebody who's actually watching us. Or watching me, specifically."

I put my glass down, my stomach coiling into a tight ball. "That doesn't sound like a joke, does it?"

"Hard to tell. But first, hear me out on one thing." Adam turned my face toward him in the darkness. "If things get bad, forget the wedding. We'll go to the justice of the peace and say our vows and leave town. We can't risk our lives because of some madman, if he really does exist."

I hugged my knees, feeling a sudden shift of cool breeze against my bare calves, raising gooseflesh. "It won't come to that, Adam. We'll figure out who it is."

"Well, promise me anyway."

"I promise." I nudged him. "Besides, I don't have much pulled together anyway. I don't even have a wedding dress. And if I let Ashley in on this. . ." I let my sentence die.

Adam stayed silent a while then shifted his feet uncomfortably. "Can I say something? I know Ashley's annoying, and I'm still mad at her for making you feel guilty over your mom's death." He stroked his fingers through my ponytail. "But I'd like to meet her anyway. You're family, no matter how distant. And you don't have much family, Shiloh."

116

"Thankfully."

"I know, but. . ." Adam twirled the ends of my hair around his finger. "You're a Christian now. You're starting over. Maybe you could give her another chance?"

"So Ashley can take over my wedding and boss me around? Say rude things about you and my friends and make a laughingstock out of me?" I blew out my breath. "You don't know her. She's a pain."

"Well, so are we from time to time."

"Right. From time to time. We don't live that way permanently." I made a face. "Or at least you don't. I can't say that much about myself."

Adam smoothed my bangs back from my forehead and laughed. "We all have our moments. But those kids you teach at Sunday school think you're pretty wonderful."

"They drive me nuts, too. I'm thinking of sterilizing myself."

"Please don't." Adam smiled, kissing my cheek lightly. "But that's the thing. You don't like it, but you do it anyway. You've got courage. You left your old life for God, and you're staying in Staunton to be with me."

I didn't say anything, staring off into the deep blue-black shadows of the summer evening.

"You're hard on your family, too, Shiloh. Why don't you just breathe a little? Relax? Let them be who they are. Everybody has crazy family members."

"Why, Adam?" I turned to face him. "Why is my family so important to you?"

He shrugged. "I want to be part of your life. Part of your family, however it is. Part of you." He laced his fingers tightly between mine, making me catch my breath. "When we join, we join for better or worse. My family's no bunch of saints either. But that's how we learn and change."

I thought suddenly of Mom and her unopened letters. All those returned envelopes cinched sadly together with dark blue ribbon.

"Some of those changes come too late though." I spoke my thoughts out loud, softly, staring at a twinkle of fireflies over the shadowy grass and trying to remember the last words I'd ever spoken to my mother. When I closed my eyes, stinging green spots still hovered.

Adam rested his head against mine, and for a second I felt his breath match mine as we sat there together in silence.

"Can I ask you something?" I turned my face slightly, my smooth cheek brushing his stubbly jaw. "Why don't you ever. . . ?" I wanted to say "kiss me," but for some reason the words sounded gauche, pushy. I let out an annoyed breath.

Adam shifted uncomfortably then tugged his cap off and scratched a hand through his sandy hair. "I think I might know what you're talking about," he finally said, not looking at me. "Is it—?"

The stink of cigarette smoke sifted abruptly through the clean scents of pine and summer grass, and I let my face fall into my hands. No way we'd get to talk now.

"Stella?" I peeked over the deck railing, ashamed at my irritation. Stella was a good friend. Christie raised her head and started to get to her feet, tail thumping against the wooden boards. Which desperately needed another coat of stain.

Yet another thing screaming for my attention. Well, maybe I'd just leave the deck with faded stain and let Adam's Uncle Bryce deal with it.

I saw the orange glow of Stella's cigarette first and then her shadowy figure shaking the peony bushes that bloomed along the back side of her house. Everything backed by her giant satellite dish.

"Hiya." She waved in our direction, letting the bushes fall back into place. Her hair-sprayed puff of hair cast a spider-like shadow. "Looks like somethin's eatin' my peonies again. Aphids, ya reckon?"

A toe ring glinted over her flip-flops, catching yellow porch light. Topped by the faded hem of her billowy, orange-and-pink-flowered housedress.

Adam got up from the steps, Christie trotting after him, and walked through the short space of grass between Stella's house and mine. He knelt by Stella's bushes, checking the leaves and then the base around the roots. I observed the two of them, curious, as Stella puffed in silence.

"Leaf blotch. See the purple spots?" Adam pointed to a clump of leaves illuminated by my porch light. "It's a fungal infection. Probably from all the rain we've been having." He tore the leaves off, making the bush shiver. "You've got to get rid of all these infected leaves so it doesn't spread. What fungicide are you using?"

"Me? I just throw some fertilizer on 'em ev'ry now and then. That's all Mama ever did, an' hers grew as big as dinner plates." Stella gestured with her hands, breathing out a mouthful of smoke.

But hey. At least Stella hadn't stooped to "planting" plastic flowers in her flower bed like the neighbors up the street.

"You should probably increase the potassium levels of your soil, too, but you definitely need a fungicide right away," said Adam, interrupting my thoughts of tacky Snow-White-and-the-Seven-Dwarves lawn ornaments and pink flamingos. "Preferably something organic. There's a mixture of water, baking soda, vegetable oil, and castile soap I can whip together for you. Works as good as the commercial stuff but doesn't kill beneficial insects." Adam checked the lower leaves again then stood up. "I'll bring it next time I come, if you want."

I watched Adam as he talked to Stella, checking her petunia bed for something else. Wishing I could protect and heal and shelter like Adam did. Instead, the little crab apple *bonsai* tree he'd made me last Christmas had started to wilt, shedding leaves all over the windowsill.

I'd even managed to squeeze the life out of that, too.

"Y'outta see this green-tea panna cotta I've been making," Stella puffed, turning to me. "It's kinda like a puddin', but better."

"Green tea?" I looked up, mouth watering at the thought of bitter *matcha* powder. "Really?"

"No joke. I got to researchin' Asian stuff when I did that sushi cake for yer s'prise birthday party and figgered I might branch out a little. Try somethin' exotic." She tapped her cigarette. "An' doggone if people don't eat it up! Jer asked for a double order this week."

"That'll go great with the recipes we're recommending him."

"Exactly what I thought. In fact. . ." Stella turned from her plants at the sound of a car, shielding her eyes from distant streetlights to see the road. "Hold on a sec. That can't be. . .naw. Forget it."

A sedan rumbled slowly past our houses, casting a shadow on my newly mown lawn. Headlights out. A glimmer of gray flashed from the roof as it eased through a puddle of streetlight.

"That can't be who?" My pulse quickened. I scrambled up from the porch and through the grass, stopping at Adam's side.

"Aw, nobody." She slapped her thigh like something occurred to her. "Shucks, I know that car. That's ol' Mac Turner. He's probably jest checkin' on Wilma to make sure she ain't cheatin' on him again. She done two times already, you know, with that Smith fella. But she keeps singin' her innocence." Stella shook her head and took another puff on her Marlboro. "They's both in the phil-a-telic club with Jer, ya know."

I grinned to myself, hearing Stella say "philatelic." She might overdose on hairspray, but the woman wasn't dumb. Probably a lot of people were smarter than I gave them credit for.

"I didn't know Jerry collects stamps." I waved smoke away from my face and grimaced. "But who did you think was driving that car just now?"

Stella squinted in the direction of the road. "Nobody important. That ol' Townshend kid."

I drew back, bumping into Adam. "Who? Jim Bob?"

And this time both Adam and Stella wheeled around to look at me in astonishment.

—⁂—

"How do you know about Jim Bob?" Stella leaned closer, hand on her hefty hip. The cigarette between her fingers continued to send up a swirl of smoke.

"I don't know much. Just what somebody told me at the office." I shrugged lightly, not wanting to worry Adam. "Why would you think Jim Bob was driving that car?"

Stella coughed, a frown crinkling her lined forehead. "Well, it's real funny. He's been gone a long time now, years and years. But I could swear I saw him the other day, pickin' up some meds from the pharmacy for his pappy. And his mama used to have a car kinda like that. Won it from some prize giveaway."

"You actually saw Jim Bob here recently?" I choked out the words, my fingers growing cold on Adam's arm. "In Staunton?"

"Well, yeah. Him an' his folks lived up on that mountain over past Goshen, before he moved off to West Virginia or wherever. He checks on his pa ev'ry now and then, ya know. Seems like the ol' fella's havin' some spells lately."

"Oh." I jutted my head back in surprise. "Well, he can't be too bad of a guy if he's taking care of his dad, I guess."

"I reckon not." Stella lifted her cigarette to her lips, turning again toward the street. "But he's real funny. Don't talk much to nobody. Heard he made it big-time in some business. Loads a money. Guess he thinks he's too good for the likes of us." She snorted, making her housedress shudder. "Ya'd think with all that money, though, he'd buy himself some hair."

"Sorry?" I scrunched my brow.

"You know. Like from Hair Club for Men or somethin'. Guy's had a receding hairline since high school. Big bald patch on the back. Don't they make hair weaves or somethin' nowadays?" She puffed. "I saw some kinda toupee on the shoppin' channel the other day that'd suit him jest fine."

Stella coughed again, and I jerked my head in her direction. "Stella. You really need to stop smoking."

Up to now I'd minced around the subject Japanese-like, putting out humble little self-abasing suggestions, but Stella didn't sound so good. Blame it on the buzzing streetlight along the road, but her complexion struck me as kind of green. Waxy.

I thought Adam would nudge me, but he nodded. "You do, Stella," he said without hesitation. "That cigarette smoke is killing you. I can fix your peonies, but I sure can't fix your lungs."

We stood there in an awkward silence, which Stella only broke by coughing again and pounding on her chest. "Ya got me." She grinned sheepishly, giving a deep wheeze. "I tried to quit before, ya know, but it always come back to bite me in the rear. Reckon it's too late for this old dog to change her ways."

"You're not a dog. And it's not too late." I let go of Adam and put my arm through hers. "I'll help you. Whatever it takes. Do this for me—for us—if you won't do it for yourself. Please."

Stella sized us both up. "What's next? Ya'll gonna try an' git me religion, too?"

"You never know." I bobbed my eyebrows. "I'd start with the smoking before you give us any more ideas."

Stella shook her head and chuckled then put out her cigarette and ground it in the grass with her flip-flop.

———

"There's one other thing about Jim Bob," said Stella as we watched Adam's truck back out of the driveway. The long day had run its course, and my eyes felt sticky from sleepiness. My forehead burned where Adam had kissed me, his lips warm against my skin.

"What about Jim Bob?" I said over my shoulder.

"I don't know how he managed to make so much dough with that bum hand of his. Broke it jumpin' off a barn roof or some such nonsense. He weren't real smart, ya know. But he was good with precision stuff. Little bolts and lug nuts and whatnot. He used to work over at the mechanic's shop. The one over on Greenville Avenue."

Stella reached over her shoulder to scratch her back. "But he wasn't much good with those li'l parts after the accident. Lost all the feeling in his right hand an' broke the bones in six places. Never will be the same."

She grunted and stretched. "Anyhow. I'll see ya 'round. Need my beauty sleep."

I hadn't moved a muscle. Still stood there, staring at Stella as she waved and headed into the house, fidgeting with her now-cold lighter.

Bald. Cast on his hand.

And I turned and raced to the door, stumbling into Mom's room and jerking open the trunk.

Snatching out her sheaf of unopened letters.

Chapter 14

*T*here are some things I must tell you, even if you don't want to speak to me," Mom had written. I'd tried to read this letter before, the night I'd dug through her trunk for her transmission warranty, but choked up. Now I searched the lines again with my finger, perched on the edge of her bed.

I'm sure I'm overreacting, as I know I do. But I don't want anything to affect you or your life because I didn't tell you.

Affect me? What from Mom's life could have possibly affected me back then?

I glanced at the date—just three months before Mom's death. I'd been in Tokyo at that time, interviewing the Japanese prime minister and writing award-winning articles on the Nagasaki bombing. Schmoozing with the bigwigs of journalism and studying journalistic ethics online for my master's.

As far as I knew, Mom was simply on one of her desperate kicks to turn her life around and start over with me when she sent this slew of correspondence.

But as I read again, brows creasing, something dark began to lurk in the corner of my mind.

You'll think I'm crazy, Shiloh, but hear me out. Have you ever, in all your wanderings, been to Staunton, Virginia?

The words hit me with surprising force, as if someone had thrown my glass of cold mugicha tea in my face.

What could Mom possibly have been talking about? When she died, I didn't even know what state she lived in.

I jerked the letter closer, the crackle of paper echoing in the stillness of the bedroom.

I get the eerie feeling that someone in town knows you.

"Knows me?" I shouted, making Christie look up from her makeshift bed on the braided rug, head against my leg.

A bald guy with a sprained or broken right hand. Have you ever met him?

I threw my head back in surprise, nearly sliding off the bed.

Okay. Maybe "bald" is too strong a word. But he's got really thin hair. He keeps it cut short, and you can see his scalp in a patch in the back. I don't know his name.

Maybe you know him from college? Or one of your newspaper jobs in New York?

I keep telling myself that's the answer—and surely there's a simple explanation. But something inside me doesn't sit right. I can't explain why, but that's the truth. He's called twice asking to talk to you, and he knows you're my daughter.

And he seems to expect that you'll arrive here soon.

Every last ounce of energy slipped from my joints, and I had to reach up and shut my jaw with my hand.

A year and a half ago, and somebody had asked for me? Here? In redneck western Virginia?

Anyway, please call me. If this guy is indeed a friend of yours, I'd like to know it, and I'd be glad to put him in touch with you. But if not, then we really need to settle this right now because his manner is a little disturbing.

Be careful, okay? I'll write you again next week.

Chapter 15

"**M**eg, this is by far the most bizarre thing I've ever heard in my life," I said into the phone, collapsing onto the sofa. The cup of green tea I'd poured with shaking hands, spilling onto the placemat, sat untouched on the kitchen table.

I thought briefly of Tim and Becky's cow-tipping adventure and hesitated. "Okay. Not the most bizarre thing. But it sure tops the charts."

Piles of letters sprawled across the sofa cushions, the deep blue ribbon coiled in an empty spiral. Papers everywhere. Cardboard boxes gutted, their contents strewn across the living room. Stuff from Mom's trunk.

"What's bizarre?" Meg's voice came across the line in a burst of clarity. Little clattering scrapes in the background.

"Mom's letters. Wait 'til you hear this one." I paused, hearing a spoon clink. "I'm bothering you, aren't I? Sounds like you're cooking."

"Shrimp and grits." Meg smacked her lips. "Soy shrimp, of course. I found some at Trader Joe's in Charlottesville last week. They taste like fishy cardboard, but it's the thought that counts, right? So much about food is mental anyway. You ever take a swig of milk when you're expecting orange soda?"

"Gross." I grimaced.

"Exactly. And. . ." She shuffled, pouring something. "Organic grits. I just had a hankering. And no, you're not bothering me. Go on."

"I read a couple of Mom's old letters that got. . .returned." My face heated slightly. "I never read them. But she talked about some baldish guy in town with a bum hand asking about me."

The clattering stopped, and I heard dead silence on the other end of the line, except for a distant laugh track from some sitcom. "You mean somebody from here asked about you. . .in the past? When your mom was still alive?"

"Around a year and a half ago. I'd never set foot in Virginia."

"Well, maybe it was a friend. A buddy. Somebody who knew you and recognized your mom."

"None of my high school or college friends met Mom. I made sure of that." I drummed my nails on my teacup. "She was in and out of mental hospitals and just. . .a mess. Dangerous sometimes, too."

"They recognized her name maybe?"

"She changed it when I started at Cornell. To Moonlight Sonata."

"No way."

"Way."

Meg snickered. "Cool. Your mom musta been pretty chill, Jacobs."

"She wasn't all there, Meg." I swallowed, my eyes slipping up to a photo of her smiling face on a side table. "At least for a long stretch of years. Anyway, she changed her name back a few years ago. But regardless, how could one of my friends expect me to arrive here—and ask for me? I never planned to come to Virginia."

Meg stayed quiet, obviously trying hard to think of something to say. Finally she spoke. "You've never done any time traveling, have you?"

"Sorry?"

"I mean, it'd be really cool if you have. I won't spill your secret." She dropped her voice to a whisper. "There's that time-travelers' convention, you know, at MIT. Is that why you're here?"

I sat there stupidly, speechless, and Meg gasped. "I'm right, aren't I? Did you come from the future or the past?"

"Meg! I haven't time traveled. Come on." I sipped my tea irritably. "I just want to figure out who Mom wrote about. Her description sounds an awful lot like Jim Bob Townshend. I mean, it could be a coincidence, but he worked at that repair shop where I got my transmission replaced. The same place Mom took the Honda to get the transmission installed the first time. I found the warranty, remember?"

"So you really haven't time traveled?" Meg's voice fell to a bitter low.

"Of course not!" I banged my teacup down. "Stay with me, Meg. I wanted to see if you'll help me."

"Help you with what?" Meg, miffed, started clattering bowls and spoons again.

"Help me find out about Jim Bob. Stella said he's come back to town. I'd like a good, hard look to see if I recognize him, or if he's just some loco crackpot."

"Where does he live?"

"According to Clarence, on some mountain near Goshen, wherever that is."

"Oh, I've been there. It's on the other side of Craigsville."

"The little town where I once saw seven jacked-up trucks parked in a row?"

Meg snickered. "That's the one. Keep going and you'll come over the mountain, and if you get on the interstate west, you'll hit the Allegheny range. Clifton Forge and Covington and all these little coal and railroad towns. After that, you'll run smack into West Virginia."

"Which is where they say Jim Bob's been living."

"Really. Hmm." She paused. "Cooter goes hunting all over that area. I bet I could dig some info out of him."

"Would you?" I let out my breath in relief. "I'd like to find out, Meg. Mom's comments bothered me. She said the guy had a weird manner, and. . ." I rested my head in my hand. "I really wish I could find some more of her letters."

"Maybe she didn't write any more."

"Maybe not." I shook the tea in my cup, staring down into the glistening circle of chartreuse-green. "But she sent one letter every week like clockwork the last year or two of her life. I'd be really surprised if she suddenly stopped."

We sat without speaking, and I sipped my tea. "So I'll see you tomorrow at the city council meeting then?"

"I'll be there. Taking pictures of old, angry fat guys in an auditorium with horrible lighting. Try making those photos look like winners." She clinked a spoon. "So are you going to tell Adam about the letters?"

"I guess so. But he won't like it."

"Of course not! So maybe he's better off not knowing, huh?"

"I can't do that." I shook my head. "I don't want to keep secrets. And besides, he's getting strange phone calls, too. It might be good for him to keep a lookout for Jim Bob himself."

I started to say good-bye, but Meg stopped me. "You don't think it's that skinhead, do you? He certainly fits the 'bald' description, unless he's grown his hair out over those tattoos."

I took a deep breath, blowing it out. The rings of light in my tea shook. "I thought maybe so at first, but the timing sort of rules him out. I mean, the Confederate reenactment happened last fall, and Mom wrote these letters months before that."

"You'd never seen the skinhead before?"

"Never." I shook my head firmly. "It was a random mugging. A bunch of guys looking for trouble and extra cash."

"So you think."

I drew back. "What do you mean? It's impossible. I told you—I'd never come to Virginia until last year."

"Maybe you did meet him. Maybe he wasn't in Virginia."

I ran a hand through my hair, trying to make sense of Meg's words. But instead I came up with an image of sputtering Porky Pig on those old Looney Toons cartoons.

"I'm not following you, Meg."

"Maybe the attack in Winchester wasn't random."

I started to protest, but something cold flitted through me. "You mean. . ."

"Maybe he knew you—or only saw you—in New York. Japan, even. Maybe he followed you here."

Her voice fell to an eerie tone. "Or he followed your mom here—hoping to find you."

Chapter 16

You should have seen the ruckus that went on in here, Ashley," I said into my cell phone, my voice sounding lost in the now-empty elementary school auditorium in Waynesboro. "They're having another city meeting in two weeks, and you can bet that guy's going to find some way to weasel out of admitting all the bribes he took."

I put my tape recorders away, my movements echoing against the hard, gold-curtained stage and rows of folding chairs. The local news truck had left nearly an hour ago, packing up its giant cameras and lights.

"Huh." Ashley made a sound like turning pages. I rolled my eyes. She could at least pretend to be interested. But I'd done it. I'd called her and invited her to join my wedding party, which was as far as my half-sisterly duty went.

But that meant I had to. . .well, talk. About something. Something that Ashley couldn't take over, boss me around about, or blame me for.

And since this was rural Virginia, that left (1) cows, (2) llama fencing, or (3) the muddy Dodge pickup that dinged my fender while pulling out of the grain elevator behind the new Starbucks. The Starbucks that recently moved from the Staunton Mall, which stood—ahem—right across the street from J's Tractor Supply.

Unfortunately, none of these topics sounded conducive to conversation with Ashley.

"Kyoko sent me another package," I tried again. "Since she's moving, she cleaned out her dresser and found some of my old things. No letters from Mom though. But something of Mom's that's pretty important to me."

Jennifer Rogers Spinola

"A deed to another house?" Ashley sounded bitter. "I mean, she left you everything else, right?"

"I meant important for sentiment's sake. Nothing of any monetary value." I said the last words carefully, trying not to arouse Ashley's jealousy again after she'd tried to horn in on my inheritance. Going so far as to claim she'd hired a lawyer.

But even Ashley Sweetwater wouldn't care about this package—stuffed full of Kyoko's weird-isms—or the little shrink-wrapped mini pecan pie Kyoko had pulled from my old apartment corkboard in Tokyo. It was beyond gross now; Mom had mailed it to me nearly a year before her death. I'd promptly skewered it by the corner with a thumbtack: a symbol of all the things I considered absurd about our relationship and her new life in the South.

But now, after Mom's death and my own changes, it felt unspeakably special. Priceless, even.

I'd pulled it out of Kyoko's smashed cardboard shipping box and tucked it carefully in my purse, grateful it had finally come home.

"Ashley?" I checked again for eavesdroppers in the auditorium and lowered my voice to a whisper. "Speaking of Mom. She didn't ever mention anything to you about a certain guy here in Staunton, did she? A guy who—"

"Interesting," said Ashley with a breezy yawn, cutting me off. The thump of a book closing. "So, red roses?"

"Excuse me?" I froze, her words catching me unaware like a Frisbee in the throat.

"Wedding flowers. What colors have you decided on? Red to match the bridesmaids' dresses?" Ashley gave a stiff sigh, as if pained to have to deal with a simpleton like me. "You are getting married in something crazy like a month and a half, correct?"

"Yeah. Almost."

"So what's it going to look like? Decorations, music, what?"

"Well, there's not much to tell." I hesitated, nervous at Ashley's rapid-fire demands. "Adam lined up some relatives to play the violin and piano. My coworker Meg's doing the photos. You should see her work. Absolutely stunning."

Even if she did shoot photos of partially clad hippies, clouds shaped like John Lennon, and a close-up of a cow with long eyelashes chewing a dandelion. Maybe I could use the cow on the cover of our wedding album.

If, that is, Meg actually remembered to show up for the wedding.

"Your coworker." Ashley's frosty voice enunciated each word with calculated exactness.

"Sure. And for decorations, let's see. . .some Japanese lanterns, square candleholders, bamboo, and. . .you know. . ." My voice trailed off as I tucked my tape recorders in my reporter's bag, embarrassed. "We can't afford a lot, and we're busy, too."

"*That's* what you call plans?"

Blood rushed to my face as I closed my notebook then flipped off the lights and closed the heavy auditorium door.

The gleaming, wood-paneled school lobby sat mostly empty, guarded by a long glass case displaying blue-ribboned student posters and glossy black plaques. A clump of people from the council meeting still mingled in the shadows, heads together as they gossiped in low tones.

School buildings always struck me as creepy at night, so lonely and empty, lit only by red fire-exit signs and dim fluorescent lights. I shivered as I capped my pen and slipped it in my reporter's bag.

"Hold on a second," I whispered to Ashley, shouldering my stuff. "Let me go drop my stuff in the car, and I'll put you on Bluetooth. But I can't talk long. Adam's coming by the school here to meet me after his meeting in Stuarts Draft. He's kind of worried with this whole mystery-murder thing, so. . . Ashley? Did you hear me?"

I tucked the phone under my chin, Ashley's voice still yakking away. I waved good-bye to Meg, who was packing up her camera equipment and arguing over the phone with Cooter about the World Series.

"How can you not have any plans? Are you crazy?" Ashley hollered when I put the phone back up to my ear. "When I got engaged, Mama and I went shopping like a year ahead of time! She had my wedding dress altered by a friend who sews for the Vera Wang models in New York, and we hired a really famous caterer, and. . ." Ashley blabbed on, oblivious to my mom-less state.

A wedding at the gun range sounded better and better.

"Well, at least you had somebody to help you, huh?" My voice came out in equally cold tones.

"Sure I did! Everybody does. I don't know a mother who's not crazy about her daughter's wedding." Ashley seemed to realize she'd blundered because she broke off abruptly. "Sorry. I forget sometimes

131

that Ellen's gone, and. . .well, why don't you let Tanzania help?"

"Dad's belly-dancing wife who's practically our age? No thanks."

"Tanzania's great. Stop being so cynical and give her a chance."

Ha. I'd rather be spat on by one of Fred Brewer's llamas.

I slapped my notebook in my bag and zipped it up, throwing the strap over my shoulder in a huff and checking to make sure I still had my purse. Wait. I didn't.

I stalked back into the auditorium and flipped on the lights.

"Sorry to break it to you, Shiloh, but your mom wouldn't have been much help with a wedding anyway. She was too. . .weird. Okay. Let's call it 'Bohemian.' You'd be getting married in tie-dyed robes or something."

Stay calm, Shiloh. Breathe. I inhaled deeply, reminding myself that I was supposed to be a Christian now and be nice, or something along those lines. Even to Ashley Boss-of-the-Universe Sweetwater.

I slipped through the rows of folding chairs where I'd been sitting, but no purse.

Wait a second. I whirled around, trying to locate my exact seat. I'd sat in the second row when I arrived, and when I moved up to speak to the president of the city council, I sat right there by the. . .

"For pity's sake, Shiloh! I've repeated myself ten times! Are you going with straps for the dress or not? I personally think you're too waifish for strapless, and you don't have enough up top to fill it out either, if you get my drift. So I'd recommend. . ."

There—my purse. Barely visible in the shadows under one of the folding chairs. I blew out my breath in relief and snaked through the narrow row. I loved that purse—a juicy strawberry-pink leather Kate Spade leftover from my big-spending days in Japan. I looped it over my shoulder, cut the lights, and headed back into the lobby, feeling suddenly exhausted. No wonder. My watch pointed to quarter after ten.

And talking to Ashley used up any energy I had left.

I waded through the remaining people in the lobby and pushed the metal door handle with my hip, the metal hinges groaning with the familiar squeaking sound I remembered from my childhood.

"Here's the thing, Ashley. I want our wedding to be simple. Not a lot of fuss, okay?" I headed down the concrete steps in front of the school. "I've told you our budget's small. Dad hasn't offered to help. So I'm not having designer dresses and famous caterers."

"You're not getting married in New York, are you?"

"No. Who do I know from New York anymore?" I switched my stuff to my other arm, phone under my chin as I made my way down the steps. "I'll probably invite a few people, but that's it."

"Really? That's perfect then!" Ashley giggled with excitement. "We'll have your wedding in Chicago, just like I wanted to begin with."

"You. . .you wanted what?"

"I knew you wouldn't get married in small-town Virginia, but I wasn't sure about New York. So Chicago it is! In fact, I've already done a bit of nosing around for you."

"Chicago?" I caught a glimpse of my reflection in the windows of a car pulled up at the curb: My hair pulled back in a messy bun. Red sweater cinched over a floral blouse with a skinny black patent leather belt. And my mouth hanging open at Ashley's utter absurdities.

Everything bathed in dull lights, illuminating shrubs and the brick school front.

"Of course! We'll do it at Millennium Park with the fountains that spit water. I've already checked the availability list, and you'll just have to move your wedding back about two months. Your fiancé's family won't care, will they?"

I dropped my purse. Right there on the sidewalk. I swiped for the strap in the boxwood-scented night air, fuming, while Ashley rambled on about the modern art in the park we could use in the photos, except for this gruesome pig-shaped thing, and about a really good hot-dog stand out front.

"Ashley. Chicago? You can't be serious. Nobody but you and Wade would be able to come!"

"Well, do you want something nice, or do you want a lot of people?" Her tone cut, bossy, the way I remembered—in nightmares, usually—from our few growing-up years together. "You just don't know anything about weddings, Shiloh. Face it. You need help."

"I know I do, but Becky said—"

"I'll start by sending you a copy of our wedding vows." Ashley cleared her throat crisply. "And you're lucky I had my bouquet preserved. Since you seem incapable of coming up with your own ideas, I'll allow you to copy it. Our colors were china blue and off-white, which won't look so great on you, but. . .oh well. So what's the budget? I want numbers."

My mouth still hung open. "Ashley, I appreciate your offers, but—"

Jennifer Rogers Spinola

"My advice: get a real photographer and toss the Asian theme. If we leave it up to you, we'll have squid on the buffet. Or those nasty Japanese fish things you're always crunching."

Ashley didn't wait for me to reply. "I've already called a seamstress in Falls Church—it's close enough, right?—and she can sew a wedding dress that'll make you look a little less. . .hmm. . .boyish, let's say. And I'll want a distinctive matron-of-honor dress, since I'll be virtually responsible for your entire wedding, and. . ."

Boyish?!

"Falls Church?" I cried. "It's nowhere near Staunton!"

"Closer than Chicago. Unless you want it done here when you come. My friends and I can be the bridesmaids, since your guest list sounds pretty short, and I've already picked out these cool turquoise dresses for us that'll—"

"I'm not getting married in Chicago!" I hollered, stopping in my tracks.

My voice echoed off the lonely parking lot and long brick school building, shrouded by silver maples around the edges. Only a few cars pulled out of the exit and into a dreary side street.

I threw my head back and took a long, deep breath of fresh night air, wishing I could scream and hurl the phone a mile away.

Finally Ashley spoke, her voice like ice. "Fine. Have everything *your* way. I thought you needed help, and I offered. But forget it."

I shook my head and plodded toward my car in too-tight, pinching heels. One of the giant lights in the parking lot was out, like the black gap of a missing tooth.

"We're supposed to be family, you know," Ashley said in clipped tones. "You said so yourself in that ridiculous letter you sent a few months ago. Or have you changed your mind about that, too?"

"Family?" I repeated incredulously, walking faster. Ashley and Dad hadn't been close to me in years—until Mom died, and suddenly they were all I had left. But to tell the truth, I didn't know how to "be" family. I tried, but it still felt like mincing forward in Japanese *geta* sandals: clumsy, off-balance, and about to fall on my head any second.

"It's not that I don't want your help, Ashley," I managed, trying again. "I appreciate it. I really do. I'm. . .happy you're going to be a bridesmaid." The last sentence wasn't exactly true, but I squeezed it out through clenched teeth, giving a last clumsy attempt at grace. "But I want to make some of my own plans, too."

"Go ahead. Do what you want. You always were selfish and independent."

That did it. I blew out my breath, fuming. "You know what? This is exactly what I told Becky would happen. And I was right. She can feed her 'people ain't what you think' speeches to her hound."

"How dare you blab about me to your silly redneck friends!" Ashley bellowed.

"Becky isn't silly!" I raised my voice. "She's one of my best friends! And I want you to come to our wedding, but not like this!" My fingers shook, cold, on the cell phone. "Always fighting. You always bossing me around."

I paused to catch my breath. "I want you to be in my life, Ashley. I miss family. But this isn't working."

"Not working? You're the one who's always overreacting. Just like Ellen." She huffed out her angry breath. "She never gave Dad any peace."

"Okay. I'm done." I clenched my teeth together, my blood beating in my ears.

"Fine. Whatever."

I clicked off my cell phone then unzipped my purse and dug for my keys, sifting through lipstick and pens. Chewable aspirin for those moments when the story, or quite often the subject, gave me a headache. In fact, now seemed like a good time for some.

But no keys.

I groaned out loud, tipping the opening of the purse toward the nearest floodlight and sorting through everything piece by piece. Shaking my purse to hear the jingle. Again, no.

Great. Shiloh P. Jacobs strikes again. How on earth had I possibly managed to bungle this one?

I rolled my knuckles against my forehead, wishing I was home in bed. At the office, even. Anywhere but stranded in an elementary school parking lot in the middle of redneck nowhere, Ashley's words still grating in my ear.

But with no keys, there'd be no drive home, unless I hopped in Adam's truck when he arrived and left my car in Waynesboro.

I sighed and headed back toward the entrance of the school.

—⁂—

It took me a good twenty minutes of crawling around on my hands and knees to find my keys. They'd apparently fallen through a gap in my not-quite-closed purse zipper, slid through the seat cushion, and fallen on the floor—where they promptly got kicked six rows behind and wedged next to one of the thick metal feet that attached the chair to the floor.

Man, do I have the worst luck!

I brushed off my black skirt and tights and clumsily got to my feet then slid out the row of folding chairs and finally the auditorium. Hoping I'd never have to see that stage and rippled velvet curtain again. I'd had enough of Waynesboro Elementary School for one night.

By the time I got out to the lobby, the school building had hushed to an eerie silence. The doors still opened though, and overhead lights burned at the entrance.

"Lockin' up," said the man at the door impatiently, checking his watch and smoking.

"I'm waiting for somebody." I reached again for my cell phone, sending a quick text to Adam to hurry. "What am I supposed to do, wait in my car?"

"Reckon." His smoke breath made me cough. "Or over at the gas station if it's still open."

"Thanks for your consideration," I said sarcastically, snapping my cell phone shut. No way I'd sit around in some empty parking lot after the notes and roses—or hang around with Mr. Creep-o with the elementary school keys. I'd just dump my stuff in the car and head over to the Texaco station and text Adam on the way.

Good thing this is rural Virginia, not Brooklyn, I thought, clicking over to my car in my heels. Once I'd left my wallet on the hood at a busy local restaurant for two hours while I interviewed the proprietor and staff, and nobody touched it except the woman who turned it in (intact) to the manager.

I stuck my keys in the lock and reached for the door handle.

And there behind me in the car window, framed by the reflection of a thin, sliver-shaped moon, loomed the dark silhouette of a man's head and shoulders.

Just inches behind my own.

Chapter 17

I whirled around, but before I could make a complete turn, he'd slammed me into the car, wrapping an arm around my neck. My keys splatted across the asphalt.

I clawed at him, turning my head enough to sink my teeth into a thick bicep, but he shook me loose and started dragging me away from the car. Fingers from his other hand clamped across my mouth.

And in a liquid second, a sensation of ice slipped across my throat in a fine line. Cold and sharp, pressing into the tender flesh just above my collarbone. I felt my pulse throb against it, pinching painfully.

A knife. The guy's got a knife. The thought jumped into my stunned brain like the memory of a whole frozen groundhog in Tim's freezer—hovering just one step above ludicrous. Where was this anyway? Hickville, Waynesboro? Where people spat tobacco out their truck windows at stoplights?

I reached for the car door and tried to hang on, but felt my balance shift and then falter.

The knife dug deeper into my throat, making me cry out, and my knees crumpled as a rush of real panic set in.

He was pulling me—dragging me—and my fingers slipped off the car door and into nothingness, clutching at the thick arm he'd forced under my chin. I dug in my nails, but he swatted me away.

I stumbled, one spindly Jimmy Choo heel sliding on the asphalt, and gasped for air. The seam under the arm of my floral silk blouse ripped as I twisted against his chest and struggled for my footing, my hair falling down over my face and tangling in his fingers.

He removed the knife just long enough to yank hard on my purse.

The strap tugged sharply against my arm, making me yelp, until I managed to loosen my arm and let it slip partially off.

Air. I need air. I pounded him with my elbow as he tightened his chokehold, but he only yanked my arm harder, making me double over. Slashing the purse strap with his knife, he tore it from me.

The whine of a car engine rumbled in my ears, sounding far away and distant like I was hearing it from inside a cave, cotton in my ears.

The knife dropped with a startling clatter on the pitted asphalt.

I tried unsuccessfully to kick it under my car and out of reach and finally managed to suck in a shallow, jagged breath. At the same time I whacked him full in the face with my fist. Feeling the thick black material of a ski cap. I ripped at it with adrenaline-shaky fingers, hoping to unmask him, just as two impossible beams of yellow light sliced through the parking lot.

The whine of an engine jerking into PARK—the slam of a car door—and footsteps running, coming closer. Just as I lost my balance and tumbled down.

A familiar voice, a shout! And the sound of my own gasping lungfuls of air while my assailant abruptly fled, his panicked footsteps rustling bushes in the thin woods at the edge of the school yard. Disappearing into a dingy alley.

Wait a second—my purse. I patted my empty shoulder. *He got my purse.* WITH MOM'S PECAN PIE TUCKED IN THE POCKET.

"You coward!" I hollered, scrambling up off the asphalt and tearing off my high heels. "Get back here!" I waved at the woman running toward me in the parking lot. "Help me, will you?"

And I tore off after him in stocking feet.

—ɷ—

"He got away! I can't believe it." Meg bent over next to me in the parking lot, gasping for breath. "You okay, Shiloh?" Her chunky earrings jingled, hair pulled back in a surprisingly chic twist.

I leaned back against the side of my Honda to catch my breath, unable to juxtapose the images that made no sense—my scattered heels, the dingy shadows of the parking lot, and Meg's face. In Waynesboro, Virginia. Black dots swam behind my eyes.

"Hey. You're not going to faint, are you?" Meg shook my shoulder lightly.

"No. I'm okay. I'm just. . .mad. The guy got my purse." I brushed myself off, unspeakably glad I did stories with Meg and not Chastity—

who'd have left me there to get knifed.

"What happened, Jacobs? Who was that guy?"

I glanced back over my shoulder in the direction my assailant had gone. "I have no idea." I spun back around to face her, my teeth chattering in the late-night cool. "What are you still doing here? I thought you left ages ago."

"Are you kidding? That school board guy with the keys locked me in. I told him I needed to use the bathroom, but apparently he forgot. I'd have been stuck in that school building all night if I hadn't hollered." Meg's lip curled in a scowl. "Sexist jerk. He brought coffee to the TV guys, but me? I had to remind him three times I'm a *Leader* photographer!"

"Where'd he go? He didn't do it, did he?"

"The school board fellow? No. He left when I did." Meg hooked a thumb toward the parking lot exit. "But listen—we've got to get you out of here—now. In case that masked bandit comes back."

Before we could move, bright headlights cut the darkness, and the familiar rumble of Adam's pickup echoed against the long brick school building and barren asphalt.

Meg ran up to his truck, dragging me along by the arm, and stuck her head up to the window while he rolled it down. "Boy, are you a sight for sore eyes," she said, shoving me in his direction. "Quick! Get her out of here before something else happens. It's not like I carry Cooter's machete to city council meetings, although I might have to start."

"Sorry?" Adam's eyes bounced from Meg to me, widening at the sight of my rumpled sweater and messed-up hair. "You okay, Shiloh? What happened?" He cut the engine and threw open the truck door, nearly knocking me down as he scrambled out.

"She'll tell you on the way to the police station." Meg bobbed her eyebrows sternly. "And if I were you, I'd get her car out of here, too, so the creep doesn't track her plate number or something equally evil." She gave us a push. "Go on. I'll follow you guys to the station."

Meg waited in her car, engine running, while Adam and I sprinted over to my Honda. I felt around the tires for my keys and tossed them to Adam, and he shoved me into the passenger's side. He jammed the keys into the ignition and squealed out of the parking space.

"It was him, wasn't it?" A vein bulged angrily in Adam's neck. "That guy your mom wrote about in her letters? With the messed-up right hand?"

It took me a second to register Adam's question, and I jerked on my seat belt as he swerved around his truck then gunned the accelerator into the street.

"Could you see his face? Try to remember, Shiloh!" Adam reached over with a shaky hand and pressed it to my cheek.

The knife. The ski mask. I blinked, snatching bits of stress-seared images from the recesses of my brain.

"I felt hair under the mask." I swallowed, trying to conjure some moisture into my parched mouth.

"You're sure?"

"Yes." I hung onto the armrest as Adam turned sharply at the intersection. "When I reached for the mask, I felt bulk at the top, like hair. I don't know how much, but the stretchy material didn't slide like it would on a perfectly smooth surface."

"Did he wear glasses?"

I considered this. "No. I hit him in the face, so I would have felt them."

"How about his hand or wrist? Was it weak or twisted or. . . ?"

"Not at all." I closed my eyes and replayed the scene like a slow-motion movie. "He held the knife under my chin with a strong right hand. Perfect dexterity. I couldn't pry his fingers off."

—⁂—

"I can't believe the jerk took my purse," I mumbled, standing at the counter at the Waynesboro police station while Adam's warm hand nursed the back of my neck. I'd tried to put my hair back in place in the dingy bathroom, but brown chunks still hung out of my impromptu ponytail, strands sticking up.

"Your purse? I'm just glad you're okay." Adam kissed the top of my head. "But I'm sorry he got your ID and money."

"My debit card. Driver's license. Wallet. All that stuff. Yep." I shook my head in disgust as I scrawled in my phone and license plate numbers, thinking thoughts toward my assailant that would have had me arrested if the deputy on duty could hear them.

"You sure you called all of them to stop any withdrawals?"

"Meg did on her cell phone before she left. I don't have that many cards, you know." I raised an eyebrow. "Me being the consummate nonspender these days." I rubbed a hand across tired eyes, trying not to smudge my mascara. "And the consummate queen of confusion. I have no idea if this guy is linked to the roses or Mom's letters or what. Nothing makes any sense!"

"But you've told the police everything."

"Every detail." I blew out my breath. "I've already given them all the florist's cards, too. Mom's letters."

I caught my breath, remembering Shane Pendergrass the cop—the one who'd sent me roses last year. Who practically WAS the Staunton Police Department. Everybody knew him and loved him. The Pendergrass family held a swanky, low-slung power over most of the police force—like a friendly Mafia of grouse-hunting hillbillies. Just sophisticated enough to make the local girls swoon.

"On second thought," I said, "I probably should've made the report somewhere else."

I looked up as the officer on duty came toward us with a sheet of paper. "Believe me, I never thought I'd get mugged in Virginia," I muttered to Adam. "And this makes the second time—that fiasco at the Civil War battle reenactment being the first. New York's looking less and less dangerous every day, you know that? Maybe we should move back to that cold-water flat I shared with Mom where the woman upstairs stabbed her husband to death with a frozen sausage."

"She. . .she what?" Adam leaned toward me, incredulous.

"She sharpened it to a point while it was soft. Pretty clever, don't you think?"

I looked up as the officer leaned over the counter facing me, pen poised. "So could you please list the contents of your purse, ma'am?" Officer Rodunk, as his nametag read, scratched the back of his freckled neck, tapping the pen impatiently.

"Debit card, wallet, the whole bit." I crossed my arms, fresh anger making my hands clench. "I told you that already. Plus the new Shiseido lipstick and blush Kyoko sent me—from their premium line." I paused. "The purse is a Kate Spade original, in a limited-edition pink—if that means anything to you. I probably sank more money into that thing than I make now per year."

He raised an eyebrow and shifted his position. "Anything else in the purse?"

"A pecan pie."

He glanced up. "A. . .pie?"

"Right. You know. One of those little gas station snacks." I gestured with my hands. "The little pecan pies in a metal tin. Only this one's about two years old. Maybe more." I clasped my hands together. "But it's important."

Officer Rodunk's pen wobbled. "Ooookay." He tipped an eyebrow. "Um. . .anything else?"

"A glow-in-the-dark jellyfish. Plastic." I wiggled my fingers. "With little sucker tentacles. The kind you can throw against walls and they stick."

This time even Adam's eyebrows shot up. Officer Rodunk tapped his pen again, not writing anything down.

"Kyoko sent it, Adam!" I put my hands up. "Do you want the contents of my purse or not, officer?"

"What else?" His voice turned sour.

"A package of gummy shrunken heads, a dangly Japanese cell phone strap with a cartoon character made of blue cheese, and a wind-up plastic sushi toy." I thought hard, trying to recollect all the ridiculous stuff Kyoko had sent me. "And. . .I think that's all."

"You reckon?" Officer Rodunk glared at me. Over his shoulder a female officer looked at me through angry slits-for-eyes, as if she'd like to leap over the counter and taze me.

"What a waste of our time," he mumbled. "What are you, a Wilson kid?"

"Sorry?"

"He means the school," Adam said in low tones, stepping up to the counter. "No, sir. She's not from here originally. And not. . .not in high school." The corners of his mouth twitched.

"High school? Excuse me?" My eyes popped.

"Not from here, huh?" Officer Rodunk jotted something on the corner of the form, and I thought I made out the word *Yankee*. "And you claim you got mugged."

"I *did* get mugged!" I stepped forward indignantly. "He held a knife to my throat, for your information!"

"A knife." He seemed to hide a smile. "What kind of a knife?"

"How am I supposed to know? A knife!" I spread my hands to show the size. "A sharp one."

"Oh, a sharp one." He was mocking me. "You a witness to this alleged mugging with the. . .um. . .sharp knife?" He nodded at Adam.

"No, sir. I arrived right after the guy ran off."

The two officers exchanged knowing glances.

They don't believe me. I took a step back from the counter, the room contorting into a haze of disbelief.

"No, wait!" Adam protested. "It really happened."

"Officer Podunk." I'd just launched into my "I'm an ethical journalist" speech, cold hands clenched in fury, when I realized what I'd just called him. Adam coughed, and the room turned deathly silent. "Rodunk!" I waved my hands. "Rodunk. That's what I meant to say, sir."

A fly buzzed against the glass of a nearby window while Officer Rodunk turned an ugly shade of pink. His knuckles clenched on the pen.

"Call Meg West, officer," I tried again. "She saw my assailant."

"Meg West? The photographer at the paper?" He turned up cold eyes.

"That's her! You know her?" I let out a sigh of relief. "I work at *The Leader*, too."

"Oh, I know her, all right." He made another note on the form. "That crazy hippie caught a trailer on fire once burning incense—and I wouldn't trust a word she said."

———

Adam walked me to the exit door, holding it open for me. Night air snaked in through the opening, balmy and fragrant with the sweet perfume of daylilies and juniper. I followed, shaking with anger and humiliation.

I waited until the door closed and Officer Rodunk stood out of earshot. "Did you see that?" I sputtered, waving my arm toward the police station. "They don't believe me!" I kicked the concrete step. "Bunch of rednecks."

"I know. I'm so sorry." Adam wrapped his arm around me, and the lines between his eyes turned hard. "That masked guy could have killed you, Shiloh! Do you realize how serious this is?"

"Sure I do! But I've gone to the police, and all I did was make a laughingstock of myself." I sniffled, so mad I could cry. "What else am I supposed to do?"

"I don't know, but we've got to make some hard decisions. If this mugger is related to whoever's sending you roses, then both of us could be in big trouble. You especially."

"The skinhead from Winchester used a knife. Maybe it's him."

"I thought of that." Adam wrapped his arm tighter around me. "And if you ask me, this mugger didn't match the profile of that Odysseus guy so far—no sneaking around from a distance and sending flowers or e-mails."

"Besides, why would a stalker want my purse?" I rubbed my arms, feeling chilly.

"We can't know for sure until something more concrete turns up.

But I still think you should play it safe and stay with somebody until all of this blows over. Maybe Faye and Earl. And don't go out running by yourself anymore."

I hated how pinched my freedom felt suddenly—all on account of a man I didn't even know.

"Faye's already offered their spare room." I fell into step beside Adam, biting my lip. Resigning myself to the lousy treadmill in Faye's laundry room. "And I might ask the police to run a background check on Clarence Toyer, too—since I've already requested one for Jim Bob Townshend."

"Who's Clarence?"

"Our mail guy at work. He may have left that note on my car."

Adam stopped on the sidewalk. "Note? What note?" He spoke so sharply that a passerby on the sidewalk looked up, cell phone to his ear.

"A silly message left under my gas tank flap. I didn't think to tell you, Adam. It just never crossed my mind."

A flash of anger passed through Adam's eyes, and the set of his jaw hardened. "You should have told me about the note, Shiloh! We're going to be married soon, and I don't want secrets between us."

"Secrets? You think I'm keeping it a secret?" My nerves had frazzled, and I raised my voice. Tears threatening to spill over.

"No. I'm sorry. I didn't mean that." Adam rubbed his eyes with his hand and sighed then drew me into a tight embrace. "You've never kept anything from me. But whatever happens to you affects me now, too. I want us to share things. To always be on the same page."

"Well, I'm trying," I retorted, wiping at a corner of my eye.

"I know you are." Adam rested his chin on the top of my head. "It's not your fault. I'm worried about you, is all."

I want us to share things," Adam had said. He was right; in less than two months we'd share an apartment. A name. A bed, even, its sheets tossed casually across us like a cascade of fallen leaves in the predawn darkness. That hand with the scar across its knuckles entwined in strands of my hair.

Until now it had always been me—alone—on my own. And suddenly I wouldn't be.

My breath snagged in my throat as I looked up at Adam, his eyes glinting back white and copper from the streetlights, like stars. This complex web of accountability took me by surprise—so new and startling and impossibly grown-up—and my knees trembled again.

"We'll get to the bottom of the roses," I said, finding my voice. "Tammy from Rask hasn't called me back yet, remember? When she does, we might know more. Until then we can't speculate."

Adam slipped his arm around my waist, and we walked together toward my car. Sitting pale and lonely in the little police station parking lot. He silently unlocked my car door, swinging it open for me. I got in and nodded my thanks, buckling up while he went around to the driver's side.

"In fact, you're the one I'm worried about," I said as he locked the door and started the engine. "Ray saw *your* face on the letter. Not mine."

"Nah. I'm sure he's mistaken. I mean, I'm a pretty normal-looking guy. And anybody could have a scar on his chin like he indicated." Adam flicked on the headlights. "Maybe I'm wrong, but it doesn't scare me. What does scare me, though, is something happening to you."

We pulled out of the parking lot in silence, and Adam ran his free hand across my cheek as we turned into the street. "How about something to eat before we head back?" He glanced over at me.

"Eat?" His words sounded out of place, like an invitation to a monster truck rally over caviar. I touched the raw line on my throat where the knife had nicked my skin, unable to think of much but shadowy parking lots and ski masks.

"Yeah. I think it'll help you feel better." He trailed his thumb off my cheek. "You cold? I can go back to my truck and get my jacket."

"You're right. I guess I should eat something. I didn't have time for dinner." I perked up slightly. "But I'm not cold. Thanks."

Adam turned down a side street. "Dairy Queen's over here. We'll be in and out in a few minutes."

But Adam couldn't have made a worse prediction.

Chapter 18

For starters, the drunk guy loitering outside the Dairy Queen who gave me a slow once-over and mumbled something about Adam and me being the "perfect couple" didn't help. Nor did his dull, brownish teeth as they curved into a leering grin. Reminding me a little too keenly of Clarence Toyer.

Adam pushed past him with his arm around me, and since the restaurant was closer than the car, grabbed the door handle and pushed me in first.

And as soon as we stepped into the brightly lit, ice-cream-and-french-fry-scented interior, we saw them: teens in tuxedos and frothy turquoise and coral-pink gowns, gathered in noisy clumps at the tables. Packing into overcrowded booths like colorful fish eggs falling off a piece of sushi.

"Prom," Adam sighed, checking his watch. "Wilson or Waynesboro High. Boy, do we have the worst luck tonight."

"Prom? In June?"

He shrugged. "It depends on the snow days they have to make up at the end of the year. We had so much snow one year that we didn't finish until nearly July."

School in July? Ugh. As much as I loved to study, the idea of ratcheting up the air conditioners while the sun beat down outside the algebra classroom windows made me squirm.

"You want to go somewhere else?" Adam leaned down to talk into my ear over the noise.

"No. Here's fine." I stifled a yawn. "We'll hurry."

I found a table as far from the mayhem as possible and sat while

Adam ordered, watching the couples giggle and holler over one another. Boys with still-pimply foreheads wore black jackets and bow ties, gesturing wildly while they told animated stories, sitting backward on the table. The more fashionable girls ran manicured fingers through unnaturally straightened and highlighted hair, smoothing strapless, silver-sequined gowns; the country girls stood out with their hair-sprayed, curling-iron-styled bangs and simple puffy-sleeved dresses.

One couple, red-faced and laughing, pretended to waltz between the tables to Aerosmith piped through the cratchity overhead radio. A long spiral of overcurled hair dangled down the girl's back.

Adam ducked his head as he walked between them with our tray, his short, sandy hair and simple plaid button-up shirt standing out against the riot of hot pink, yellow, and sea-green satins.

None of the girls giggled or batted their eyes at him. Of course not. He was. . .well, Adam. Simple and plain, yet I sensed something extraordinary about him—something that made the tense lines in my face relax. He struck me as country but not redneck; just a strand of dusty barbed wire away from preppy.

And a thousand cow pastures removed from anyone I'd ever imagined for myself until this year.

"Did you go to prom, Adam?" I asked as he set down our tray.

He slid into the booth across from me and leaned closer to hear. "Me? Yeah." He put my straw in my Coke for me, scratching the back of his neck like he felt uncomfortable.

"Really?" I wrinkled my nose, having a hard time imagining Adam in a tux with a girl. "With who?"

"Guess." He rolled his eyes.

"Eliza Harrison," I teased. "Your old flame."

"You mean my parents' old flame. And yes, that's who."

"Right." I snitched a french fry. "I guess you've disappointed them then."

A brief stab of pain darted through Adam's eyes, and I immediately wished I could take back my words. "No," he said, brow creasing in a slight frown. "They wanted me to be happy. But they didn't know me as well as they thought. I've always wanted more than a girl who thinks marrying and having children is her whole life—with no other goals or thoughts whatsoever. Except maybe crocheting doilies."

I laughed into my paper cup of Coke and pulled the straw out of my mouth.

"Don't get me wrong. Family and children are important. Really important. But what if we can't have children? Does anybody ever think of that?" Adam pulled his straw out of the paper and stuffed it in his drink. "And what about life outside of changing diapers and mashing potatoes? I don't want stupid kids, Shiloh. I think both of us should be well-rounded people so our family can be well-rounded, too."

"Well said." I tapped my cup to his. "The mashed potatoes I've made were pretty bad, by the way."

"That's okay. Mine aren't any better." Adam smiled.

I didn't speak for a minute, smoothing the flimsy plastic lid on my cup. "So you want kids?" I braced myself for his response, which I pretty much already knew.

"Sure I do." Adam's eyes softened. "Kids are amazing. They're. . . well, I can't even describe it. Like my brother Todd. I love him." He looked away with a distant smile. "I think I've always wanted kids ever since Mom and Dad brought Todd home from the hospital. I wasn't even a teenager yet. I loved looking after somebody smaller than me. Teaching him how to ride a bike and do math problems."

I pictured Adam laying a squirming baby on the changing table. Awkwardly trying to fasten a diaper. Bouncing a ball or pushing Todd on a tricycle.

"I'd like to have kids, too, I guess." I poked at my fries. "But what if I don't feel that way as much as you do?"

One of the waltz-dancers crashed into our table, nearly overturning Adam's Dr Pepper. They gasped apologies, covering their giggly mouths in horror. He nodded tersely. I, not so inclined to polite niceties, shot them a cold look through narrowed eyes.

"So?" I turned back to Adam. "Did you hear my question?"

"I heard you." Adam set his cup upright and took a long drink then set it down and leaned his face close to mine. "I'm not marrying you for the kids you'll give me, Shiloh," he said in almost a whisper, his breath tickling the tendrils around my ear. "I'm marrying you for *you.* God knows what's best for us."

Unexpected tears sprang into my eyes, and I felt my heart throb and bounce in my chest like air turbulence on a plane. A startling shiver that began cold and spread out through my veins. I looked down, the tray suddenly turning watery. "You're sure about that?"

"Very sure." Adam's eyes were so close I could see their grayish irises. The short brown lashes that framed them, not quite black.

"Then why haven't you kissed me yet?" My voice came out in a quivery whisper. Surprising me as much as it appeared to surprise Adam.

"Huh?" He drew back, startled, and knocked his hand against the table. He rubbed at it, wincing.

"You haven't kissed me," I said, my eyes bouncing from my tray to his face and back again. "Not even on the day we got engaged. Just on the cheek. Not that I mind. Exactly." My hands shook again, and I fumbled with my straw paper, twisting it. "But. . .I don't understand."

"I know. I'm sorry." He glanced at my mouth with a look that struck me as almost hungry, his pupils widening slightly. Drawing a single finger across my lips in a tingling line. I still felt it after he brushed my hair behind my shoulder and chastely folded his hands on the table. "Don't think I haven't wanted to. A lot." He fumbled with his napkin, those blunt nails of his clipped super short as if he'd cut into flesh.

"Then why?"

He swallowed, the lines in his throat bobbing. "I just can't yet. I want to wait a little longer. For me. For you. For us."

"Wait?" My mouth fell open.

"Yeah." He blinked faster, looking away.

"What if I don't want to wait? Did you ever think of that?" My voice cut, cold and hard. I reached out quickly and took his hand, trying to soften my words. "I'm sorry. But I don't. . .understand you sometimes. I mean, it's just a kiss."

"I know." Adam blew out his breath. "But that's it precisely. It's not 'just a kiss.' At least I don't want it to be. It's meant to lead somewhere, Shiloh." His eyes searched mine. "And I'm not ready to go there yet."

My anger flared suddenly, and I felt heat rush to my face. My pulse roared in my ear. "Are you saying that because I've had boyfriends and fiancés before—more than you have—that I. . .that I'm dangerous? That I'm trying to push you somewhere you don't want to go?"

I half stood in my seat, fingers cold and quaking. A sudden nausea swirled in my stomach, like the first time I'd seen the truck blasting country music across the street from Mom's house. Me, fresh off the plane from Japan and horrified at the idea of being stuck in a small, run-down country town like Staunton.

Everyone around here was completely insane. Nuts! All of them! Clarence, the mugger, the drunk outside the Dairy Queen, and Adam J. Carter. And maybe me, too.

Jennifer Rogers Spinola

My jaw quivered as I tried to get a rein on my tongue before I spewed something hateful. Deer-blasters and ultra-right-wing freaks! THIS is what I'd chosen for my life?

"No! For goodness' sake, Shiloh. Sit down." Adam grabbed my hand and pulled me back down to the booth. "Stop thinking I'm judging you. That's not what I meant at all. I meant I wanted to wait for your sake. *Yours*, do you hear me? Mine, too, but I was thinking mainly of you."

He exhaled, tracing my fingers with his. Making those little shivers of sensitive flesh echo up and down my arm. "You're beautiful, Shiloh. I love you. Don't you know how easy it would be to. . .to. . ."

"To what?" I felt tears smart again behind my eyes.

"To do a lot more than just kiss you." Adam let out a long, shuddering breath, closing his eyes. Those brownish eyelashes quivering before he opened them again. Color gathered in his face, across his cheeks, and under the blondish hair that fell over his forehead. "Please try to understand me. And if you can't, then just do this for me. Like you said to Stella with her smoking."

His lips, redder and suddenly beautiful in their firm lines and touch of moisture, pressed together as he thought. "I've made mistakes before. Maybe not to the extent that you might think is important, but it was for me. I don't want to do that. Not with you."

"Why not with me? What makes me so different?"

"You're. . .you're precious." Something like tears glimmered in his eyes as he reached out to cup my cheek. "I want everything to be right. No regrets."

I didn't reply. Just sat there thinking, remembering what he'd told me on the grassy banks of the lake where he'd asked me to marry him, slipping a ring twisted out of grass on my finger. After I'd reminded him that I would never be the pristine, sugar-sweet bride of a protected youth. *"I'm not asking you to be me,"* he'd said. *"I'm asking you to be you and marry me."*

Adam abruptly leaned forward and brushed my cheek with his lips. Warm lips, and soft. Then he sat back in the booth and unwrapped a clean napkin, dabbing gently at the corners of my tear-swollen eyes.

I reached out and accepted the napkin with a nod of thanks, sniffling in the rest of my tears. And abruptly jerked myself out of the booth, wondering how I'd gone and gotten myself engaged to stubborn Adam Carter, Mr. "you-don't-know-Virginia-Beach" who nixed my beautiful Morning Sun honeymoon package.

"I've never heard of anybody doing something as crazy as waiting for a kiss," I managed, my lips quivering. "Do you know that?"

He reached out for my hand. "Well? Then maybe we can be the first."

I stared at him as his fingers slipped through mine, not sure if I should call the old Western State Lunatic Asylum in Staunton and have him committed—and maybe me, too—or press my head to his chest in a tight hug. Just like most people in the South: infuriating and irresistible at the same time.

Instead I wordlessly turned on my heel, pushing my way through the prom stars to the dinky Dairy Queen bathroom.

—◆—

Adam's face tensed with worry when I slid back into the booth. I'd more or less composed myself inside the frigid, over-air-conditioned stall, trying not to look at the graffiti scrawled in the new metal walls. "You okay?" He reached for my arm. "I didn't mean to. . . It's just an idea, you know."

"An idea. Right. A pretty different one though, I'd have to say."

"Weird, you mean?" Adam asked, rubbing his thumb across my arm.

"Hmm. Yeah. Maybe that, too." But I tried to think of something else to talk about. Think about. I started unwrapping my cheeseburger, hunger stirring with a surprising fierceness. Like just after I'd finished a ten-mile run, body craving carbs. Fries. Oh, they looked so good.

"So how about you?" Adam asked in a brighter tone, perhaps trying to lighten our emotions. "I guess you went to prom, too, right?"

"No." I shook two french fries free from the paper sleeve. They'd cooled to a dull lukewarm—the bane of fast-food fries—but still looked tasty, if not a bit oily. I ate them and licked the grains of salt from my fingers.

"You didn't go to prom? Why not?"

"I was too busy rushing Mom to the hospital after she overdosed on some psychedelic tea her guru gave her." I chewed another fry. "I almost lost her that time." I cleared my throat, feeling my breath congeal. "And I told her. . ."

Adam put his hamburger down. "Told her what?"

"That I hoped she died." I swallowed, the fries morphing into starchy clumps in my esophagus. "Guess I got my wish, huh?"

Adam's hand found mine through the mess of greasy papers on

our tray, and he linked our fingers together. We sat there together in silence, and I was glad that for once he didn't try to say something to assuage my guilty conscience. He simply wiped his fingers on his napkin then lifted my palm to his mouth and kissed it. Resting my hand gently against his stubbly cheek.

My eyes flickered down to the paper tray liner, where we'd squirted a splotch of garish, orange-red ketchup. Pooled by our fries like blood. My free hand flitted to my throat, tracing the line where the knife blade had pressed into my skin.

"Are you afraid to die, Adam?"

I whispered it so quietly that Adam had to lean forward to hear. One of the high school boys at a nearby table spun a tray on his finger like a basketball, grappling for it as it careened sideways and clattered on the floor. Punctuated by an explosion of laughter and applause.

"Afraid to die? No. Not really." He kissed my fingers again as he let them go.

"Everything in Japan's about avoiding death." I finished un-wrapping my burger and picked it up. "The number four. *Shi*. It sounds like the word for death. Nobody gives gifts in fours. It's a bad omen." I took a bite of my burger, which gushed melted cheese and salty dill pickle rounds. "You don't stick chopsticks upright in your bowl or pass food chopstick to chopstick because that's how they deal with rice offerings and cremated remains at funerals."

Adam's eyes widened over his cup.

"Lots of things, really. You don't sleep facing north because that's how people are laid out for cremation. And so forth. Never write somebody's name in red ink."

As soon as I said it, I choked on my bite of burger, the gritty pieces of meat lodging in the back of my throat.

"What's wrong? You don't believe that stuff, do you?" Adam reached across the table to pound me on the back.

"No way. Not anymore." I coughed again to clear my throat. "But the note on my car was written in red ink. And both florist's cards from the bouquet."

Adam's face paled. "Red ink? Is that supposed to mean something?"

"I have no idea." I took a sip of my Coke. "But it's. . .yes. A little weird. Do you know anybody who regularly writes in red ink?"

"My dad. A math teacher."

"Right." I tried another bite of burger. "And Clarence prefers red

152

pens when he does his crossword puzzles. You better believe I'm going to talk to the police about Clarence." I chewed in frustration, wishing I'd never had reason to suspect Clarence. My coworker, of all people. Why couldn't the note on my car have blown away in the wind, like so many of my worries about Mom's death?

"But that's the thing, Adam. Everybody tries to avoid death. Most of Mom's guru chasing and cult following was about that, too— finding a way to prolong life and earn points for the next one. I know differently now. But the idea of death still bothers me." I chewed a while in silence. "It's terrible no matter how you look at it. I've written up a few car accidents that gave me nightmares. Even as a Christian, I don't like it."

"I guess nobody does." Adam looked across the table at me. "And that's why we put our faith in Jesus. He's the only one who's ever beat death and lived to tell about it."

He glanced over at the raucous crowd of prom-goers, where two couples made out in the corners of the booths. The others toasted noisily with chocolate-dipped ice-cream cones. Girls dabbed delicately at their lips with paper napkins, heads bent together as they reapplied lipstick with shining compact mirrors.

"Most people go on acting as if life's forever and the afterlife is some sort of cosmic lights-out." Adam balled up his napkin. "Without a care in the world. There's no judgment. No accounting for our actions on earth. Faith is irrelevant. But. . .that's not the way it is."

The pulse of the electric guitar on the radio died during an unexpected lull in the teen chatters, and I heard Adam's voice come clearly. "We only have one life, Shiloh. We have to live it for Him. That's all that matters."

I looked over at a neighboring table as Adam's words swelled the walls of my heart. One of the tuxedoed guys clumsily balanced an ice-cream cone on his nose, arms spread. I wondered if he'd ever considered that when he walked out those glass doors with his date on his arm and climbed into his car, a drunk driver might veer across his path. Or a deer, for crying out loud. Goodness knows deer crashes killed enough people in Virginia every year. I wondered if he was ready to face death—there in his tuxedo, a silly grin plastered across his face. Plans for love and college and a future dancing in his head.

Was I ready? I picked at a sesame seed on top of my bun, remembering the cold steel of the knife.

Jennifer Rogers Spinola

"Well, I know one thing for sure. As much as I love Jesus, I'm not looking forward to dying." I wiped my fingers on a ketchup-stained napkin. "And I could never live with knowing that I caused somebody else's suffering and death."

"Let that go," said Adam gently, wiping a crumb from my chin. "Leave it with God. He knows better than we do."

"I know." *But.* I bit into my burger and didn't finish the rest of my thought. "It's so easy for you, isn't it, Adam?" I blurted, mouth half full. Wondering what my life would be like now if I'd grown up here in the Bible Belt, listening to sermons and going to Sunday school. Laughing with my prom date at a small-town restaurant instead of stepping over discarded syringes on my way to the homeless shelter in Brooklyn after Mom got evicted for the third time. Hoping my neighbor's leering boyfriend wouldn't try to kiss me again while I cracked open their bullet-ridden apartment door, begging her to call 911 after Mom passed out in the hallway.

"Easy?" Adam stopped chewing. "Maybe you're right." He wiped his mouth on a napkin. "But I'd die for Him, Shiloh, without a second thought. And for you." He ran his hand over my silver engagement band. "I guess that ups the stakes a little."

I glanced up at Adam as I balled up my napkin, feeling in the well of my stomach how different we were: a man who wouldn't kiss me or even come in my house alone—engaged to a woman who hadn't cared when her ex-fiancé roomed with another woman. Or pretended not to care, rather.

Adam's short, conservative haircut and simple Gospel answers slammed up against my quaking fears and old superstitions. His fishing tackle box versus my sleek cherry-blossom-patterned teacup and Japanese fashion magazines.

Can we really do this, God? I felt my heart beat painfully in my chest as my ring glimmered in the light. A spark of fluid silver, both cold and alive. Liquid fire. A paradox wrapped around my finger.

For one shimmering moment I didn't know who was right—me or the drunk outside the door who'd proclaimed us the "perfect couple."

Maybe both.

Or maybe neither.

Adam's cell phone vibrated suddenly, buzzing against the table where he'd dropped it with his keys. He frowned at the number and punched the button with the heel of his hand, wiping his fingers on a napkin before putting the phone to his ear.

"Yes, sir?" He sat up straighter, mouthing "police" as his eyes jerked up to meet mine. "Did you find him? Oh. Okay." His expression sagged. "Thanks anyway."

I heard a faint voice speaking, and then Adam's face crinkled in surprise. "Yes, it's my truck. We're getting ready to drive home. Why, is something wrong?"

"Your truck? Why's he asking about your truck?" I whispered, mad that they hadn't found the creep yet. Now I'd have to try to sleep knowing he was out there somewhere with my purse, helping himself to my debit card.

As soon as we finished eating, I'd drop Adam back off at the elementary school parking lot to pick up his truck and get us both out of there. For good.

Matt the intern could do the next city council write-up, the loafer.

Adam hit the SPEAKERPHONE button, and I heard the officer's voice loud and clear: "Well, driving home might be a problem."

"Sorry?"

"Your tires are slashed. All four of them."

"What?" Adam and I gasped at the same time, nearly banging heads as we leaned forward to hear better.

"And that's not all. Seems like whoever did it left a message for you, unless you regularly carve words in the side of your truck with your keys."

"What message?" Adam sputtered. "What do you mean?"

"Somebody scratched a big, 'STAY AWAY' in all caps on the left side of your truck. You'd better come see for yourself."

Chapter 19

What is this?" I dropped my old burgundy-brown purse in a heap on the carpeted office floor. All my excitement about going wedding shopping this coming weekend with Becky dissipating like a tired Japanese blowfish.

"What's what?" Meg looked up from holding a stack of papers upright against my gray cubicle wall, signing something.

"That." I pointed.

"That would be a standard office chair, although a little on the cheap side." Meg raised an eyebrow and pushed some long strands of taffy-auburn hair behind her ear before turning back to her paper.

"Not the chair. I'm talking about that." I pointed again, trying to ignore her foul-smelling mug on the corner of my desk. "That padded envelope. How long has it been here?"

Meg pursed her eyebrows in a "you've lost your marbles" grimace. "Since the mail rounds, probably. Clarence probably brought it. Why? What's the big deal?"

"It's from California." I took off my lanyard and poked a corner of the package with my glossy ID tag. "I don't know anybody in California. Clarence used to live there though."

"What's the return address?" Meg peeked over my shoulder, her musty patchouli scent making my nose itch.

"Santa Clarita. There's no name."

She sobered suddenly and lowered her papers. "You don't think it's related to what happened in Waynesboro, do you? Or the roses? Mercy, Jacobs. You're starting to scare me."

"I don't know what to think." I reluctantly picked up the envelope and squeezed it, feeling something thin and hard inside. I slit open the edge with scissors and dropped the envelope sliver in the trash. A cracked CD case fell out into my hand.

"The Judybats?" Meg picked it up with her fingertips. "Who in the world are they? And what happened to this case?" She turned over the cracked and dented plastic, which looked like it had been chucked from a moving car at top speed and into a road sign. Several times. And mended with bubble gum.

"Don't ask me." I pulled the case open by its rickety joints and dislodged the equally scratched CD. One scuffed edge was mottled with something sticky.

"There's another CD in there." Meg peered over my shoulder. "And. . .something in the middle?"

"Oh boy," I muttered as a thin, flat, cardboard packet plopped onto my desk from between the two CDs. "What next? More roses?" I sliced carefully through the stiff square with the scissors.

"Don't say that." Meg shot me a stern look. "After the other night, I'm afraid to let you out of my sight."

I cut one more time, and the cardboard fell open. Revealing a gleaming, razor-sharp throwing star. Like the kind ninjas throw at people in cartoons. One sparkling edge glinted in the overhead light.

"Shiloh Jacobs." Meg flung the battered CD case on the desk and backed away. "Who's sending you throwing stars? Do you have any idea how illegal that is? Sending knives through the mail?" She leaned closer to my desk, pulling the throwing star partially out of its sheath with the tip of her pen. "Although they did a pretty good job of hiding it from the X-rays." She fiddled with the CDs, holding them together like a sandwich with the throwing star between them. "Huh. Check it out."

She tore a sheet of paper from my note cube and ran it across the razor edge of the blade, eyes widening in admiration as it sliced through the paper as easily as butter. Leaving a thin paper curl.

"Great. Now I'm supposed to figure out who sent me this." I threw up my arms in exasperation. Phil and Priyasha turned in their chairs at my loud rant, and heads popped over cubicles. I bobbed an involuntary "I'm sorry" bow, Japan-style, and dropped my voice. "I don't know anything that's going on lately, Meg!"

Fuming, I scooted the whole mess to the side of my desk with my keyboard and plopped in my chair to think.

157

"Jacobs," Meg hissed and threw a manila folder over the whole pile of envelopes and cardboard, scooting the throwing star out of sight. "You can't just leave that there! Somebody'll see it. Kevin'll have a heart attack if he finds reporters carrying weapons into the office."

"Do I look like I'm carrying anything?" My voice rose testily.

"No, but still. Get a grip." Meg lowered her voice to a whisper. "Take it home or whatever on your lunch break. Put it in your car. Just get it out of here."

"You want it?" I glared at her.

"Are you kidding? Cooter would have my head."

"Why, is he antiweapon, too?"

Meg frowned in surprise. "What do you mean, 'too'?"

I turned to look at her. "Aren't you against guns and all that?"

"Against guns? Jacobs, I own two .22 rifles, a .45 automatic, and a Glock. I've been squirrel hunting more times than I can count."

"Squirrel hunting?" I shrieked, quickly lowering my voice before Phil glared at me again. "I thought you're vegan!"

"I didn't say I eat them. But the suckers keep eating my corn and getting in Cooter's still. Making a mess out of the eaves and clogging up our gutters. Gotta do something. Cooter swears they're the best thing he's ever eaten. So have at it, I say."

She looped her thumbs through the belt loops of her jeans. "But he'll be mad if I show up with a throwing star that's better than his. He makes knives, you know. Pretty terrible ones. But he's really proud of his throwing stars." She shrugged a shoulder. "If you can call them that. They're more like metal Frisbees."

Not a single word came to my mouth. I just sat there, immobile, until Meg pulled the empty envelope from under the folder and peered again at the return address. "Hey, aren't throwing stars illegal in California?"

"Illegal? Try a felony!" I shook my hand in the direction of the pile. "Perfect. All I need is some wacko sending me weapons and another stupid note from Clarence on my car."

"A note from Clarence?" She snorted a laugh, tapping her corky sandal on the carpet. "Was it obscene?"

"No. It didn't make any sense. Just a bunch of numbers and more drawings of an eye." I turned back to my desk, wishing I could crawl back in bed and start the day over. No, the week. Maybe more than that.

"At least you haven't gotten any more roses." Meg patted my shoulder. "There are some real fruit loops out there, you know."

"Yeah, and speaking of fruit loops, it's fortuitous that you weren't in Waynesboro last week, Shiloh," said Matt the intern, butting into our conversation as he leaned back in his chair without a squeak. A conference room chair with nice cushy padding. *Grrr.*

"Why do you say that?"

"I had to update the crime listings. Some chick got mugged at knifepoint." He chuckled. "What a goofball, loitering on elementary school property at inappropriate hours of the night. Serves her right."

I swiveled slowly in my chair to meet his eyes. "That was *me*. I did the city council report, remember?"

Matt paled from the roots of his long, dark brown ponytail to his slightly double chin.

I scooted my chair across the carpet, coming face-to-face with him until our noses nearly touched. I spoke through my teeth. "The meeting didn't even finish until ten o'clock. I'm not a goofball. Got it?"

"Whoa, whoa, whoa!" Meg wheeled me back over to my desk and grabbed an empty chair from Phil's cubicle, ignoring Matt's sputtered apology. "Did you say the guy had a knife?" She sat down, crossing her long legs. Jeans frayed along the bottom hem and dragged on the carpet over her Birkenstocks.

"Sure he had a knife! I said so in the police report."

"I didn't see a knife!" Meg's eyes bugged. "I just saw the guy take off, and you told me he'd swiped your purse!"

"Well, it was dark, and we barely had a chance to talk before Adam showed up and took me to the police station." I sagged back in my seat. "Now I'll have to call the police again and report this stupid package. No, you know what? Maybe I'll just do it all this afternoon when I go by there to report all the weird hang ups on my answering machine. Who knows? Maybe I'll have something else to report by then, too." I scowled.

"It's the same guy!" Meg reached out to shake my shoulder. "He threatened you at knifepoint, and now he's sending weapons in the mail."

"We don't know that, Meg! There might be no connection whatsoever."

"Right, but you can't rule anything out." She waved a hand in front of my face. "Look at me, Jacobs. I don't want to be taking photos of a crime scene with your name slapped across the headline. Got it?"

I sighed. "I'll take everything to the police this afternoon, okay?"

"You'd better." She raised an eyebrow. "I thought that God of yours was supposed to protect you. Looks like He's been dozing off on the job."

"On the contrary." I put my hands down and soberly met her eyes. "I think He's done a pretty good job. And He used *you*." I reached out and poked her in the arm. "You're the one who scared off the guy so all he got was my purse. Did you ever think of that?"

Meg fell ghostly silent, finally reaching over to sip from her foul-smelling mug. "Well, anyway. You'd better be careful."

"I am. Christie and I are staying at Faye and Earl's for a while. I only know about the answering machine messages because Faye and Adam took me home to pack."

I swiveled around to my desk to somehow try to work then glanced back to Meg. "The police did give me one tip though. Although I'm not sure what to do with it."

"A tip? About Odysseus?"

"Maybe. About the guy who mugged me last night."

"Tell me."

"Copper shavings." I turned on my computer. "They found minute copper shavings in the elementary school parking lot by the place I'd parked, and a few more specks near the trees where the guy ran away. They think the shavings must have fallen off his clothes."

"So you're saying our stalker is a metallurgist?"

"Could be. Or a plumber. A welder. Something. Or someone who spent considerable time with one."

"You said Jim Bob used to be a mechanic. Half the stuff under a car hood is made of copper."

"You're right." I massaged my forehead as I thought. "Good thing I asked the police to check him out." I mulled through my list then opened the Internet and typed into some search engines. "Knife makers use copper, too. Not that I'm suspecting Cooter. It's just a fact."

"Oh, I could imagine Cooter doing something ridiculous like that. I mean, come on. The guy cheers for the Colorado Rockies! Give me a break." Meg made a face while my jaw dropped. "I'm kidding, of course. It wasn't him. We were arguing about the lousy World Series while you wrestled the Man in the Iron Mask."

"Your boyfriend's a good guy, Meg! It can't be him. Besides, I've never even met Cooter."

"You think you haven't met him." She flicked an eyebrow in warning. "Be careful, Jacobs. When it comes to stalkers, you can't be sure who you know and who you don't. Remember that." Her eyes bored into me. "It's important that you don't rule out anybody. And if he's half-cocked, as many stalkers are, what makes sense to them might not necessarily make sense to us."

Meg scooted forward. "When you're not playing with a full deck, reality shifts. People are who you want them to be." She put her hands on her hips, staring off into space. "For example. Have you noticed something?"

"About what?"

"About the perp's messages. He uses numbers a lot."

"I saw that." I dug through the papers on my desk and pulled out the newest paper I'd found on my car. "Threes. Fours. Twelves. A lot of them."

"Maybe he's an accountant."

"Tim's an accountant," I blurted without thinking. "But. . .but there's no way Tim would. . ." I crumpled up the paper and threw it in the trash. "This is craziness! Anybody could be a suspect if I keep thinking like this."

"No!" Meg dug the paper out of the trash. "That's just it! You can't rule people out. I'm sure it's not Tim, but stick with your gut. We know a couple of things—like, the guy reads literature."

I felt ill suddenly, remembering the *Julius Caesar* book in the back of Tim's truck.

"Stop. This is too much."

"He knows enough about security to hide his fingerprints." Meg scratched out a list in my reporter's notebook, raising her voice over my protests. "He uses some sort of trick to hide his handwriting and his knives. And he possibly works with metal or spends time near someone who does."

"Something else." She shoved the paper closer. "He knows you like roses. Or he thinks you do. *Red* roses." Meg tapped the pen against her chin thoughtfully. "He spray paints in red—if it's the same guy. Maybe the color red means something? Or at least it does to him?"

"I've thought about that. But I don't know what to do with it." I raised my hands. "Any more than I do the copper shavings."

"Well, keep it all in the back of your mind. And remember one thing." She turned me to face her. "He wants you to ditch your fiancé and your wedding. For *him*."

"What's that supposed to mean?"

"I have no earthly idea." Meg shook her head. "But it's pretty clear he's serious about it. So watch yourself."

—m—

Breathe, Shiloh. Just breathe. Relax.

I scooted forward and took a shaky sip of steaming green tea, its bitter, slightly fruity, earthy flavor reminding me of Japan. Which made my nerves relax a bit, inhaling memories of plum-blossom-strewn sidewalks and pulsing neon signs. A far cry from greasy chicken gizzards and deep-fried Pop-Tarts—which yes, I'd actually seen at a diner in town.

What I needed right now was to shake Staunton's gritty dust off my Prada heels and feel the blast of a Japanese subway on my face. The noise of busy sidewalks and the chirp at the black-and-white crosswalk. The low hum of the JR train as it skimmed along the coast, salty sea breeze blowing my hair.

Going somewhere. Far away from cow-ridden western Virginia.

Wait a second.

I grabbed the padded envelope and squinted at the address. Then I snatched up the Whatever-Bats CD case with a tissue and turned it over in my hand. Staring at the faded photo of the band members, one of whom boasted thick, stand-up hair like one of Mom's spider ferns.

And I tore open my purse, rummaging through it for my international phone card.

—m—

"Kyoko Morikoshi." I tried to keep my voice down, but even so, I could still hear it over the clacking of keyboards and rattle of the old air-conditioning system. "Did you send me a *shuriken*? A very sharp one?"

"What? Hold on a second."

From across the line something ripped in my ear, loud and grating. I pulled the receiver away. "What on earth are you doing?"

"Packing boxes. I need more tape." Kyoko grunted, and the stiff tape made a groaning sound as she wrapped it around the box. Marker squeaked. "There. That one's done. So what's your question again?"

"A throwing star. Did you send one to my office?"

"Me? No." She snorted.

Oh boy. The colors of the room rippled, as if I were seeing underwater. "But I asked my brother to. Did he?" Her voice sparked

162

with sudden excitement. "Are you serious, Ro? He really sent it?"

"Does he live in Santa Clarita?" I growled.

"Yes! That's him! Wow, I'm so impressed!" Thumps muffled into the receiver as Kyoko apparently put down her stuff, snatching the phone closer. "Tell me—what brand is it? A Cold Steel?" she bubbled, excited. "I figured it was better for my bro to send it than mess with customs, but I didn't know if he'd really do it. So does it fit in your purse? And did he do the CD thing I told him?"

I just sat there in my chair, shaking my head back and forth. "I can't believe this. You know it's illegal for him to have one in California, don't you?"

Kyoko snorted. "Since when has Kentaro cared about illegalities? Please. That's the least of my worries right now. You got mugged, Ro! I told you this would happen if you didn't stay out of trouble."

"And how exactly am I supposed to do that?" I threw my hands up in the air.

"Move to a real town." Kyoko enunciated her words with cold exactness. "Or at least stop hanging around weird places like Civil War battlefields."

"Oh, and elementary schools?" I scooted my chair forward stiffly, stung. "I was doing my job when that guy snatched my purse, Kyoko. No different than you wandering around Okinawa."

"I beg to differ. I didn't get mugged in Okinawa, did I?" I heard her scratch something on the side of the box, marker squeaking. "Although I got one mug of a sunburn on the beach. It still hurts."

I wrapped the phone cord around my hand, staring up at a dried, dark red rose petal that had fallen onto the desk. Half hidden under folders. "Well, you're right about one thing. I'd love to move. And now that Adam's uncle is buying my house, it might be easier. Who knows? Maybe we can move to Harrisonburg about half an hour north of here—where Adam's college is." I still sounded dubious. "Although it's not a whole lot bigger than Staunton. And it smells like dog food."

"Dog food?"

"Harrisonburg's where they process the turkey and chicken parts. Like for Purina."

"Ro-chan." Kyoko sighed.

"Okay. Forget I said anything." I scooted the rose petal into the trash. "But don't give me a hard time, okay? I'm doing the best I can. I just need a little time to make some sense out of things."

"No, you need a bodyguard—and maybe a few more shuriken. But this is the best I can do for now."

I felt myself smile despite my best efforts. "Well, thanks, Kyoko. For the. . .uh. . .thought, anyway. The CD case thing was clever. I guessed it had to be you once I saw the guy with the big hair. Some '80s band, I figured."

"What?" Kyoko's shriek startled me so much I nearly dropped the phone. "Kentaro sent you my Judybats CD? I love that one! I knew I shouldn't have let him borrow it! Tell me, Ro—is it still in good shape? 'Cause that's a limited-edition special release, and I paid big bucks for it. If he let anything happen to it, I'll. . ."

I tipped the phone to the side, Kyoko's ranting still blaring out, and met eyes with Meg in a grin as she headed out. Camera slung jauntily over one shoulder.

—⁓—

I was reaching to hang up when a crazy thought sprang into my mind, as jarring as if Phil the sportswriter had slapped me with the strap of his Cannon. Which, given his grumpy, hotheaded nature, he'd probably like very much.

"Kyoko." I jerked the receiver closer to my mouth. "Let me ask you something. Do you still have any of my things from my old apartment? The one back in Shiodome?"

"Before you got fired?" Her tone needled.

"Thanks for bringing it up." I scowled. "Just answer me. What happened to all the rest of my stuff I didn't want to pay to have shipped?"

"The pecan pie? I sent you that."

"I know. I mean like. . .maybe my old books. Letters." My heartbeat picked up. "I'm pretty sure I left behind a couple of letters."

"Oh, that kind of stuff. Why?"

"I'm. . .curious. And I need some of the letters if they're still there." My heart thudded, remembering Mom's stacks of unopened envelopes and dark blue ribbon. Hoping I'd stashed any others she might have sent—or ones that arrived for me after I'd already left Japan.

"Well, AP policy is to throw away unclaimed belongings after the apartment's been returned, unless the renter leaves a postal deposit."

That painful acid returned to my throat, and I felt my fingers turn cold.

"But."

"But what?"

"You're talking to *me*." I could almost hear Kyoko smile over the line. "I've been. . .how shall we say. . .keeping your junk for you."

"You have? How?"

"Oh, I stored a bunch of it in a couple boxes labeled 'extra photocopies of the safety handbook' in the office storage room. Of course nobody's bothered to open it." She yawned and made a groaning sound like she was stretching. "And then I sort of. . .um. . .appropriated them. So they've already been shipped as part of my belongings. To your address, of course. Which I've designated as a storage unit."

I sat there with my hand pressed over my mouth, hardly believing my good luck.

"And believe me, your house is pretty small, Ro. I've seen it. In fact, you might consider renting an actual storage unit and moving there instead."

I didn't bother to reply to her jab. "When do you think the boxes will get here?"

"I dunno. I sent 'em two weeks ago. You want the tracking numbers?"

Right then and there, if I could have gotten down on my knees and kissed Kyoko's chunky spike-heeled, metal-studded boots, I would have.

Chapter 20

"Come on. Quit starin' at 'em." Becky tried to pull me away from the glass display at the wholesale flower shop, where a thick bouquet of dark red roses nestled behind frosty glass. Tied with silver and burgundy ribbon.

"It looks so similar, Becky. I can't stand it."

"Put a cork in it, woman!" she scowled, steering the stroller with her free hand. "Quit thinkin' about that stuff! You're weddin' shoppin' now. Ain't nobody gonna get ya in here."

The stroller wheels squeaked as she pushed it around a corner, but Macy didn't stir. Black lashes closed in sleep, and one brown hand curled against her flushed cheek. I traced her softer-than-silk skin with my finger, pushing a sweaty black curl out of her forehead. Her hair was longer now; Becky had fashioned the little tufts into two tiny pigtails, one on either side of Macy's head.

I helped Becky steer the stroller, wishing Macy would hurry and wake up. A whiff of baby-powder scent reminded me of her weight in my arms as she sipped water from a bottle and played, for five rapt minutes, with a silken corner of the transparent scarf at my throat.

Macy had come to the Donaldson house in bitter February, two months old and barely the size of a newborn. But now, as her chubby cheeks flushed slightly with sleep, you'd never know she'd been an at-risk preemie.

What a difference a little love—and a lot of God's grace—can make in the heart of a child.

Becky put her hands on her hips. "Maybe ya'll do things differently back in Japan, or New York, or wherever, but weddin' shoppin' means lookin' for *weddin'* stuff! Forgit ev'rything else. I mean it." She tapped her foot. "Lands, if it's gonna be this difficult, mebbe y'oughtta just sign some papers at the justice of the peace!"

I put my hands up quickly in surrender, recalling Adam's comments on Mom's deck at nightfall. "Fine. You win. I'm just not good at all this, you know? Flowers and stuff. I said last year that I'd like grape hyacinths for my wedding, but it's too late in the season for spring bulbs."

"Well, think of somethin' else."

"But you know I like potted things."

"Too bad. I ain't puttin' ferns up the aisle, and that's final." Becky shook her head. She dislodged the stroller wheel from an overly exuberant stand of lilies and pushed it ahead.

I trailed along after her, brushing my hands against petals. The air smelled loamy and sweet, just a degree or two warmer than comfortable: a gardener's paradise. Hanging baskets of orange and white impatiens hung over the black tubs of carnations and frilly spades of snapdragons. Waves of yellow and pink and green stretched as far as I could see.

"Sorry, Becky. But I'm furious that somebody's interfering with our life and harassing Adam. You know about the e-mails, don't you? The scratches on his truck?"

"Y'all told me." Becky sighed. "Glad the police is lookin' into things. And I ain't coldhearted, ya know. I jest wanna see your weddin' day be really special, is all."

"I know." I tucked an arm through hers. "Anyway, just so you know, I've been talking to the prosecutor for my assault case in Winchester, too. And he doesn't think it's Jed Tucker."

"Well, I shore don't know what Adam's got to do with ol' Amanda what's-her-name anyhow. Why, he never met the gal!"

"I know." I sighed and scooted a bucket of peachy-pink snapdragons next to a pot of deep amethyst African violets, admiring the color contrast.

"Mebbe it's Tim's cousin Randy. He did like ya an awful lot. Told Tim he was gonna marry ya, but I reckon he done gave that up by now." Becky snickered. "Seein' as how the competition got a little steeper."

"Well, good for him." I helped Becky push the stroller over a garden hose, remembering Randy in his gray Civil War reenactment garb—and me pushing his sneaky arm off my shoulders. At least he hadn't sent me any more pictures of us Photoshopped together in a while.

Becky lifted a bucket of china-white tulips to her nose and sniffed then checked the price. "Besides Shane, ain't nobody else who sent ya roses, is there?"

I didn't answer, fingering a bleeding heart stem. The little pink hearts dangled off the leafy green arch like jewels.

"What?" Becky put the pot down and turned to face me. "Is there somebody ya ain't told me about?"

"No. But I keep forgetting about Shane." I ran my finger over the hearts, watching them quiver along the stem. "About the roses."

"Why? What's he got to do with anything?" Becky's eyes popped as she apparently got a handle on my thoughts. "You ain't suggestin' Shane is sendin' ya all this stuff, are ya? He's a good guy! He was in our weddin', for cryin' out loud. He'd never try ta horn in on Adam."

"I know. That's why I didn't think anything, but. . .doesn't he drive a dark green sports car?"

"Don't be silly! It ain't Shane." Becky pushed me back toward the bucket of tulips. "So do you like these? They look real nice."

"They do." I put one to my nose and inhaled the scent of spring. A fruity perfume, like heady apricot jam. "But I'm sure they're out of my price range."

"Well then carry *one*."

Becky grinned and pushed the stroller through the jungle of plants like an expert, stopping only to fix Macy's sock and find the pacifier that had submerged itself under the blanket. I watched her there, remembering how we'd met for the first time in an empty church parking lot—where I'd been dumb enough to run out of gas in my rental car. She still beamed that same bright smile, same sassy laughter.

Which was exactly what a grump like me needed.

"You're right." Becky straightened up. "I'm stumped. Maybe it's Santa Claus." She played with a bunch of lavender lisianthus, its rose-like whorl of petals matching Macy's soft corduroy overalls. "You got any enemies then?" Becky rolled her eyes. "Better forgit I said that. Your list'll take all day."

"Hey, any enemies I have certainly aren't *my* fault."

"Don't matter. Ya still got 'em." She shook her head, sizing me up. "I've spent all twenty-six years a my life in this town, and ain't nobody done nothin' to me but steal my gym shorts an' hang 'em on the flagpole. But you? So far you've managed to git mugged not once, but twice—and then practically shot by Trinity's psycho ex-boyfriend. What's his name? Chad?"

"Chase Fletcher."

"That's the one. You must have a force field or somethin' that attracts weirdos."

"Like I said. Not my fault." I sniffed the lisianthus, but it didn't smell like anything. Just leaves. I put it back in the bucket, disappointed.

"Besides, Chase has been gone for ages. I know he blamed me for breaking them up, but I haven't heard a squeak from him since last December." I ran my fingers across a lily petal, smooth as satin. "Anyway, he hated my guts. Why would he send me love messages?"

"Don't ask me. I'm jest guessin' stuff." Becky tucked a strand of blond hair behind her ear and gathered a bunch of indigo-blue irises. "Look. These are real pretty. But you're gonna go with red, ain't ya? For your flowers?"

"Red?" My mind hadn't moved past Chase Fletcher.

"For your weddin'!" Becky pretended to smack me in the forehead. "Lands, if you don't have a short memory!"

"Sorry." I gave a rueful smile. "Brain overload."

"Listen. I jest want you to relax an' have some fun tonight, ya hear?" She took my arm. "I bet this whole thing'll blow over in no time. Some silly mistake at the florist. An old high school crush. Somethin'," she said, scooting the stroller forward. "B'sides, ain't you the one who always says nothin' never happens in Staunton?"

Funny. She was right. And maybe—just maybe—she'd be right about all this rose stuff, too. A week from now it would all be ancient history, and I'd be back to cow tipping.

"Okay. Well then let me ask you something." I dropped my voice slightly. "Since we're talking about wedding stuff."

"Or s'posed to be."

"Right. Well, it's about Adam." I twirled the iris pot around, running my fingers over the sword-like leaves. "Has he always been this. . .how shall we say. . .opinionated about things?"

"What things?"

"I don't know. Life. Stuff." I hunched my shoulders in a nervous shrug, not ready to throw my dirty laundry all over the flower shop. "You've known him practically all your life, so maybe you can help me understand him. I mean, I love him, but he's so. . .so. . ." I put the pot back, searching for the right word.

"Stubbern?"

"Yeah. For starters. And he has all these weird ideas about things." I flipped a price card upright. "Not that they're bad ideas. They're just. . . different. And once his mind is made up, he doesn't do much in the way of negotiations." I thought back to the Virginia Beach honeymoon package fiasco. His crazy "saving a kiss" speech. My mouth tingled, remembering how he'd trailed his finger across my lip.

Becky tried to hide a smirk. "Sounds like somebody I know."

"Who?"

"You." She poked me. "Stubborn and hardheaded. And picky, too."

"I'm not picky!" My cheeks flushed. "Are you making fun of me? I asked you for advice."

"Aw, simmer down." Becky rested her arm on my shoulder. "I ain't makin' fun of ya. But we all got things we gotta work on, Shah-loh. Adam ain't perfect, and neither are you. You were a real snob when ya first showed up here, you know?"

I started to protest, but Becky shushed me. "But you had a good heart. We all couldn't help but love ya. And. . .well, we've been hooked on ya ever since. You're family now. Always was." Her eyes softened. "Same with Adam. Ya gotta roll with it. Let him change things on his own, and don't always demand that he do stuff your way. He loves ya, but he's gonna make mistakes."

"But that's just it." I crossed my arms. "I like my way. I know how to do things."

I started to blurt something about how Adam didn't even have a college degree yet then slapped my lips shut. As if my educational background somehow gave me superiority. Ha! I was the one who'd gotten fired for plagiarism while studying *ethics*, of all things.

Becky leaned close. "Well then, why are ya gettin' married, if you like your own way so well?"

Her question baffled me. I twirled a hanging pot of begonias, watching it untwirl in lazy loops. The layered coral petals, crystalline, twinkled back at me like tiny diamonds.

"Well, I love him. I want to be with him. But I don't want to lose my voice and become a. . .a. . .pawn. A figurehead. I don't know."

"He ain't askin' ya to mouse around and not say nothin'. But ya gotta give a little, too, sometimes, Yankee. Love ain't all about callin' all the shots. Makin' all the decisions and havin' ev'rything your way like you're Miss Independent. Men, especially, don't take to that too well."

"I guess not," I muttered.

"Ain't no guessin'. God made a man and a woman differ'nt. And sometimes ya gotta sit back and let him do his job to protect ya. To step up to the plate an' make some decisions." She pushed me playfully. "Might be even better than the ones you make. Who knows?"

I didn't answer, thinking.

"I know you've lived on your own a long time, decidin' everything for yourself. But that's gonna hafta change. A lot."

Her voice hushed, almost wistful. "Matter of fact, love's more about givin' things up than anything else. Men can be real pains in the neck, ya know?"

"Tell me about it."

"Naw, I'm serious. It's the truth. Why, Adam ain't no saint. Shoot, Tim ain't! But if you're gonna wear his ring, you're gonna hafta learn to forgive. Stop arguin' all the time. Be sweet anyway when you git your panties in a wad. That sorta thing."

"How on earth am I supposed to do that, Becky?" I ran both hands through my hair. "There's not a sweet bone in my body."

"Sure there is!"

"No there isn't. I'm telling you. You were just born that way or something."

"Shucks." Becky laughed. "Ain't none of us who like to git our feelin's hurt or follow somebody else's idea when ours is better. You jest gotta let God teach ya!"

"How am I supposed to do that? Spell it out plain for me, Becky. I don't know anything about this stuff. I've been a Christian what, a year? Less?"

"Practice! Ya gotta get in the habit sometimes when it don't come so natural. Turn the other cheek. Be positive. Smile. Ask God to give ya grace, an' sometimes to keep your trap shut when ya wanna say somethin' nasty—'specially when he deserves it! Like any new thing, like ridin' a bike, it takes a while. But it gits easier, an' sorta becomes a part of ya."

The stroller quivered, and I saw a chubby brown arm flail, intersecting my thoughts. Becky bent over the stroller. "Aw. Look who's awake." She reached down to unclip the safety belt and then scooped Macy, still limp with sleep, up into her arms. Resting the little curly head on her shoulder.

"Finally." I ran a hand through Macy's curls, tracing the tip of her delicately curved ear. One chocolate-brown hand, its palm soft and pink, dangled. "I've been waiting the whole time for her to wake up. May I?" I held out my arms.

"Shore ya can." Becky showed bucky front teeth in a grin. "Just lemme make shore she's good an' awake first. She's a li'l bit crabby when she falls asleep this late. Ain't ya, sugarplum?" She bounced her shoulder slightly, kissing the back of Macy's curly head.

Macy yawned in response, showing white baby teeth poking through pink gums. Then she rubbed her eyes with two brown fists.

"Come on, Macy." I rubbed her back and offered my upturned palms. "No?"

She yawned again, contorting her face like she might cry. And buried her eyes in Becky's shoulder.

"Sorry, Shah-loh. She don't mean nothin'. Just hold on a bit." Becky shifted her slightly, putting a clean cloth under her shoulder and reaching for a bottle of warm water from a thermal bag. "You see, she's started stickin' to us like glue these days. Not wantin' nobody else."

"Well, that's good, I guess." I stroked my fingers through one of her stray curls. "I miss her though."

"Don't worry. She'll come around. Adoption agency says that's actually a real good sign, ya know? When she starts gettin' attached to us." Becky's eyes took on a glassy appearance. "We ain't been with her that long, and after bein' passed around from nurse to doctor night and day, never findin' the same two people to think of as Mama and Daddy." Becky's voice trailed off, and she looked away, brushing her eyes quickly with the back of her hand. "Gimme that container a milk, will ya? It's all measured."

"I'll make it for you." I poured in the dry milk and twisted on the bottle top, shaking it up as I'd seen Becky do a hundred times. Only I forgot to tamp the end of the nipple, and milk sprayed out, splattering my pretty green-flowered dress.

I laughed, wiping myself clean with the corner of Becky's cloth. "Sorry. I'm not a pro like you are."

Becky rolled her eyes. "Shoot. I don't know nothin'."

"Oh, you do. You kept the nursery at church for years."

"Right. Like feedin' a bunch of kids Cheerios means I know somethin'. I'm as clueless as they come, my friend." She shifted Macy up to her chin, nuzzling her cheek. "But you know what? When ya got love and an open heart, that's all they need. Love covers over an awful lotta mistakes." She winked at me. "And that goes for the fellas, too."

Open heart. Mistakes. Love. My thoughts reeled back to Adam, sitting on that picnic table by the lake when he'd asked me to marry him. Thinking of how many things about him I didn't have in common, and frankly, would probably never understand.

And my stomach clenched in a tight ball, glad I'd said yes.

"We'd better get out of here soon, huh?" I said in disappointment, glancing back at the rose case as I shifted Macy on my shoulder then lowered her back to the stroller. "Macy's got to get home, probably. And I've got to finish up a story."

"I reckon." Becky sighed. "I'm jest sorry we didn't find nothin' for ya. We got some ideas though."

"Exactly. We'll figure it out. Don't worry."

Becky checked a couple of things off on a little planner she'd designated "Shiloh's Wedding Stuff" on the cover. "How 'bout decorations for the church? You thought about 'em yet?"

"Sort of." I pushed the stroller toward the exit, shoving pots and overeager leaves out of the way. "How should I do it?"

"If you're goin' with somethin' Asian, it oughtta be real easy. Think about what ya like and go from there."

"Like. . .what? I haven't been to a lot of weddings. I couldn't go to Ashley's wedding, and the Shinto ceremonies I saw in Japan bring back nightmares of giant moon-shaped white hats and too many cups of *sake*."

Becky's face clouded into a look of absolute pity. "You really don't know much about this stuff, do ya?"

"No. I keep saying that, and nobody believes me."

"Well, I was thinkin' more along the lines of candles and whatnot. Maybe some ribbons for the aisles, or ya might wanna scatter flower petals. Stuff like that."

"Oh. Sure. Well, Wal-Mart, I guess. Right?"

"Wal-Mart's good. Harrisonburg's got a Target. But you can do the Asian thing, I reckon, if you find cheap enough stuff." Becky turned to a new page in her planner. "Mama knows some craft place in Charlottesville that might have somethin'." She scratched down some notes. "She can run ya by next week. Then once Ashley buys them red bridesmaids' dresses, we can settle on some flowers to match."

Becky started to head to the exit then paused by a section of loose-cut flowers for do-it-yourself arrangements. I watched as she stood piecing them together, bloom by colorful bloom, into a pretty bouquet.

"What do you think a this?" She handed it to me—a striking mixture of pinks and purples—with a bit of yellow statice to brighten it up.

"It's nice, Becky. You're good at this." I turned the bunch around.

"Yeah. Well. The Fashion Nazi ain't the only one who can match colors. I'm learnin' a thing or two." She passed me another bunch. "How 'bout this'n? Stargazers smell real good."

I sniffed a super fragrant lily, its petals curled back like graceful eyelashes, then put it back. Too much like the smell of Mom's funeral lilies.

"You know? Maybe I won't carry a bouquet."

"Why in the world not?" Becky looked up from wiping Macy's milk-dribbled chin like I'd announced a wedding on Mars.

"I don't really like cut flowers. Even cut Christmas trees."

"Well, ya shore ain't gonna carry no potted plant up the aisle," said Becky, making a face at me. "An' you say my fashion sense is weird!"

"Well, that's why maybe I won't carry anything."

"Why, for Pete's sake? Cut flowers are pretty, too."

"That's just it. All they do is die. You cut them—and snip! They're gone. Their days are numbered. Maybe even their hours."

I shook a cut stem of a white snapdragon for emphasis, remembering the wind on my unfeeling face as I stood by Mom's fresh grave. Her photo on my cubicle wall, smiling back at me. Ray's sad eyes. Kate Townshend's lonely photo of Amanda on her mantel.

"A minute ago it was growing and blooming, but now it's going to die."

Becky fell unusually quiet as she smoothed Macy's overalls that had scrunched under her legs. A tender gesture probably nobody else had noticed. "I don't wanna say this the wrong way, Shah-loh, but we're all gonna die."

"Of course we are." A drop of water fell from the end of the snapdragon stem. "But I prefer not to kill my flowers before their time."

"Well, cut er not cut, we're all goin'." Becky spoke so soberly that I turned my eyes to her. "Ain't no stoppin' it. You know that."

"Sure I do, but isn't it a waste? All that beautiful bloom for what—an hour?"

"Mebbe in some ways, but. . ." She gathered a handful of roses and freesia, delicately perfumed, and pressed them in my hands. "Ya gotta remember though—this was their purpose all along. And they did it to their fullest. It's their gift."

I felt strangely moved, standing there with shoppers laughing in the background. And me looking down at those beautiful, doomed flowers in my hands, their glowing colors trembling with drops.

"But it's such a waste, Becky!"

"Or a sacrifice. Depends on how ya look at it. They lived and bloomed, jest like they were made to do. And when it was time to go, they gracefully said yes."

She ran her hands over the petals, which gleamed like bits of satin. "We're seein' their last magnificent moments and enjoyin' 'em. If you was a flower, wouldn't that make ya happy to know you'd done what you was born ta do? Even if ya didn't get to do it very long?"

I swallowed hard, thinking of things far deeper than flowers. Thinking of Mom. Of her shining life given over to God. A sacrifice, cut down in its last and brightest hour.

"One last flourish," she'd written in her journal. *"Ill-timed but unspeakably beautiful in its quiet fanfare. . . . Come, fall! Come, winter! I am not afraid. I will keep on singing until my last petal falls."*

The freesia blooms swirled together in a blur, and I turned the bunch over in the light, watching their petals glisten.

"So I don't think it's wrong to carry a weddin' bouquet. We're jest rememberin' why we're on this earth."

I glanced at Macy, who was sucking contentedly on her bottle—a tiny soul, still destined for great days to come. Becky and her strong-hearted faith, facing the future as she had faced her childless days: tender, yet unafraid.

Like Mom. The new Mom I wish I could have known. But would one day meet face-to-face in heaven, with a body that would no longer wear out and a mind that would never again know pain or depression.

"What you sow does not come to life unless it dies," the apostle Paul had written to the people of Corinth. I'd learned that in church. "The body that is sown is perishable, it is raised imperishable; it is sown in dishonor, it is raised in glory; it is sown in weakness, it is raised in power; it is sown a natural body, it is raised a spiritual body."

None of us knew when God would call us home. And that would be the response of a believer in Christ: to bow our head and bend our will and gracefully say yes. No matter how new the stem or how bright the bloom.

Adam's words in Dairy Queen: *"I'd die for you,"* he'd said. *"Without a second thought."*

"I think maybe you're right, Becky," I said finally, tears stinging my eyes.

I chose two bright stems of freesia, one for me and one for Becky, and carried them up to the register to check out.

Chapter 21

"**Q**uiz. Who won the last NASCAR race?"

I nearly dropped the phone, typing away at a larceny story at the Sprouses' walnut kitchen table—post five-mile run on Faye's ancient treadmill. Her sunny yellow kitchen walls and checked curtains gleamed back at me, all trimmed with new sunflower decor.

"Kyoko? Why are you asking about NASCAR at this hour?" I took off my old Prada glasses and rubbed my eyes. My sprig of yellow freesia smiled at me from a vase in the midst of my mess: notes, tape recorders, info printouts, and a tube of mod-red nail polish.

"Which race? The Quaker State 400 in Kentucky ?" I shook my feet to dry my freshly painted toes. "I think Vic Priestly won that one because. . ."

The line fell silent. I groaned. I'd walked right into Kyoko's trap.

"Okay, okay," I snapped. "I only know because Tim told me."

"But you REMEMBERED! Seriously, Ro, you're disturbed. I'm sending you a spittoon as a late birthday present."

"A. . .what?" I ran my hand through my damp hair, still grapefruit-jasmine scented from my shower.

"Never mind. I give up. You're past all hope."

"Probably. I can send you the race scores if you want though. There's a website."

"See? The fact you know that is scary."

I took my hand off the keyboard, sensing impending doom. Normally I'd push Kyoko's buttons and rant about gun racks and Confederate flags, but I wasn't in the mood. "You're leaving Japan, aren't you?"

Jennifer Rogers Spinola

"Yep. My flight's this afternoon."

I fell silent, imagining Kyoko's empty apartment, stripped of its punk-rock records and posters, dark Indian elephant tapestries, and the purple lava lamp that bubbled. Her skull-and-crossbones purses. The weird smell of incense and musty books.

"Ro? You still there?"

"I'm here."

"What, you're going to let me waltz out of Japan without so much as a good-bye? You're worrying me now."

"I always worry you."

"Good point." She harrumphed. "By the way, you might be interested to know that my transfer request has been approved. It's all set."

"Really? To where?"

Please say Japan, Kyoko! Please, please tell me you've changed your mind! Or at least California, where you're only a short flight away.

"Italy."

"Italy?"

"Correct. Land of cappuccino and gelato. I think even you'd be proud."

"Italy," I repeated, imagining Kyoko climbing crumbly, ancient steps surrounded by fountains, snapping photos. Driving an old Fiat up narrow streets. Picking olives.

"That's great." I tried to sound excited.

"Dave said the housing's better than in Germany, and they're kind of short-staffed. They'd welcome me with open arms. I'll stay in the US until August for training and then go straight to Genoa." She yawned. "Birthplace of pesto. Can't be all bad."

"Congratulations." I didn't mean to sound sarcastic, but it sort of came out that way. "I know you'll do great there." I swallowed, my throat tightening. "Just tell me, Kyoko, before you go—what will you miss from Japan?"

"Besides giving you a hard time about Carlos? Not much."

"What? You mean there's nothing you'll miss?" It pained me to imagine my last link to Japan slipping away—and Kyoko not even appreciating her loss.

"Definitely not the pickled plums."

"*Umeboshi*? I love those!"

"You're sick. Those things are salty." Kyoko grunted moodily.

178

"Okay. I guess there is one thing."

"The cream puffs?" My ears perked up as I remembered Beard Papa's and the moist, delicious little puffs covered with powdered sugar.

"No, doofus. I can't eat that stuff," she crabbed. "My hips are plenty wide as it is."

"Stop it. So what will you miss then?"

The front door opened, and I turned around to wave at Earl Sprouse. Covered in grease and carrying his toolbox and an armful of wrenches and pipes, his gray hair a mess. He grinned and waved back, and I heard Faye's footsteps from the laundry room as she came (*ahem*—rather quickly, I noted) up the stairs to meet him.

"Hello? Kyoko?" I faced the table again to give them some privacy.

"I answered you. The thing I'll miss most from Japan is the *wa*."

"You mean, like the balance?"

"Yeah, sort of." Kyoko heaved a cranky sigh. "I know it's weird, but life here is very ordered. To a fault. I mean, sometimes it's nice to know what to do in each and every situation ahead of time. Like picking out your dinner from a row of plastic models that look just like the real thing, and you know exactly what you're going to get. You say all the preprogrammed phrases, and everybody's happy. Nobody disturbs the wa. If you do what you're supposed to, you never really make mistakes. It's all anticipated—even the compliments. If only real life could be so gaffe-proof!"

I didn't know what to say. Kyoko was so free and unordered that this revelation surprised me.

"On the other hand, though, it's what drives me crazy. I hate walking out of the bathroom in my toilet slippers so everybody stares and gasps at me. 'Oh no! She's done it wrong again!'" Kyoko grunted. "We foreigners crash all over the wa and stomp on it."

"No, *you* do. I always remembered my toilet slippers."

"Kiss-up. I bet you were teacher's pet in school, too."

"That goes without saying." I smirked.

"Ugh. Excuse me while I go throw up." Kyoko made gagging sounds.

"I am kidding. My teachers hated me because they always had to buy me lunch."

Silence. "Ouch."

"I know. But I'll have you know I eat very well these days. Especially at Faye's." I pictured the crispy country-fried steak she'd served at dinner, complete with mashed potatoes, creamed corn, and buttered yeast rolls. Maybe staying over at someone else's for a while wasn't. . .such a bad thing.

"Good for you." Kyoko heaved a long sigh. "Okay, since you forced me, I admit I'll miss the subways. They're so pristine. And of course I'll miss the anime."

"Those creepy comics? Yuck. Not me."

Kyoko fell silent, and I sensed something emotional coming. Like tremors before an earthquake. "Once I visited my homestay family after almost a year, and when I left, they walked out to the train with me. Stood on the platform until the train came." Her words came out almost husky, completely un-Kyoko-like. "The mother's tears made streak marks on her cheeks. And they waved as the train took off, until I couldn't see them anymore. When we came around a bend, they were still bowing and waving—even the little tiny grandma. Just specks in the distance."

She made a sniffling sound. "I saw cherry blossoms on the hillsides behind them like snow."

I looked up at smooth walls and framed photos of Faye's wedding, barely seeing any of it. "You finally get it, Kyoko."

"Get what?" Kyoko barked, hastily backpedaling from anything remotely sentimental.

"Japan. That's what I miss, too."

She didn't answer for a long time. I heard her bumping and moving stuff and doing what sounded like folding clothes. Taping more boxes.

"I miss my brothers more," she said in an "I-don't-care" tone. "And that San Francisco smog, doggone it. Never thought I'd miss that." I heard the click of her suitcase latches, as if to close up the memories.

"What are you taking from Japan?" I sniffled, reaching for a tissue in my purse.

"Books. CDs. Some ugly gargoyle from Okinawa." I heard the crows again outside her window, crying from bicycle-and-pedestrian-crowded streets. Venders probably putting out their bunches of green onions, round *nashi* pears, and imported bananas for the day. "It's not like I have space for a lot of stuff. My whole apartment here could fit in my carry-on bag."

I stayed quiet, listening to Kyoko's last day in Tokyo.

"Listen, is there anything else you want me to send you from here?" Kyoko abruptly switched subjects. "I've already mailed you some seaweed paper, miso paste, and a bunch of stuff."

"You're really great, Kyoko. Thanks. I'll love whatever you send." I remembered the throwing star and caught myself. "Let me rephrase. I'll love whatever you send that's not illegal or gross or a hazard to myself or society."

She snickered. "That does constrain me a bit, doesn't it?" I heard a thump. "Hope you like *yukata* fabric."

"Huh?"

"You know. Fabric for making yukata. Girly colored stuff with bunnies and flowers and other nasty things. Mrs. Oyama gave me a ton of it as a going-away present, and I have no idea what I'll do with it. Have you ever seen me in sugar-pink with cherry blossoms and lavender? Geesh." I heard her shudder. "A nice thought, of course, but I get the creeps just looking at it."

The two green and navy-blue yukata my homestay mom made me still hung in my closet: pretty, cotton kimono-style robes in cheerful patterns, with wide, colorful *obi* sashes tied in the back. Girls wore them to festivals in sandals, hair pulled up, fanning themselves with bright paper fans. "I'd love it. I'll use the fabric to make bags and pillows and things."

"That's actually a good idea," said Kyoko in admiration. "Wow. Did you think of it yourself?" She paused. "Or did you download it off the Internet, copy it, and hand it to your former editor Dave Driscoll with your name at the top?"

My eyes popped. "Of all the—!"

"I'm kidding, Ro. Take it easy." Kyoko laughed lightly. "Really. Maybe it's bad taste, but. . .I just couldn't resist." She grew surprisingly sober. "What's done is done, and I'm leaving in a few hours anyway. Your plagiarism goof-up is actually putting us on the same continent for a while."

"Are you ever going to forgive me?"

"For making me share a work space with Nora Choi, no. But for getting fired, yes. We all do things we shouldn't. We make mistakes. We. . .you know. Learn that way."

I heard her clip another suitcase closed. "Water under the bridge, my friend. You'll do things differently next time. And I think. . ." Her voice trailed off.

"Think what?" I pouted.

"You'll be okay there with Adam." Her voice softened. "If you can

181

just stop putting yourself in harm's way for five minutes."

"I'll try."

Neither of us seemed to know what to say.

"Well, my flight's in a couple of hours," said Kyoko, grunting as she stretched. "I'm just calling to say *sayonara*."

In the distance I heard the roar of a little delivery moped, probably taking *ramen* noodles or a *bento* (premade lunchbox) to someone in her building. The faint *ping-pong* of the doorbell, distinctively Japanese.

"It's not *sayonara* for good-bye. It's *mata ne*. See you later," I corrected, trying to swallow the lump that had formed painfully in my throat.

"Yeah. But it's. . .well, sayonara to an era."

"Did you have to say that?" I flared.

"I know, I know. But. . .it's true, Ro. I'm sorry." Kyoko could be brutally honest. "But it was good while it lasted. And. . ."

I waited.

"And I wouldn't have enjoyed it half as much without you." Her voice turned uncharacteristically husky. "You made it fun. And when I think of Japan, I'll always think of you."

My eyes burned. I glanced over at the severed stem of freesia, its cheery yellow petals already starting to wilt a bit on the edges. One leaf curled at the tip.

Yet they raised bright faces, crocus-like, in reckless golden joy.

"Well, you know where I live. We can pick up where we left off." I cleared my throat.

"Of course. And now it'll be easier for me to send you stuff and harass you about your budding redneck roots." Kyoko paused. "If you'll forgive my cliché, the best is yet to come. Even that Jesus of yours saved the best wine 'til the end, didn't He?"

The best is yet to come.

Trading the old for the new. My top-of-the-line Japanese cell phone for Adam's simple old gray one. My single days for married ones. My will for God's way. And my brash independence for a life spent yielding and growing with someone else.

Strange and scary paradoxes, all of them. Mingled into one astonishing life called mine.

I glanced around at the house that had been my second home all these difficult months, filling my Japan-aching heart with fresh and tender memories. In the town that had started all this, taking me away from Tokyo in one swift phone call.

This was where I belonged. Where my heart had settled, even against my will.

A death of sorts. To all I once wanted.

I traced my ring, the color of moonlight and tears. Remembering the rattle of dirt on top of Mom's casket. The door closing for the last time in my Tokyo apartment. Kyoko's good-bye as I boarded at Narita International Airport last summer, until I could no longer see her.

"Very truly I tell you, unless a kernel of wheat falls to the ground and dies, it remains only a single seed. But if it dies, it produces many seeds. Anyone who loves their life will lose it, while anyone who hates their life in this world will keep it for eternal life."

My freesia trembled in the breeze.

"Can you hold the phone up to the window?" I sniffled.

"What?"

"Can you hold the phone up to the window? So I can hear?"

Amazingly, Kyoko didn't make a wisecrack. Didn't say a word.

The next thing I heard was the raspy *caw* of a crow. Faraway, distant, over the muted noise of traffic. Car horns honking. The ring of cicadas. The roar of a delivery truck pulling away from a shop, and the faint *chirp-chirp-chirp* of the crosswalk, bird-like. Haunting.

The opening and closing of a door, like the opening and closing of our days in Tokyo.

Women's voices, drifting up from the street. "*Domo arigatou!*" they were saying, probably bowing, faces lit with smiles. "Mata ne! See you later!"

Mata ne, old Mrs. Inoue and your shop. The handfuls of ginger candy you used to give me when I bought green onions and cold jasmine tea. Mata ne, Momiji fried pork and noodle stalls and whir of the subway, blowing my hair. Mata ne, Tokyo. Mata ne, Japan.

The best is yet to come.

Kyoko waited respectfully almost ten minutes and then informed me that her hand was about to fall off. Told me she'd charge me the ticket if I made her miss her flight.

But I was okay. I'd listened to the city I loved and said good-bye.

"Thanks, Kyoko," I said in a steadier voice. "You're a good friend. I'll miss our Japan days."

"I'll miss them, too, Ro. Come to Italy. We'll make more memories there."

"I'd love to. And you'll be in Europe now, so I can still send you NASCAR races on DVD," I sniffled. "I've downloaded a whole bunch for you."

A pause while Kyoko decided if I was serious. "I'm not gonna ask," she finally said. Then, "I'll see you in August."

"I'll be waiting."

"Mata ne, my friend."

"Mata ne."

Chapter 22

I t's too crowded up front. Let's get these out of here." I pulled at the side of a table while Jerry pushed, making a new walkway between the entrance of The Green Tree restaurant and the alcove we'd opened up in the back.

I stood back and surveyed our work, my old apron wrapped around my waist. New paint gleamed from floor to ceiling—a bright, pale blue-green somewhere between earth and sky tones—and Jerry's gorgeous, sand-colored flooring glistened with a fresh coat of wax. All the mirrors of different sizes Adam had hung to the side of the alcove in a thick scatter and around the bare walls reflected back golden spangles as if the moon and stars had come unglued and gotten stuck in a restaurant in Staunton, Virginia.

And the most amazing part of all: the smell of fresh herbs and clean plants. Potted plants. Living plants. Adam had tossed the idea of cut flowers (which had to be replaced daily) with dollar-friendly potted plants on the tables: Mini sweet-bay trees. Basil plants. Rosemary shrubs trimmed in circles like topiaries. Each in a hammered metal pot.

Besides that, he'd convinced Jerry to use real trees instead of the dusty old plastic ficus—placing them in pots near the windows and under strategically lit spaces. Their branches stretched up toward the aqua sky, and the whole place felt like we'd magically stepped outside.

As for the menu, Jerry and I studied gourmet cooking magazines and restaurant recipes until our eyes crossed. Rewrote trendy recipes. Taste tested.

I'd written my restaurant contacts back in Japan and Thailand for Asian noodle and rice recipes with exotic ingredients like coconut milk, ginger, and curry that packed loads of flavor in a little (inexpensive) punch—and Jerry threw in an unexpected Southern twist. Why? Because locally grown produce and poultry trumped imported ingredients in the cheapness department. So: Japanese fried tempura eggplant and Southern squash with dipping sauce. Shenandoah Valley goat cheese instead of Jarlsberg on crostini with red onion and rhubarb marmalade. Hominy polenta. Local greens and pine nuts.

It was unconventional, but it worked. Or at least I hoped it would.

After all, this was The Green Tree. *Jerry's* Green Tree. And I couldn't let a bunch of lousy reviews flush it down the drain. Staunton needed this restaurant—if only to have one place in town that didn't chuck everything in the deep fryer.

"It's time." Jerry checked his watch, fingers shaking. "This is it, y'all. Doors open at eleven, and it's three 'til. The crew from *Fine Dining* is comin' at eleven fifteen sharp. You think we're ready?"

"The place looks great." I peeled off my apron. "They'll love it. You'll see."

"Yeah, well, I hope so." Jerry mopped his sweaty forehead. "This place means the world to me. And you." He pointed. "You're an angel."

—∞—

I stumbled slightly, grabbing a chair back to catch myself. Odysseus's words sifting back like a bad memory: *"To my angel. I can't wait to share my life with you."*

Jerry gave me a funny look, one eyebrow raised, as I let go of the chair. "You ain't been tippin' the wine back in the kitchen, have ya?"

My heart calmed down as I looked around the clean lines of the dining room. Dawn, the hostess, organized papers by the already neat register. The familiar clink of glasses rang from the kitchen, accompanied by faint strains of the cooks, Flash and José, singing off-key bluegrass tunes.

"Don't mention it, Jerry. You'd do the same for us." I looked up as the glass doors opened, and Dawn slipped out to greet our first clients. "Call after the critics come and tell me how it goes."

"Will do." Jerry nodded. "And I have a feeling it's gonna be good."

I stepped out into the balmy sunshine and headed for my car, summer wind blowing the sweet, dusty scent of geraniums from Jerry's new window boxes across the sidewalk. Flags fluttered along the street, and heavy clouds towered overhead in a hazy blue sky.

I watched the edge of the horizon darken and thicken as I drove back to *The Leader* office and parked, smelling rain in the distance. I shut and locked my car door, praying that *Fine Dining's* review would be good and Jerry could stay in business. Maybe even—

Cell phone. Again. I'd only been gone an hour, and Chastity had called me three times to ask me about Phil's sports page mock-up. Could she not read my name placard? I didn't do sports—I did crime.

"Meg? What's up?" I squinted up at the clouds through my sunglasses as I headed toward the building. "I'll be there in two seconds. Tell Chastity to quit calling me and ask Phil herself."

A motorcycle roared by, and the noise sucked up her reply. I pressed my other ear closed. "Sorry, can you repeat? I thought you said something about a bouquet." My stomach did a flip. "You didn't say that, did you? I've only been gone an hour."

"No, not a bouquet."

"Oh, good." I let out my breath and pushed open the door to the building. My sweaty neck and forehead begged for air-conditioning. "You had me worried there for a second."

"*Three* bouquets. All identical to the others you've received so far."

—⁂—

Even from the far end of the cubicle row, I could see them. I dropped my keys on the carpet, staring at three full, lush bouquets of plump, dark red roses. *The Leader* staff seemed to part like the Red Sea as I stormed over to my desk, everyone huddled in an eerie silence while I tore the florist's card from the center bouquet with a tissue.

"How do you like the roses, angel?" read the card. *"Do they remind you of old times? I thought your heart was dark, my love, but now I know it's white. Three times you've shaken up my life. Three plus four was wrong, but I see it now—three times four is twelve. I can't wait to marry you."*

"Nuts! The guy is nuts!" I slammed down the card.

"Kevin wants to see you about this," whispered Meg, nibbling a nail. "He's not happy."

"Are you kidding? I'm not happy!" I tore through my notes for Rask's number and shoved the vases aside. Knocking folders and notebooks onto the carpet.

"Kevin's worried, Shiloh. I think he's going to kick you off stories altogether for a while."

"I knew it; I knew it," I seethed through my teeth as I dialed. "All because of some weaselly little. . . Hello?" A woman picked up and mumbled something unintelligible. "Is this Rask Florist?"

187

"Yes, ma'am. Home of quality floral service. How may I help you?"

"I don't care whose home you are as long as you can connect me to Tammy immediately and explain these rose bouquets!" I stormed. "I've called your shop multiple times and received zero information, and that better change right now."

"Simmer down, honey. This is Tammy. You must be the gal the police called about. Am I right?"

I plopped down in my chair and tossed my purse on the desk near the bouquets. Shoving leaves and petals out of the way. "So you're Tammy. And either you've been avoiding me or Brandy's worse than I thought about leaving messages. Because I've been trying to reach you for a while."

"Oh, that gal? She's gone. She wasn't much help anyhow. Temp, ya know. And it took me a while to get back on my feet after my surgery, ya know?"

I bit back a nasty response, letting my angry heartbeat calm to a steady rhythm. "Well, can you tell me who sent me these three bouquets just now? It's really important."

"Sorry. I just got to the office. But I'll see if I can find the receipt. Brandy threw out a bunch of stuff though, so there's no tellin' what's here and what's gone."

I gave her the dates and my information then tapped my nails on the desk impatiently while I waited.

"Oh yeah." Tammy picked up the phone again. "I remember that first one from a couple weeks ago 'cause I took the order the morning before I went in for my surgery." Tammy's voice rang into my ear. "It was kinda strange."

"Strange? What do you mean strange?"

"Well, here's the thing. I don't really know who sent it. The customer paid cash—which we found in the mailbox."

"Huh?" I dropped the keys.

"Yep. In the company mailbox. In a sealed envelope with your name on it and all the delivery details, including what to write on the card. The color of ink to use. All that stuff."

Hairs on the back of my neck tickled. "You're serious? Did the sender leave a return address? Postmark?"

"Nothin'. No postmark. Didn't look like it'd been mailed—just dropped in the box. Although it did have a funny stamp."

A funny stamp, huh? *Amanda Cummings collected stamps.* The

thought rocked through me.

"I thought the whole setup was sorta odd, but he—I'm guessin' it's a he—included exact payment, to the penny. So we delivered the flowers to his specifications. We're a florist, ya know, so we get lotsa unusual requests. People order anonymous bouquets all the time."

"But. . .but you don't have a name on my order? Nothing? Not a clue who it's from?"

"Nope. Sorry."

My shoulders sagged in disappointment. "Well, do you still have the letter? I'd at least like to look at it."

"Sorry, honey. Brandy threw all that stuff out."

Wonderful. There went my hope of evidence.

"Was the handwriting distinctive in any way?" My fingers tightened around the receiver. Like, maybe, his *A*'s? I hoped so, to close the net on Amanda's possible killer. And at the same time, I desperately hoped not—because that meant he might be after *me*.

"Nope. Nothing unusual at all, that I recollect. He'd written in cursive. Real neat handwriting, all the letters smooth and straight. I remember thinkin' how I wish my kids could write like that. Bunch a chicken scratch, both of 'em."

So much for the handwriting theory. "Well, can you find out who took the order this morning? It's urgent, Tammy. I need to know." I swallowed, feeling a crazy panic climb up my throat.

"I think Dean got that one," said Tammy. "Wasn't me. I just got here, and the place is a mess. Hold on."

She put me on hold again, and I held in my breath. Nervously twirling a pen between my fingers. "Yep," she said finally. "Dean rung it up. Same story. Envelope in the mailbox—and again, no postmark."

My pulse quickened. "So it seems like a local order, if he just dropped it in the mailbox. Although that's against the law, you know, to put anything in a federal mailbox." I leaned forward. "Does Dean still have the letter and envelope? The police asked Rask's entire staff to hold everything related to my name."

Tammy covered the phone line, and I heard her speaking. First in softer tones then louder. Someone protesting in the background.

"I'm so sorry, hon." Tammy sighed. "Dean said the police told 'em to watch for flowers for somebody named Sheila. Sounds like Brandy or whoever copied your name down wrong. It's right here on the note she left—plain as day. Sheila Jacobson."

"Sheila?" I hollered, flinging the pen. It bounced off Matt's empty chair and onto the floor as Clarence's ugly grin spread through my mind. "Did she write it down wrong, or did the police bungle my name?" My eyes narrowed. Or was Brandy in cahoots with Clarence somehow?

"Dunno how your name got mixed up. My guess is Brandy."

"You're not kidding," I grumbled. "So where's the letter?"

"Dean said he tossed it since the name didn't match the one the police said to hold."

I scrambled to my feet, still holding the phone to my ear. Eyes bouncing to the clock on the wall. "The trash hasn't gone yet, has it?"

"The trash? Naw, I don't reckon so. But we've done emptied it in the outside bin." She paused. "Why, you ain't gonna—"

"Hold your trash!" I hollered. "I'll be there in twenty minutes."

Chapter 23

grabbed my purse and stuck a note on Kevin's door then texted Adam while I ran down the stairs in my strappy heels. Tiny pearl raindrops fell like a mist, sprinkling down from a thin cloud bank and darkening the sidewalk. Heat steamed up in a sweltering haze.

I drove a couple of blocks over to Rask then wedged my Honda in a dumpy-looking parking lot and sprinted over. My long strand of retro beads clinked together as I gathered up the folds of my crisp navy-blue work dress, and I jumped the curb and jerked open Rask's glass door.

"Hi, is Tammy here?" I stood at the counter, out of breath, and smoothed my flyaway hair back in its clip.

"You Shiloh Jacobs?" A woman with graying, peach-colored hair in a big pouf and too much eye shadow peeked over the counter at me from behind a vase of spring-yellow daffodils.

"That's me." I lifted the photo ID on my lanyard. "May I?"

She lifted a sparse eyebrow at me. "Be my guest. The Dumpster's out back. I done called the police to let 'em know, but ain't much we can do, even if you do find the letter. Unless he left some fingerprints on it or somethin'."

My patience frazzled at her offhanded tone. "But that's the whole point!" I raised my voice a touch. "It should have been kept as evidence for the police."

The other clerk on duty—who I assumed was the "Dean" character Tammy'd mentioned earlier—poked a flushed, angry face through the doorway to an adjoining workroom. His blond hair, shining in the overhead fluorescent light, nearly matched the daffodils. "She wrote the

191

name wrong. I swear! You saw it yourself, Tammy!"

Tammy waved him away and came around the counter through a stand of lilies. "I'm so sorry, honey." She patted my shoulder. "But this surgery's just thrown me for a loop. When I'm around, things are always in order. I promise you that."

My hard look melted slightly. "I'm sure you're right. Rask's been in business a long time." I inhaled the dizzy fragrances of lavender and lily of the valley. "And your flowers are beautiful. But I need to find that letter, no matter what."

"I gotcha. You go right on ahead." Tammy squeezed my hand with ring-laden fingers. "And I'll make it up to ya, you hear? Let's talk after ya dig. How's that?"

"Fine. But how long do I have before the trash comes?"

"Probably another hour or two, but not much more than that. They don't leave the trash sittin' around long, and it's due for a pickup."

"So long as you're diving in, why don't you look for my earring back?" Dean snipped from the back room, shooting me another hateful look. "It's kind of gold-colored. Fell off this morning."

I spun around to face him. "Excuse me?"

"You sicced the police on Jim Bob Townshend," he mumbled through clenched teeth, rising to his feet. "Why, I oughtta. . ."

"Ought to what?" I stalked toward him. "And what business of yours is it who I tip off to the police?" I narrowed my eyes. "Wait a minute. You're friends with Jim Bob?"

Tammy shushed Dean, pushing him back through the doorway and slamming the door. "Ignore him." She shook her head in disgust. "He's just a little worked up. Thinks everybody's trying to make his friend look guilty."

I froze. "Who, Jim Bob? Guilty of. . .what?" I stilled suddenly, turning over the snatches of Dean's flushed face that I'd seen in those brief moments. The sound of his voice. Wondering, if by some odd possibility, we'd met before—or if he'd met Mom.

Or if he'd tried to knock me off with a knife to cover for his pal Jim Bob. After all, the masked marauder did have hair.

"Hey, wait, doll— What's your name? Shiloh?" Tammy interrupted my thoughts as if interpreting the dark slant of my suspicions. "Don't you worry no more about Dean. You want a trash bag or somethin'?" She gestured toward the back of the counter. "How 'bout some tissues to wipe your hands or somethin'?"

I hesitated. "You've got trash bags?"

"Shore! Here's a fresh roll." She tossed me a cylinder of black plastic. "Knock yerself out!"

I tucked the trash bags and a wad of tissues under my arm and burst out into the gray morning.

" 'If ya find my earring back, dig it out for me,' " I mimicked to myself, stepping around a concrete divider and shimmying over a section of prickly hedges. Deciding right then and there that I'd ask the police to check up on Dean, too. I didn't recognize his face, but a setup right there at the florist, with Brandy and maybe even Tammy herself as an accomplice, could answer a pile of questions.

I minced around puddles in broken concrete and slipped behind the building—where old power lines sagged and exposed pipes ran down brickwork from more than a hundred years ago. All culminating in the perfect picture of neglect and desolation.

And there: the Dumpster. A rusted, corrugated metal box of filth, right under a dripping, blackened gutter and streak of stained brick.

I wiped raindrops from my face, wondering how one was supposed to root through a trash bin without destroying clothes and shoes or contracting foul diseases. All without an umbrella or rubbing alcohol or a surgical mask.

I blinked up at the gray sky, cut into sharp squares by the old brick buildings, lines of rain sifting down toward me in pale streaks. A black construction tarp flapped over one corner of faded brick.

The tarp gave me an idea. I jerked the roll of trash bags from under my arm and tore off a sheet of black plastic then fitted it over one leg— wishing to goodness I'd worn pants instead of a dress. I cuffed and knotted it over my knee like odd, bulging hosiery then tore long strips from another bag and tied them around the cuff for reinforcement.

Then the other leg. I punched a hole in the bottom of a third bag, cinching it in the waist to make a shiny black plastic skirt.

I repeated the process all the way up, finishing with a trash bag over my head, the eye and nose/mouth holes punched through with my finger. A trash bag over each hand.

And. . .here we go. Good thing I got a tetanus booster last year. I lifted the lid and awkwardly pulled myself up over the rusty metal rim, all my plastic armor shivering and crinkling as I dropped into the soggy piles of trash. Landing smack on a tangle of bent florist's wire.

Copper wire.

193

—⁓—

"Shiloh?"

I squatted on stacks of old newspapers and pitted, crumbly, green floral foam. Mounds of cut stems and leaves in various stages of decay. Ribbons and dead carnations and the proverbial banana peel piled around my trash-bagged feet. Soggy cardboard boxes. The inside of the Dumpster was stained with old brown grease that had dried in waxy streaks, and I breathed through my mouth to avoid inhaling the stench.

"Shiloh? Where are you?"

I jerked my head up toward the familiar voice. Quick footsteps echoed against the brick buildings and empty asphalt, and I dropped the discarded receipt tape and price tags and hauled myself to my feet, one black-covered hand on the lip of the bin. And I popped my head up over the dented side.

Just in time to see Adam jump back in horror at my shrouded face, tripping backward over a chunk of broken concrete. Feet tangling, arms flailing, and finally sprawling into the wet gutter.

He picked himself up and brushed off his brown UPS uniform pants while I tore at the trash bag covering my head. "Adam! What are you doing here?" I searched for a foothold to boost myself up.

My foot slipped in a pile of rotten cabbage from a neighboring vegetable market, and down I went.

"For goodness' sake." Adam splashed through a puddle on his way to the Dumpster, looking irritated. "What in the world are you doing in there? You look like Darth Vader."

He reached out a hand to help me up, and I reluctantly shook off my trash-bag mitten and took it. Brushing cabbage scraps from my hair with the back of my wrist.

"What is this, some kind of trash bag gas mask?" He gestured to the plastic bag I'd draped over the side of the bin.

"Believe me, if you offered me a gas mask, I'd accept." I let go of his hand long enough to right myself as a cardboard box crumbled beneath my foot. "Sorry. I'm just crazy to find out who's sending this stuff. If the letter's there, I want to see it myself."

"I want to find the guy as bad as you do, but I can't believe you, of all people, are digging through a Dumpster." Adam screwed up his face as he plucked a piece of flower stem from my bangs. "You really think it's in there?"

"I'm pretty sure, if Dean threw it away this morning. Unless he's lying, and that's a different story." I gestured to mounds of plant clippings and dead leaves. An empty Bud Light can. "But if the letter's here, I haven't found it yet." I scrunched back the plastic bag on my other arm and glanced at my watch. "Look at the time! Kevin's going to kill me."

"Don't you dare say that." Adam glared.

"Sorry! Just an expression." I shrugged meekly. "I'd better call him though. Can you hand me my phone? It's in my purse." I leaned over the side of the dumpster to point. "Thanks." I wiped my hand on my other trash bag sleeve before reaching out to take it.

I called, and Kevin yelled at me about safety and told me to be careful, for pity's sake, and to get my rear in his office when I got back. Then I placed the phone on the edge of the bin, balancing it against the hinges.

"I guess I should give up, huh?" I sighed, catching myself as the mountain of florist's foam and ribbon shifted under my feet. Adam grabbed my shoulder and helped me stand up then straightened the trash bag I'd poked my head through. Which now hung like a dirty choir robe over my beautiful navy-blue dress. A section of bead grinned through the torn neck opening.

"You're sure they threw everything in here?" Adam flicked a piece of stray green florist's wire off the edge of the bin.

"That's what Tammy told me."

"This morning."

I glanced at my cell phone and checked the time. "One hour and six minutes ago."

Adam sighed and shook his head.

"What? I'm just trying to find some evidence. The guy's bothering you, too, Adam. You should be more thankful." I put my nose in the air and reached again for the rim of the Dumpster to pull myself out.

"You have no idea. The street outside our house got spray-painted last night."

"What?" I staggered back. "Spray-painted? Like. . ."

"With red paint. And a weird message. Dad's really upset. We found it this morning, and we've already called the police."

"What did it say?"

" 'I'm watching you.' "

My heart thudded against my chest. "What did the *A* look like?"

"Weird. Just like you told me about the previous messages. A sort of odd curlicue-hook thing and slanted funny." He swallowed. "And. . . there's more. That's why I stopped by to meet you."

"What do you mean, 'There's more'?" I stepped back.

"He left a letter for you in the mailbox. A fat one with your name on it. Stamped, with an odd stamp I've never seen before. Although not postmarked." Adam patted his pants pocket. "I've got it right here for you. It's wrapped in paper in case of fingerprints."

I reached out in disbelief and took the letter between two of the tissues Tammy had given me. Adam slit the envelope open with his pocketknife, and I pulled them out: tiny slips of paper—like they'd been put through a shredder—reading "*Cilegna*." Hundreds of them, handwritten. Falling out of the envelope and littering the trash piles like sick Easter grass.

I hastily scooped them up, not wanting to lose a single bit of evidence. "What's 'cilegna' supposed to mean?"

Adam studied it a minute, his jaw tight with anger. " 'Angelic,' " he finally said. " *Angelic* written backward."

I pulled out a tiny folded note, scrawled on notebook paper: *"Shiloh + Odysseus forever. August 3."*

I felt defiled, like I'd found my name scrawled on the bathroom wall.

Something still made a hard shape in the envelope, tucked among paper shreds.

Three somethings: a distant photo of me pushing open the door to The Green Tree in a Givenchy dress, magazines under my arm. A snapshot of Becky and me laughing in the flower shop. And another of my white Honda, parked outside the mechanic's shop.

Fury burned in my veins, and I clenched my hands into fists. "Adam, this is terrible! And all the more reason we need to find this stupid bouquet order." I wiped my face with the crook of my elbow as Adam turned toward his truck. "Wait, where are you going?"

"To cover myself in trash bags like the Lone Ranger here," said Adam, attempting a smile over his emotion-tight face. "So I can figure out who this guy is and punch his lights out."

I gripped the rim of the dirty bin with both hands. "You mean you're going to help me?"

"Why not? I've got thirty-five minutes before my next delivery. What else do I have to do but paw through somebody's potato peelings?"

He ruffled my hair before bending down to pick up the roll of trash bags.

—m—

"Is that your phone?" Adam raised his head from a stack of waterlogged papers. Interrupting our stimulating conversation about tuxedo prices.

"I'll get it." I waddled over to the other side of the Dumpster. "It's probably Meg calling to find out where I am." I wiped some moisture off the screen. "No. Not Meg. Wait a second." I put the phone under my chin and adjusted the trash bags over my hand. "Hello?"

"Hi. Ray Floyd here."

"Oh, hi, Ray." I shook drops off my trash-bag coverings, which were beginning to deteriorate. "Can I help you?"

I listened and nodded, pressing the SPEAKERPHONE button. "I'm fine, thanks. What am I doing?" Adam and I exchanged smirks. "Just. . . um. . .some summer cleaning. You?"

"I'm packing up to leave town, Shiloh. My street got spray painted last night in front of my house."

"You, too?"

Ray paused, sounding weary. "What do you mean, 'too'?"

"Well, it seems like you're not the only one." I pressed my lips together. "What did the message say?"

" 'I'm watching you.' In red paint."

I gasped. "The same message!"

Ray cleared his throat. "Listen, I've talked to the police, and I think I'm going to leave town a while. I'll be closer to my girlfriend, and there's just too much happening here. I don't feel safe anymore."

"Good move on your part. I agree."

My gaze fluttered over to Adam again, wondering with a sinking stomach if he—or his whole family—should leave town, too. Or me, for that matter.

"You're taking Ginger, aren't you?" I finally asked, trying to keep my voice cheerful.

"Of course. I've never been away from her. She'll keep me company." I could hear him patting her furry side, license tags clinking. "I won't have Internet at my buddy's place, but I'll e-mail you my phone number and address before I go in case you or the police need to get in touch with me."

"Thanks." I bit my lip. "Just one unrelated question before you go, if you don't mind."

"Shoot."

"My mom—Ellen Jacobs—wasn't one of your music students, was she?"

"I don't. . .think so. What did she play?"

"Guitar. She took beginner lessons, I think. Several years ago."

"I don't remember her. I mainly teach piano and sax. In fact, Jim Bob was the one who messed around with the guitar. He was pretty good, I heard. Before he broke his hand, of course."

"Did he ever give lessons?"

"No idea."

"Well, maybe you can tell me what this song is then." I hummed a few notes from the paper I'd found in Mom's guitar case. "She seemed to like this one a lot."

Ray paused. "It sounds familiar, but. . .sorry."

"Maybe she wrote it. Who knows." I shrugged. "Anyway, be careful, Ray. *Bon voyage.*"

"You're welcome. Stay safe."

I pressed off the phone just as Adam abruptly jumped to his feet, holding up a scrap of stained paper and crumpled envelope. "I think this is it!"

"You found it?" I whirled around.

"The envelope's addressed to Rask. Written in cursive. Look." He passed it to me with his plastic-covered fingertips. "And it's got your name on it."

"No postmark." I snatched it up, looking through each line for a hint. But nothing stood out either in the writing or the words—as standard and straightforward as if I'd written it myself. Just the order specifics and my name. Except. . .

"Shiloh! Look at this!" Adam grabbed my arm and jerked me toward the envelope.

Chapter 24

"S o, you make a habit out of Dumpster diving?" My editor, Kevin Lopez, didn't smile, but the lines on his cheeks deepened in mirth as he crossed his arms in his leather chair. Phil and Priyasha clicked away on keyboards outside his office door a little too quietly, whispering, and almost certainly listening in on our conversation.

"Definitely. You should try it sometime. It improves my personal aroma." I'd stripped off the garbage bags, but I still felt filthy. I needed a shower. Bad. My hair felt staticky from a too-close encounter with plastic, rain, and vegetable scraps. Something sticky had crusted at the end of one strand.

"So you wanted to talk to me." I glanced longingly at the fresh Starbucks cup on his desk circled by a cardboard holder. It had been too long since breakfast, and I needed a nice hot shot of sugared caffeine.

"Yep. But first of all, did you find anything?"

I held up the soiled letter. "I'm not sure what it means exactly, since I don't recognize the handwriting, but look"—I pointed to the battered envelope—"an old stamp I've never seen before."

"You're kidding! I collect stamps." Kevin grabbed a tissue to cover his fingers and reached for the letter. He picked up his reading glasses and held the envelope up to the light. "Whoa. The 'double-love' stamp. Also known as the 'broken-heart' stamp because of the way the printer hit the paper twice and smudged, making effectively two hearts. One cutting into the other."

He raised dark eyes to meet mine. "This is worth a lot of money, you know. Or it was, before it got smeared with whatever they threw in the Dumpster. What a shame."

"The year's significant, too—when Amanda Cummings was born. Coincidence?"

Kevin raised a thick eyebrow as he turned the envelope over. "Wow. That's big, Shiloh."

"It means the person sending me roses is probably the same one who allegedly did away with Amanda twelve years ago." I let out a shaky breath. "And he's been purposefully disguising his handwriting in the notes on my car. Using stencils, up until the letters I got today. Maybe even getting someone else to write the letters for him."

On the street below, an ambulance screamed by, siren flashing, and I flinched.

"This is why we need to talk. Have you taken the letter to the police?" Kevin reached over to adjust his blinds, peeking out through the slats at the old brick buildings that lined the street. A gesture that made me nervous.

"I'll take it by right after this."

He crossed his arms, his leather chair squeaking as he leaned back. "This is serious, Shiloh. I've seen these stalker cases before, and they can get ugly." He dropped his hand down to his glass-topped desk and drummed his fingers. "So I'm taking you off duty for a while. Matt can cover for you."

"Off duty?" I sputtered. "What am I supposed to do? Sit around at Faye's house and knit? I'll be a sitting duck! And besides, I need something to keep my mind off this mess. I'll go insane doing nothing."

"Do weather or something." Kevin's dark brows knit together. "You can help Priyasha with marketing. From home."

WEATHER? I groaned inwardly. It hurt to give up my hard-won post at the news desk. Crime was mine, after all. Mine! And now nasty Matt Tellerman would take my place, bragging to all his college buddies that he'd been promoted.

Kevin's nostrils twitched. He pulled the plastic lid off his Starbucks cup and sniffed then cocked his head. "Is that. . .you?"

"Is what me?"

"That smell. Sort of like old banana peels." He sniffed again, lip curling. "And maybe sour coffee grounds."

"You're good, Kevin." I pointed a finger at him. "So can I go now?"

"Straight to the police station. Carefully. Look behind you while you drive, and call 911 if you see anything suspicious." Kevin put the lid back on his cup. "And do me a favor and call a psychiatrist or something. You'll need one if this mess gets any worse."

"Oh, don't worry. I've already scheduled an appointment with one this afternoon."

Kevin groaned and massaged his head with both hands.

"And then I'm scheduling a planning session with Meg about photos."

"With Meg." Kevin instinctively reached for the drawer where he kept his Maalox.

"For the wedding. I'll get this wedding organized if it kills me." I grimaced. "Bad word choice."

"No Dumpster photos?"

"Hmm. Now that you mention it. . ."

Kevin rubbed his face with his hand. "You know what? See if you can schedule a visit with the psychiatrist for me, too."

———

Jerry. The Green Tree. If I couldn't run a few miles and knock all this stress out of my lungs, I needed to talk to Jerry and hear some good news. I pushed open the door to the parking lot and dialed Jerry twice, but he didn't pick up. So I dialed Trinity Jackson instead as my heels clicked across concrete.

"Trinity?" I asked when she answered. "How did *Fine Dining*'s visit go?" Instead of the exuberance I expected, Trinity sighed.

"What's going on?" I checked my phone to make sure I'd dialed the right number. "Didn't they show up?"

"Oh yes. Unfortunately."

"Unfortunately? What are you talking about, Trinity? The menu was perfect! We even researched what the editor of *Fine Dining* eats for breakfast! We repainted and redecorated. The place is gorgeous!"

"It is. But we still flopped." She sighed. "And you forgot your payment."

"My payment?" I sputtered. "What are you talking about? And what do you mean we flopped?" I stopped short on the sidewalk, my voice rising to shrill tones. "Where's Jerry? Why isn't he answering his phone?"

"I mean we flopped, Shiloh. Big-time. One crazy thing after another. You won't believe it." Trinity's voice sagged, tired and listless. "But Jerry still paid you. He left a check for you and Adam. Said that if you didn't come by to get it, Flash would put the cash in your bank account."

"Where's Jerry?" I tried to hold back tears.

Jennifer Rogers Spinola

"The last time I saw him, he was headed to his office with his head down."

—∞—

Trinity told it in pieces: A sewer main had broken down the street from The Green Tree, making an unwelcome stench, and without warning a leak from an adjoining building gushed into the kitchen—putting out electricity for half an hour while crisp fried noodles grew soft in the frying pan. The freezer went out. Ice dribbled into puddles, turning Stella's once-magnificent ramekins of green tea panna cotta into soggy sponges.

Jerry improvised, throwing together a gorgeous plate of blue cheese and green apple slices on bitter frisée lettuce, all drizzled with honey and walnuts. But the *Fine Dining* photographer shrieked about nut allergies—after Trinity had asked twice about special diets or requests.

So Jerry withdrew the offending plate and reseated the party—thanks to the photographer's complaints about "nut particles in the environment"—and, wouldn't you know it, placed them next to the top food critic's most hated rival from her college days.

And when the food critic turned back to Jerry, he saw an ugly gleam in her eye—like a glance of light off the pointy tines of a fork.

"Trite and overrated," she mumbled under her breath to the photographer. Just loud enough for Jerry to hear.

—∞—

By the time I'd dried my face from bawling, stopped by the police station, negotiated a photo-shoot plan with Meg by phone, showered, dried my hair, and changed into clean, crisp Hollister jeans and chic heels, I was late for my appointment with Dr. Geissler. The one thing I probably needed more than anything else. Who knows? If he had one of those long, comfortable sofas, I might curl up and ask him to prescribe something that'd put me out for about. . .oh, three weeks. And wake up in time for my rehearsal dinner.

If, of course, The Green Tree still existed then. Which at this point looked pretty impossible.

I sped across town toward Dr. Geissler's office, following my printed-off address from the Internet, and parked. I let myself into the neat white office and identified myself to Melina, who promptly escorted me back to the doctor's office.

No sofa in sight, but a soft armchair in pastel tones did the trick.

I sank into the cushy padding, playing with the fringed pillow, and had just started to nod off when the door opened.

"You must be Ellen Jacobs's daughter." Dr. Geissler extended a white-clad arm with a warm smile. "Shiloh, right?" He glanced at his chart as we exchanged pleasantries.

"That's correct." I sat up straight and attempted to rub the sleep from my face. "Sorry. It's been a long week." I tried to smile, smoothing my hair and stretching my leg to reach a rogue shoe that had slipped off. "A very long week."

Dr. Geissler sat down on a chair opposite me, crossing one leg comfortably over the other and flipping through a thick file. His gray-white hair lay back, neatly combed, and his cheeks were vibrant and clean shaven. A stethoscope hung around his neck, and gentle gray eyes folded in soft laugh lines at the corners. "A long week, Shiloh? What's up?"

"Me? Oh, I'm not important. I'm here to find out about Mom. Whatever you can tell me that won't jeopardize your patient-physician confidence. I understand all that." I squirmed to sit up straight in the foamy cushions, which turned my muscles to butter. "Not that I don't have my own issues right now, but I'm sick of talking about stalkers."

The doctor jumped. His eyes widened, blinking in visible confusion. "Sorry?" He jerked his head from me down to Mom's file and began thumbing through it. "What did you just say?"

"About Mom? I wanted to find out a little more about her health before she passed away. Her blood pressure, particularly." I picked at a spot on the chair arm, ashamed to meet his eyes. "We didn't get along well her last few years."

"No, no. The last thing you said about a stalker."

"Oh, that." I sighed and waved it away, remembering what Melina the receptionist had said about Dr. Geissler's slow descent into Alzheimer's—and wondering if the effects would begin this early in our session. "I'm just tired. One can only take so much police talk, restaurant sabotage, and rummaging through trash bins."

I stopped short, realizing how utterly ridiculous I sounded. "Forgive me. I'm running off at the mouth again."

"No, Shiloh." He looked up from his file with a piercing look. "You must tell me what you meant about a stalker. It's extremely important."

I jumped, startled, at his sharp tone, which sounded too urgent and calculated to belong to a man with no memory.

"I did mention a stalker," I said, dropping my gaze and running my fingers through the fringes of the pillow. "But it has nothing to do with Mom. I simply—"

"Nonsense." Dr. Geissler pulled a sheet of paper from her file. "How long has this stalker thing been going on?"

Discomfort crept up my shoulders, making my hair prickle. "I don't know. A month or so."

Dr. Geissler scooted his chair closer. "Your mother spoke to me about a stalker in her last weeks."

The high-heeled shoe that had been dangling off my foot fell with a muffled *clomp* onto the soft oriental rug. "Excuse me?"

"A stalker, Shiloh. Your mom had a stalker. A mystery man who'd begun to follow her. Call her. Leave strange messages on her car and at her office."

My mouth fell open, and I didn't bother to close it.

"And here's the clincher." Dr. Geissler leaned forward earnestly. "She said he was looking for you."

"There's no way she meant that," I managed, my fingers gripping the sides of the armchair. "In one of her last letters, she mentioned a guy who made her uncomfortable, who seemed to know me, but a stalker? Come on." I shook my head, not even bothering to pick up the pillow when it tumbled to the floor.

"I assure you she did mean that." Dr. Geissler adjusted his glasses and paged through the file. "It's documented in her sessions several times. Here. She mentioned finding a letter at her office." He pointed with his pen. "Inside he'd folded a love note for her to give you, and his rapturous assurance that you'd come soon."

I nearly forgot my manners and jerked the file out of his hands to see. "You're sure the guy meant *me*?"

"Your mother was certain of it. He knew your name. And he even called you by some sort of affectionate. . .well, nickname."

My heart began to pound. "What nickname?"

"Here it is." The doctor held up a page. " 'Angel,' he called you. 'My beloved angel.' " He closed the file. "And he sent your mother some gifts to pass on to you. Bouquets of red roses. Lots of them."

Chapter 25

"Doctor. Listen." I leaned forward, my hands trembling so much I knotted them together. "Mom wrote about a bald guy with an injured right hand who supposedly. . .knew me." I paused and studied his face, wondering how much I should tell him. "She asked if I had a friend here who was expecting me, and she said he made her uncomfortable. She said. . ."

The room felt too cold suddenly, over-air-conditioned and stuffy. My teeth chattered.

The doctor studied me, waiting. "She said what?"

"The guy expected me to come to Staunton. But that's impossible."

"You'd never visited your mom? Never passed through town, even briefly?"

"Not once. After I graduated from college and moved to Japan, my life was there." I broke off, pressing both hands to my head as if to squeeze some sense into it before insanity took over. "If I hadn't gotten fired, I would have stayed there the rest of my life. I'm telling the truth, doctor—I don't have the foggiest idea who my mom was referring to!"

I sat back in the chair. "Her description matches somebody who used to work at her mechanic's shop, but to my knowledge, I've never met the guy."

"The auto shop." The doctor stroked his chin, straightening his glasses as he leafed through the papers. "She mentioned that detail. Yes. He even left some letters for you there when she went to pick up her car."

I leaned my head against the back of the armchair, rolling it back and forth. "It makes no sense. I promise you."

"Well, the whole issue worried her enough that her blood pressure soared. She had anxiety problems. Couldn't sleep." Dr. Geissler sandwiched his fingers together. "I prescribed her a natural calmative and increased her blood pressure medication because of her heart. Ellen's health was quite good, but she did have significant hypertension." He shook his head sadly. "And it may have played a part in her death, I'm afraid to say—although at her age it isn't so unusual to. . ."

Dr. Geissler was still speaking, but his words floated past me, gibberish-like.

"Sorry?" I was staring at the fibers on the rug. The forest-green weave made a wash of magenta when I lifted my eyes, haloing the doctor's face.

"I asked why you're so concerned with your mother's blood pressure readings."

My heart pulsed loudly in my ears. Faster. Faster. A rush of hope roaring through my veins. "Did you say her blood pressure increased because of the stalker?"

"I did." He dipped his chin in a nod. "I've got all her records right here."

"She didn't increase her medication because of our fights and dysfunctional relationship?" I blinked back tears, but not fast enough. One made a hot streak down my cheek.

"I'm sure all that latent stress didn't help her numbers, but as far as I can recall, your relationship dynamics didn't play a major role in her spike in blood pressure. No."

The doctor studied me with sympathetic eyes, quietly handing me a tissue box. "Ellen had a history of dysfunctional relationships, you know. She'd become quite accustomed to them, unfortunately. In fact, she may have even had borderline schizophrenia from descriptions of her earlier years and some of her medical reports, although those are pretty spotty." He sorted through the file. "She experienced panic attacks. Possibly bipolar disorder."

Dr. Geissler closed the folder and adjusted his glasses, his voice gentle. "Ellen wasn't. . .*well* for much of her life, Shiloh. But she loved you. Deeply. I'm absolutely certain that, more than anything, she wanted you to know that."

My eyes streamed. "But the letters," I gasped as I fumbled for a tissue. "The letters I returned. They hurt her. I know they did." I wiped at my cheeks, hands trembling so badly I could hardly hold the tissue.

"And that's when her readings went up."

His own eyes filled, and he took off his glasses to wipe them. "Because you didn't read what she'd written regarding the mystery man who'd morphed into a stalker. She worried about you—and your safety." He shook his head, sliding his glasses back in place. "But she didn't harbor bitterness. She wasn't broken. And I'd already adjusted her medication by that point."

The timbre of his voice turned hoarse, barely audible. And he reached out awkwardly and clasped my hand in his wrinkled one. "Let it go, Shiloh."

The room fell so quiet I could hear the gentle rattle of the blinds against the window glass as the air-conditioning vent ruffled them.

Time stopped; my eyes riveted to the doctor's gently lined face as he opened his mouth to speak again.

"All of it. Let it all go. Because here's the thing: even if you had caused her death, she would have wanted you to leave all of that behind and go forward. She adored you." His eyes glistened with fresh tears. "Until our last visit, she couldn't stop talking about how much she loved you."

I tried to speak, but my throat choked up. And I slid my head into my hands, sobbing.

—⁑—

I could barely compose myself in the restroom, washing my face repeatedly with cold water. Sponging my cheeks with paper towels. Old-style paper towels, brown and rough, cranked from a metal dispenser like the ones in my high school bathroom.

Then I dug in my purse for eye drops and mascara and dabbed some concealer over the red spots.

I looked back at my reflection, the green and gold flecks in my eyes standing out in brilliant tones amid the teary red.

Eyes like Mom's. I ran my fingers over my wet lashes, trying to remember the contour of her eyelids. The graceful slope of her elegant high cheekbones. The sound of her voice, which had diminished so swiftly in my memory over the months that I could barely recall it.

I rinsed my hands in a stream of water, remembering how I'd stood in the Barnes & Noble bathroom at the Staunton Mall a year ago. Talking to my coworker Jamie about life and eternity and Jesus, and feeling my unbelieving, shut-up heart open just a bit against my will, like a crinkly Japanese fan.

And when I believed and prayed to let Jesus in for good and gave Him my heavy burden for His easy one, the weight lifted from my shoulders. I felt washed, clean, new.

Just like Mom, when He set her free.

And now, for the first time in her life, she truly was free. Forever.

I turned off the water and dried my hands then picked up my purse and slipped back into Dr. Geissler's room. He was gathering up his files and checking his watch, and he turned when I came in.

"There, now," he said in a grandfatherly way, lightly patting my arm. "Doesn't it feel better to know the truth?"

"It does." I sniffled again, trying to clear my head. The sun slanted through the blinds in a stream of gold, as if I'd stepped into a different room. "I still have more questions about the stalker though. And Amanda Cummings."

"Amanda Cummings." His chin bobbed in surprise. "Now there's a name I haven't heard in a while." His eyes grew fond. "I can't reveal anything about our consultations, but I can tell you this: she could have made something of herself. A smart young lady, that Amanda. A bit of depression, but otherwise in top shape." He sighed and rocked back in his seat, studying me. "May I. . .ask you something first?"

"Sure." I reached for another tissue and folded it into a tiny series of triangles, Japanese-style, one on top of another. My mind still filled with the doctor's hope-filled words.

"Were you aware of a change in your mother's behavior in her last years?"

"You mean related to the stalker?" I unfolded my tissue triangle and wiped my nose.

"No. In her personal life." The doctor lifted his hands as he tried to explain. "She. . .changed. Quite a bit. By the time your mother passed away, she'd cut back on some of the depression medications I'd prescribed. Not all, but some. She glowed." He looked wistfully into the distance. "I'll never forget the day she came into my office with the Gospel of John and told me I needed to be saved."

"She said that?" I laughed through my tears.

"That and a lot more. She left me a copy of the New Testament and told me to read it." He chuckled. "It's still up there on my shelf."

"Did you?"

"No." He chuckled again. "I admired her spunk and enthusiasm, but I've seen too many broken people to believe there's a God. Cases of abuse and abandonment. Besides, science has pretty much ruled God out anyway. Although. . ." He massaged his mouth as if in thought.

"Although what?"

"When I was younger, I used to think there might be a God, but. . ." His voice trailed off. "That was a long time ago. I'm an old man now, Shiloh. It's a bit late for somebody like me to change his tune, even if I did believe."

"You sound like my next-door neighbor." I heard myself speak again, strong and unexpectedly bold as I scooted forward in the armchair. "It wasn't too late for my mom, and it's isn't for you either. You said yourself that something transformed her life. Well, that's the power of Jesus—and He can change you like He changed her."

I felt funny using such bold language—like a preacher or something—but to my own surprise, I didn't duck my head or take back my words.

"I don't know. My memory's failing." Dr. Geissler ran his hand through his white hair, eyes wincing with something like humiliation and sorrow. "If there is a God, He's letting me fall apart, bit by slow bit. I can never forgive Him for that."

"What if, for argument's sake, you should have lost your memory long before now, but God's giving you extra time so you can reach out to Him and believe?" I shrugged. "Besides, doctor, my friend Becky reminded me that we're all going sometime. What matters is how we've lived—and if we've lived for Him or not."

I leaned forward, oddly encouraged by his silence. "You mentioned all the broken people you've seen. But what about my mom? What about the way God transformed her from. . .well, death to life? You can't consider one without the other."

Dr. Geissler slowly took off his glasses and wiped them again, even though they didn't need any wiping. He let his breath fall in a sigh and then shot me a smile. "I just don't know, Shiloh."

"Will you read the Bible she left?"

"Think it'll do any good?"

"Sure it will. It changed my life, too—and I'm not an easy nut to crack." I considered. "Although the nut part is pretty much right."

He squinted at me. "You sound so certain about what you believe. I'm surprised. You seem a bit too educated for this Gospel stuff. Forgive me if that's offensive."

"All the education in the world won't matter when God opens His

Book of Life to see if my name's written there. If I believed in His Son, Jesus." I paused to take a breath. "That's all that matters, doctor. And Mom found it. Before I did."

The room fell so silent I heard the tick of my watch. A muffled voice down the hall, and the slight reverberation of the walls as someone slammed a car door outside.

"I'll think about it." Dr. Geissler put his glasses back on and turned in his chair to face me. Reaching out to tightly clench my hand in his. "Promise?"

"I promise. I'll read it, and I'll give it a fair chance."

He blinked several times and tipped his head as in confusion. "So what were we talking about? Before you left for. . . Where did you go again?"

"The bathroom?"

"Oh, right." He smiled, but his eyes still squinted as if trying to remember. "We were discussing. . ." He adjusted his glasses and leaned over the folder, sorting through the papers.

"My mom. Her stalker." I swallowed nervously. "You remember, don't you, doctor?"

His hand stopped on a paper, and he jutted his head back with a smile of recognition. "Oh, that's right. Red roses, wasn't it?"

"Precisely. So if all this stalker stuff is true, why didn't Mom go to the police?"

"I told her she should. Repeatedly."

"So why didn't she?"

"She was afraid to. For two reasons. First of all, if this guy was a fiancé or romantic interest of yours, as he claimed to be, she didn't want to intrude. She felt she'd meddled enough in your life already, and she didn't want to give you more fodder for resentment toward her."

"Wait. Wait. Wait." I waved my hand. "Did you say fiancé?"

"That's correct. He stated on several occasions that the two of you were going to be married."

"Now that's crazy!" I shook my head vigorously. "I just got engaged this March, and I'd never met Adam until the day of Mom's funeral."

"Were you engaged before then?"

"I was." I twisted Adam's silver engagement band on my finger, embarrassed. "But we broke up after I came to Staunton."

Dr. Geissler gave me a hard look. "And you're certain this first fellow didn't follow you here with a broken heart?"

"Positive. And he broke *my* heart, not the other way around," I added a bit tartly. "But either way, the dates don't add up. Carlos and I called it quits after Mom's funeral. Not before. And according to you and the postmarks on Mom's letters, all unusual contacts from this unknown man started several months before her death in June."

Dr. Geissler searched through his file then shrugged. "You're correct. I really don't have any explanation."

"Well, what's the second reason she gave you for not going to the police?"

"She feared internal politics."

"Come again?" I cocked my head.

"Staunton's a small town, Shiloh." He dropped his voice. "She worried things might turn around on her if she implicated someone on too-friendly terms with the local police force. She didn't give names or specifics. But until the very end, she refused—reluctantly—to report it."

My fingers clenched. "What do you mean, until the end?"

"On your mother's last visit here, she promised me she'd go." Dr. Geissler met my eyes. "The threats had become too intense, and she said she'd take her chances and report it." He paused, pressing his lips together. "But as you know, she never got that chance."

"Dr. Geissler. I need every scrap of information you can give me about the man my mother suspected." I whipped out my trusty tape recorders and reporter's notebook and clicked open a pen. "Please. It's urgent."

He turned to his desk and spread out a thick smear of pages. "I'll do my best."

I waited as he shuffled through the pages one at a time, scanning and lifting them up. Lips moving as he read through the reports.

Minutes ticked by, slowly, slowly. The slant of sun shifted so that it fell across my arm in honey-colored stripes, glinting on the pen tucked anxiously between my fingers.

And still the doctor read, massaging his brow several times and shifting in his seat.

"Doctor?" I finally asked. "Have you found anything?"

"Sorry?" He looked up, a page between two fingers. And an embarrassed smile on his lips. "I apologize. What exactly. . .did you need from me?"

"Clues. To my mother's stalker."

"Stalker?" His eyes popped open in obvious confusion. "I'm so sorry, but what's your name again?"

"Shiloh Jacobs." I dropped the pen. "Don't you remember? We spoke for nearly an hour about my mother."

"Your. . .mother?" Dr. Geissler looked down at the file and then at me in a sort of blank apology, shaking his head. "Have we met? I don't. . .seem to have a file on you."

Alzheimer's. Poor guy. I held back tears, not sure what to say.

The doctor's gaze had drifted into the distance, as if unseeing. Confused. He rubbed his head, the confident expression melting into one of helplessness. Fear.

I quietly dropped my pen and notebook back in my purse and gathered up my tape recorders. Then reached out to touch his limp shoulder in grateful thanks.

He didn't look up when I slipped out the door.

—◊—

My cell phone buzzed with messages as soon as I turned it on. Evening sun slanted red-gold across the parking lot, and dizzying summer heat swelled up from the maples and pines that dotted the road.

"Adam? Hi." I unlocked my car, careful to look over my shoulder before getting in. "I saw you called several times. Everything okay?"

"Just checking to make sure you're all right." Adam sounded relieved. "How did your meeting with the doctor go?"

"Wait 'til you hear." I checked my rearview mirror and backed out of the parking lot, sticking my Bluetooth in my ear. Pulled on my sunglasses.

"Tell me everything. But first, I've got some news for you."

"Good or bad?" I blew out my breath, letting out my pent-up emotions before I bawled.

"Good. Mostly. I think."

I scowled as I flipped on my signal and turned onto the main road. "That's not very encouraging."

"I found us an apartment."

My mood brightened. "You did? Where?"

"Harrisonburg, near the JMU campus. It's not a great place, so don't get your hopes up," he warned. "But it'll be available next month. The landlord said we can make the deposit any time, and she'll hold it for us until after our wedding."

"Wow." I pondered this new piece of information as I pulled up to a stoplight. "Is it nice?"

"It's. . .well, you'll have to see it."

Oh boy.

"The place is okay," he said, as if trying to conjure enthusiasm. "It's not great, but it'll do for a while. Seeing as how we won't have much money while I'm in school and you'll be spending more on gas to commute to work. If you decide to continue at *The Leader*, of course."

"Oh. Right." I startled, thinking for the first time what I'd miss if I left my job. "I guess we'll have to find a new church then, too?"

"Unless you want to commute about forty minutes to Covenant Baptist every Sunday and church event, then yes."

I bit my lip, feeling an uncomfortable wave of anxiety splash over me. No more Sunday morning banter in the beginner's Sunday school class, where Darryl and Brad and Lyle took turns on the whiteboard diagramming how to skin a deer—all the while discussing Abraham's covenant with God in Genesis, which brand of grape juice was better for communion, and arguing the ramifications of baptism. No more rowdy kids gluing cotton ball sheep haphazardly to construction paper while I told the story of Jesus the Good Shepherd and wished I'd brought more aspirin.

And most importantly, no more mile-a-minute gab sessions with Becky and Tim, or Trinity's grandmother Beulah, or Faye and Earl while we joined the noisy influx of churchgoers into the bright, airy sanctuary. Home-baked honey ham and sweet potatoes at Beulah's house postservice. Photos of missionaries we prayed for and letters from the jail ministry.

"Shiloh? You still there?"

"I'm here. Sorry." I rubbed my face. "Just thinking."

"You don't want to move?"

"I thought I did, but. . ." I put on my turn signal and shifted slowly into the other lane, my throat tightening as I imagined all our boxes piled into the back of Adam's pickup truck. Mom's empty kitchen, the walls bare and floors shiny with pine-scented cleaner. "It's fine though. I'm happy about the apartment. Really. It'll just take some getting used to. A new town. A new life."

And all of it in another place nearly as redneck as Staunton, Virginia. What were the odds?

"Does the apartment allow dogs?" I asked suddenly, jerking to a stop at a stoplight.

Adam hesitated. "No."

I just sat there when the light turned green until the Suburban behind me honked.

"I'm sorry." Adam sounded disappointed. "It's not exactly how I hoped things would turn out, but it's the best I can find right now. Maybe Christie can stay at my parents' place."

"We'll. . .figure it out." I forced a smile when I wanted to cry and bang on the steering wheel. "Together."

"Exactly." His tone brightened. "And hey, you'll never guess who called me."

"Ashley?"

"Ha. No. Thankfully."

I snickered. "Who?"

"Kyoko."

I did a double take, swerving and narrowly missing a pothole. "Kyoko called you? Why?"

"To check on you, like everybody else. And let you know she's arrived safely in San Francisco."

"Oh, good." I let out a sigh of relief. Bittersweet as it was to know Kyoko had left Japan forever. "Is she glad to be back?"

"Exuberant. She kept hollering about how much she's missed the Iranian bakery where nobody speaks English, and the graffiti, and the drunk guy on the corner who wears nothing but a shower curtain."

"What?" I shrieked.

"I kid you not. Don't worry—she says she'll call you as soon as she wakes up and for you not to do anything crazy. Whatever that means."

"Kyoko thinks everything I do is crazy."

"Then whatever you do, don't tell her about the Dumpster."

Chapter 26

"Somebody seriously has a screw loose," I muttered, tearing off my sunglasses as I followed Becky up to the shiny glass door of the dress shop in Stuarts Draft. The brick on the strip mall looked new, if not a little pompous. Which meant everything inside was probably way out of my budget. "If I get another message from that creep, or another stupid bouquet, or photo, or whatever he decides to stuff in an envelope, I'm going to. . ."

"Mercy, Shah-loh!" Becky gawked at me, stopping right there on the sidewalk. A puff of hot wind blowing her pale hair. "Photos of you?"

"Yep. Sitting in the auditorium at the city council meeting, or walking into *The Leader* building. They're not good photos, usually taken from far away with a zoom lens, but they're me all right."

"But none of you with a cow, right?"

I pointed a finger in warning. "Don't even bring that up. Got it?"

Becky slapped a hand across her smile. "It ain't that hippie photographer friend a yours, is it?" she asked, sobering. "Practicin' for the weddin'? She went there with ya."

"Meg? No way." I waved it away. "There's another photo at Ray Floyd's house, taken from the window while I interviewed him on the night of the crash."

"She was there, too. Remember?"

"Becky, it's not Meg." I knew Becky was trying to help, but I felt my blood pressure start to soar. "We thought maybe the guy who drove the car that crashed into Ray's house snapped it, but we can't find a connection. And police reports show him too drunk to take steady pictures of anything on the night of the crash."

215

"Well, that don't make no sense. Didja tell the police?"

"Yes," I grumbled. Dumb old Shane Pendergrass had given me the once-over like he'd done the night he met me and let his fingers brush against mine a little too long when I handed him the photos.

If Adam had been there, he'd have decked him.

"Hey, isn't Shane's birthday on August third?" I asked, squinting at Becky in the bright sunlight. "He invited me to some birthday beach party last year. And I didn't go, in case you're wondering."

"Yep, August third. On your weddin' day, ironically." She grinned. "He'll be tore up, won't he?"

I paused, heel on the edge of the sidewalk. Not liking the ugly suspicions boiling up inside me. "He hurt himself a few years ago."

"Yep. Pulled a tendon in his wrist or somethin'. Jujitsu, I think. Whatever that is." Becky wrinkled her nose. "Why you askin' all this stuff about Shane anyhow?"

"Call it journalistic curiosity."

"Well, come on." She linked an arm through mine. "Curiosity killed the cat, you know, an' I ain't in the mood to talk about murder! Now git in there an' act like a bride for two seconds. Git!" She shoved me forward. "We still don't got a dress for ya, an' ya ain't gittin' hitched without one. So hurry up!"

We pulled open the shiny door and found ourselves greeted by rows of white wedding dresses all draped in plastic. Sequins sparkled in the overhead light. Price tags carefully angled so I couldn't read them without digging inside the plastic. Huh. Nice trick. I knelt to see better then stood up quickly when the overly enthusiastic saleswoman named Pamela scooted over to "see if we needed any help."

"We're jest lookin'." Becky tipped her sunglasses up on her hair. "But thanks anyhow."

I felt nervous suddenly, surrounded by expensive satin and tulle and lace. Everything perfect; all the billows of satin pale and bride-y.

In contrast, I had trouble keeping myself away from (1) muggers, (2) dirt, or (3) grimy accident sites for even a few hours. I always chose the darkest blue jeans I could find for exactly that reason: to hide all my stains and food/tea spills.

I ran my hand over the shiny plastic as Pamela retreated with a bloodthirsty smile. "Before I buy anything, I wanted to tell you something, Becky. I'm starting to wonder if I should leave town until the wedding."

"You reckon?" Becky dropped the sleeve of a white lace gown. "I mean, gracious, Shah-loh. I shore as fire don't want nothin' to happen to ya. But ya think it's come to that?"

"I don't know." I shrugged nervously. "I'm just wondering if we should get married somewhere else, or change the date, or. . ." I pushed some dresses across the rack, their tiny pearl beads glinting. "I mean, the perp knows our wedding date, and with the engagement announcement in the paper, he could walk right into the service if he wanted to."

"You gotta do what's best, my friend. But I'd hate to see all our plans warshed down the toilet. You done chose bridesmaids' dresses—those gorgeous apple-red ones that your half sis is gonna buy." She sighed and flipped through her schedule book. "Those pretty *washi* homemade paper invitations with flowers and leaves and whatnot. Them paper lanterns and candles. Rehearsal dinner at The Green Tree. It's gonna be real pretty the way ya got it all planned—even on a budget."

She teared up and rubbed her nose with her palm. "But you know best. Lands, Shah-loh! I never thought things'd git so ugly."

I fixed a strand of her hair that had tangled in the hoop of her earring as she closed the planner. "I'm not giving up yet, Becky. I'm just letting you know what's going through my mind. Staunton's pretty safe, but this whole stalker thing's turning into a big deal. I'm being followed. A lot." I glanced uncomfortably around the shop.

"I'm so sorry." She looked up at me with sympathetic eyes. "You don't deserve all this. It's your weddin'! You oughtta be havin' fun."

"I am having fun." I hugged her. "And I'm not giving up yet. But I thought you should know."

"Well then." She managed a grin. "Let's shop."

We sorted through racks of lace and satin, nodding and shaking our heads. Then Becky herded me over to the fitting area, arms full of snazzy gowns with a million buttons, bows, layers, and frills I'd never wear—thanks to the minimal Japanese "less-is-more" mentality that had warped me forever. Pamela helped Becky hang all the gowns on a shiny rack and unlocked an enormous mirrored fitting room for me then left us in polite privacy.

"You're going to have to help me," I warned, looking at the complicated buttons on the first dress. Even the hook-and-eye under-garments and fluffy crinoline slip freaked me out a little. "And I'm not coming out of here looking like a Las Vegas showgirl." I glared at a sequin-studded number.

"Well, of course I'm gonna help ya. Shoot, I couldn't even bend over an' put on my own shoes in mine!"

Becky kept her back politely turned while I put on the undergarments and slip. She hooked up the back and helped me wiggle into the first dress—a traditional thing with big, puffy sleeves and lace appliqué. An intricate lace train that would probably reach from the dress shop to The Green Tree restaurant.

"I don't like it," I said as Becky started on the first of about half a million tiny buttons up the back. "You'd need to tease my hair because I look like I'm on some cheesy daytime soap."

Becky grinned. "Actually, ya kinda do." She yanked me back in place. "Now hold still. 'Cause it ain't done yet."

I made a face and turned back to the mirror and caught a startling glimpse of myself in a *wedding dress*. My dark brown hair, my multicolored hazel eyes, and a cloud of white. Becky's face behind me, serious with concentration.

"Ya got a honeymoon place picked out?" She glanced up at me with a knowing smile.

I heard two other girls in the fitting rooms next to us, so I dropped my voice to a whisper. "Kind of."

"What's kind of?"

"Well, Adam's looking at a cabin in the mountains." We hadn't discussed it with anyone, but I trusted Becky with every detail of my life. "I'm not a nature girl, but he said it's really nice. A fireplace and whirlpool bath and a loft. We wanted to stay a week, but. . ." I broke off, picking at a seam on the skirt.

"But what?"

"I think we'll downgrade to two or three nights."

"Money?"

"Yeah. But it's okay. It'll be nice anyway." I shook my finger at her. "And don't give us any more, hear me? I found that check you left in my car."

"Aw, that. Shucks." Becky looked embarrassed. "Ain't nothin'. Wish it could be more." She fluffed the skirt. "There. Whaddaya think?"

I raised an eyebrow, turning sideways in the mirror. "I don't think so. Sorry."

Becky studied my reflection a minute. "Yeah. Mebbe you're right. It's kinda bulky on ya, anyhow. G'won an' take it off, and I'll git the next one."

I waited for Becky to release me from button prison and stepped carefully out of the dress. I helped Becky drape it on the hanger then waited obediently while she grabbed the next one.

"You're kidding. That?" I balked, foot halfway into the opening. "It's got stripes across it."

"Yeah. They're real fashionable. Y'oughtta know that, Yankee!"

"It looks like surgical gauze. And fashion is a complicated thing." I let Becky zip me up and straighten the skirt. "So where did you and Tim go on your honeymoon?"

"Pigeon Forge, Tennessee. Stayed in a cabin part a the time an' in a nice hotel the rest. Mom 'n' Pop helped out a bunch, so it was way nicer than we coulda done on our own. Went ta Dollywood, all that stuff." She grinned and waggled her eyebrows, hitching up the back of my strapless bodice. "But we didn't do as much shoppin' as I'd thought!"

I coughed and tried to change the subject.

"A good honeymoon's real special, Shah-loh," she said, as if letting me in on a secret. "One a the best mem'ries of yer life."

I gulped. "I'm sure it is."

"My friend got some cheap deal package on the coast, but it turned out to be a dump. Dirty, nasty. Full a roaches an' further away from the beach than Kansas! Had a horrible time."

My eyes bugged out, remembering the pages I'd printed off on the Internet. "What was the deal called?"

"I don't know. Somethin' Sun Package at Virginia Beach. Big rip-off."

"Morning Sun?"

"Yeah, that sounds right. Somethin' ya gotta sign up for real quick. The pics on the Internet look snazzy, but they found somebody's hairs in the bed 'n' toenails on the bathroom floor."

The hairs on the back of my neck tingled, imagining what else the "morning sun" might have turned up if I'd had my way.

"But at least Tim's and mine was fine. I'm jest thankful to God for that, 'cause I'd been plannin' my honeymoon since I was a kid." Becky poked me in the back, making my ticklish nerves contort.

"Really." I shook my head at the dress in the mirror, hoping Becky would change the subject. "I think Ashley's right. I don't look so good in strapless."

Becky twisted her mouth to the side. "Mebbe she's right. Your shoulders are kinda small and so are. . .yeah. Spaghetti straps might suit ya better." She sighed, flipping through the rack. "But jest about

Jennifer Rogers Spinola

all of 'em's strapless. Guess that's what people wear."

"People who have shoulders."

"Well. Yeah. And a little more. . .hmm." Becky pulled at the zipper. "Don't worry. We'll find somethin' jest right for ya. Anyway, like we was talkin' about before. It's always a plus to marry a man who's a real romantic—and a real good kisser." She laughed and hung up the dress. "So whaddaya think?"

"About the dress? Definitely no. I felt like The Mummy's Bride."

"About Adam." Becky rolled her eyes. "Is he a perty good kisser? 'Cause Tim sure is. Gracious!"

I smoothed the puffy skirt of the next dress, which shimmered with layers of soft ruffles and tiny crystals. And tried not to think of mullet-ed Tim kissing anybody—or the burping contests he held with Todd. I felt heat rising not just to my cheeks, but creeping up all the way to my hairline.

"It's awfully hot in here." I reached suddenly for the doorknob.

"Hold yer horses, woman! Unless ya wanna go prancin' out there in your undies." She gave me a smug smile in the mirror. "An' ya still ain't answered me about Adam."

I looped my arms through the lacy straps and pretended I hadn't heard.

"Well, it's all right," said Becky gently, fluffing out billowy tulle. "Those things take time, ya know. It don't all happen overnight like they show in the movies. I mean kissin' and. . .well, other stuff, too, once you're married."

"I don't know if he's a good kisser or not," I finally managed, seeing the conversation creep off in an unexpected direction.

"What'd ya say? Speak up."

I tried again, but Becky scrunched up her nose as she turned me around. Pulling at the ribbon lacing in the back. "Huh? Did you say you haven't kissed yet?"

"Yes!" I whispered in humiliation, covering my face with my hands.

"Yes you have, or yes you haven't?"

Becky could be exasperating sometimes. I flung my arms out. "We haven't kissed yet, okay? Adam and me. So I don't really know if he's a good kisser or not!"

Becky's hands stopped on the lacing. "Are you serious? Y'all haven't kissed yet? Even once?"

"Why don't you say it loud enough for everybody else to hear?"

220

I snapped, but Becky ignored me.

"I mean, yer engaged! Why would ya not. . ." She saw my crossed arms in the mirror. "Sorry, Shah-loh. Ain't none a my business."

"Well, it's a little late now," I huffed, glaring. "Now you know. And so does everybody else around here."

"Aww, I'm sorry." Becky hung her head meekly. "I didn't mean anything by it. I'm jest. . .surprised, is all. I was thinkin' how you don't have no mama to talk about this stuff, so I thought. . . I'm sorry. Fergive me."

Becky looked so repentant that I dropped my scowl and looked away. "It's okay. I'm just. . .a little embarrassed, I guess. I mean, most people would've kissed a long time ago."

"Well, yeah, but it ain't like a rule or nothin'. Ya do things however's most comf'terble for the both of ya. I mean, there are some things that are off-limits 'til ya tie the knot, but. . .ya know what I mean."

"Adam isn't ready to kiss yet."

"Are you?"

"Maybe, but it's not that simple. He doesn't. . .want to yet."

She shrugged. "So? He's differ'nt. He's careful. It's nice."

"At *all*," I emphasized, catching Becky's eye. "Not until the wedding."

This time her propriety came undone. "What?" she squealed. "Adam said that?"

"Yeah. We talked about it the other day." I covered my flaming cheeks with cool palms. "I know it's strange, but it's what he said he wanted to do. Or *not* do, rather."

"Until the doggone weddin' ceremony? Are you pullin' my leg, Shah-loh?"

I cringed as Becky's voice rang off the sides of the dressing room. "I'm serious," I whispered, shushing her. "He's thought like that a long time. You know, wanting to save everything. . .and I mean *everything*." I crossed my arms stiffly. "So that's it. That's how we're doing things. Now you know, okay?"

Becky forgot about the back of my dress and turned me to face her, ignoring the last sarcastic words I'd flung at her.

"Doggone it all!" She laughed and wiped her eyes, digging in her purse for a tissue. "That's gotta be one a the sweetest things I ever heard! I mean, I knowed Adam was differ'nt from way back, but I didn't know. . . Shucks, you're a real lucky woman." She blew her nose. "My oughtta-be-brother done made me proud! And you, too,

Yankee—'cause the wrong woman would ruin him always tryin' ta change him."

"Well, it's not the only way to do things," I said before she got any ideas that I was Mother Teresa. "It's just an idea."

She stuck the wrinkled tissue in her pocket and tugged on the laces again, turning me around. "Good thing, 'cause I hafta tell ya me an' Tim kissed an awful lot before we got married, Shah-loh. An *awful* lot! We weren't no saintly Adam Carter. Why, when we was on our second date we. . ."

I covered my ears and sang loudly to shut out the details. I could hear her laughing even with my ears plugged.

"But that's it!" she said, yanking my hands off my ears. "We stopped there, for the record. Although it was mighty hard! Sometimes I wonder if mebbe we'd a been better off ta do like Adam, but. . ." She grinned mischievously. "We were young fools!"

Becky beamed at me, red-eyed. "Y'all are a match made in heaven, ya know?"

I gazed back at her reflection, remembering the drunk outside the Dairy Queen who'd called us the "perfect couple." Wondering if Becky was equally insane—or if they'd both noticed something I hadn't.

"I can't tell you how happy I am an' proud of ya both. Mercy! Ain't life the best?"

"Don't tell anybody," I warned quickly. "It's not supposed to be a big deal. Just something he decided with me."

"Done." She pretended to zip her lips closed.

Becky sniffled and finished lacing up the back, fluffing the skirt out. "But I'm tellin' you, Shah-loh Jacobs, waitin' for love's the best thing ever! Don't let nobody tell you differ'nt! Why would you wanna tear the wrapping off the package before it's your birthday? You gotta wait, an' God'll honor yer waitin'."

She smoothed my hair to one side and straightened the straps. "Don't mean ev'rything's gonna be smooth sailin'. Life's rough. Marriage is rough. But you'll be *blessed*."

Her last word rang through the dressing room like spangles of light from the crystals on the dress.

"I used to think all that waiting stuff for Christians was silly," I said, avoiding Becky's eyes in the mirror. "I thought a lot of things were silly. But now. . .well, I look at things a bit differently." I shook out the skirt and watched it fluff down, crystals sparkling.

Carlos's chiseled face flashed briefly through my mind while Becky tried unsuccessfully to pull the lacing through the next loop. In a cold instant I replayed Carlos's honeyed words. Other guys I'd dated. Other kisses. Other things I wasn't proud of.

"I just wish I'd had more sense before this." I picked at a hem.

"Ain't none of us perfect," said Becky gently. "On Judgment Day we're all the same—sinners in need a His grace."

I felt tears in my eyes as I ruffled the long, billowy skirt. It fell in light layers, cloud-like. When I twirled, it swished. A soft rustling sound like gentle rain.

In the mirror I saw Becky's face sober. "You know, it's sorta like them flowers I showed ya at the wholesale shop. The cut ones."

"What about them?" I scrubbed a hand over my cheek.

"You gotta die."

"Die?" Visions of red roses and ugly letters flung themselves into my brain.

"To yerself. To yer flesh. Deny yourself and take up yer cross. That's what Jesus said." Becky picked at the errant hem. "That's why we wait for what seems good, even if it's just a kiss. Or whatever God puts on our mind to keep holy."

I looked up, surprised to hear Becky Donaldson wax spiritual and use the word "holy." The last time I'd stopped by her house, she was slathered in a dark blue facial mask, screaming at Dale Earnhardt Jr. on the TV screen—a half-eaten MoonPie in one hand and a cow-shaped baby rattle in the other.

"You hafta give it all up. Your expectations of how a husband's gotta be. How he's gotta act, your demands and your selfishness, and all the bitterness you wanna store up against him when things don't go so hot. You kick it in the grave, cover it up with dirt, and don't look back."

She dropped her voice to a husky low. "And then, my friend, that's when you'll learn to truly live."

—∞—

The dress wasn't quite. . .*it*. We loved the billowy cut, but it made me feel like I'd fallen inside a wedding cake—so full and frothy I could hardly find my own feet. Different straps, I said. A-line skirt, said Becky. And less "stuff" on it (and under it).

So we left the shop empty-handed, stopping for lunch at a greasy Mexican restaurant with cilantro-loaded salsa. Next on our shop-a-thon: the Salvation Army, and after that, the Staunton Mall. And because of

Jennifer Rogers Spinola

the mall's dearth of acceptable stores, I figured my chances of finding a decent dress were about the same either way.

Thrift stores are surprisingly good sources of scuffed coffee-table books on macramé from the '70s, dusty plastic houseplants, and dented suitcases with the locks broken off. Sweaters in ugly, pilled color bands with stains on the sleeves.

I ran my hand over the rack of party dresses, letting them fall apart one by hideous one: bright mustard-yellow and peach, with ugly cuts from thirty years ago. Dingy. Musty. Sweat-stained.

Until the white dress appeared, shining dimly in the dull overhead fluorescent light. I flipped back then pulled it off the hanger in surprise.

Wow. Pretty. I sucked in my breath. *Really* pretty. A surprisingly high-class brand with all the perfect seams in an unusual cut. An A-line skirt that tumbled to the floor, hem trimmed with intricate silver-kissed lace. Short, fluttery sleeves that reminded me of kimono sleeves. Just my size, or close enough that an alteration would fix it easily.

I sniffed nearly transparent layers of white, bracing myself for cigarette-smoke odor. But none lingered. Just the slight damp smell of being kept too long in someone's basement.

I turned the dress over, eyeing the touches of lace around the neckline and bodice. Smooth, simple lines.

"Becky!" I called. The dress draped pretty and fresh across my arm, a puddle of pearl-white, as if it had been waiting for me. *Fifteen dollars.* The cheapest dress I'd found new cost more than ten times that—and it was fringed like a cowgirl's.

"Did ya find somethin'?" Becky asked in surprise, wending her way through shelves of old books.

"Look at this!" I spun the dress around, listening to the tulle swish underneath. "Isn't it beautiful?"

And then we both saw it: a hideous mustard-yellow stain on the left side. Almost as big as my hand, right in the waist area. And we groaned together.

"It's real nice," said Becky, lifting it up for a closer look. Shook her head. "But that stain ain't never gonna come out, prob'ly."

She rubbed the garish splotch then turned the dress inside out and checked the back of the material. Shook her head again. "I'm so sorry."

"Yeah." I hung it sadly back on the hanger. "You think stain remover might work?"

"No way. It'll tear up the material."

"It's just fifteen dollars." I chewed my lip.

"You got fifteen dollars you wanna throw away? 'Cause that ain't comin' out. I can tell ya right now."

My shoulders slumped.

"A weddin' dress needs to be white—real white. Can't have no spots or nothin'. Which is why it's hard to find one used." Becky gave the dress a pat. "I prob'ly got a whole mess a stains on mine. That's jest the way a weddin' dress is."

I hung it reluctantly on the rack, fluffing the skirt. "Bleach?"

"Shucks, no!" Becky's eyes popped in horror. "Not that kinda material. Didn't anybody ever teach ya how ta warsh clothes?"

I plodded out with Becky to her oven-hot car and sat deep in thought, air conditioner blowing full blast on my face. Trying to invent some way to save that dress. And just when she'd flipped on her signal to pull out into the road, I grabbed her arm.

"Go back, Becky! I've got an idea!"

"Fer what? That bookcase you was lookin' at?"

"No, the dress!"

"The weddin' dress? You gotta be kiddin."

"Nope."

Becky wrinkled up her brow and sat there, turn signal still blinking. "You crazy? What ya gonna do about that big ol' ugly stain? Git a blowtorch an' burn it off?" She scowled, grumpy from our spate of bad shopping luck.

"No! I've got a better idea." I practically leaped out of my seat. "Go back or I'll get out here."

Becky grudgingly turned off her signal and backed into the parking lot, and she parked while I hastily unclipped my seat belt.

"I'm warnin' ya." She glared through her sunglasses. "Don't come cryin' ta me if ya bleach the daylights outta that dress an' it turns yella."

"I'm not going to bleach it." I threw open the car door then ran inside and grabbed the dress. Counted out fifteen dollars in cash and slapped it on the counter. Then I ordered Becky to hightail it over to Faye's as fast as she could.

And reached over the seat back to grab Priyasha's bag of bridal magazines.

—⁂—

"A what?" asked Faye Sprouse over her glasses, turning the dress over and smoothing the satin. Fingering the stain.

"An *obi*. Like on a kimono. Have you seen one?"

She wrinkled her brow, running a hand through her graying hair, curled in an attractive cut. A little longer and more modern than she used to wear it before Earl. "A. . .a what?"

"An obi. Like a belt." I gestured. "It's wide and colorful, and it wraps around the waist and ties in the back. In a bow or some other complicated design."

"And ya wanna put that on the dress?"

"Yes! Like this. Look." I plopped a bridal catalog down on the table and opened it to a marked page. "See how this dress has a belt-thing around the waist? Well, what if I used a Japanese fabric—like red kimono silk? And had it tie in the back, in a nice bow—with those long sweeps down the back of the skirt?"

Becky's eyes widened. "It'd be Asian, all right." She looked at the picture and held up the dress. "An' this real simple dress style is jest the right match, ain't it?"

"Exactly!" I grinned, giddy. "And it would cover the stain. Look." I placed my hands over the waist area. "It looks perfect to me. Could you do that, Faye? I know you sew."

"Well, I think so," she said, turning the dress over again. Looking inside at the seams. "That'd be real simple, if you could find the fabric. Silk's prob'ly real expensive."

"Oh, that's not a problem. I've probably got something I can use, or Kyoko does." I held my breath. "So you could do it?"

Faye nodded. "You bet. In fact, if ya want, I could draw the ends of the silk out like a train. Maybe trail on the floor a bit."

I looked at Faye in delight then at Becky. A slow smile spread over Becky's face, and she shook her head.

"The Fashion Nazi strikes again!" she hollered. "Fifteen doggone bucks, woman!" Then she jumped on my back and hugged me like a crazy woman while I staggered, trying not to drop her or careen sideways into Faye's kitchen table.

"I've got my wedding dress! I've got my wedding dress!" I shouted when Becky let go and I got my breath back. And I ran through the halls with the dress flying out like a white banner, Becky whooping behind me.

Chapter 27

The only detail about the dress I hoped no one discovered was the silk fabric for the obi. It was a table runner. One of Kyoko's, which I fell in love with after she sent me photos. Red silk with a pink Japanese flower pattern delicately overlaid. Stunning, shining silk, with that gorgeous iridescent sheen.

"You're going to use a table runner for your dress?" Kyoko sputtered out of my cell phone over a haze of the summer-hot parking lot, still sweltering at three in the afternoon. I smelled rain in the distance. A dusty wind whisked from down Greenville Avenue, bringing scents of Hardee's hamburgers and burned-out grease from the mechanic who'd just penciled me in next week for a nearly due inspection.

After—ahem—I nosed around about Jim Bob. With zero results. The guy who jotted down my name with grease-stained fingers had never heard of him.

"Yep. The table runner'll work perfectly." I tipped my sunglasses down off my hair and dug for the car keys, holding Christie's leash with one hand while she sniffed and strained at the chain. "Our vet visit this morning was free. And good news at the mechanic—the inspection's cheaper than I expected."

"Why, what'd you do, sweet-talk them all? You sure do a number on police officers and redneck cousins, you know."

"Give me a break. Our vet's a woman."

"Well, I'd wager your mechanic's not. So anyway, how about that transmission? Is it working okay?"

"Perfectly. I didn't have to pay a cent, thanks to Mom's old warranty, remember. And. . .I'm driving Faye's old Escort just to be safe." I jingled the unfamiliar keys for Kyoko's benefit.

On top of that, I'd done the unthinkable to disguise myself: for the first time in my life, I'd donned a pair of (gulp) *cowboy boots*. Real brown leather boots, borrowed from Becky Donaldson. A flowy green-and-cream-plaid dress. Sunglasses.

If the Escort didn't throw off Odysseus, the cowboy boots would. Since they were pretty much the last thing Shiloh P. Jacobs would ever wear in her right mind.

"Well, that's great about the transmission, Ro. A new one can set you back thousands of bucks. What'd you do, visit a temple or something? Buy another *omamori?*"

"I don't need good-luck charms." Drops slid down my neck under my ponytail as I unlocked the passenger's side door. Then I rolled down the windows and let the car air out a bit. Christie jumped up into the towel-covered passenger's seat. "And I definitely don't need to visit any more temples. I threw enough coins away on that silly stuff when I lived in Japan, and it didn't do me a bit of good."

"Maybe you didn't give enough money."

"Maybe I didn't want to accept what life dished out." I settled Christie carefully on the seat, clicking off her leash while she alternately licked my chin and smudged the freshly washed window glass with her nose, tail whapping me in the face. "Or take responsibility for my actions."

"That, too." Kyoko's reply came surprisingly soft. "You've changed, Ro. And I mean that in a good way. Except for the. . .um. . .table runner thing. That's just goofy. Back in Japan you would have called in sick rather than step out of the house sans Prada. Or whatever snooty brands you wore."

I shuddered, thinking of my cowboy boots. If Kyoko heard about them, I was in big trouble.

"Well, life's thrown me a Salvation Army wedding dress." I shut the passenger's side door and circled around to the left side, pushing my heat-straggly bangs to the side and out of my eyes. "As long as you don't mind parting with that table runner. It is silk, after all."

"Of course not! We never used it. But how's it gonna look? I've never heard of a wedding dress with an obi in my life, Ro. And believe me, I've seen some weird wedding getups."

"Yeah, like your aunt's gold bridesmaids' dresses. I've been thinking about those."

"Don't tempt me, my dear," said Kyoko dryly. "You have no idea what a thrill I'd get out of it."

"I think we'll stick with mine." I slammed my door and turned the air-conditioner vents toward Christie and me, adjusting my rearview mirror and backing out of the space.

"So, has Ashley actually bought our bridesmaids' dresses yet, Ro-chan? I mean, it's not August yet, but I'm Type A. I like things done in advance. And this is WAY past the 'advanced' stage."

"I know." I sighed and pulled out into Greenville Avenue's Friday afternoon traffic, sun glinting off Faye's hood as I passed fast-food restaurants and pizza places. Trying not to get uptight every time I thought of Ashley. "She said she found the dresses in our sizes."

"Did she buy them?"

"I. . .I think so."

"Did she say so?" Kyoko growled.

"I'll ask again. I promise."

"Well, maybe I should bring some of these gold babies for backup."

I almost said yes in jest then thought better of it. If there were two women in the world I had to watch, they were Kyoko and Ashley. For entirely different reasons.

"So you've sent the table runner already?"

"Yesterday, overnight express. You'll probably get it tomorrow though, with all the bad weather in the Midwest." Kyoko hmm-ed. "Should I have included a place setting with it? Maybe to cover some larger spots, like—"

"Just the runner." I glared.

"It's yours. Enjoy."

I tapped out a little dance with my feet. "My wedding dress! Can you believe it? For fifteen dollars."

"I hope you're happy." Kyoko's voice held a warning tone. "Remember, I told you I'd pay for a decent dress."

I smiled. "I know. Thanks. But you're already paying for all the Japanese stuff you're bringing. Plates and teacups and *mochi* and everything."

Mochi. My mouth watered, remembering the sweet, squishy little pounded rice cakes Japanese served at traditional festivals.

"And not just any mochi," added Kyoko. "Cherry blossom mochi to match your wedding cake. Which supposedly Stella is concocting in her blessedly smoke-free kitchen. Am I right?"

"You got it. She's been clean for two weeks or so. I hound her every day by phone and buy her lots of chewing gum. At least cooking for her catering business keeps her busy because she'll lose business when Jerry's restaurant closes."

"Good luck with your charity cases, Ro. But don't even think of trying to get me to quit. I like my cancer sticks, thank you very much."

"I know you do." I bit my lip. "I'll find some way to convince you though. Don't worry."

"Oh, I do worry. Believe me. Hey, speaking of mochi." I pressed the Bluetooth to my ear in a vain attempt to keep up with Kyoko's split-second subject changes. "A lot of elderly Japanese people choke on mochi every year and die. The rice is pounded so densely that the mochi balls are hard to chew and easy to swallow. And curiously enough, they fit exactly the size and shape of a human windpipe."

I felt ill. "Maybe we shouldn't serve mochi at the wedding after all."

"Did you know that a woman once saved her husband from choking on mochi by shoving a vacuum-cleaner hose down his throat?" Kyoko rattled on, as if she hadn't heard. "AP. Go through the archives."

"So where are you going now anyway?" She switched subjects again, probably trying to catch me off guard. "Your car's fixed. You've got no business prowling around town doing anything else after this, so you'd better be heading home. Hear me?"

"Take it easy. I've just got to—"

"Got to nothing! Do you have the throwing star in your purse? If you don't, you're in big trouble." Kyoko's tone turned as sharp as one of those sparkling razor edges.

"It's in there." I adjusted my sunglasses in annoyance. "Simply because I haven't had time to think of a hiding place Christie won't find at Faye's. She ate Earl's entire stash of Kit Kats, you know? I told you we went to the vet this morning."

"Wait, isn't chocolate toxic for dogs?"

"I'm surprised at you. Are you getting soft toward animals?" I stuck the Bluetooth deeper in my ear.

"Please," she snorted. "I don't care, really. The chocolate thing's simply scientific fact. Anyway, she'll like the box I sent then, with your old apartment stuff from Tokyo. I threw in some cucumber-flavored Kit Kats."

"Cucumber?" I howled.

"That's Japan for you. Always messing with the flavors. It was either cucumber or banana, and banana seemed so. . .normal."

I rolled my eyes. "Well, the scientific fact is that Christie's fine because apparently Kit Kats don't contain that much actual chocolate. We had her last vet checkup an hour ago. I did feel pretty terrible, though, when I found all the empty wrappers." My smile faded as I recalled my worried face as I rushed Christie to the vet in tears, patting her fuzzy head in the passenger's seat. "I guess I'm not so good at keeping things alive."

That was pretty true, actually. I'd let Mom's rose garden dry out last year, although Adam—by some miracle—had managed to save it. His bonsai tree wasn't so lucky though. Even though I'd taken it to Faye's and prodded it with fertilizer and filtered water, I found it dead three days ago. A mass of wrinkled leaves. I'd bawled like a baby.

"Hmmph." Kyoko sniffed. "I'll be happy if you just keep yourself alive. And you still haven't told me where you're going before Faye's. And it better not be to run. I swear, Ro, you'd give the longest suffering priest a heart attack."

The sun disappeared in a wash of darker clouds, and the humid, rain-heavy air felt like a stifling blanket. Two heavy drops splattered on the windshield.

"I'm running on Faye's treadmill, okay? And I'm just going to the post office to pick up the box you sent with my old apartment stuff. And now some garishly flavored Kit Kats, too, apparently."

Kyoko let out a long breath. "Fine. I'll give you permission this time. But don't push it."

I chuckled as I came under the railroad overpass, driving by a giant metal flower-pot display with zinnias spilling out in all colors. A patch of carmine impatiens peeked from a planter—reminding me of red roses.

I took a deep breath and turned away from the flowers. "There's one more thing I should tell you though, Kyoko."

"Oh great. Here it comes." She let out a groan. "More Odysseus stuff, right? I'd like to strap that guy to a moving truck."

"That makes two of us." I gently pushed Christie's head back as she tried to nose her way onto my lap. "So here it is: the police found my purse that got snatched."

"Well, that's good news, isn't it?"

"Yes and no." I pushed Christie's bottom back on the seat again, more firmly this time, and navigated through the hilly, narrow, one-way streets. Stuart Hall, the preppy girl's school, slid by on my left. "The good news is that everything's inside—even my spare change. All my cards. A woman found my purse in a trash can about two miles from Waynesboro Elementary."

I winced, picturing my beautiful Kate Spade jammed up against somebody's wrinkled orange peels and cigarette butts. Its handle sliced when the guy ripped it off my arm.

"But."

Kyoko moaned. "I knew there was a but!"

"Just hear me out, okay? The weird thing is that somebody apparently left a gift in one of the pockets."

"A gift. For you."

"Possibly."

"What, mochi? A table runner?" Kyoko sounded exasperated— and if I judged her tone correctly, a little bit weary. After all, worrying (an action somewhat akin to dreaded affection) taxed her reserves.

"A paper *sensu*."

Kyoko fell silent.

"You still there?" I jiggled the Bluetooth.

"Sure, I'm here. I'm waiting for the punch line."

"There's no punch line, Kyoko. That's it. Somebody stuck a little white paper folding Japanese fan with a ribbon on the handle in one of the pockets."

Light rain spattered, and I turned on my windshield wipers. They made knife-like movements across my windshield, whisper-like.

"A sensu. The kind people give for gifts." Kyoko cleared her throat sharply. "Ahem. *Wedding* gifts."

"Right." I hunched my shoulders nervously as Christie, blissfully undisturbed by our conversation, poked a smiling, toothy snout out the crack in the window.

"They found the sensu in your purse."

"Yeah."

"And you didn't put it there and—let me guess—have never seen it before. And no fingerprints."

"Exactly. No fingerprints. Just like all the other letters and cards. How'd you know?"

Kyoko sighed. "I just figured it'd be something ridiculous like that, knowing you. So what's this supposed to mean? That your mugger thought you needed a cool-down in the summer heat?"

"I. . .I don't know." I lifted my shoulder in a nervous shrug. "I just thought it was strange."

"You think?" Kyoko's voice turned to steel. "I don't know how to say this, Ro, but there was a really gory case in South Korea a few weeks ago where this guy showed up at his ex-wife's house with a traditional wedding robe and a very, very sharp—"

"Kyoko!" I shook my head vigorously, flipping off my wipers as the drizzle subsided. "No more talk about murder, okay? I just wanted to tell you. In case you remember some strange Japanese significance about paper fans that I don't."

"Besides the wedding thing, no. Did he write anything on it?"

"*Tenshi.* Angel. In some kind of drippy kanji with an ink brush. He did a pretty good job, actually."

Kyoko grunted. "The angel thing again. Have I mentioned before that angels, since they're supposedly part of the supernatural afterlife, usually symbolize death? Or in some cases—"

I cut her off. "You've mentioned it."

"Fine. Remember that," she growled. "So our mugger knows something about Japanese culture then."

"Or thinks he does. The brush strokes for the kanji were good, but you can tell the stroke order's wrong."

"So he'd copied the kanji rather than drawing it himself from rote. Dead giveaway of a *gaijin* foreigner trying to pass himself off as a Japan-ophile."

Kyoko fell silent a long time, and I tried in vain to turn her attention to other topics. Until she gave a loud gasp.

"What?" I jumped. "Don't do that. You're scaring me."

"What color ribbon did he tie on the sensu?"

Dread pooled in my stomach like noxious water. "Why?"

"Just tell me. It wasn't red, was it?"

Ohhhhh boy. I inhaled a long, shuddering breath. "Yes. Does that mean something? I know red has to do with love in Japan, but it's a bit obscure."

"Oh no. It's far more than simple love, Ro." Kyoko's voice sounded ominous, like the thicker bank of dark clouds brooding in the eastern sky. "In old Japan, red ribbons meant connectedness—destiny—two souls meant to be together. Similar to the Chinese idea of a 'red string of fate.' No matter where the two go, the string cannot be broken."

—⁓—

I said good-bye to Kyoko and drove toward the familiar little brick post office in Churchville, its American flag quivering in a dull, humid breeze as if trying to rouse itself from sleep. Then I parked between two vans in a side lot of a hardware store to be safe, keeping Faye's Escort out of sight.

I clacked my way across the post office parking lot in my boots, Kyoko's words about red ribbons ringing in my ears, and tied Christie in a rain-free overhang—just long enough to retrieve my precious box of apartment stuff. All covered with Japanese customs forms and clear ribbons of tape.

"Here ya go." Sandra the postal worker hefted it onto the counter as I pushed back my sunglasses, inhaling sweet post office scents of stamp glue, cardboard, and inky stamp pads. A hefty woman to my left counted out change for a roll of stamps, taking her time. "What'd they send ya, bowling balls?"

"With Kyoko, that's entirely possible."

I'd just thanked Sandra, shouldering my box and preparing to push open the glass door, when she waved me back. "I think we got an overnight for ya, too, Shiloh. Hold on a sec."

"Already?" My heart leaped. "From California, maybe?"

"That's the one. It come this mornin'."

Sandra rummaged in the back until she found the thick padded envelope, and she pushed it across the counter toward me. "Here ya go. Have a good'n."

She slapped the counter in her friendly way and turned to help Stamp Woman, who was fretting over a missing nickel, turning her coin purse inside out. But I just stood there, savoring the final missing piece of my wedding dress tucked in thick paper. Afraid to open the envelope and yet straining to hold the silk in my fingers. Feel the heft and turn it in the light.

I set my Japan box on the counter and ripped open the envelope tabs, fingers shaking. Removed the thick layers of tissue paper. And pulled out a gorgeous stream of scarlet, which puddled in my hands like water. Soft as petals. Delicately embroidered. I wrapped it around my waist with a whispering sound, the long ends rippling down, weightless, like water.

"It's perfect," I breathed, turning the silk in the light to see it shine.

"You gonna wear that?"

I glanced up to see Sandra quirking an eyebrow at me. The bell on the door tinkled another customer's entrance, and I straightened up, embarrassed. "Oh. Sorry. It's for my wedding dress."

That sounded even more stupid. But before I could correct myself, the next customer stepped around us and up to the far side of the counter, dirty baseball cap pulled low over his eyes. Hands nervously clenching and unclenching. Face obscured as the woman finally pushed a triumphant nickel across the counter.

"Package for Townshend," the man mumbled. "J. B. Townshend."

—⁂—

My heart leaped into my throat, and I nearly dropped the silk. My fingers turned clammy as I dropped my sunglasses over my eyes and eased backward, straining to see his face. But he'd turned away, picking at his nails with his keys. Shoulders hunched.

Stamp Woman took her goods and scooted outside in a cloud of bad perfume, and suddenly all that separated me and Jim Bob Townshend, former fiancé of Amanda Cummings and possible killer, was one measly cardboard box covered in customs labels.

No, two—as Sandra, like I was seeing double, pushed a nearly identical box onto the counter. Wrapped in customs forms just like mine.

I reached for my box, palms sweaty, just as he reached for his. And at that exact moment, a wail of police sirens wafted from down the street, making us all turn.

Jim Bob muttered something under his breath and scrambled for his box, eyes fixed on the street through the blind-slatted window. He careened into me as I whipped around, box in my arms. Jolting my sunglasses loose and knocking my packages and purse onto the floor. Tissue paper and red silk spilled across my cowboy boots.

He never glanced my way. Never apologized. Just scooped up his box and threw open the glass door then bolted toward the parking lot. Jerking his head over his shoulder toward the sound of sirens and barreling toward his car.

A silver-gray Taurus with a plastic-covered, broken back window.

Before I could say another word, he'd already squealed out of the parking space and toward the exit in one overanxious swerve. Face turned away from me. Careening away from the police sirens at top speed, lurching over a curb.

Sandra and I stared openmouthed in the direction he'd gone.

"Was that. . .Jim Bob Townshend?" I finally managed, putting my sunglasses back on my hair and bending to pick up my stuff.

"Dunno. I ain't never met him. Heard he's been in town though."

She shook her head. "Rude fella, ain't he?"

"And acts like he's nervous or guilty. Running off from the police like that." I hefted my box back up onto the counter and stooped to retrieve errant tissue paper.

Sandra started to turn away then stopped with a start. "Shiloh? Lands, this ain't yer box!"

"What?" I froze, hand in midreach for the tissue paper.

"This'n's that Townshend guy's. He musta took yer box by mistake."

I scrambled to my feet and grabbed the box, flipping it around to read the label: *J. B. Townshend.* From a Toyota shipping center. I let out a cry of frustration. "He can't take my box! I need it!" My hands clenched into fists. "Mom's letters!"

"Well, he did." Sandra ran the computer surveillance videos and shook her head. "See here? He just heard them cops and took off. But I'm shore he'll bring it back when he sees the address."

"Not if he reads Mom's letters."

I stalked back out with my sloppily stuffed envelope, shaking with anger and my near brush with Jim Bob Townshend. I unclipped Christie and helped her into the Escort then climbed in and locked the door behind me. Pushing back her exuberant wet snout.

"It's just silk, Christie," I said, crabby, as she nosed her way back, sniffing at the envelope. I stuffed everything back in, but not before she'd snatched a piece of tissue paper.

"Give me that." I grabbed most of it back. "And quit sniffing. You're not a police dog, and there's nothing in here but silk."

Although Kyoko had sent the package. Cucumber-flavored Kit Kats were the least of my worries.

I jabbed the keys into the ignition in frustration and then stopped when my cell phone jingled. I dug it from my purse. "Meg?" I answered stonily, too cranky for conversation.

"I saw him! I saw him!" Meg was shouting. So loudly I nearly flung the phone across the car.

"Calm down!" I hollered back, mashing down the VOLUME button. "Saw who?"

"Jim Bob Townshend."

My other hand froze on the envelope. "You saw him, too? Where is he?"

"He's here, Jacobs! In Staunton, headed away from Churchville on Route 254 at crazy speeds. Cooter's with me, and he swears it's him.

He remembers him from shop class. And he's driving that same old Taurus, but now there's a tarp taped over one of his back windows."

"I'm in Churchville." I tried to keep my breath steady, whirling around to retrieve a shred of tissue paper from Christie's mouth. "Did you get his license-plate number?"

"No. We tried to, but his plate's kinda smudged. I can send you some photos of the back of his head, but they're blurry." Great. Like the back of somebody's head would help—unless he had a Confederate flag or something tattooed there. I wiped sticky fingers slimed with dog slobber and tissue paper on the towel covering the passenger's seat. Then I pried open Christie's mouth and dug around her tongue and teeth to make sure she hadn't hidden any more paper slivers.

This dog, if I didn't accidentally poison her with Kit Kats first, was going to drive me nuts.

Meg let out a bitter cry as I released Christie's tissue-paper-free mouth and scrubbed my fingers on the towel again. "I'm sure it's Jim Bob. And you won't believe what he's got in his car."

"What?" My heart raced.

"Copper tubing. We stopped at a red light right behind him, and you can see it in the back."

I jerked my head back in surprise. *Copper shavings. On the ground at the Waynesboro Elementary School.*

"Something else," Meg spoke again. "Remember that Dean guy you were curious about? The one at the florist? His last name's Papadakis."

I let her words sink in, feeling my insides shift. "Greek. Like the Odysseus character in Homer's book." I tipped my head. "So how do you know all this stuff?"

"Cooter taught shop at Buffalo Gap, remember?"

"The high school?"

"Yep. He's got three fingers on his left hand, like an extraordinary percentage of shop teachers. Know why? He had this buzz saw, see, and—"

"Focus, Meg!" I shouted, mad. "Tell me what Cooter knows about Jim Bob!"

"Oh. . .right. Well, teachers catch more of the local gossip than you'd think, especially in a cow town like this. Free entertainment, ya know? Why, Cooter knew this one gal back in the day who. . ." As much as I loved Meg, sometimes I felt like shaking her till her teeth rattled. "Wait. We were talking about Jim Bob, right? Okay, guess who was Jim Bob's best friend during all his growing-up years?"

"Amanda?" It came out shaky.

"No, actually. But close. Dean Papadakis. And. . .drum roll please. . . Deputy Shane Pendergrass."

"What?" I hollered.

"You got it. All three of them hung out together, pulling pranks, reading poetry, and trying to pick up chicks. They called themselves the 'Dead Poets Gone Bad,' or something equally ridiculous. Dean and Jim Bob were especially tight, except for a brief falling out over a girl in high school. Guess who?"

I squeezed my eyes shut. "This is too much, Meg."

"Uh-huh. Amanda."

The phone wavered in my hand, but Meg didn't stop. "Hang on, Jacobs. It gets better—or worse, however you want to take it. We were wrong. Cooter says Amanda *was* Japanese."

"Sorry?" I shook my head, which felt ready to overflow with too much information. Christie licked my chin in response, nuzzling my neck. My wet bangs stuck to my forehead and cheekbone where she'd slobbered.

"We got it backward. Amanda was Kate Townshend's *biological* granddaughter—her genetics just favored her dad's side of the family. Jim Bob was the relative by marriage. And no, Amanda and Jim Bob weren't blood related. In case you're curious."

"So Jim Bob might have known a thing or two about Japanese culture then from Amanda."

"Almost certainly. Cooter says they exchanged paper fans for their engagement since they couldn't afford rings."

"You're kidding." I could barely move my lips.

"Nope."

"They tied red ribbons to the handles of the fans, didn't they?"

"Yeah." Meg silenced then began to sputter. "Hey! How'd you know?"

A cold coil of dread and adrenaline-pricked urgency tangled together in my insides, making my skin tingle. "Where did you say Jim Bob's headed?"

"Away from Churchville, but he took a side road like he's going to circle back. Probably headed to Goshen again to see his dad. We followed him as far as that big barn by the BP station, and then a chicken truck cut us off. Feathers everywhere. We're going two miles an hour."

Meg heaved a bitter sigh. "Our case against Jim Bob so far is circumstantial, and the cops are gonna let him squeak out of here without so much as a parking ticket if we don't come up with some evidence against him. And I mean *hard* evidence."

"Especially if Shane's covering his sorry tail." I gritted my teeth.

"Exactly. We don't even know if you recognize him. If you did, that could explain a lot of things."

I jerked my keys into the ignition and swerved out of my parking space, picturing an Augusta County map in my head. And the closest route Jim Bob might take to Goshen. Then I pushed the accelerator through Churchville, hoping to cut Jim Bob off at the intersection and catch his license-plate number. And hopefully get a glimpse of his face when he pulled out onto the main road.

I passed a little fender bender and the police squad car that had caused Jim Bob's panic and zoomed away from the tiny town limits and farther out into the county. Down winding, two-lane roads, past endless green fields and farmhouses, until I came to the intersection I figured Jim Bob would use.

And sure enough: a graphite-silver Ford Taurus, easing out of the side road and pointed toward Goshen.

AHEAD OF ME. And too far away for me to catch a glimpse of his face. I was a minute too late. An old pickup pulled in between us from a farm road, its bed packed with construction supplies, and I stomped on the brake. Which cut off my view of his license plate.

"Noooo!" I gave a cry of frustration, banging my steering wheel. Then I flicked on my turn signal to pull into a driveway and turn around.

Jim Bob 2, Shiloh 0.

I buried my face in my hands, thinking of my precious Japan package that might hold Mom's letters. Jim Bob's grubby hands as he grabbed my box without looking back, dumping my silk on the dirty post office floor.

"The police need hard evidence," Meg had said.

If I didn't do something now, the only hard evidence the police might find was. . .well, *me*. Or my face on the back of a milk carton.

Out of the corner of my eye I spotted my reporter's notebook poking out of my bag where I'd tossed it all on the floorboard. *My tape recorders tucked inside.*

All at once I turned off my turn signal and punched the gas, pulling my sunglasses down over my eyes.

—⁓—

A light rain began to fall as Jim Bob's Taurus zipped through wooded mountain roads ahead of me, just past Buffalo Gap. Making a beeline through dusty little towns like Augusta Springs and Craigsville.

Heading straight toward Goshen as Meg predicted.

The roads grew curvier and less posted, with thick stands of forest and pastureland interspersed with railroad tracks, rickety-looking double-wide trailers parked in gardens of spinning lawn statuary and windmills, and rumbly jacked-up trucks plastered with faded Confederate flags.

Adam's going to have my head for this! I nibbled nervously on a nail, wondering if I should call him all the way in Stuarts Draft and interrupt his training seminar—or better yet, turn around and get my Yankee tail out of Dodge. Or wherever the flip I was.

But when I thought of Mom's high blood pressure and the aneurysm that eventually took her life, my pulse burned. I stepped on the gas, half wishing Jim Bob would stop the car so I could get out and scream at him. And maybe bang him over the head with one of those copper tubes.

The rain increased as the road began to slope upward, winding through forest that thickened with each serpentine turn of the gaunt asphalt. Dilapidated log cabins flashed between stands of ancient hickories and pines, some sporting old-style multiple structures with separate smokehouses and kitchens. Thin lines of smoke rose from ancient chimneys. It felt eerie, watching time turn backward, like encountering Tim on my front porch last year in his gray Civil War battle reenactment uniform.

When Jim Bob's car turned onto an unmarked dirt path, kicking up sloshes of muddy water, I hesitated. But through the trees I saw a rough cabin, and the taillights abruptly vanished. I pulled off the road and into a little thicket of pines. I stiffened as Faye's Escort, which had probably never been used as an off-road vehicle, inched down a muddy ditch, scraping slightly on the underside. My jaw jolted with a bump, and I eased between two tall pines. Wet branches pulled along the windows, lightly scraping the glass.

I cut the engine and whispered for Christie to stay. Drops pattered on the windshield, breaking the sudden, thick silence.

"Don't bark, okay? Don't do anything. Just stay," I ordered, pulling on my jean jacket. "I'll be back in a second."

I patted her head then eased the car door open and climbed out. Closing the door behind me with a catch of my breath. Christie watched, her furry face pressed up to the rain-spattered window and pointy ears pricked, as I slipped through wet, leafy shrubs and twigs in a dull roar of rain. The boots were heavier than I expected; I had to crouch and sort of hop, trying not to make too much noise.

I crept closer to a leaky, old, thatched-roof log cabin with sorry-looking chickens rooting and scratching under a gnarled old tree. A grizzled hound, probably deaf with age, lay stretched across the front porch in openmouthed sleep. Forest surrounded us on all sides, as far as I could see. No power lines. A crumbly brick chimney smoked like a sullen old man with a corncob pipe, and the front porch sagged.

A closed wooden shed loomed behind the cabin, and in front of the double shed doors sat the oldest, most rusted pickup I'd ever seen. Both headlights out. Bumper falling off in pieces. Its dented hood yawned partially open, propped up with a section of crooked tree limb.

The Taurus engine revved loudly, and I jerked my eyes back to the front of the cabin.

Jim Bob's sedan had sunk into a patch of mud, and he pushed the gas several times, trying to back up. But his right wheel sank deeper in a muddy groove, and dirty water spun. A sharp *clunk*, and he cut the engine.

I waited, peeking through the leaves, as Jim Bob got out of the car and bent toward the right tire, crouching and muttering under his breath. Tall and strong, with a thick build. *And a stiff right hand.*

He pushed against the front of the car with his left arm, his face obscured by the baseball cap plus a curve of the hood and windshield. He finally got back in the car and revved the gas again. Door slightly ajar.

Nothing about his gait or manner struck me as familiar. I sniffed the rain-laden wind, smelling smoke and damp woods. And an odd perfume that reminded me, with uncanny accuracy, of the heavy rose fragrance of Odysseus's bouquets.

I pushed my way through a patch of wet saplings on my hands and knees, trying to get a better view.

And there, planted all around the front steps, stood a thick smear of gorgeous rose bushes—their intense color visible even through the rain. The most beautiful dark red I'd ever seen.

Exactly the deep, velvety shade of ruby that I remembered from every single bouquet Odysseus had sent to my office.

—◊◊—

Thunder rumbled in the distance, a terrible sound, as Jim Bob swung open the squeaky door to his Taurus and got out again, digging in the back of his car for something. I strained to see him from my vantage point—sassafras twigs poking me in the side and a leafy vine wrapped around my bare shin. What did Tim say about poison ivy? "Leaves of three, let them be"? Or was it, "Leaves of three, a friend of thee?" All those Southernisms about coral snakes and storm clouds ran together in my head.

I'd probably be bleaching myself for a month from chiggers, too.

I pulled a toothy wild briar from my dress, hoping Jim Bob would hurry up and show his face. My wet hair plastered to my neck and ears, arms tightly wrapped to keep myself from shivering.

Jim Bob reached suddenly for his baseball cap and shook it off, revealing a close-buzzed head and large, shiny forehead. He plopped the cap back on his head and slammed the car door shut. Not bothering to lock the car, like so many trusting Southerners. Then without warning he whirled around—staring RIGHT in my direction.

I ducked my head behind a thick poplar. Not daring to move a muscle. A twig snapped under my boot, and I sucked in my breath. Praying, praying for God to protect me in spite of my obvious brash stupidity.

Chapter 28

When I peeked again, I saw Jim Bob's face. I blinked back raindrops, confused.

Never, in all my life, had I met Jim Bob Townshend. Not once. I held back my shivering and leaned closer through the rain-wet leaves, trying to unroll the years and imagine him a little younger, a little chubbier, or with slightly more hair. But not a single feature on his face brought back any memories. A large, blunt nose with a slight downward crook. Thin lips. A curved jaw and dark eyes framed by darker brows.

None of which brought back the slightest recollection.

But then again, Meg had warned me—stalkers could be total strangers. Most of which probably weren't playing with a full deck.

Jim Bob took a step toward me then turned back at a slight scratching sound on the porch. The hound on the porch reluctantly roused itself, scrambling stiffly to its feet, license tags jingling. Jim Bob patted it clumsily on the head and then knocked on the cabin door, the dog limping along after him.

"Pa?" Jim Bob called, rapping again with his knuckles. His *left-*hand knuckles, I noted. "Y'all right?"

His accent pitched so thickly I could barely make out the words. I crawled a few paces forward through wet leaves, teeth chattering, to hear better and then stuck my tape recorder through a gap in the trees. Praying it would pick up Jim Bob's voice.

He put his hands up. "Don't shoot! It's me. Jim Bob. I got 'em. But my axle's broke again. I'll have to fix it 'fore I git your truck started. Mebbe t'morrow."

The door opened just a crack, and the dog snaked inside, tail bobbing. Jim Bob put his hands down. "Doggone rain. You shore y'all right, Pa?"

And he disappeared inside, shutting the door behind him.

I waited there in the rain a few minutes then slipped over to the Taurus in the mud. Mincing my way through puddles. I grabbed a leaf and wiped some mud off the license plate—a Texas license plate, not the West Virginia plates I'd imagined—and scrubbed at the numbers. Jotting them down in my reporter's notebook.

Then I leaned closer, picking at a corner of something at the metal corner of the plate.

Well, what do you know. A fake plate. A reflective sticker of some sort with neatly printed decals to match. All covered with a grimy film of dirt and exhaust that actually made it look pretty realistic.

No wonder Jim Bob sprinted out of the post office at the first sound of police sirens.

I picked a spot away from the dark windows of the cabin and shakily straightened up, circling my eyes with my hands to keep the rain out as I leaned toward the back window. Trying to make out the shadowy shapes in the dusty seat.

Wrenches everywhere. A spare tire. Nuts and bolts, and a metal toolbox. A tire jack and old slide hammer. A fluke meter for checking electrical voltage. All mingled with a bunch of cables and auto parts.

Mechanic's tools. Including the copper tubing, which Jim Bob could easily work into auto parts to fix his dad's truck. With his *left* hand, after years at relearning his trade without the use of his right. Leaving tiny, nearly indiscernible shavings clinging to his shirt and in the folds of his pants.

My breath frosted the glass, and I slipped closer to make it out: the square shape of a cardboard box on the backseat, all covered in customs labels.

I reached through the crinkly plastic tarp, peeling it away from the broken glass, and reached for my box. I eased it through the window opening and backed away. Then I ducked and clomped my way back into the woods at a fast clip and raced toward Faye's car.

—⁂—

My cell phone didn't pick up a signal as I drove down the mountain in the rain and thunder, passing trailers and double-wides of all sorts huddled in the trees. Trucks with monster tires and crooked mailboxes illuminated by pulses of blue-white lightning. My soaked dress clung to my skin, muddied in large patches, and my wet ponytail hung in messy strands.

I wended my way through small towns on my way back to Staunton, rain lashing the Escort in noisy waves. My windshield wipers pumped at top speed, clearing a small space so I could see the asphalt. A skin of raindrop-pocked water danced across the surface of the road, flood-like.

As I inched around wet curves toward Faye's, I saw it in the distance: a fallen tree stretched across the road in a heap of leaves. Lightning, probably. Splintered limbs and chunks of trunk splattered across the bend in an ugly, traffic-stopping mess. Taillights from stopped cars in front of me glowed against the shiny asphalt, reflected in scarlet beads on my windshield.

I tried my phone again with no luck then turned the car around in a patch of sodden embankment and headed back toward Churchville to wait out the storm. The rain heaved, and I followed the road home by memory. Past lonely Buffalo Gap High School surrounded by cow pastures. Past the little country church and then left into Crawford Manor, nestled at the blue-gray base of Crawford Mountain.

I started to turn into Mom's familiar gravel driveway then thought better of it—in the off chance that someone tried to follow me—and pulled instead into Stella's shrubby driveway. Broken leaves and puddles littered the gravel. Her house stood dark and silent, the porch light still shining from when she'd left the house in the early morning.

I hid Faye's Escort behind Stella's yellow school bus and thick stands of butterfly bushes and grabbed my precious cardboard box. Then I opened the car door for Christie and threw my jacket over my head, racing together through the lightning flashes for Mom's house.

I hastily locked the door behind me and tried Adam again on my cell phone, dropping my damp jacket and shaking the water from my hair and dress. Leaving those horrid muddy boots at the door.

Adam's voice mail picked up, and I left a message for him and then for Faye before the signal went down again. I finally clicked the phone off and tossed it in a kitchen chair. Probably most of the county would have trouble getting signals in this storm.

I toweled off Christie's wet paws and legs to keep her from dirtying the floor then walked barefoot through the empty kitchen to Mom's old guest bedroom. The room I'd called my own for nearly a year. Now most of my photos, books, and colorful Japanese wall hangings lay in taped, labeled cardboard boxes for the move. My movements echoed against the bare walls and floors in an unfamiliar rattle, and I felt—for the first time since my early days in Virginia—like a stranger in Mom's house.

The bookshelves had been emptied. Extra towels and sheets boxed up. Curtains taken down in the library and her bedroom, leaving stark white blinds.

I undid my messy ponytail and shook my wet hair loose then peeled off my filthy dress. Threw on a dry pair of jeans and striped T-shirt from one of the boxes. Layered on a soft gray cardigan. I stepped into socks and, since my Japanese house slippers were over at Faye's, a pair of cheap sneakers I'd picked up at Payless to replace the tennis shoes I'd practically ruined with cow poo that night in the pasture.

I made a cup of hot green tea, warming the chilly kitchen, and pushed the blinking answering machine button while I rinsed out the pot. Flipping past so many hang ups that my finger hurt as I deleted them.

Until I heard Ashley's voice. I paused, letting the message play.

"Shiloh? Hey. It's Ashley. Got some news for you! You probably won't like it, but just hear me out, okay?"

Her voice sounded too cheerful. Too shrill. I paused, water dripping off the pot in my hand.

"Well, there's this cute baby contest on the weekend of your wedding, and I think Carson can win. He's adorable, you know? So. . .sorry I won't be there. Oh, and the bridesmaids' dresses. . . uh. . .well, I've been busy getting Carson registered for the contest, so. . .maybe you should buy them somewhere else, okay? Sorry."

I swatted the answering machine button off as the rain roared outside. Perfect. All I needed was Ashley bailing on me now—and leaving one of the groomsmen without a partner. And two bridesmaids without dresses. Those dresses were gone now from the catalog along with pretty much everything else we liked. The last catalog I saw showed winter fashions already—and how absurd would August bridesmaids look in long-sleeved velvet?

We'd have to start all over again.

I sighed and bent over the counter, rubbing my weary face in both hands.

But there was no time for fuming. Not with Jim Bob on the loose and all my hard evidence consisting of inaudible tape recordings of small talk and a fake license-plate number.

So I plopped down on the living room sofa with my cardboard box, Christie coiled in a damp, spike-haired heap around my feet.

I cut through the heavy packing tape, hoping that if nothing else he'd left a few fingerprints on my box that might match something on one of Odysseus's notes or photos, and I pulled the box flaps open. I sorted through packing peanuts, old AP forms and documents, reporter's notebooks, weird-smelling Kit Kats, and a random freeze-dried octopus Kyoko'd obviously tossed in there for fun.

And then I drew them out: three unopened envelopes addressed to my Tokyo apartment, lettered in Mom's familiar blue ink handwriting.

My heartbeat quickened as I spread the letters carefully on the sofa in order by date, savoring the moment as rain drummed on the porch and rattled in the gutter. A final word from Mom—and perhaps the last I'd ever hear this side of heaven. Thick mist huddled outside my darkened windows, making the yellow light of the room feel cozy and warm.

I opened the first envelope, withdrawing three sheets of blue lines. And I curled up against the soft curves of the sofa and began to read.

    It all started at the mechanic's shop on Greenville Avenue. It seemed harmless at first—a glance over the counter at one of your photos I'd printed off the Internet and carried in my wallet. A simple shot with your hair pulled back and your eyes bright.

    "Who is she?" the young man asked, bending over to see better.

    "My daughter. She's beautiful, isn't she?"

    "Gorgeous." And he reluctantly handed back your photo, asking for your name.

    I hesitated, not wanting to give away too much of your personal information. "Shiloh," I finally responded when he prodded me again with a little more enthusiasm. "And that's all you need to know."

    I gave him a warning look and tucked your photo out of sight, and he laughed, making me laugh, too—the overzealous young admirer versus the overprotective mom. The stuff of comic shows and jokes.

    "Does she live here?" he asked.

    "No. But I'm sure she'll come visit me soon."

Jennifer Rogers Spinola

*He waved good-bye, and I left the shop, relaxed and at
ease. My transmission running smoothly. And I thought no more
about it.*

*Until all the phone calls began. The letters. The roses. My
life in upheaval, and my heart in my throat at every turn. And
now I have begun to fear for your life—and mine.*

My green tea grew cold while I read, devouring each word like
morsels of the last Japanese mochi rice cake I would ever taste—
savoring its color and texture and flavor against my tongue. Mom's
words. Her life. Her threads of sentences, weaving patterns of her
memories and thoughts, by some miracle falling fresh on my heart
more than a year after she'd gone Home.

*And so I kept the letters for you—nearly all of them. I've
stored them in my guitar case. Inside the lining. So if he comes
looking, by some chance, he won't find them.*

I leaped up from the sofa and raced to the bedroom, where Mom's
padded guitar case leaned, closed and zipped, against a pile of boxes.
I felt around the black curves, looking for an opening of some kind.
And sure enough, a subtle slit in the bottom seam.

I pushed my fingers through and felt paper. Thick paper,
folded. And withdrew a handful of cards and letters sporting hand-
drawn paintings and drawings. My multicolored eye. Japanese kanji
characters. Fat envelopes addressed to "My angel love," decorated with
broken hearts and flattened from more than a year of being pressed
against the rigid guitar case. And as I tipped the first one, out poured
a cascade of dried, dark red rose petals.

My cell phone rang, startling me, and I dropped Mom's letter on the
kitchen table. Still puzzling over her lines about the drawing she'd
made.

*I saw him once, I think, she'd written. Only once. And I
stayed up all night, trying desperately to sketch his face. I didn't
draw it very well, I'm afraid. But the strangest thing is that it
looks nothing like the young man in the auto shop. Perhaps he's
sent someone else to find you?*

*At any rate, the drawing unnerved me so much I destroyed
it. Not well, perhaps, but at least after that I could sleep again.*

I stepped over sleeping Christie for my cell phone. "Hello?"

"Shiloh Jacobs." Adam's voice, loud and angry, rattled in the
empty kitchen. "What on earth are you doing at your mom's house?
I've been worried sick about you! The roads are a mess, and I couldn't
get a cell signal to save my life until just now. I'm still in Stuarts Draft.
Where have you been?"

"I've been here for the past two hours or so, Adam," I answered a
bit defensively. "I called as soon as I could get a connection."

"You were supposed to go to the vet, the post office, and straight
back to Faye's. Why didn't you do that?"

I opened my mouth to protest, hit by two emotions at the same
time: (1) guilt that, no, I hadn't called Adam before my flight to
Goshen and (2) indignation that he expected me to meekly hand over
my schedule like an incompetent weakling.

"Jim Bob Townshend grabbed my box by mistake at the post
office," I sputtered, temper flaring. "And I wanted to see if I recognized
him. I'm fine, okay? And I got my box back."

"You what?" Adam hollered. "You went after him?"

I blew out an angry sigh, stiffening. "Listen, you don't have to
worry about me, okay? I'm old enough to know what I'm doing. Older
than you, actually. I'm not a kid you can't trust."

"It's not you I don't trust, Shiloh! It's him!"

"Well, Jim Bob isn't going anywhere. His car's broken down. I'll
drive back to Faye's as soon as the rain lets up and tell everything to
the police."

"What if the stalker's not Jim Bob? As a matter of fact, I don't
think it's him. And if you'd asked me before you went after him, I'd
have told you why." Adam's voice heated.

"Of course it's him! He's got a perfect motive for hating Ray
Floyd—and Amanda, too, for dumping him for Ray. Mom said herself
in her letter that he asked about me years ago."

"You're forgetting something."

"I'm not forgetting anything!" I raised my voice, on the verge of
tears. Less than a month before my wedding, and here I stood, arguing
with my fiancé in the house where we'd sat outside in fragrant nightfall
talking about life and family.

"Oh yes you are. Those paintings are meticulous. Detailed. Tiny. Jim Bob can change fan belts, but I don't believe he could paint like that with his left hand. And besides—you said the guy who mugged you had hair and used his right hand."

"But. . .but. . ."

"The requests to the florist weren't mailed, Shiloh. They were dropped into the mailbox. Locally. Jim Bob doesn't live here. He just showed up in town over the past few weeks or so."

"Right. When the roses started."

"No. I think if you draw the timing out, you'll see that the roses came first."

A sick sensation oozed into my stomach. I snatched up Mom's letter and reread the part about the sketch. The face that didn't match. I squeezed my eyes closed, trying to make some sense of it.

"But. . .it has to be Jim Bob! Or Dean, then, working as some sort of go-between. I don't know!" I ran both hands through my hair, feeling like pulling it out.

"That's exactly why we need to be working on this together!" Adam snapped into the phone, his tone hard and accusing. "I told you before—if we're going to be married, we have to share everything. No secrets."

"Then you can't flip out when I have a different opinion than you."

"I don't do that!"

"Yes you do! Once your mind is made up, there's no changing it. And that's really hard to work with, you know?"

I heard Adam spit out an angry breath, more furious than I'd ever heard him. But when he spoke again, his voice sounded choked. "Look, maybe I am a bit stubborn with my ideas."

"A bit?" My throat swelled at the raw emotion in his words.

"I grew up that way, always having to put my foot down so I didn't get pushed in directions I didn't want to go. I can. . .you know. Work on that." He blew out a violent sigh. "But I can't live with you keeping things from me. With you. . ."

"With me what?"

"Always going off on your own and doing things yourself. Your own way. You're a competent woman, Shiloh. Amazingly tenacious, and independent, and intelligent. Probably more than me. I admire that. But I can't compete with you."

"Compete with me?" I yelped, hearing my cell phone bleep in my ear to indicate a low battery. Of course. While my charger sat plugged into the wall at Faye's. "Why would you think something like that?"

"Because that's what I feel like I have to do sometimes." His voice quivered slightly. "Like you don't. . .need me. You can do just fine on your own."

A stab of guilt pricked through my heart, all my emotions roiling together in one pounding mess, like the raging rain outside. Lightning flashed through my darkened windows.

And at that exact moment, my lights went out.

Chapter 29

The fridge hum coughed to an eerie silence. The ceiling fan over the kitchen table spun squeaking as it shuddered to a stop.

Everything plunged into darkness. Thunder growled over the mountains, and rain lashed the side of the house. Wind howled around the porch eaves.

"The power's out, Adam. Stay with me, okay?"

I fumbled in the kitchen drawers for a flashlight, wishing I hadn't packed up so much stuff for the move. But with Uncle Bryce coming in just a few weeks, I was already behind. Now Adam and I would probably spend our wedding rehearsal hauling boxes to a moving truck. Good thing UPS gave him plenty of practice.

"Shiloh!" Adam yelled again. I pulled the phone away from my ear.

"I'm fine, Adam! Just stay on the line. Please. The storm will pass."

"You need to get out of there now."

"I know, I know." I jerked open another drawer and felt the cool cylinder of the flashlight. "Hold on. I've got light." I pressed the button, and a warm glow spread across the kitchen, gleaming back from the shiny microwave door and metal lines of the stove. The beam made golden spots on the walls as I focused on the light switch, stepping over Christie to flip it on and off.

"I'm leaving. Right now." I threw all the letters and things into my cardboard box from Japan then hustled Christie to the door. Keys in hand, rain sifting down outside in black sheets. "I'll call you the minute I get to Faye's. I promise."

Christie whined at the door, pawing, while I unlocked it. I pushed open the screen door a crack, and before I could grab her, she'd nosed her way through. She took off like a shot through the rainy evening, leaving me standing there holding the door.

"Argh. The dog." I rolled my head in my hand. "Now I'll have to wait until she comes back."

"She's gone? You let her out?"

"No, she just went! We've been over this before." I sighed, bone weary and wishing I'd never gone on this stupid wild-goose chase with Jim Bob. "But Christie can't stay out long in this mess. She'll be back in a minute, and we'll leave."

And just as I closed the door and locked it, it hit me: Mom's paper shredder. Up in the attic. I'd seen it there when I looked for her transmission warranty, and from what I'd heard of that particular brand of shredder, it was a piece of junk.

If she'd destroyed her drawing of Odysseus in the middle of the night, with swift but not-so-perfect results, I might've just stumbled on my biggest clue of all.

"You'd better go straight to Faye's," Adam huffed, still mad. "Don't stop your car for anybody. Just get your things and go."

There he went, ordering me around again. I knew he meant well, but it made my skin prickle.

"And make sure you have your ID with you."

"My ID? For what?" I was already pulling down the attic ladder. Still feeling cranky at his bossy-yelling thing. Which, if we were supposed to live together, I'd probably have to put up with—because heaven knows men don't change much after they slap a ring on your finger.

Even Carlos had taught me that. *The cheater.*

"Meet me at the courthouse at 8 a.m. sharp. I think this whole thing has gone far enough."

I froze, my foot on the first rung of the ladder. "To. . .to get married? You're serious?"

No answer. I shook the phone. "Hello? Adam?"

A blank screen stared back at me, its insolent gray rectangle reminding me not so politely that I'd let the battery run out.

"So everything's my fault, as usual." I stuffed my phone in my jeans pocket and climbed up the rough pine stairs to the attic.

I found the paper shredder by the flashlight's glinting beam and carried it down to the kitchen table, holding my light steady as I opened the front of the plastic canister. Spilling thick paper shreds, some still stuck together by the blade's dull edge, onto the kitchen table.

I sorted through them by flashlight, illuminating flashes of brown and white.

Wait a second. I jerked up the slip of paper, which looked like Mom had sketched something in brown marker, and held it up to the light. Then I sorted through the loose wad of paper strips covered with sketch marks.

I started fitting them together, turning them this way and that until the sketch marks matched. Joining them to reveal the lines of a man's heavy jaw, a curve of hair behind his ear. A large, angular face. Long, thin nose.

I leaned closer, sensing something familiar in those full lips and that set of square jaw. Something. . .I'd seen before.

"Wow, Mom, I didn't know you could draw so well," I said aloud, my flashlight beam flickering against the paper strips. Shadows of my hands stretched black fingers across the wrinkles. "You should have minored in art instead of me."

I reached for another strip of nose and eased it into place, working my way up to the eyes. "And you're right. He looks nothing like Jim Bob so far. I'm so confused."

A tremor of ice passed through me as my fingers fit together the lines of his face. The face of a man who'd stalked my mother, gotten me kicked off the crime beat, and ruined my wedding. My hand shook as I reached for the next piece.

I heard something. A soft sound on the side of the house.

"Christie?" I called, dropping the paper slips. I grabbed the flashlight and hurried to the door, pushing back the curtains on the side window. My hand on the doorknob.

But when a flash of lightning illuminated the wooden boards of the deck, it gleamed back empty. No Christie.

Maybe she'd gone to the other door. I marched through the living room and scrunched the sheers aside, straining to see the front porch through the large picture window.

Again, no Christie.

Something thumped against the side of the house, its movement reverberating through the walls. I felt it against my arm, and the window glass rattled slightly.

Without warning, a large shadow fell across the curtains.

A man's shadow. Tall and angular, just a few inches away from me. Separated only by a thin pane of glass.

Chapter 30

I let the sheers fall back together in a silent second. Instinctively I grabbed for the flashlight and switched it off, plunging the house into darkness. But at least I could hide my location and buy a little more time.

The doorknob jiggled as he tried to force it open. Then again with more strength, shaking the door frame. The lock held, and I caught my breath. And then he slipped out of my field of vision, toward Mom's window. Half shrouded by gangly shrubs and a trellis thick with clematis and climbing roses.

Call the police, for pity's sake! Now!

I scrambled to my feet, stumbling over scattered packing peanuts as I hurled myself toward the kitchen. Grabbing the phone in one swift movement. My breath loud in my ears as I dialed.

Too loud. "Where's the dial tone?" I whispered, jiggling the cord.

No response. Just silence. And a peal of thunder that shook the walls of the house.

Of all the lousy luck! Leave it to Shiloh P. Jacobs to shut herself in the house with a madman outside. No cell phone, no landline. And no Christie.

Poor Christie, out in the rain by herself with a maniac. Where was she? If that creep so much as laid a finger on her, I'd bite him in the leg myself.

The shadow reappeared, slipping along the edges of the picture window, and I wondered briefly if he was watching me.

I hung the phone back in the receiver without a sound and dropped to my knees, racking my brain for anything I could use as a weapon. But with everything boxed up, my options were limited. A plastic take-out fork? One of Stella's ugly garden gnomes?

Wait a second. The freezer. I jerked it open and pulled out a hefty leg of venison, plastic-wrapped and hard as a rock. Not that a piece of deer meat would help much if somebody slit the window screen and climbed inside—knife-toting wacko that my stalker had turned out to be.

But it was better than nothing, right?

As if mocking my thoughts, the screen in Mom's bedroom window squeaked as he tried to push it up. And when it groaned in hesitation, I heard the dull crunch of something like clippers or shears cutting through the screen.

I clapped cold fingers over my mouth, freezing in midstep. Those windows opened as easily as a Twinkie wrapper. Once I'd jimmied open my bedroom window with Becky's Blockbuster card when I left my keys at her house.

I eased down the hall toward Mom's room, clutching the venison leg like a baseball bat, but the shadow disappeared. I whirled around, terrified. The only thing worse than a shadow outside my house was a shadow that kept disappearing.

The rain switched directions, spattering against the windows, and the rattling of the window screen abruptly silenced. I took advantage of the pause to crawl back to the table and feel for my cell phone, determined to squeeze every last drop of juice from the battery. Just one call would do it.

At the first push of the button, my cell phone turned on, sending a blue glow into my cupped fingers, and then unceremoniously blinked off.

I unzipped my purse and dug through it frantically in search of my work pager, in hope that I could send a frantic page to Meg or Kevin. I dumped my purse upside down on the table and pawed through it, dropping coins and rumpled tissues and pens. A checked-off wedding planning schedule. Kyoko's throwing star, which wouldn't accomplish a thing through panes of glass. Tubes of lip gloss rolled onto the floor.

I shook out my purse, but no pager. Probably still in the car.

A scrape of rusty metal screen at the far end of the house made me jump, knocking pens and breath mints off the table. I heard my bedroom window screen stick and then suddenly—in one ugly screech—slide up.

Instead of retreating, all my weeks of worrying and checking over my shoulder suddenly boiled in my mind like storm clouds. The spray paint and notes. The worries I wouldn't make it to my wedding. The arguments with Adam over roses, and the fear in Mom's letters.

I wasn't Amanda. *And I wasn't about to disappear.*

I tripped over lipstick and keys littering the linoleum floor on my way to the bedroom, smacking the wooden window frame hard with my leg of frozen meat. Nearly breaking the glass. "Get out of here!" I yelled, raising the venison to swing again—and hoping it made contact with his head.

Spine-chilling laughter shook the glass, and he pushed at the pane again, trying to force it up.

I swung and smashed the window frame again, this time miscalculating and cracking the glass. *Bad idea.*

Laughter again, louder than before—sounding vaguely familiar. But not familiar enough to place. It was maddening, all this ducking and hiding and guessing.

"Get out of here!" I shouted. "My neighbors have probably called the police already!"

"*Never!*" came the muffled shout through fractured glass. And he punched it with something blunt, probably the shears he'd used to cut the screen. A chunk of glass fell onto my bedroom floor, and I jumped back, shielding my eyes from splinters.

In a dull flash of lightning I saw a man's gloved hand appear, and I swung again with my trusty leg of venison, trying to keep a grip on the slippery plastic wrapping. The frost coating melted on my nearly numb palms. More glass shattered down, but to my horror, choked in the uncut portions of the screen and fell inward rather than outward. Spilling all down my carpet in glittering pieces.

Making a perfect hole for him to reach through, and as I swung again, grab the thick venison leg. I slid across the carpet as he pulled me forcefully toward the window.

I stumbled and let go of the frozen meat just as he reached through the window and grabbed my cardigan sleeve, and somehow I managed to pull myself loose and scream. Floundering through the darkness of the room, banging into boxes as I lurched for the doorway.

In a lull between thunder and rain, I heard the sound of breaking glass. I slammed the bathroom door behind me and locked it then leaned against the door—my racing brain trying to process one last piece of ridiculous information. *He's coming in after me.*

And all I had for defense was a stinkin' hairbrush! I rummaged through the bathroom cabinets, stuff spilling out of the drawers and onto the rug. A tube of toothpaste. Some bad-tasting mouthwash. A couple of old hair elastics. Perhaps I could make a slingshot with the brush and hair elastics, à la David and Goliath, and let fly a few bars of peach-scented soap?

And then suddenly over the din came a loud shotgun blast. *BLAM!* The house shook.

I dropped the hair elastics.

"I don't know who you are, but you'd better git the tarnation outta here!" blared Stella's voice from the front of the house, loud and strident.

"Stella?" I crawled to the bathroom door and pressed my ear to wood.

"You mess with me or my friend an' I'll blow yer fool head from here ta kingdom come, ya hear?"

Another blast. *BLAM!* My knees shook as I felt the vibrations, like earthquake aftershocks.

"Yeah, you better run! Run, you mangy dog, before I. . . Where the blazes are ya?"

I stayed silent, waiting, hearing nothing but my breath. Then jumped back as someone pounded on my front door. "Shiloh?" came Stella's muffled voice. "You okay? The rascal musta run off."

"Stella?" I called, shaking, raising myself a few inches.

"He ain't comin' back! An' I'll be standin' here till the police come. Ain't nothin' gonna move me outta the way!" She paused a minute. "Say, what's all this trash on yer porch?"

Police sirens whined in the distance. "Hold on. The po-lice is comin'!" Stella called. "Sure took 'em long enough."

The sirens increased to a high-pitched wail, and Christie's barking rang against the walls. The sound of an engine. I cracked open the bathroom door, hoping I didn't find Odysseus's shot-ridden body slumped outside my bedroom window.

"Shiloh!" Stella pounded on the front door. "Answer me! Ya okay in there?"

In the faint crack of streetlight from Mom's bedroom window across the hall, my bathroom rug glowed ruby red. Red like the string of fate. The color of Odysseus's roses. The color of my bridesmaids' dresses. The color of the wedding dress obi I'd never wear.

"I think Stella shot somebody," I murmured out loud, feeling strangely light-headed.

And I bent over right there on the rug and forgot everything else.

—⁊⁊—

When I came to, someone was pounding on the front door so loud my teeth rattled, and Christie barked incessantly. Loud, harsh sounds that made my head ache.

I felt around for my venison leg, not finding it, and heard the distinct squeal of a police dispatcher. I crawled out of the bathroom and ventured into the hallway. The living room curtains blinked white and blue. Through the window I saw a uniformed officer I didn't recognize on my front porch, hand on his holster.

I jerked the front door open, still feeling dizzy. OFFICER T. WHITMAN, read his police badge. Stella hovered worriedly next to him, one hand nervously flicking a lighter. Flowered housedress. Curlers. No gun in sight.

"You the resident of the house, ma'am?" Officer Whitman, short and thick-shouldered, looked dark and serious in his hat and badges.

"I think so," I said, rubbing my forehead in a daze. "The guy's already gone though, right?"

"All this junk on the porch yours?"

He shined his light on a huge mess of flowers—red flowers—fresh, dark red roses, all mixed with red ribbons, red crepe paper streamers, and silk flowers that looked like they were pulled from somebody's front lawn.

"For what hath night to do with sleep?" read a poorly lettered banner, smeared by the rain. *"If not victory, revenge!"*

I snatched up a silk carnation stained in ugly shades of blue and red. Cemetery flowers! I'd seen some flowers just like these at Green Hill Cemetery on my last visit to Mom's grave. The guy had left roadside daisies and random things like American flags, too, maybe pulled from the same cemetery. All lying in sodden heaps on my rain-soaked front porch.

"Holy smokes," Stella breathed. "There's a bunch a letters and numbers on all these papers, and newspaper clippin's, too. Regular wacko, this'n." She prodded something with her toe. "And what's all them photos of the mechanic's shop? Ain't that the one on Greenville Avenue? I don't get it."

"I'll check out the house." Officer Whitman gruffly stalked into my darkened living room. "And then I'll ask you both some questions."

"Wait a sec," called Stella, reaching for his arm. "Ain't Shane on duty tonight?"

"Called in sick an hour ago, Stel." Officer Whitman flipped at my light switch to no avail then switched on his flashlight.

"Why, I jest saw him at the Barbecue Barn not more'n two hours ago!" Stella flung her hands up. "He was flirtin' with the waitress and eatin' the daylights outta some pulled pork. He shore looked fine ta me!" She dropped her shocked expression just long enough to give a sassy wink. "An' I mean *real* fine. If he was older an' not my kin, of course."

That's right. Stella and Shane were distant third cousins or something. By marriage, she'd told me. But at the moment, just thinking about nonforking family trees made me nauseated.

Stella followed Officer Whitman inside, and I threw my arms around her.

"Did you shoot somebody, Stella?" My teeth chattered as he searched the dark house by flashlight, leaving us in the darkened living room. "I swung that leg of venison, but it didn't stop him."

"Venison? What the sam hill you talkin' about?" Stella blinked at me through the darkness.

"I heard two shotgun blasts, and the guy ran away. You said so."

Stella looked at me like I'd lost my mind. "I didn't hear nothin'! I just come runnin' over when that dog a yours whined at my bedroom window like nuts, an' I saw the fella take off runnin'."

I blinked, wondering if I'd gotten confused. But I'd heard the shotgun blasts. Both of them. Stella steadied my shoulders. "You're jest feelin' kinda woozy. Sit down a bit."

I crumpled onto the sofa, and she lit a candle with her lighter. Poured me a glass of water.

"But you said. . ." I rubbed my head, trying to remember. "And I heard. . ."

"Lands, look at that knot on yer forehead!" said Stella, staring at me. "You pass out or somethin'?"

I touched my forehead, and sure enough it had swollen, tender. I winced and brought my cool glass up to ease the swelling. I'd probably hit it when I fell over on the bathroom floor.

"Good lands, gal! No wonder ya ain't makin' sense!" Stella chided me. "Lemme see that knot."

Officer Whitman came through my front door, his face tight. "I think I know why your power's out."

"The storm. I guess everybody around here's lost power."

Stella cocked her head. "Now that's the thing, Shiloh—mine ain't off."

I ran to the window, and sure enough, my neighbor's porch light smiled back at me. Fuzzy through light rain.

I swiveled my head back to Officer Whitman. "You mean. . . ?"

"Your power and phone lines have been cut. Come take a look."

Chapter 31

"It's too bad you've found your wedding dress already." Kyoko, oblivious to my traumatic night, chirped into my cell phone as I drove to Faye's. Stella had lent me her phone charger that plugged into the car cigarette lighter. "I found a website you'd love."

I glanced at the clock on the dash, suppressing a yawn. Almost three in the morning. Christie had curled up on the passenger's seat, head on her paws. In the rearview mirror, Stella's headlight (yes, singular, her right one was out) beamed into my bleary eyes as she followed me to Faye's, along with Officer Whitman's squad car. To make sure Stalker Freak didn't try to intercept.

Since, of course, I didn't stock my car with frozen game meat.

"Right, like I can afford a wedding dress online," I retorted to Kyoko.

"Well, you miiiight change your mind. It's. . .perfect for you."

Something about the way she said it raised my suspicions. "I don't have Internet now, Kyoko. I'm not at home."

She paused, obviously disappointed. "Okay, spoilsport. It's called 'Simply Camo.' You've gotta see it! They sell wedding dresses in white satin and camouflage."

"Please." I rolled my eyes.

"No, really! So which pattern do you want, 'desert sand camo?' " I heard her clicking a keyboard. "Nah, I think 'snow camo' will suit you better. Tiffany—that's what it says the model's name is—has fallen branches across her skirt. Wonder if Bobbie Jo here's hiding a grouse under that fishtail hem?"

My mouth fell open, and I barely registered the bump of a pothole that jolted the car.

"They've got prom dresses, too." Kyoko snickered. "Ro? You there?"

"I'm here."

"Good, 'cause I've got a bunch more sites in case you don't like that one. Look—a John-Deere-themed bridal party! Everybody's decked in green and yellow."

"You think just because I live in Staunton that I'd get married in Tim's hunting gear? Like. . .Bobbie Jo?" I shouted, forgetting about my bad night for a second.

"Actually I think the table runner's what did it for me." She guffawed to herself. "But hey, you could have a nice ceremony with one of those camo dresses. Maybe on a shooting range."

"The shooting range thing's been done. Becky's cousin."

"The guy who made a swimming pool out of his pickup truck bed?" Kyoko sounded worried.

"Yep. I think he's single again if you're interested." I drove in crabby silence, scowling.

"There's this other dress with electric lights under the skirt and one made entirely out of newspapers," said Kyoko helpfully, switching subjects. "But I can always point you to Goth Bride if you prefer. My fave. They use the coolest skeleton mannequins." I heard her typing, and then the keystrokes stopped abruptly. "Hey, did you say you're not at home? At three in the morning?"

My throat suddenly swelled, tight with tears, as I thought of my wasted wedding plans. All down the drain because of some psychopath who called himself after a Homer character.

"You're not off on a story, are you?" Kyoko roared. "If you say yes, I swear I'll knock you into next week!"

I sniffled, reaching over to scratch Christie's head and eliciting tail thumps against the dashboard. "I'm not doing stories anymore. I'm not doing anything. The wedding's off, Kyoko."

Thick silence filled the line. I heard the gentle whir of smooth, wet asphalt under my tires, punctuated by hissing splashes as I drove through puddles. "Ro-chan. I. . .I'm so sorry," moaned Kyoko, nearly in a whisper. "I know I gave you grief about living in Virginia, calling Adam a farmer and everything, but he's really okay. I mean, he might look more respectable if he grew his hair out and got a tattoo or something, but he's nice. I liked him."

"No, no!" I corrected, annoyed. "Adam and I are still getting married. We just won't have a wedding." I wiped my eyes with the back of my hand. "The whole thing's a mess. I'll tell you about it." I sighed, dreading the recap. "But I'm worried. I haven't been able to talk to Adam since it happened."

"Since what happened?"

"I called him—we all did—but he doesn't pick up. Maybe he left his cell phone off before he went to bed. I texted him a bunch of times though, so he'll find out when he wakes up." I jabbered on, barely hearing her. "And you know something else? Maybe I dreamed it, but I could have sworn I heard Stella fire a shotgun."

"How do you know what a shotgun sounds like?" Kyoko sputtered.

I felt heat flood my face. "I just. . .do."

"Sorry. Not good enough."

"People shoot birds all over the neighborhood. And squirrels. You know that. You were here last year."

"Well, they definitely don't use shotguns for squirrels. Unless you want half your front lawn blown away."

"What do they use then, gun expert?"

"Twenty-twos, mostly. I have brothers, remember?"

"Isn't that illegal?" I gasped. "Just plinking pigeons on your front lawn? What if a bullet hit somebody?"

"Of course it's illegal! You're never allowed to discharge a firearm in a residential area."

"Well, then, there's no way Stella would've used a shotgun." I flicked on my high beams to cut the murky mist. "She wouldn't be able to handle it anyway if the kick's as strong as you say."

"I. . .think she could handle one."

"Right." I made a face.

"In fact, I'm pretty sure she's got one. Sawed-off."

"Stella?" I shrieked, bursting into laughter at the thought of her taking aim in her housedress, curlers and all. "No way."

"Um. . .I'm not sure how to tell you this, Ro-chan, but I saw it. The time I visited and you were always running to work or church or wherever. She invited me over for pancakes—pretty good ones, too—and the sawed-off job was standing in the corner, plain as day."

A wave of horror swept over me. "You think Stella scared the guy off with a sawed-off shotgun?"

"Don't think, Ro," Kyoko warned as my car went down an enormous valley and up a hill as if suspended over night skies. "Just be glad she scared whoever you're talking about away. She probably just shot it in the air once or twice and put it back in her kitchen. Mission accomplished."

"And didn't tell the police." I let out my breath in astonishment.

"Would you? And what guy are you referring to in this nuts-o story?" Her tone turned testy.

"I wouldn't have a sawed-off shotgun in *my* kitchen," I retorted, deliberately not answering her question.

"Maybe you should. And you still haven't told me how you know what a shotgun sounds like."

I didn't answer for a long time. "Okay," I finally said. "But promise not to laugh."

"Nope. Not gonna."

I sighed. "Fine. I heard a shotgun at the shooting range, okay? With Tim and Becky and a bunch of their relatives. They shoot tin cans and metal turkeys and targets. And skeet. . .something. Whatever they're called. Clay things they throw in the air and shoot."

"*You?*" Kyoko hooted. "You went to a shooting range?"

"Well, once for Becky's cousin's wedding, and the other times for—"

"*Times?*" she cried. "As in, plural? You didn't shoot any guns, did you?"

I fidgeted with my Bluetooth.

"Did you?"

"Wow, this connection's really bad," I said. "Guess I'll have to call you back later."

———

I parked at Faye's house in the damp predawn, drops falling from the maple tree in her front yard as I grabbed my stuff from the backseat and let Christie out. Christie had saved my life; I should upgrade her from generic puppy biscuits to an actual name brand.

I trudged through the wet grass toward the glowing porch light, glancing back over my shoulder at the pasture where I'd dodged cow pies with Tim and Becky in their cow-tipping spree. And before that, on the morning I lost my AP job a little more than a year ago, I'd stood right here under this very tree, watching dawn rise pink over the mountains—believing my life was over forever.

I looked up as the squad car eased into the driveway, giving a squirt of siren. Blue-and-white lights pulsing. I waved back, and the car hovered there, finally cutting its engine.

Stella pulled in after the squad car and parked behind my Honda.

Trusty Stella. What a boon she'd turned out to be. People could say whatever they wanted about her hair-sprayed 'do, but the woman had guts. And enough illegal weapons to keep Crawford Manor safe.

I pulled Christie along on her leash toward Stella's dark blue Chevy, shouldering my bags. My teeth rattled in the misty chill, and I tugged my cardigan tighter as her door squeaked open.

"Stella. Thanks so much for taking care of me."

"Ain't no trouble, sug. You jest git on in the house. Lands, that dog a yours is gold, Shiloh. If she hadn't shown up. . . ?" And Stella burst into tears, her back shaking. "Sorry. I'm jest a little shook up, is all. Everything fallin' to pieces—like that year it snowed in July. Nothin' makes sense."

"Snow in July?" My eyes bugged. "Clarence tells some whoppers, but that's ridiculous."

"Ridiculous? I was there!" Stella's hands shook so much she dropped her keys. "Lands, an' the world's comin' apart again. Losin' your mama first, and now this is happenin' to ya? Boy, do I need a smoke."

"No you don't. Relax and take a deep breath." I leaned over and patted her back. "We'll make some tea. Come on inside with me." I held out my hand. "Faye's opening the front door now."

"Naw. I gotta hit the road." Stella pushed the car door open and hauled her hefty frame out, grunting with effort. "I got a party to bake for today." She squeezed her eyes in misery, her hands trembling. "C'mon, Shiloh. Jest one li'l Marlboro ain't never hurt nobody! Promise I'll quit tom'rrow. Honest."

"No." I crossed my arms and used my bossiest voice. "If you give up now, you'll always give up. Sometimes you've just got to stick with it, especially when it's hard. That's when it really counts."

My mind flashed back to Adam and the angry words we'd exchanged. Feeling, a bit guilty, like I should take my own advice.

"I'll try." Stella wiped her eyes. "But it ain't gonna be easy. I'm tellin' ya." She jingled her keys. "And if I'm gonna have one whit of willpower, I better get some shut-eye."

"Well, would you mind going by Adam's before you head home? To make sure he's okay?" I fidgeted with my purse strap. "Officer Whitman said they'll go by the house, but I'm worried. If he's awake, tell him I'll be there at eight."

"Be where?"

"He knows what I'm talking about." I glanced around at the dark fields, suddenly nervous about who might be watching. Or listening. "I'll fill you in later."

" 'Course I'll do it. You go on." She pushed me toward the house, where Faye was unlatching the screen door. "I'll call ya. And watch your car, ya know? My car got broken into the other day. Didn't take nothin', but threw all Jer's stuff around like they was lookin' for somethin'."

"Oh, that's right. I forgot Jerry's borrowing your car." I shivered and rubbed my arms, glumly remembering our last-ditch efforts to save the restaurant. All of which flopped.

Just like my life.

"I'll be careful." I watched Stella over my shoulder as she got in her car and backed toward the road, easing close to the squad car. Window down. And she stuck her head out to talk.

And why not? Stella was related to Shane and probably related to Officer Whitman, too. That figured—probably half of Staunton was related in some way or another.

My cell phone vibrated suddenly in my pocket as I headed toward the front porch. Faye was hurrying down the driveway to meet me, hugging herself in the early morning chill.

"Adam—finally." I dug for the phone. Then I held it up to see the screen and paused, not recognizing the number.

"Who is this?" I frowned, checking the number again as I turned toward Faye.

"My angel," whispered a voice. "We almost made it. But don't worry—next time we will."

"You. . .you. . ." I stopped in midstride.

"Just one thing, my love. About the justice of the peace. Don't go. It's a bad idea. A very bad idea. You broke my heart once, but I won't let you break it twice." His words hissed like a serpent sliding through rain-beaded grass, ready to strike. "If you go, I promise it's the last thing you'll ever do. Don't even bother calling the police. They won't find me before it's too late."

I stood rooted to the ground, unable to move. Speak. Breathe.

"But I know where to find you," he whispered.

Chapter 32

"There's still time for us to do things the way we planned—on our special day. Our wedding day." The caller's breath caught. "I know you remember, my angel. It's why you came. Just like I knew you would."

The call ended suddenly, and the phone silenced. Limp in my hand.

A death threat.

A whisper of vengeance. Of love turned sour—like the broken-heart stamp—and of lost chances.

"If not victory, revenge!" The words from the wet banner I'd found on my porch swirled through my head, sounding vaguely familiar. A line from a book I read back in college. An essay I'd written, and a lit exam.

Something about the fall of man—a divorce. A breakup. Adam and Eve's sin and leaving the Garden of Eden forever.

And most importantly: angels. Lots and lots of angels.

That was it. Milton's *Paradise Lost*.

"Shiloh. Come on in here, honey," called Faye, coming toward me with worry puckering her lined brow. She wrapped a blanket around my shoulders and rubbed my arms, and I blinked back, unseeing. "You all right, doll? We're worried sick about ya. Becky's on her way over. You jest go in and rest."

I moved like a robot, stiff, up the wooden stairs, wishing for one terrible moment that I'd never set foot in Staunton, Virginia.

—⁂—

"Lands, Shah-loh. I'm so sorry." Becky's face was pale, and her hands trembled on the steering wheel as she checked in her rearview mirror. "I never thought in a million years things'd git this bad."

268

I pressed my elbow to the door of her car, staring listlessly out the window. My eyes ringed with dark circles from a sleepless few hours before dawn. "I shouldn't have gone back to Mom's. I shouldn't have investigated."

"The police couldn't track that phone number?"

"Calling card. It's impossible to trace."

Becky shook her head. "Well, as long as you an' Adam are together, everything else'll work itself out." She checked the rearview mirror again, her green eyes tense and narrowed in the reflection.

"I just wish Adam would call me. It's not like him to be so silent." I picked up my phone again, which still felt warm from my hand. "Stella said his truck wasn't there, but his bedroom light was on. He'd left a note on the door saying he'd see me in the morning." I pressed my lips together. "And he texted me a while ago saying, 'Waiting for you at eight.' So I guess he's okay. I texted back that I'd be a few minutes late because I need to stop by the bank first."

"He's probably packing. Y'all are gonna leave town after ya sign the papers, ain't ya?"

"Yeah. Jerry opened The Green Tree so I can pick up my paycheck for helping him and cash it when the bank opens. Then I'll meet Adam at the courthouse. The whole marriage process shouldn't take more than a few minutes." I forced a smile. "Hey, you can be a witness if you want."

"Aw, no. I'm holdin' out for that red dress your half sister said she'd buy." Becky eased into a parking space along downtown Staunton's historic streets, empty in the early morning glow.

"I know. I never should have trusted her." I sank my face into my hands. "Everything's ruined."

"Not ev'rything. Keep that chin up, Yankee."

"Yes, everything. Everything except the house selling. We're sharing a moving truck with Adam's Uncle Bryce, and Adam's making the deposit on the apartment right after the wedding." I caught myself, nearly forgetting the change in wedding dates. "So I guess that means sometime this week."

I'd changed into fresh jeans and a pretty white cotton top with lace edging, which I thought might scatter some bride-like sentiments on such a momentous occasion. But sturdy enough to last several hours in the car, on the run with Adam, as soon as we signed the marriage documents. White lace headband. Leather sandals. A rainbow-colored cloth messenger bag from Guatemala hung over my shoulder.

Yep, the Fashion Nazi was about to get married in jeans and a messenger bag.

At least I hadn't stooped to cowboy boots. *Yet.*

My cell phone rang suddenly, startling me. I fought with my partially unclipped seat belt, freeing my hands, and grabbed for it. "Hello? Adam?"

"Shiloh? This is Bryce Carter. How are you doing?"

"Bryce? Hi. I'm. . .well, okay. Long story." I leaned back in the seat, feeling one last spark of comfort as I imagined handing over the key to Mom's house. The house that brought me to Virginia. And the house that would slap triple digits, for the first time in years, into my bank account. "The house'll be ready for you in a couple days."

Bryce sighed. "Shiloh, I don't know how to tell you this. . .but we're not moving. We'll have to back out of the real-estate deal. I'm so sorry." His voice trembled a bit. "The company folded, and instead of getting a promotion, I've just been laid off."

―――

"Oh, my friend." Becky looked over at me with sympathetic eyes, shaking my shoulder as I buried my face in my hands. For Mom's house, yes, but also for Bryce Carter. "I'm so sorry."

"They've got three kids," I murmured, rolling my head back and forth. "Everything's falling apart, Becky! How do I manage to ruin everything? Tell me that!"

"Shucks." Becky took the keys out of the ignition and reached over to hug me. "Must be a special gift, I reckon. 'Course from my view, not havin' Ashley show up in town for your weddin' might be the best part a the deal."

"Maybe so." I chuckled and wiped my eyes with the back of my hand.

"Maybe nothin'. You shore know how to stir up some life in this li'l old town!" She ruffled my hair. "Well, c'mon, Yankee. You're still a bride, remember? Git 'er done!"

And she marched around to my car door and flung it open, giving a silly bow.

―――

"I don't like this," I said, stepping up onto the sidewalk near The Green Tree. A cool breeze ruffled our hair and clothes, poststorm, and a hint of peach glowed along the horizon through fine breaks in the clouds. "It's not like Adam to keep his phone off this long. I'm going to call the police station and see if they've heard anything else."

"He's prob'ly jest busy gettin' ready, but it won't hurt nothin' to call." Becky shrugged, tugging on The Green Tree door and then knocking when it didn't open. " 'Specially with some madman on the loose."

I dialed the police and talked to Officer Whitman while Jerry unlocked the door, his hair a mess and eyes haggard with dark circles. He ushered us in, his sleeves rolled up and shirt damp. Wiping his shoes on an old towel.

"Sorry, ladies. The sanitizer hose broke again, and I'm jest gonna replace the whole doggone system. I've fixed it a hundred times, but it's never worked right—and I can't get a single plumber to fix it properly. So be it." He sighed. "I reckon I'm jest fixin' it up for somebody else to enjoy, but as long as my doors are open, we're gonna do our best."

He wiped his forehead on his sleeve and reached to shake our hands. "Shiloh Jacobs." He wagged his head back and forth, those round glasses of his spattered with drops. "If you ain't a magnet for trouble. And I mean that with all due respect."

"Um. . .thanks, I guess."

"Stel called me this morning, and lands! Scared the daylights outta me. If ya ask me, sounds a bit like. . ." He broke off, his eyes narrowed in deep thought.

"Sounds like what?" I took a step forward.

"Aw, nothin'." He waved it away. "Jest this case I heard once about some gal named Amanda. She disappeared, ya know. Real sad story. I never met her, but my heart broke jest the same. Take care, ya hear?" He reached out and touched my arm soberly. "And if ol' Jer can do anything for ya, jest let me know. Anything at all."

"I'll be fine." I made myself smile. "Adam and I will come see you when this is all over. And Jerry." I caught his sleeve as he turned back toward the kitchen. "I'm so sorry about the restaurant. *Fine Dining*. The whole mess. I really tried to help."

I scuffed my shoe against that beautiful golden flooring, wishing I could sink through a giant hole right there in the dining room. "Shiloh." Jerry snapped his fingers for me to look up at him. "You listen here." His voice turned stern, and tears swam in his eyes. "Every single thing you gave me was a gift, you hear me? And it don't get better than that. If I could do it all over again, I wouldn't change a thing. Not a daggum leaf on them trees. This place looks better than it's ever been, in all my years." He reached out and gently touched a potted basil on a nearby

271

table. "Sometimes your streak of good luck runs out and the hard times come. But that don't mean you ain't been given a gift. You gotta take the good with the bad and be thankful for all of it."

Adam. I closed my eyes, remembering the feel of his fingers through mine.

Jerry pointed at me. "Now git that chin up, and go get your paycheck. It's at the register." And he disappeared into the kitchen, the double doors swinging closed behind him.

"G'won." Becky gave me a push, smiling through her tears. "You heard the man. Git."

I slipped behind the register counter and dug through stacks of neatly ordered receipts and register tapes. Accounting ledgers and vouchers. Not finding anything resembling a paycheck. I bent down and dug through the cabinets, coming up with nothing but extra menus and a stray peppermint.

"Hey, Shiloh. You lookin' for yer check?" Flash the cook leaned over the counter, the white apron tied around his scrawny middle, wet and stained with grease. "It's back in Jer's office. Jest g'won in and git it."

"You're sure?" I stood up.

"Yep. Jer's awful forgetful these days. Lot on his mind, I reckon." He clapped my shoulder affectionately, his sideways grin showing a missing tooth. "And worried sick about ya. We all are."

Becky waited at the register, checking her watch and trying to call Adam while I followed Flash back through the kitchen doors. From across the kitchen I saw Jerry on his back in a puddle of water, reaching up with a wrench and twisting at a copper pipe, grunting with effort. Reaching into a bucket piled with plumbing supplies.

"G'won. I'll go he'p Jer." Flash cracked open the office door—a glorified closet, really—and I ducked inside. I flipped on the bare overhead bulb and gingerly moved some papers around on his desk, feeling like a crook as I sorted through somebody else's things.

The desk bulged with books—recipe and cooking books—and under them *Julius Caesar*, *Romeo and Juliet*, and a collection of classical Japanese poems. I smiled, lifting them to look through the stacks of documents underneath.

And out of one of the books fell a crumpled note.

"I love you, my dearest," it read in scratchy red ink. *"How can I count the ways? I think of you over and over, throughout my longest days, and watch the minutes to see you again."*

Chapter 33

snatched up my paycheck and fled out of the office, finding the dining room empty. Becky'd probably gone to the bathroom or something. But I didn't wait. I threw open the glass doors to the street, stumbling against the side of the building as I fled headlong away from The Green Tree.

"Becky!" I gasped into my cell phone as her voice mail picked up. "Where are you? You've got to get out of there! Now!"

I scrambled between two crumbly brick buildings and bent over in the back alley, my stomach churning. Crouching to my knees and trying not to heave.

Thinking of Jerry. Of those beautiful trees and noodle plates, and his hand on my arm.

My cell phone rang, and I snatched it up.

"Shah-loh? Where the blazes are ya?" Becky chirped, her words high-pitched in irritation.

"I'm a block behind The Green Tree. Come get me, Becky. Please."

In the background I heard Jerry's anxious voice, but I snapped the cell phone off and waited, shaking, until Becky's sedan screeched around the corner.

"Yankee, I outta clobber you good!" she shouted angrily from the car, flinging open the passenger door. "Why, you up an' ran outta there like. . ."

She stopped short when she saw my tear-streaked cheeks. "What happened?" Becky rolled her head into her hand and muttered under her breath. "Lands, woman, yer gonna give me a heart attack!"

She pulled back into the street, hazard lights blinking, while I clumsily shut the door and choked back a sob.

Becky shook me till my teeth rattled. "Speak, woman, or I'm goin' to the police!" She glared. "An' ain't gonna be no Shane Pendergrass there ta he'p ya out."

"Not the police!" I choked. "Not yet! I just can't. Go to the bank. Please. And then I'll figure out what to do."

"What to do about what?"

"About Jerry."

Becky ran over a curb and careened back into the street with a screech. "You think. . .you think Jerry's. . . ?"

"Odysseus. Yes."

To my surprise, Becky's face glowed with furious color. "Now, hold on one cotton-pickin' minute!" she shouted, her eyes flashing. "You done gone too far this time, Shah-loh Jacobs! Jerry ain't been nothin' but nice ta any of us! You're jest stressed is all. Not that I blame ya. But you gotta cut out all this Jerry nonsense before ya—"

"Pull over."

"What? I ain't gonna pull over for no—"

"Pull over!" I shouted, and Becky jerked the car into a gas station. She threw it into PARK, seething.

And I shoved my cell phone at her.

I watched as she flipped through the photos I'd snapped, one by startling one: red card envelopes and red ribbons. A Japanese kanji writing guide for foreigners. A glossy volume on Japanese culture.

"*Your eyes are like stars,*" he'd written on a scrap of notebook paper in red, several words scratched out. "*Shining their beautiful warmth to my soul. I can't wait for the day when we can be together. . . .*"

Some little abstract doodles of hearts, Japanese kanji, a piece of sushi—and. . .an eye. A *woman's* eye, with long lashes.

And a thick, brown, leather-bound volume labeled *Paradise Lost* in block script.

Like a sick Dali painting, Becky's angry face morphed into disbelief, then hurt, then a puddle of tears. Her hands shook on the cell phone.

"Copper shavings." I could barely speak. "Jerry was fixing copper pipes just now."

"I don't believe it," Becky said, wiping her face. "I don't care what ya say! Somebody planted everything. Cain't be Jerry! No way under the sun he'd—"

"He collects stamps. And there's one missing on the page of the year Amanda was born." I pointed to an empty yellowish square in a dark blue album. "The double-heart stamp. It's gone."

Even Becky startled into silence.

"But. . .that Odysseus fella kept talkin' about broken hearts," she finally said, fumbling for a tissue. "What's that hafta do with Jerry?"

"I left him."

"You never dated him, Shah-loh! Ya only worked there." She raised an eyebrow. " 'Less I was mistaken about them long hours."

"Of course not, Becky!" I smacked her. "But maybe. . .in his mind it meant something else."

I slumped back in the seat. "I mean, taste-testing recipes in a kitchen full of servers and cooks hardly seems like a romantic tryst, but. . ." I wiped my eyes on the back of my arm. "Jerry lied to me just now."

"Jest now? Shoot, he ain't even here!"

"No. In the restaurant," I snapped. "He said he'd never met Amanda Cummings."

"Well, maybe he didn't!"

"Amanda worked at The Green Tree as a waitress before it was The Green Tree. I researched." I blew my nose. "It was called The Red Barn back then, and it sold country-style fare. Macaroni and cheese. Salty country ham. Green beans. That sort of thing."

Becky slapped her own cheek in disbelief. "No, Shah-loh. Please tell me yer kiddin'. Jerry owned The Red Barn? I mean. . ."

"Jerry Farmer in the flesh. And his first restaurant venture."

"Mebbe he got too busy to remember all the names?" She started to tear up again. "I mean, I bet he had lotsa servers, an'. ˙. ."

"Three. It was a small place."

Becky sank back in her seat, speechless. "But. . .but wasn't the anonymous painter left-handed? And bald, yer mama said?"

"Jerry's left-handed, Becky. And he's whacked his hair off to the skin more than once—enough to be confused with a bald guy. So either my purse snatcher's unrelated, or Jerry set him up. And one more thing." I clicked the phone off, sniffling back tears. "Jerry's related to Shane Pendergrass. Which is why Mom was afraid to go to the police. And probably why Shane called in sick just now—to help Jerry out."

—⁂—

"Lands, if this world ain't one gigantic mess." Becky pulled jerkily back into the street, swerving around a rogue squirrel. Her driving wasn't great on a normal day, but now I hugged the armrest as if my life depended on it. "I better git ya to the bank and the courthouse first before Adam tans my hide."

Tan my hide. Another one of those Southern expressions I needed to write down. The only hide, in fact, about to be tanned was probably Jerry's. And maybe Shane's, too.

But instead of feeling satisfaction, I felt awful all the way through. Responsible, even. Guilty. Sick.

"Hold on. Somebody's calling." I reached for my phone then narrowed my eyes at the voice. "Well, well. Shane Pendergrass. Hope you're feeling better," I minced, my words cold.

"Yeah, kinda, but. . .listen. Can ya come by the station?" His sober tone held a mix of nerves and dread that unsettled me.

"Come by the station? Think again, buddy."

Becky pulled into the bank parking lot and parked. Badly. Half in a parking space and tire rammed into the curb, her eyes round as Japanese teacups.

"It's Adam, Shiloh," Shane said in almost a whisper. "We. . .uh. . . found his truck on the side of the road. Seems like he was headin' out to your place in Churchville from Stuarts Draft."

I felt the blood drain from my face. "I don't believe you. This is one of your tricks, isn't it?" My voice rose. "To make me come out to some empty parking lot again? Well, forget it. He already texted me saying he was fine."

Shane paused, speechless. Just as Becky's phone buzzed with a text message. She jerked her keys out of the ignition and answered, gasping back a scream.

"It's from Adam's parents!" she managed, clapping a hand over her mouth. Turning to me with horrified eyes. "They're all worked up and tryin' to reach ya."

"Shane?" I gasped into the phone. "What did you say about Adam? Where is he?"

"We. . .dunno," Shane replied, sounding shaken. "That's what I was trying to tell ya. He's gone. Nobody knows where he went."

———

I squeezed into a ball on the seat in a fetal position, rocking back and forth. Becky jerked open my car door and wedged herself onto the edge of the seat. She held me tight, sobbing into my hair.

I clung to her arm, wishing I'd never gotten up this morning. Never seen a red rose. And never set foot in stupid Staunton, Virginia, where all my dreams died like flies stuck to fly paper. One by horrible one.

"C'mon, Shah-loh," Becky sniffled, obviously trying to pull us together. "Think with me. We gotta cash that check so you can have some money on ya, 'cause you need ta leave town pronto." She wiped her face and steadied her breath.

"But the courthouse!" I bawled, not moving. "I promised!"

Becky's eyes spilled over. "Pray, Shah-loh. Pray hard. And come with me. Ain't no time to argue."

My watch read six minutes after eight when I pushed open the glass doors to Planters Bank. The teller waved me up to the counter, and I stood there in blank stupefaction until Becky pushed me ahead. "Cash it," Becky finally said for me.

The teller took my check and raised an eyebrow at the amount. "All of it?"

What did she mean, "All of it?" I pulled the check back and felt my heart leap into my throat at the amount: *five thousand dollars.*

My mouth turned to cotton, and I just stood there, staring down at the check. "Why did Jerry give me so much?" I faltered. "Generosity? Or. . .or some kind of sick bribe?"

"Ask questions later. Jest cash a thousand and put the rest in the bank," said Becky. "Here. Gimme a deposit slip." She reached over my shoulder and helped me fill it out.

I signed, and the teller counted out some bills into my hand. Becky finally took them for me and stuffed them into my purse then guided me toward the exit.

A hand brushed mine, reaching for the door handle at the same time I did.

I jerked my bleary eyes up, surprised to see none other than Ray Floyd, looking at me like he'd seen a ghost. His face pale and clammy.

"Shiloh?" he said in surprise. "You're—you're here?"

"Sure I'm here. I bank here," I replied a little tartly, despising pretty much everybody in my vicinity. "Aren't you supposed to be in Washington?"

"I came back to talk to you." He moved closer and lowered his voice. "Because I've figured out who's stalking us. I've got evidence."

Becky narrowed her eyes. "Who are ya, and whaddaya want? 'Cause she's in a hurry."

Ray stuck out a hand and shook hers. "Ray Floyd. I'll be quick.

But Shiloh, could I speak to you a second? You're not safe. I know what he's planning next."

"Who?" I pushed through the door and into the misty morning and spun around to face Ray. "Jerry Farmer? Do you think he took Adam?" Adam's name brought fresh tears to my eyes.

Ray came through the door beside me and stopped in midstride, giving me a startled nod.

I grabbed Ray's arm. "Help me, Ray! Do you know where he might have taken Adam? Is Shane in on this, too?"

Ray started to speak again then glanced around and motioned me away from the entrance. Finger to his lips. "I'll tell you everything I know. But hurry."

He grabbed my arm and pulled me toward his car, unlocking it with a chirping sound.

"Wait. That one?" I stopped so suddenly Becky rammed into the back of me. "I thought you had a burgundy Volvo."

"I've got two cars. What's the big deal?" He gave me a push. "Hurry, Shiloh! There isn't time!"

"That's a Mercury." I took a step back. "A dark silver color."

Ray's eyes turned hard, and he grabbed my arm again. Rougher this time. And he pulled me away from Becky. "We have a lot to talk about, you and I. And we'll start with that fiancé of yours. Adam, I think his name is, right?"

"What about Adam?" I cried, trying to free my arm. And I realized, in a flash of horror, that Ray hadn't released me. He was dragging me. Toward his car.

I started to pound on his back. "Let me go, Ray! What are you doing?"

Becky screamed. Ray broke into a run, throwing his other arm under my throat in a kind of headlock and yanking me along. *Exactly the way my purse snatcher had done in Waynesboro.*

I bit his arm and pounded his face with my free hand, trying to knock off his glasses, but he moved too fast for me. Bending my head down with crushing force.

"No! You're not leaving again!" he hollered.

I punched him in the stomach as hard as I could, but the arm across my throat cut off more oxygen than I'd expected. I gasped for breath, wrenching his fingers as I tried to breathe.

"Stop him!" Becky shrieked, tackling Ray from behind like a

football player and smacking him hard across the head with her purse. He temporarily loosened his grip, but only long enough to shove me into the driver's side of his Mercury sedan, banging my head on the side. *The dull-colored car that had skulked outside Adam's house.*

"I'll shoot!" he yelled, firing a very real and very loud gun, shattering glass in a nearby car. Becky and I both screamed.

I kicked and punched, prying his arm away from my throat just enough to see Ray dodge Becky's purse, which she flung at him with full force.

That square jaw. Those thick shoulders and full lips. Long, thin nose. *Mom's drawing.* It was him. Ray Floyd.

"He's got a gun!" I shouted to Becky. "Stay back! Call the police!"

But my words were lost in the slam of the driver's side door as Ray threw his keys in the ignition and hit the automatic door locks, practically sitting on me. I yelled in pain and lunged for the passenger's side door, but couldn't reach with that oaf on my leg.

"Oh no you don't!" Ray hollered, grabbing my arm as I swung at him. He stormed right over a concrete parking lot divider, hitting it with such a loud bang I thought he'd shot me. Then he squealed out of the parking lot, the force throwing me against the dashboard and then against the window, smacking my head.

When the stars disappeared from my vision, I saw the floorboard of the car covered in dark red roses.

"You're Odysseus!" I cried, grabbing a handful of roses and flinging them at his face.

"And you're my angel," he said in a strange, quivery voice, pointing his gun at me. "And this time you won't get away."

Chapter 34

'm not your angel!" I braced myself as he slammed over a concrete divider and into the oncoming lane, horns blaring. He turned at the last minute, skidding down a road that led out of town. "And where's Adam? What have you done with him?"

He was accelerating faster than I could keep up with, speedometer rising. I reached for the door, but I couldn't jump out now at these speeds.

"You're my angel, all right!" Ray shouted, shoving the gun closer. He trembled, wild-eyed. Beads of sweat trickled down his pallid brow. I warned myself to watch it, or he might shoot me. He'd come that unglued.

Keep calm, I told myself, forcing my racing pulse to slow, and remembering—on a supersonic level—Becky's "treat-a-man-nice" advice in the flower shop. I figured it applied to lunatics as well. *Keep quiet, be gentle, and help him calm down. You'll have a better chance if you can get him thinking straight. Then catch him off guard.*

"Could you please put the gun away?" I asked, holding the seat with both hands as he lurched over a pothole. We were heading farther away from buildings and into some rural side streets, and nothing looked familiar. I tried desperately to memorize our turns.

Ray didn't answer. He glanced over at me with wide eyes, his thick, curly hair disheveled like a madman's.

"Please, Ray? I'm scared. Please put the gun away." *Remind him that you're human*, police always advised victims. *That you're a person, and that you have feelings.*

"Becky's probably worried sick about me by now, and. . ."

The gun wavered just an inch, and then he shoved it back in my face again, touching my cheek. "I'm not stupid! You'll run, just like you did last time! You ruined my life!"

I had the sudden urge to grab the gun and smack Ray's heavy rectangular glasses off with it, but I kept my hands curled in my lap. He was too dangerous.

"There's no way I can run, Ray! You've got the doors locked. What am I supposed to do?"

"Don't call me Ray!" he shouted, sounding angry again. "I'm Odysseus! Stop pretending you don't know me!"

"Okay." I put my hands up. "Odysseus. Sorry. Now will you please put the gun away?"

"Shut up! And don't even think about unlocking the door."

"I won't."

"You do and you'll be sorry." He kept the gun trained on me for a few seconds then slowly let it drop. I pretended not to notice and stayed calm when he put it in his pocket under his shiny, putty-colored jacket.

Thank You, God, I prayed silently, trying to stop shaking. *At least now it won't go off if he hits another pothole.*

"You left me!" Ray shouted, turning angrily back at me. He tossed the handful of roses I'd thrown at him back in my lap. "Why did you wait so long? And why did you *deposit* money at the bank? Are you crazy? What were you thinking?"

The two questions hit me at the same time, spinning my head. "Why did I wait so long for what?" I finally managed, choosing one.

"You know what!" His face contorted with fury again, and his hand fumbled as if to grab his gun.

"Because I was. . .scared," I replied, making it up as I went.

"But you promised you'd be there! Twelve years ago, angel!"

"Angel?" I blurted, rubbing my head where it smarted. "Why do you keep calling me that?"

"My angel. You were everything to me! I waited all this time for you, and when you finally showed up at the bank like we agreed, you *deposit* money? Instead of taking it?" His face flushed with anger. "I saw you there at the counter with the deposit slip!"

Twelve years ago. We hit a bump, and I braced myself. And forced myself not to react when another car passed us and he swerved too close, tires squealing.

Amanda Cummings disappeared twelve years ago. "You think I'm. . .

Jennifer Rogers Spinola

Amanda Cummings," I ventured.

"Of course you are! I recognized you the minute I saw your photo that day in the auto shop! You can dye your hair, but you can't disguise those eyes. I've never seen another person on earth with eyes like yours—all green and gold. I loved you! And you walked out on me." He gripped the steering wheel with bulging knuckles.

Your photo. "Did you say you saw my photo?" I turned to him, still hugging the armrest. "Like. . .the one my mom carried in her wallet?"

Ray looked over at me with a sudden flash of warmth. "You remember."

"In the mechanic's shop where Jim Bob Townshend worked." I leaned forward, steadying myself against the dashboard while we squealed around a curve.

"It *is* you." Ray reached over with a distant smile and stroked a hand through my hair, and I slapped him away. "I knew you'd remember. I was standing in line behind your mom when I saw your face. 'Shiloh,' she told him. 'That's all you need to know.' " He let out a ragged breath. "And that's when I realized you'd been waiting for me—just like I'd waited for you. It was all part of your plan."

"Ray." I waved a hesitant hand in front of his face. "You know I'd never met you, right? That my mom simply printed off a photo of me from the Internet? I'd never even been to Virginia."

"Don't change the subject!" Ray yelled, flaring up again. "Why did you walk out on me, angel? Why?"

"Amanda," I corrected cautiously. "Don't you think I'm Amanda?"

"Have you forgotten everything? Our middle names?"

I stared blankly, and he scowled. "Angela. Remember? Your middle name."

"Amanda. . .Angela?" I tried. *That's right. Amanda Angela Cummings. Angela. Angel.* I groaned inwardly. *How could I have been so dense?*

"Of course! Those were our nicknames for years. Nobody knew them but you and me. You were the only one who called me Odysseus."

"After your middle name," I guessed, trying to piece things together.

"Otis. Which sounds a bit like Odysseus, I suppose. Or at least you thought so back then," Ray snapped. "And if anybody knows love, it's me—just like the ancients did. With poetry. Prose. Anguish." His face contorted as if he might cry, and he squeezed the steering wheel tighter. "And we had all that, angel! You and me. We were going to shake the dust of this crummy town off our feet and. . ."

Then his face hardened. "But you couldn't wait for me! You robbed the bank yourself with that Townshend kid and disappeared. And I've been in anguish the past twelve years—until you showed up again."

Robbed the bank? My jaw dropped open, despite the placid pose I'd tried to affect.

"What? Surprised?" Ray shot back, his arm moving toward his pocket like he might dig out the gun. "Surprised I know? Everybody thinks you disappeared, but I know the truth. We planned that holdup together for August third—every single detail. Every angle. And then I wake up two days before and check the Staunton news online, and what do I see? You've already done it! You double-crossed me!" he roared.

August third? I flinched, remembering the strange year Clarence told me about when it snowed in July. Amanda's disappearance. The bank heist. Could Amanda really have robbed the bank, or did Ray just fabricate another story?

"You're sure Amanda robbed the bank? With Jim Bob Townshend?"

"Of course I'm sure!" he snarled, reaching out to grab my arm. "Don't you remember?"

I jerked away, trying to stay calm. "Why didn't you turn her into the police then, if you knew she did it?"

"I didn't turn *you* in because I loved you," said Ray in a choked voice. "I couldn't believe you'd really left me. But then after all these years. . .seven, at first, because three plus four is seven. . .and then twelve. Perfect twelve. Your birthday, you know. Three times four makes twelve."

"Wait. Wait. Wait." I put a hand up, math calculations spinning in my head. "Are you saying you expected me seven years after Amanda disappeared? Because of your. . .three plus four thing?"

"Sure I did. Twelve minus seven is five. Five years ago."

Ohhhhh. I get it now. Sort of.

"I sent you flowers and everything. Left you messages." Ray ran a hand through his hair, making it stand up in wild tufts. " 'You were my first.' "

"But that's just it! I wasn't your first. You'd been engaged before, and so had Amanda."

Ray laughed, a cold sound. Almost like a shudder. "Oh, no. You were my first true love. First—and last. Never forget that." His eyes caught mine. "And when I saw your picture in the auto shop the first time, I knew you'd come. Twelve years after you left. Just as I thought."

He wiped his face with a sweaty palm. "A crazy plan, but I knew you'd come back for me."

The man needed help. Seriously. I rubbed my forehead, feeling woozy again.

He pointed a trembling finger at me. "But you were going to marry another man on *our* wedding day. Not even Jim Bob, but that Carter guy! Why him?"

Ray blinked rapidly as if deep in thought. "Maybe it's. . .it's part of your plan, too? To throw off the police?" He wiped a moist cheek, breaking into a watery smile. "I'm right, aren't I? Did I misjudge you?"

I thought of rolling my eyes, but I didn't want to set Ray off again.

"August third," he whispered. "The day we were supposed to rob the bank together and run away. Marry. Because we were always meant to be together, you know. You wouldn't back out on me."

In an instant I understood all the numbers. The reminders. In his twisted way, Ray'd been trying to give me another chance. To make things right again.

Because he still believed my heart was white, innocent, and we were tied together with a red string of fate.

I would have banged my head on the dashboard if it wasn't already smarting from two blows.

"So that's what this is all about?" I demanded. "A jilted wedding and bank robbery from twelve years ago?"

"I've been following you for weeks, trying every possible way to tell you I love you. To tell you I remember and we can still do things right—and be together again just the way we planned."

"Ray. I'm not Amanda." I lifted one palm, my other hand still clinging to the armrest.

"Oh yes you are. I saw your debit cards and driver's license. Everything's the same. Your birthday. Your Japanese stuff. Your artistic talent. I know all about you." He lowered his voice as if confiding a secret. "I checked all your cards and information that night I visited you in Waynesboro. Did you know I used to be a wrestler? I won some championships, actually. I'm ambidextrous. Takes people by surprise every time."

For Pete's sake. I groaned inwardly. That explained a lot. "So you're the creep who stole my purse."

"Oh yes." Ray smiled sweetly as if announcing a summer picnic. "I went to the city council meeting and slipped your keys out of your purse so you'd have to go back inside. You should pay more attention, angel."

"You wore contacts?" I glared.

"Certainly. Glasses don't work well in a mask." He punched the accelerator, turning down an even more deserted farm road. "But I left you a wedding gift, like we exchanged for our engagement. A paper fan."

"Oh, that's original." My mouth twisted. "Amanda did that with Jim Bob, too."

"And I did it to make her forget him. The jealous beast." Ray's lip curled. "He planted all those roses at his dad's house for her, you know? But I won anyway."

He turned abruptly. "You don't still love him, do you? You followed him in those funky cowboy boots. I saw you."

"You know I followed Jim Bob?" I shouted, sitting up straight. "And no, I don't love him."

His face distorted into a bitter smirk as he jerked the wheel, skidding around a fallen branch. "No. You love that UPS guy. Believe me, I know. I've been trailing you for weeks now. Watching you price invitations and price wedding dresses. That one with the puffy skirt Becky picked out seems like it would have suited you just right. I got a picture of it after you left."

"You liked it?" I tipped my head. "I don't know. It was kind of fluffy, if you ask me."

"Hmm. Maybe a little." He stroked his chin. "If they'd take out some of the tulle underneath, though, I think it could work."

Wait a minute. What was I saying? "Just where, Ray, do you get off following me around?" I bellowed. "You had no right!"

"My name's Odysseus!" He swerved again, hard, so that my teeth banged together. "I've been watching you—just me and my camera. At work. At your grandmother's house."

"I don't have a grandmother!" I waved my arms.

"Sure you do. Kate Townshend." Ray pushed on the gas. "And I saw you at the doctor's office. He was my doctor, too, you know, before he was Amanda's."

"Sure. Because you're sick," I muttered under my breath.

"I've watched you in Food Lion. Driving home. Everywhere. Waiting for the perfect opportunity to take you back." He shrugged sadly. "I almost did last night. But? Foiled again."

Ray seemed to forget reality and gave me a hazy smile. "But I'll never forget seeing you in person for the first time after all these years.

Right there in my den, covering your story."

I glanced at the door handle, wondering if I should risk flinging it open at this speed—or if Ray would shoot me first. He saw and pressed on the gas, laughing at my panic.

"That's impossible! You were in the photo with me."

He looked over at me with eyes full of love and anger, but mostly pain. "We had coffee together, remember?"

"Yeah. It was really good."

"It was, wasn't it? Colombian." His face relaxed to a fond look.

"I knew it. Bold and rich, with a hint of acidity. More body than Guatemalan."

"Precisely! It's quite robust." He tipped his head toward me like we were old friends. "Organic, of course. I prefer it to Sumatra—too earthy for me."

For a moment I thought I might be out of my mind, too, sharing coffee memories with a madman. If only he weren't so doggone conversational, with such good taste in bridal wear and coffee!

Ray waved angrily. "Forget the coffee! That was just an excuse to buy a few minutes so I could set up my camera tripod outside. Timers, angel. Ever heard of them?"

I. Am. A. Moron.

"And then I stayed there watching you. You in that gorgeous kanji T-shirt, with your messy hair and perfect eyes." He closed his eyes. "The only eyes in the world with that beautiful green and gold starburst. I've never seen anything like it. I had to mix the green paint six times before I got the right shade."

So that was it. My eyes looked like Amanda's, and we shared the same birthday. *What a psychopath!*

"I invented that story about Adam's picture on the letter, too, to send him a warning. Because I knew you never stopped loving me." Ray's chest shuddered with emotion, and I looked around for something to use as a weapon. The headrest perhaps? If I dislodged it, could I smack him over the head with it?

And then I spotted it: a red ribbon coiled through the roses at my feet. My eyes darted to Ray's neck, and in a seamless second, I'd snatched it up. And looped it around Ray's throat with one fluid movement.

Chapter 35

The car swerved, and I grabbed the steering wheel as Ray clutched at the ribbon. I yanked tighter, feeling a grim satisfaction as I remembered his knife blade at my neck.

"I wouldn't do that if I were you," he croaked, groping for the ribbon. "You wouldn't want to hurt your beloved. Any more than he already is."

"What did you say?" I gasped, loosening the ribbon slightly.

"You heard me. Let me breathe, and I'll tell you where he is."

"You're a liar." Tears filled my eyes, and I pulled the ribbon tighter in vengeance, steering with one hand while the car skidded across the poorly marked lanes of the winding road. Fending off Ray's fists as he tried to free his neck.

His face turned a purplish color, and he grasped at the ribbon. "In. . .the. . .back," he wheezed.

I stomped on Ray's shoe covering the brake and stretched tall enough to tip my head over the high seat back and see—to my horror—a bulky figure slung haphazardly across the backseat and floorboards, covered by an old blanket. One lifeless arm slung across the carpet, tied at the wrist.

Adam's arm.

I screamed, pounding Ray with my fists, and he jerked the ribbon away from his throat long enough to grab the gun and shove his hand in the little space between the driver's seat and the door, pointing it straight toward the bulge of Adam's head.

"Let him go!" I cried, punching wildly.

"If you stay." Ray grinned, fending off my fists with one arm as if enjoying his little game. "You're the one I want anyway."

The car had stopped. If I flung open the door now, I could make it. I could run. I could. . .

Ray's voice came out so steely and stilled I barely heard him. "If you so much as move a finger, angel, I'll blow him away. Got it?"

"I'll stay. Just let him go." I closed my eyes.

Ray grabbed my neck in a vicelike grip and reached over to unlock the back passenger's side door, shoving my face into the fabric of the seat. At least he vacuumed often; it smelled nice. I heard him throw open the door and push Adam out into a pile on the side of the road. Without a single word or sound from Adam.

Then Ray slammed the door and threw the car in DRIVE, squealing down the road in a blaze of mud and gravel.

"Is he dead? Did you kill him?" My mouth quivered as I raised my head and inched up to a sitting position, trying to catch a glimpse in the side mirror.

Oh no. Not somebody else I'd driven to his grave. Not Adam.

Ray didn't answer. Only a faint smile played on his lips.

I clawed at the window to see, out of the corner of the glass, the supine figure of Adam Carter, still clad in his brown UPS uniform and strewn in a heap. A bloody gash on his ghostly white forehead and his arms tied together with rope.

—◦◦◦—

"Odysseus," I managed, barely keeping back sobs. "Listen to me. What would you say if I told you that you were mistaken? That you might be right about Amanda, but I'm not her?"

"I'd say you were lying!" A vein in his neck bulged.

"But what if I'm not?" I sniffled, and Ray—out of odd courtesy—handed me a tissue box from between the seats. Scented, no less. I took a tissue and nodded my thanks, scrubbing my cheeks. "What if I told you that I'm Shiloh P. Jacobs, and I just moved here a year ago from Tokyo? I never met Amanda." I balled up my tissue and reached for another one. "Think about it. Twelve years ago I was. . .what, thirteen years old?"

I could see the wheels in Ray's head spinning. Something seemed to make sense, as if he were waking to reality, then he pounded on his forehead with his fist.

"Stop it!" he yelled, eyes wild. "Stop trying to confuse me!"

He abruptly jerked his gun out of his pocket and leveled it at me, hand shaking. "You're my angel! You think I didn't see all those clues you sent me? Wearing red? You know I love red. It was our color."

"Red?" I interrupted incredulously. "You said you liked green and yellow! At Gypsy Hill Park! Remember that horrible shirt?"

"No! That's Ray's favorite color. I'm Odysseus."

I gasped and covered it with a cough. "Sorry. I thought you were kind of. . .you know. The same person."

"Only sometimes! Don't you get it?" His eyes looked wild. "Twelve years ago you loved red, angel, and so did I. Red's the color of love in Japan, as you know. The color of life and energy, like the sun, and used for celebrations. For weddings." He beamed at me. "Especially when coupled with white, like your innocent heart. *Kohaku*, I think they call that special red-and-white combination. Your school colors. Because even then you loved me."

Cornell. Deep carnelian red and white. I groaned.

Ray's smile darkened. "Although I'm not sure your heart's as innocent as I thought."

I had to hand it to him—he was pretty creative for a man losing his wits. "What are you, some kind of accountant? Messing with letters and phone numbers?"

"Statistics major. I love numbers." He smiled briefly. "Anyway, I stole that Farmer guy's stamp from his car, since I know you love stamps, and I sent you one." He narrowed his eyes. "You should have known it was me, angel. I made you a wedding ring—see? I'm an artist, too, like you."

Ray dug in his pants pocket and pulled out a gorgeous band of interlaced metals. "Silver and copper. The closest thing I could find to white and red."

I clapped a hand over my mouth. "Copper shavings. But. . .you told me you had a girlfriend! Back at the park!"

"I do." He raised his eyebrows. "You."

And then as suddenly as sun in a rain shower, Ray calmed. "Hi, Shiloh," he said pleasantly. "What are you doing here? Another story?"

—∽—

"Another story?" I gasped. "Ray, you've kidnapped me!"

He looked genuinely surprised, furrowing his brow. "Me? Don't be silly." He chuckled. "What's the story about this time?"

I stared at him, wondering if I should play along or not.

"You were just getting ready to drop me off," I said, holding my breath. "So I can finish my interview."

"Really?" Ray passed his hand across his face in bewilderment. "Out here? No way. Let me take you back to town." He took his foot off the gas. "What kind of story is it?"

"Oh, any story," I said casually. "If you'd be so kind as to let me off right here, then I can. . ." My hand hovered nervously over the handle.

A red barn appeared on the hillside, and Ray glanced at it. Then at me. Then he scowled and jammed the accelerator down.

"You were going to let me out back there!" I gasped, hanging on to the door handle.

"Shut up! Stop changing the subject! You wore red to the city council meeting to send me a message. That day in the park you wore a red dress." He waved his arm. "The night of the crash you wore a T-shirt with Japanese kanji, just like she did. You sent me a special stamp, too, on my newspaper subscription renewal."

My head reeled. "That's all random! And I don't do subscription renewals. Clarence does!"

Ray didn't seem to hear me. "And then you sang our song."

"What song?" I gripped my head in both hands.

"When you were digging through the Dumpster, you sang it. The one your mom liked."

"That was your song with Amanda?" I yelped. "I had no idea! I just found it in her guitar case!"

"Of course you knew it. That's why you sang it to me. Don't you see? It's exactly the same song I left in your gas tank as a message."

"That triumph thing was. . .a song?"

"Oh yes." Ray turned his eyes toward me. " 'Angel Band,' it's called. An old bluegrass tune about longing for heaven. You love that one."

No, no, no. . .not again! I groaned and buried my face in my hands.

"And you used to work at Jerry Farmer's restaurant. You're a vegetarian, angel."

"I'm not a vegetarian. I have a freezer full of venison!" Granted, I'd probably never eat it, but it was there. "Wait a second. I hit you with a deer leg when you came skulking outside my house, remember? You must have taken it with you because nobody found it after you ran off."

"That wasn't yours. It couldn't have been." He paused. "Although it did make a nice roast, if I do say so."

"What?"

"In the Crock-Pot. You just have to stew it long enough tenderize the meat, and a pinch of chili powder takes the gaminess out."

"So that's the secret." I pounded a fist on my hand.

Ray leaned closer. "Here's another secret. I sent you flowers at the place you grew up. You got them! The mailbox was empty."

"Where I grew up?" I squealed. "You think I'm from Deerfield? A trailer park?"

"That's where we fell in love after I moved to Virginia."

"I grew up in Brooklyn!" I pounded the seat with my fist. "Not Deerfield. Some guy named Herbert Jones got your dumb flowers and turned them into the police for tampering with a federal mailbox!"

"Liar!" Ray looked wild-eyed again, but his eye began to twitch. "You're Amanda Cummings."

"I'm not Amanda. I'm Shiloh P. Jacobs. I'm from Brooklyn, New York, and I never saw you before that day someone plowed a Jeep Cherokee into your window!"

Ray looked panicked. "Stop it, angel! Stop saying things like that. I won't let you." He waved the gun closer. "I know it's you. I loved you, my angel! I believed in you, and you. . .you threw it away."

He flexed the trigger finger with shaking hands, making me wince. I thought of grabbing the wheel and jerking us off the road, but we were speeding too fast for that.

"I wasted twelve years of my life for you, angel. And you're not getting another chance now."

"Ray," I said, dropping the name game and feeling a weird sort of pity. "I'm really sorry for what Amanda might have done to you. But I'm not Amanda. I'm Shiloh. You've got the wrong girl."

The gun wobbled, and he wiped his face with his sleeve.

"Listen to me." I tried to make my voice strong and confident. "It's easy to mistake identities. I do it all the time."

His head came up briefly, and I took a deep breath, praying for wisdom. "I judge people, Ray. I think I know them, have them figured out. Like Tim and Jerry. Who would have thought they'd read Shakespeare? But I'm wrong when I set myself up as somebody's judge. People change. People grow. Even me." I reached out a hesitant hand and—surprising even myself—put it gingerly on his arm. "Don't ruin your life by believing a lie. Admit you've made a mistake, and start over."

Ray came around a bend, his chest rising and falling with emotion. And when he turned to look at me, his eyes looked heavy with pain. "No," he whispered hoarsely. "I can't do it."

"You can. Just pull over and let me out."

"No!" Ray's voice hardened. Without warning he stomped on the brake, lurching us to a stop. Then he grabbed my face and turned it forcefully toward him with his free hand and stared into my eyes. "You're Amanda. I'd know those eyes anywhere, angel. Shiloh. Whoever you are. And you're going to be so sorry."

I almost grabbed the gun, but he'd locked his trigger finger firmly in place. It amazed me that Ray could talk, drive, and hold the gun at the same time. Must be nice to be ambidextrous. In the same situation, I'd probably shoot myself in the foot or plow into the barn.

Ray was too quiet. Pulling over to the side of the road. I needed to speak—say something—do something. Stall.

"Those are some beautiful cows," I said, hoping to distract him. "Holsteins, aren't they?"

Ray let the gun drop slightly, so I jabbered on. "Ever read the story of Abraham, Ray? It's from the Bible. He let his nephew Lot choose the best land, which probably looked just like that—all green and hilly. And then God sent angels."

Ray's head jerked up at the word *angel*.

"To destroy the evil cities of Sodom and Gomorrah where Lot lived. But Abraham pleaded with God to save Lot. Because," I added purposefully, "he valued Lot's life."

"Life? I'll tell you about life. You ruined mine, and I'll never forgive you for that." Ray suddenly grabbed my shirt collar in his fist, making it cut tight against my neck.

"Three's your number, angel. Our wedding date. We dated for three years. You double-crossed me three days early. You came into my life, left, and I found you again. Three unforgettable moments."

Three dozen roses.

"And now there's about to be four." Ray was too calm. It unnerved me.

"What's four?" I quavered, trying to keep him talking. "Not. . . ?"

Four. Shi. The Japanese number of death.

The car had slowed to a near stop, rolling slightly over gravel as Ray's foot let up on the brake. Thin, scrubby locust trees flanked a cow pasture just outside the passenger's side window.

Ray aimed the gun at me. "Good-bye, my angel," he whispered. "Forever."

Chapter 36

"Look!" I screamed, shouting the first thing that came to mind. "Squirrel!" And I smacked the gun out of his grasp as he turned his head.

We both fumbled for it, yelling and pushing as it tumbled off the seat and onto the driver's side floorboard. Ray stomped on the brake and grabbed my hair, fishtailing us to a stop and slamming the car into Park. I managed to get one hand free and lay on the horn.

The sound worked. Ray jerked my hand off the horn, and I elbowed him hard in the stomach. I knocked his glasses off when he crumpled and threw myself partially onto the floor, shoving his legs out of the way while I dug for the gun. Pulling half my hair free as his grip loosened slightly.

But Ray moved fast and had the advantage of longer arms. He pushed me aside like a pesky fly, our heads banging together, and jerked my hair harder. But too late for him—my fingers felt the pistol under the gas pedal. We both grabbed the gun at the same time, my hand on the stock and Ray's larger one squeezing mine so hard I yelped.

I felt my grip slide—felt him prying my fingers off painfully, one by one—and realized he was going to win.

Unless.

Over Ray's shoulder and curly head gleamed the precious automatic door lock. I let go of the gun. And instead I lunged over him and hit the Unlock button.

A click reverberated through the car, and just as Ray raised his head, triumphant, I punched him square in the jaw, the only place I could reach. I tugged my hair loose and kicked open the passenger door.

Jennifer Rogers Spinola

I squirmed out of his grasp and threw myself out of the car with so much force that I stumbled headlong, so close that Ray actually made a swipe for my heel.

I tore my foot away and scrambled through the thick grass toward the pasture, wind knocked out of me and gasping for breath. Scraped elbow bleeding where I'd slipped on the gravel.

My hair flew in my eyes, and I could hardly see where I was going, stumbling over patches of thick weeds. I didn't care. I just needed to be as far away from Ray as possible.

"Get back here, angel!" Ray screamed, and I heard the blast of a gun. The sound of shuddering limbs and falling leaves. A branch fell to the ground just behind me.

I dropped to my knees and scooted under the barbed-wire fence, running as hard as I could away from the car. My messenger bag flapping wildly across my chest.

Out of the corner of my eye I saw Ray sprint over to the barbed-wire fence in hot pursuit. I ran as fast as I could and then tripped on a slight roll and slammed into the ground. My jaw shuddered with the vibrations.

My slippery sandals were going to get me killed.

And Ray had already scaled the barbed wire, coming fast. So close I could see his glasses hang crooked postfight. His footsteps pounded the grass.

I threw off my sandals and scrambled to my feet, but Ray was too quick. In one flying leap he tackled me, slamming me to the ground. Knocking the breath out of me so much I couldn't even groan.

Oh God, this is it. . . .

And then before I could move, I heard something—something *heavy*. The pounding of hooves. An angry grunt.

As if in a bizarre dream, I opened my eyes to see all four hundred pounds of Liv the Llama hurl itself in Ray's direction.

"She never forgets a face," Kate Townshend had said.

Ray staggered back as Liv charged him at top speed, breath huffing from angry nostrils. Knobby legs flying, body aimed low to the ground. I dragged myself to my knees, gasping, and not quite believing my eyes. Until I saw Ray, still backpedaling and stumbling, clumsily aim the gun at Liv.

Must. Find. Something. To. Throw.

My mind moved in dazed slowness, but my fingers were faster. Working open the top of the messenger bag and digging inside. Slipping the throwing star from its cardboard package and reaching back over my shoulder. Hurling it as hard as I could.

I heard it whistle, and in slow motion the throwing star glinted against the green pasture grass. Sailing through the air with a perfect slice. Spinning in dizzy spirals too fast to see.

And it caught Ray Otis Floyd on the edge of his right knee.

Quite a bit off target, I must admit. I guess I needed more lessons at the gun range. But at least it hit him.

I heard him shout, saw him crumple. Blood stained his pants. The gun went off at a wild angle, and Liv threw her head back and ran the other direction.

And I, for one, thought that was a pretty good idea.

—⚬—

I sprinted across the field away from Liv, barefoot, dodging cow pies that had browned in the sun. On the slope to my right, cows looked up at me, curious, as I sprinted for the low knoll in the stubbly grass.

Something whizzed past me, bee-like, and I saw a puff of dirt just two feet away. Heard the slight delay of the gun as it went off. *POWWW!* It echoed against the grassy hills, making my ears ring.

I threw myself to the ground in a patch of weeds, breathing hard, flies buzzing anxiously nearby. Ray was a good shot. A really good shot. I started to wonder if Amanda escaped after all or if Ray had taken care of her for good.

He shouted, and I heard a flailing of brush as he positioned himself and leveled his gun at me.

Not this time, Ray! I took off across the pasture again. *I'm not about to be another Amanda Cummings!*

A shallow ridge curved just to my right, flanked by a tall, tree-covered hill that sloped down to meet me. If I could make it to the ridge, right before the flat knoll where cows lazed, I'd be sheltered.

The ridge stood a good distance away, but I didn't run every day for nothing.

I swerved around a patch of some kind of weed cows apparently didn't like, jumping two cow pies like hurdles, and ran hard. The wind threw my hair out of my eyes as I scrambled up the incline, which glimmered with patches of yellow dandelions. And I threw myself headlong toward the ridge.

Jennifer Rogers Spinola

Three quick explosions reverberated in fast succession: *POW! POW! POW!* The cows looked up nervously.

And as my feet hit the ground, I felt something wham me in the side, like a giant two-by-four. I landed hard and rolled onto my back.

But when I felt around on the grass, I didn't find a two-by-four. Just grass and a stray, dried cow pile. A lone bee buzzed over some clover as one of the cows looked up at me, chewing its cud and blinking long eyelashes like the photo in Meg's portfolio.

I scrambled down the slope, surprised to find that my legs and arms had turned all rubbery. My footing gave, and I slid headlong into the grass.

An engine rumbled in the distance, and through blades of stubby grass I saw Ray slam his car door. He squealed off, swerving out of sight.

I started to pick myself up, gasping for breath, when I felt something warm leaking out my side. I looked down in disbelief at the lower half of my shirt—stained bright red. Spreading slowly, like a scarlet flower opening.

I pressed my hand to my side, not understanding. Held up my palm, now smeared with blood.

Ray Floyd just shot me.

Chapter 37

Reality set in when I began to shake, knees buckling beneath me. I felt cold all over, and a strange stabbing throb crept into my side.

This can't be happening. Pain clawed at me, filling my abdomen and roiling in my stomach.

My cell phone. I dug it out of my messenger bag and tapped out a number with shaking fingers. I pushed all the wrong buttons, and a pizza guy answered.

"Hello?" I cried, fumbling and dropping the phone again. Its shape was unfamiliar to me, too new and sleek. And my hands wouldn't stop shaking. When I managed to get the phone up to my ear, he'd hung up on me.

"Hello? Pizza guy? Anybody?"

A dial tone. My palm was sweaty with blood, and the phone slipped again, down a rocky decline and out of reach.

My breath came faster, and a panicked hysteria settled over me. I shouted for help, my voice ringing off the hillside and into silence. A couple of cows looked up.

I can't believe this! Of all the stupid places for Ray to take a shot at me!

I coughed, and the grass turned red. For a second I hated the color red. I eased down through the rocks and managed to grab my cell phone then crawled forward toward the distant barbed-wire fence on my hands and knees.

What if Ray comes back for me? I paused, exhausted, and wiped the sweat out of my eyes. My legs didn't cooperate when I tried to stand.

My shirt was soaked now, and I felt light-headed. Pain pounded through my side so that I strained for breath.

Jennifer Rogers Spinola

You're going to die, whispered a panicked voice, tense with adrenaline. *In the middle of a cow pasture in Nowhere, Virginia.*

Leave it to me, Shiloh P. Jacobs, to die in a stupid cow pasture with two heifers—one brown and one spotted—chewing a clump of weeds. The indignity infuriated me. I half expected Tim and Becky to pop out from behind one, cackling and slapping their knees.

I tried to sit up, holding my middle, and hyperventilated when I saw my blood.

I screamed for help until my throat ran hoarse and then sank there, terrified, in the grass.

"God!" I sobbed. "Can't You send somebody? I don't want to die here!"

A lone hawk sailed overhead, sealing the image of vastness, and disappeared silently over the ridge.

All at once I heard my cell phone ring somewhere in the grass, absurdly out of place, as if the pizza guy had called to confirm my order. *Well, good luck delivering anything out here.*

My senses were leaving me. I reached over and managed, after three tries, to press the CALL button. "I'd like a stretcher," I quavered, teeth chattering. "With cheese."

And I rested my head on the grass next to the phone while somebody yelled. The voice whined like a pesky mosquito, demanding my location. I swiped at it, groaning in agony.

"I have no idea!" I needed quiet, not shouting. My head throbbed. "But please don't let him shoot the llama."

My white shirt dripped, staining my jeans. I looked down and felt sick, feeling my last bit of panic ooze out like my blood. *Oh, God, Oh, God. . .* I thought, unable to move my lips. *I guess this is it.*

I remembered Mom's funeral. The scent of lilies, and the piles of gladiolus and wreaths.

"She loved you," said Dr. Geissler.

My body seemed to seize up, racked with pain, and my lungs convulsed. I coughed hard, unable to stop the warm flow I felt in my side. An odd sense of peace rushed over me. *So this is how it feels to die.*

This is how Mom felt, kneeling in the grass all alone, calling out for Stella. This is how she died, and how she sang her last song.

I thought of the wedding and of Adam. . . . *Adam.* A bitter regret stabbed through me, but it passed quickly, like a needle through numbed flesh. At the edge of my blurred vision, little pinpricks of darkness closed in slowly.

I, Shiloh P. Jacobs, am going to die.

I no longer felt the ground. I seemed to be floating, losing touch with the sensation of earth, but rough blades of grass still poked me in the cheek. I couldn't explain it, really. I tried to move my arms through empty space, but they flopped against hard soil.

A blanket wrapped me. Cradled me. Exquisitely warm. My side still throbbed, making me cough and cry out, but I felt something else: the strange and powerful presence of God like never before.

"Do not be afraid. I bring you good news that will cause great joy for all the people. Today in the town of David a Savior has been born to you; he is the Messiah, the Lord."

It seemed odd, lying there in the nebulous grass, that people only quoted this verse at Christmas. It was beautiful. Maybe the most beautiful verse I'd ever heard.

I blinked up at the gray sky, remembering my lies. My plagiarism and years of arrogant running from God. The way I'd shoved Mom away. The words I'd spoken and the sins I'd committed, piled high over twenty-five years.

And the grass of another hill, two thousand years ago, that ran red with the blood of that same Savior so I could have peace with God.

"Forgiven," I imagined God saying, punching a big stamp over my long list of sins. *Forgiven! Forgiven! Forgiven!*

I have been forgiven so much!

I felt weightless, free, like the low clouds overhead, passing over the sun, and I choked back a sob as I thought of Mom. Her changed life and her powerful words. Her shining faith, which had passed itself—ironically—to me. And now I would die young as she had. Following in her footsteps until the end.

And for the first time in my life, I felt proud.

"Do not be afraid. . . . Very truly I tell you, unless a kernel of wheat falls to the ground and dies, it remains only a single seed. But if it dies, it produces many seeds."

The verses came faster and faster, reverberating through my head like thunder: *"The body that is sown is perishable, it is raised imperishable; it is sown in dishonor, it is raised in glory; it is sown in weakness, it is raised in power. . . . Death has been swallowed up in victory."*

A swell of joy surged through me, a sparkle of something alive and eternal, and I felt the weight of my old guilt fall away at last.

Jennifer Rogers Spinola

This is what Mom felt! *This* is what she found in her last moments: the Savior's hand tight in hers, taking her home for good.

No fear. No loneliness. No racking sorrow or regret. All joy! All hope! For death has been swallowed up in victory!

"Even though I walk through the darkest valley, I will fear no evil, for you are with me. . ."

For You are with me!

My eyes landed, full of tears, on a tiny yellow blossom buried in a half-chewed patch of stubble, and I remembered what Becky said about bouquets. The cut stems of freesia and roses in her hands, dripping.

A sacrifice, she'd called them. *"They lived and bloomed, jest like they were made to do. And when it was time to go, they gracefully said yes."*

"Yes, Jesus!" I whispered, shivering. "The best thing I've ever done is say yes to You."

"Do not be afraid! I bring you good news that will cause great joy!"

"Do not be afraid!"

Somewhere in the distance I heard the impossible grumble of. . . a tractor? Coming closer, its strident rattle blaring in my ears. The bellowing of cows as they lifted their heads. Agony that made me cry out and pray aloud, begging for relief. Choking coughs.

The tinkling of ethereal music, layer upon layer, and the brilliant love of God as the pasture and throbbing pain faded into darkness. Hands that felt like Mom's brushing back my hair.

"Do not be afraid!" His voice came tender, full of joy, in words that weren't spoken but felt. I couldn't see Him, but I knew His warmth and life like my own breath. Ragged now, shallow.

"I'm not afraid, Jesus!" I whispered, raising my arms toward heaven. Or maybe I thought I did, since I couldn't seem to move. Nothing worked right anymore. I tried to speak, but my mouth was full of dirt and dry grass. The roar of a tractor engine deafened my ears.

"Do not be afraid!"

And that was the last I remembered.

Chapter 38

Iopened my eyes and looked down at the unflattering hospital gown and blankets. Tubes ran from my arm up to an IV bag, and a bandage stretched across my elbow where I'd skinned it in the gravel. A drain tube ran from my stomach under the blankets. Monitors beeped.

I wiggled my toes, surprised to see them move at the end of the bed.

And then I saw him—just a foot away. Adam leaned in a chair, sound asleep. Hair disheveled and face in his hand. Stitches grinned from a gash on his forehead.

I held up the blankets and peeked at the bandages covering my abdomen, touching them gingerly with my fingertips. I groaned as I painfully shifted my weight, trying not to think of the stitches that would have to come out of that wound. *It's going to be a long time before I run a marathon or look good in a wedding dress—that's for sure.*

Wedding. Adam. My mouth fell open. He's alive? He's not. . . ?

His chest rose and fell with breath. I reached over and pressed weak fingers to his wrist, feeling warm blood pulse through his veins. *He's alive!* A miracle. I turned my own hand over in the light, gazing down at my silver engagement band. The veins pumping blood to my fingers and toes. A second chance at life—no, a third because I'd already been given a second chance when I asked Jesus to forgive my sins and change my heart forever.

I didn't care if I got married in Tim's hunting jacket. I was alive and so was my groom.

And there on my bedside table lay my Bible. I reached for it clumsily, dumping it upside down with splayed pages, and finally hauling it onto the bed. I paged through Genesis intently, looking for the story of Abraham and Lot.

"Shiloh?" Adam said groggily, jumping from his sleep and leaning forward. "You're awake?"

"He never knew," I blurted. My hands shook, and I smushed one of the pages.

He cradled my free hand between his, careful not to jostle the IV tube. Tears danced in his eyes. I'd never seen them so red, puffy from lack of sleep. But neither had I seen them so happy either.

"Shiloh, what are you looking for? You've been—"

"Abraham." I frantically scanned the lines of type and pointed. Shoved the Bible at Adam. "He never knew God answered his prayer."

"What prayer?"

"For God to save Lot. All the Bible says is that Abraham prayed, and the next morning he stood looking over the smoke of the burning city. Lot fled after the angels rescued him, and he lived in the mountains the rest of his life. So Abraham never knew God had answered his prayer."

Adam's blue eyes bounced from the Bible to me.

My tears spilled over as I remembered Mom's journal, and Adam sponged my cheek with a tissue. "Just like Mom never knew. About. . . about me. That I'd be okay, and I'd find her God."

Adam's eyelids fluttered closed, and he placed his cool palm on my forehead, brushing back my bangs. "But she trusted God anyway, just like Abraham did. Even if she never got to see it."

Adam put the Bible down and carefully wrapped his arms around me. I pressed his face to mine—soaking up the supple warmth of his skin, rough with a hint of stubble, pulsing with life. He kissed my cheek, his lips soft and tender. I turned my face toward him, basking in the sensation of his breath on my skin.

"Your mom made her peace with death." He pulled away to look me in the eyes. "The police opened her last two letters for evidence, and they let Becky and me take a look." His eyes reddened with fresh tears. "Wait 'til you read them. They're beautiful. She'd lost all her fear." He sniffled. "And she left you the lyrics."

"Lyrics for what?"

"That bluegrass song she liked." He dug around in the bedside table and held out a paper for me. "It's an old one. 'Angel Band,' it's called. It's about heaven."

Adam rubbed his nose, which had reddened with tears. "It's like. . . she knew her time was coming, Shiloh. I don't know how, but she did.

And she wanted you to know she'd be okay."

I buried my face against Adam's chest then doubled over in a groan.

"What's wrong? What happened?" He jerked his hand off my arm, checking the IV tube.

I wheezed, trying to get my breath. I squeezed my eyes closed and waited for the swelling pains to subside. This felt far worse than anything I'd experienced in the cow pasture. I leaned back against the pillows, scrunching up my knees.

"Breathe." He massaged my shoulder. "That's it."

I slowly relaxed my legs. "So what happened to. . . ?" I hesitated to say "Odysseus" again.

"Oh, Shiloh." Adam let out a long sigh, resting his head against my hand. "There's so much to tell."

"He's not still out there, is he?" I scrambled to sit up.

"No, no." Adam gently pushed me back. "You've been in surgery and under some heavy drugs for about a day and a half, so we've had a chance to piece things together a bit. The police got Ray right away. He hit a tree. He was driving like a maniac, apparently, and bleeding from a pretty deep cut on his leg."

I closed my eyes and let the news sink in. "And you—what happened? I thought you were. . .well, dead." I winced as the images sifted back.

"We're still not entirely sure what happened. Seems like he'd punctured my tire to get me to pull over and then hit me with a crowbar or something. It put me out, and apparently he chloroformed me, too—with some pretty strong stuff. I was out from sometime Friday night until Saturday morning."

"But the note on your front door! The text you sent!"

"The note *he* left. The text *he* sent. He took my cell phone."

I clung to the rails on the sides of the bed, feeling dizzy. "What about Amanda? Did she really rob the bank with Jim Bob Townshend and get away with it?"

"Now that I can't help you with—although Shane thinks it's really true."

"Shane Pendergrass?" I drew back. "You mean he had nothing to do with this?"

"Nope. Apparently he really did eat some bad barbecue. He'd checked in at the minor emergency clinic when Ray came to your house, and he didn't go back on duty until the next morning. It's all documented."

"Whoa." I exhaled. "So he thinks Amanda really did rob the bank."

"When he heard Ray's cockeyed story, yeah. The bank cameras from twelve years ago show a single intruder, small enough to be a woman, and somebody about Jim Bob's build covering her. It seems like she planned her own disappearance first to throw off suspicion. The police are looking for them both. Jim Bob'll probably be easier to catch though, since he slips back in town sometimes and supposedly lives close by."

"So he and Amanda broke up after the robbery?"

"Seems like it—if they were together at all. They might have just been old pals. She was engaged to Ray at the time, so the whole thing's a little foggy. She and Jim Bob probably divided the money and went their separate ways, although nobody knows the details. She's been gone for years."

I rested a hand on my forehead. "Then that Dean guy at Rask was innocent after all."

"Oh no. He recently bought a half-million-dollar home on a part-time income, under a false name, and police are investigating. They think Jim Bob sent him money."

"Stolen money." I blew out my breath. "Seems like Jim Bob should've sent his dad some, from the looks of that cabin." I twitched a leg where pinkish blisters had formed. "I think I got poison ivy from his woods, too."

"Well, maybe his dad didn't want a new cabin. Some people are happy with what they've got, you know? Money can't solve everything."

I squeezed Adam's hand, thinking of our budget wedding and my crazy, gorgeous table-runner dress. Still attempting to process all the details about the case. "So I'll have to go to trial again—after I deal with the skinhead in October."

"What's once more? Tell them to take a number."

"Very funny." I watched clear liquid drip into the IV tube, which reminded me of Jerry's leaky sink. "So Jerry didn't do it." A sob rose in my throat. "But he lied, Adam! He said he didn't know Amanda Cummings. She worked at his restaurant."

"She worked there three weeks. Jerry went to Missouri with his mom when she got sick. His old business partner, Dimitri, hired Amanda. Jerry never met her."

"But. . .what about all the love notes at his desk? Those poems in red ink?"

Adam lowered his voice and smirked. "Becky found this little tidbit: he's got a girlfriend."

"What?" I yelped.

"Yep. Kate Townshend has a niece about his age who's visiting for the summer from Japan. He sends her flowers all the time, and who knows? Maybe they'll get married." Adam lifted a finger to his lips. "But it's a secret. And the red ink? Jerry's color blind. He doesn't know what color pen he grabs."

"The rose at the restaurant!"

"Stella. She thought the chrysanthemums were too funereal. She came by the restaurant before we arrived, remember? Trinity said so."

My mouth opened. "*Paradise Lost.* I saw it, Adam."

"Well." He raised his palms. "Sometimes things are just a coincidence. Like you sharing the same birthday with Amanda."

I started to laugh and coughed, pain shooting through my stomach. "Can't they put more painkiller in there?" I moaned, doubling over.

The pain mounted so intensely I started to heave, and Adam quickly handed me the bedpan and called the nurse. I tried not to look at him as she came in, checking my tubes and monitors and talking cheerfully. She whisked the bedpan away and put a fresh drip in the IV.

I just threw up in front of my fiancé. Instead of being smart, pulled together, and confident, I was sponging my face and mouth with tissues and wearing a ridiculous hospital gown big enough to fit Liv the Llama.

Adam didn't laugh. He smoothed my bangs to the side, looking at me the way he did in January after sledding, when my hair looked like a tornado had sped through it.

"You're beautiful," he'd said for the first time, making a shudder of electricity pass through my stomach.

And now he was saying it again.

I couldn't laugh, so I cried instead. Which hurt almost as much as laughing, but required tissues.

When I looked up at Adam Carter, simple Southern landscaper-turned-UPS-driver from Virginia, I couldn't imagine a better match for me. Even if we were as different as grits and Japanese *gobo* root.

"So we're not moving to the Harrisonburg apartment, I guess," I said, shifting into a more comfortable position. "Now that the house isn't selling."

"I guess not." Adam studied me a minute. "I've been thinking. What if we just. . .well, move in there?"

"Mom's house?" My eyes bugged.

"*Your* house. And then, once we're married, *our* house. If you want."

I fell speechless, imagining Adam's work jackets in my closet. His UPS uniform and clipboards piled on the sofa, right next to my reporter's notebooks and trendy bracelets. His tennis shoes and my Japanese house slippers strewn among Christie's chew toys.

"I'll commute to college, and you can keep your job." Adam finished drying my face and tossed the tissue in the trash can. "And I guess you—we, actually—will both be stuck in Staunton a while longer."

I looked up, cringing. "You mean we're doomed to neighbors who throw horseshoes and spit in cups and play Hank Williams Jr. until two in the morning?"

"Yep. Looks like it. And I drive a pickup, so. . ." He raised his palms, and his mouth quirked a wry smile.

"Great. You'll fit right in." I grinned and turned my eyes to the ceiling.

Staunton, Virginia. My new home sweet home. Who'd have guessed?

Adam straightened my blankets, smoothing them along the edges. "And if you need to push the wedding date back, we will," he said gently. "I just want you to get better. You can take your time."

"You mean. . .we'll still have a wedding?"

"Of course we will. It'll be great. Although we'll probably have to cut our honeymoon with all these medical bills." He stroked his fingers across my cheek as if searching for words. "Did you know you called me, Shiloh?"

"Called you what?"

"No, on your cell phone. That day with Ray."

"I called Pizza Hut."

"In the cow pasture. You called me. Ray apparently tossed my cell phone, too, when he dumped me out of the car. I found it in the folds of the blanket."

He looked pained, caressing my fingers. "I came to when I heard it ringing, and when you mentioned the llama, I figured out where you were. I know the guy who bought Fred Brewer's llama—the only one around here. I used to trim his trees."

I sat up on one elbow. "Does he by any chance have a tractor?"

"That was me." Adam smoothed my cheek. "The guy who owns the neighboring farm is hard of hearing, so I begged him to take a shortcut through the field on his tractor. He could see it was an emergency, I guess. I had blood all over me." He slid his hand down my arm and clasped it. "And so did you. You're lucky to be alive. I promise you that."

I glanced down at the bandages. "How bad is it?"

Adam didn't speak for a while. "It was touch-and-go for a while. None of us knew for sure if. . ."

I pressed his hand, and he swallowed hard. "The bullet missed your vital organs. The doc says you look good, and so long as you heal with no infection, you're in the clear. She'll see you soon."

Somewhere down the corridor music sparkled from a TV, notes lilting and rising, and I remembered. In one powerful swell.

"Do not be afraid. I bring you good news that will cause great joy for all the people. Today in the town of David a Savior has been born to you; he is the Messiah, the Lord."

Cut carnations quivered in a vase on the table. Like Ellen Amelia Jacobs, gracefully saying yes.

Adam was holding a cup of water to my lips when his cell phone rang. "It's Becky," he whispered. "Do you mind company?"

"Tell her to git her tail in here!" I sniffled in as redneck an accent as I could manage. "And bring me something to eat!"

Adam tucked the phone under his chin. "You're hungry? I'll get the nurse. Anything special you want?"

I thought through my list of exotic Japanese dishes, none of which would be available at Augusta County Medical Center. And for probably the first time in my life, none sounded particularly palatable.

I needed something bland. Something warm and slightly salty, mushy, even, and a little. . .

"Grits!" I cried. "Ask if they have any grits!"

Adam stared at me. "You, my dear Yankee," he finally said, Tim-style, hands on his hips, "have been in Virginia entirely too long."

Before I could say another word, I heard a familiar voice crabbing about the "stupid hospital in the middle of Podunk nowhere."

"Where did you put her? Purgatory?" she snapped as she stormed down the hall. "Oh. Here it is. For the love of mercy. . ."

She barged in without knocking, snatching off her sunglasses.

"Kyoko?" Adam and I both looked up.

"Of all the stupid, idiotic, boneheaded things to do! Why on earth did you go and get shot?" She carried gobs of stuff—flowers, bags, who knows what. The flowers, orange lilies, quivered as she shouted.

"And in a cow pasture, too," I added when I found my voice. "Nice touch, huh?"

Kyoko hadn't even heard me. She was too busy waving her arms around. "Do you have any idea how long it takes to get here with all those dumb flight delays? I've been on standby for eighteen hours!"

She glared, dark makeup smeared. "You're impossible, Ro! I don't know why I stay friends with you! If you're not getting fired and jumped by rednecks and stalked by lunatics and marrying farmers, you're. . .you're. . ."

She wheeled on Adam, who put his hands up, and she jabbed her finger at him. "You, buster, better know what you're getting into!"

And Kyoko Morikoshi burst into tears, throwing all her stuff in a big heap on the floor.

Chapter 39

Becky's eyes were already running, and I hadn't even put on my dress yet. "Pull yourself together," I snapped, shoving more tissues at her while she helped me step into the dress. I stuck my arms in and turned for her to button up the back.

"I'm together," Becky sniffled. She passed me to Kyoko to expertly tie the red silk obi while Trinity Jackson dabbed more concealer under my eyes.

"What happened to you? Late night?" Trinity teased, tapping on some powder.

"Leaving flowers outside Odysseus's house," I retorted, closing my eyes while she turned my face and brushed on mascara.

"That ain't funny." Becky smacked me, digging for more tissues.

"Hear, hear," said Kyoko, pulling the obi a little too roughly. I yelped, clutching my abdomen.

"Sorry, Ro!" Kyoko gasped, instantly contrite. "You okay?"

Her eyeliner looked significantly lighter today, less vampire-like, and she'd even taken out her eyebrow ring. I should be nice. "Now that you all are here, I'm fine." I shook my finger at Becky. "And that was two words. Not *y'all*."

"I heard ya, Yankee. Now put yer head back. An' hold still." Becky was always crabby when she morphed into boss mode, and the dresses Ashley hadn't sent—hadn't bought, even—exacerbated things.

Becky started pinning up my hair. "Anyway, I'm real proud of all of ya who did show up," she said diplomatically. "Trinity saved the day, and y'all look mighty fine."

She curtsied, and Trinity curtsied back: both with hair up.

Sandals. Clad in pink flowered cotton yukata robes with tiny white and lavender details, delicately crossed at the chest. Bright red obi sashes tied around the waist—all courtesy of Faye Sprouse's sewing skills and Kyoko's friend Mrs. Oyama.

Becky giggled. "We do look kinda like them *geishas*, though."

"Geisha?" Kyoko harrumphed. "Not unless you want Trinity to paint your face white and hang stuff in your hair."

I was just glad the yukata covered Kyoko's tattoos.

"You wanted an Asian wedding," grinned Trinity, clicking the compact shut. "And you got it."

She looked every inch a model: her curly hair tastefully pulled back with a flower. Long, slim, brown arms gracefully reached for her makeup kit through long, flowing sleeves.

Meg West—sporting a tie-dyed tunic over fraying linen bell-bottoms—was a riot taking photos. Teetering sideways on folding chairs. Lying on the floor, belly up, legs pitched like an awkward yoga position. Climbing up scaffolding in a nearby construction site as we hurried to the church.

Church. Sanctuary. Wedding. My lipstick felt dry, and I checked the mirror. "Chopstick favors done?" I asked, jitters forming in my stomach.

"Check."

My chiggers itched, and I scratched at my leg until Becky smacked me. "All the lanterns hung?"

"Thank me later." Kyoko blew on her nails.

"How about the reception hall? Does it look nice?"

"Done. Beulah's hangin' the last a them lanterns, and the tables look real pretty."

My hands fluttered to my forehead. "Did we get enough *panko* bread crumbs to finish the *tempura*, or. . ."

"Ro!" Kyoko snapped her fingers. "Relax! Everything's fine."

"I still need something for people to throw when we go out of the church," I murmured, barely hearing her.

"Your half sister?" Kyoko glared.

"Panko?" I bit back a giggle.

"Cain't be rice," said Becky ominously, "on account a the birds."

"Actually, Adam says the whole rice thing is just an urban myth—like cow tipping. Birds eat rice from fields all the time. It's a grain." I shrugged. "Figures. He knows all about the birds."

"And the bees?" Kyoko nudged me. "After all, he did extend your honeymoon to about two weeks. Thanks to whoever put all that money in your account." She put up her hands. "And it wasn't me. So quit asking."

"I been nosin' around, too, tryin' to find out, but I ain't found out nothin'. Wasn't Jerry or Stella or anybody we know. I talked to the bank teller myself, and none of 'em match the description." Becky cocked an eyebrow. "Anyhow. I'm still worried about them birds. They ain't gonna explode er nothin' if we throw rice?"

"Nope. But I'm not using rice because it stings. So says Faye."

Kyoko's face hardened in disappointment, probably at the lack of bird explosions or opportunities to sting people. "Well, what else is there?"

"Birdseed?" Trinity suggested. "Bubbles?"

"Grits!" Kyoko cried. "We can all throw grits!"

We all fell silent, in various stages of shock or revulsion. Or so I thought. Until Becky spoke up, her voice tentative. "Well, ya know, it would look kinda like snow."

"It really does." Trinity nodded. "My little brother and I used to make snowstorms in our bowls with the dry stuff. Hey, do you know you can get fifty-pound bags now?"

"Where?" asked Becky.

"Costco."

"No kiddin'." She leaned back and crossed her arms over her chest. "Quaker?"

"Of course. They're really good. Grandma makes the best grits casserole you've ever tasted with them. In fact—"

"Hey!" Kyoko waved a hand violently in front of their faces, scowling. "The grits things was a joke, okay?" she barked. "I've got the throwing stuff covered."

"No shuriken." I raised my eyebrows in warning.

"Ha. You're lucky this time." Kyoko dug in a corner and unearthed a big basket piled high with rose petals in various yukata shades—pinks, whites, lavenders, and heavy on the reds. "Courtesy of your mom. And some of Stella's peonies to fill in."

"Mom's roses?" I fingered the petals, picturing my beautiful, simple bouquet: A fat white ball of Kobe roses, all edged with perfect pale pink. Tied with a red ribbon.

"The same. Just don't look at your rose bushes when you get home. They're kind of bare."

Jennifer Rogers Spinola

—⁂—

By the time Faye fluffed the veil just under my fashionably messy updo—à la Tokyo, a red flower stuck on one side—I heard the piano music change.

"Well, doll," said Faye, tears in her eyes and amethyst earrings I'd given her last year sparkling. "It's show time."

The nursery stood empty. Becky, Kyoko, and Trinity huddled at the double sanctuary doors, giggling with Rick and Todd Carter and Tim in tuxedos. Everyone fragrant and nervous.

"You're walking down the aisle just before Beulah," I said, clutching Faye's arm. "Adopted mothers of the bride. And then you'll sit with the family."

I took the perfumed bouquet of roses, cut, to remind me why I was on this earth: *As long as you both shall live.*

I heard Meg's camera clicking somewhere nearby, but I didn't see a thing. Didn't feel a thing.

"Ready, hot stuff?" Faye wiped her eyes and smiled, holding the door open while Meg adjusted my obi and snapped more pictures.

I took a deep, shaky breath. "Ready, Faye," I smiled back. "Like Becky says, Git 'er done!"

—⁂—

The doors opened. Aisle scattered with petals. A forest of potted dogwood trees and young maples from Adam's woods clustered at the front of the church and around the arch, all laced with white lights and little glowing Japanese lanterns. Fresh with leaves. Alive. Radiant. Pots of indigo grape hyacinths, dizzingly honey-sweet in their heady perfume, formed a blue-purple sea of spiked bells that wound through the trees.

Courtesy of Rask Florist, I heard. Something like five hundred grape hyacinth bulbs.

The cross in stained glass glowed overhead, faint sunlight shining through in colored slants. And I spotted Adam's smile in the distance, past the rows of faces.

I felt a wave of panic come over me, thinking of Kyoko's cracks about trailer parks and pork rinds. My beloved Japan, thousands of miles away, and nothing but a country house in a redneck neighborhood waiting for me in Staunton.

Except one thing.

I steadied my eyes on Adam. The scar on his forehead was healing,

stitches taken out. He looked crisp and clean in a tuxedo, more stylish
than I'd ever seen him—and at the same time wonderfully familiar. So
simple I could almost have overlooked him.

And yet by some miracle I hadn't.

"Do not be afraid!" I heard the verses whisper through my mind
as I forced my feet ahead. *"I bring you good news that will cause great
joy. . ."*

My nervous breath steadied. His hand in mine. The pastor's words,
something about Adam loving me like Christ loved the church, who
gave Himself up for her. Flickering candles. The scent of roses.

Adam and I climbed the carpeted steps together, under the arch
made of fresh blooms and tangled white lights, and I felt him slip a
silver ring on my finger.

His lips murmured, "I do."

And mine, softer but just as sure. "I do."

"I now pronounce you man and wife." Words that jolted like
electricity.

Man and wife.

Bone of my bone, and flesh of my flesh.

As long as we both shall live.

"You may kiss the bride."

For one instant I panicked, seeing the crowd, but Adam's hand
steadied me. "Relax," he whispered, eyes sparkling with love and joy.
"It's me."

And he kissed me on the cheek.

Wait. *On the cheek?!*

Then he leaned closer. His lips found mine, there among the
flicker of fresh leaves and glowing lanterns. A sweet breath of indigo
grape hyacinth whispering around us as he drew me closer.

———

I couldn't believe how beautiful everything was. How people packed
the sanctuary. The lanterns. The dainty little dishes of mochi and
Japanese sweets Kyoko displayed on a side table. Stella's show-stopping
cherry blossom cake, topped with Mom's pink rose petals.

Nor could I believe the surprise sushi platter Jerry created for
the occasion, and probably a good-bye gift before The Green Tree
folded: crayfish and venison sushi (cooked, of course). *Temaki* (hand
rolls) with country ham, sweet potato, Vidalia onion, and okra. Hot
sushi rolls breaded with cornbread. String beans instead of *edamame*

steamed soybeans. And a dark brown dipping sauce I was pretty sure he'd spiked with Jack Daniel's.

It was beyond ingenious: it was southern-fried sushi.

I laughed until my stitches hurt, and Adam finally made me leave the tray with Meg, who alternately snapped pictures and wiped her eyes from mirth.

"Hey, who did this?"

I looked up from the platter at Wayne Grabowsky, one of my former reporter cohorts at the *New York Post*—now turned editor. The shirt collar under his black Italian suit hung lazily open.

"Wayne?" I sucked in a gasp of astonishment. "You came? To my wedding?"

"Sure we did." Gina Watkins, my old sidekick back at the *Post*, grinned over his shoulder in a devastating pale blue silk Versace. "We got your invitation, and I talked him into it. We're doing a story in Alexandria anyway. It's not that far."

"Gina." I shook my head, the years flashing past me like bullet trains. "I haven't seen you in what, seven years? Eight?"

"About that, yeah. Wayne and I are both at the *Times* now. Wayne does entertainment—mainly food—and I'm stuck with the society pages. It's not so bad." Her collagen-enhanced cheekbones grinned back, framed by pearl dangle earrings.

"Wait a second. Food? You do restaurant reviews?" My head swiveled to Wayne.

"I do. And hey, you know what? We had the most amazing lunch today. A little hole-in-the-wall place downtown." Wayne tapped a finger on his chin, his eyes gleaming. "Gorgeous blue-cheese fig tapas, and the best spicy peanut noodles I've ever had—with sweet potato, turkey, and serrano chilies. Good ethics, too—organic and heavy on local produce. Southern fusion, no?" He closed his eyes. "I could swear I tasted a hint of maple in the sauce, and maybe balsamic vinegar. And for dessert: green tea panna cotta with blackberry reduction. Perfect."

"Oh, yeah, yeah!" Gina's silvery eye shadow shimmered. "I loved that blue-cheese grits soufflé thing! I'm a vegetarian now, so farmer fare is slim pickings." She raised a manicured hand. "The place was fabulous! The paint, the potted herbs, everything. You'd never know you were in. . . Where are we, again?"

"What's the name of the restaurant?" Wayne wrinkled his brow. "The Green something?"

"The Green Tree," I replied. My heart pounded.

"I'm thinking about doing a write-up." He squinted at Jerry's sushi platter. "But this tray is too good to pass up. You got your camera, honey?"

Gina crouched and clicked, pausing only to giggle into her bare shoulder. "Too funny. Tracy'll love it. Genius!"

And then I saw it—the slight flutter of her thickly mascara-ed eyelashes as she glimpsed Jerry's business card on the corner of the tray. "The Green Tree?" She snatched up the card. "Is this the same place?"

"You've gotta be kidding." Wayne chuckled, reaching for his cell phone. "Let me call Tracy and see if she'll let us run a two-page spread. A big one—lots of color. 'Veggie Heaven in the Valley,' we'll call it. Four-and-a-half stars, don't you think? Five if they'd offered ceviche."

"I think Jerry can arrange ceviche." I winked. "With a spicy kimchi cabbage base and a garnish of Virginia red onions, peaches, and cilantro."

"My word. I love kimchi." He breathed out a sigh. "The place'll be overrun with foodies from the North, you hear? Carpetbaggers galore. Mark my words." And Wayne tapped in Tracy's phone number, his yacht-tanned face breaking into a grin.

"Wait a second. Shiloh?" he frowned at his phone. "Is this you?"

"Sorry?" I turned back over my shoulder.

"Somebody just sent me a picture of a girl that looks exactly like you—and. . .a cow?"

"Excuse me a minute." I gave a too-white smile. "There's someone in this room I need to throttle."

—⁓—

"It was you," I whispered in Clarence's ear over the laughter.

"Who, Odysseus?" The corners of his mouth turned up. Green plaid bow tie. And it even looked half decent with his tweed suit.

"No. The little no-name guy in Verona who won the lottery." I poked him in the shoulder. "You took the article out of *The Leader* archives, but I found it anyway. And you put all that money in my account." I lowered my voice to a whisper. "The bank teller gave you away by describing your bow tie."

Clarence glanced around and quickly lifted his finger to his lips. Winked at me.

And I winked back.

—⁓—

And, somewhere between the Southern pineapple cheese ball and Kyoko's shrimp tempura, after Stella caught the bouquet, it was time

Jennifer Rogers Spinola

for Cinderella to flee. And everyone else as well, after decorating Adam's truck with shaving cream and Silly String.

I was fixing my veil for the ride when someone tapped me on the shoulder. "Shiloh."

I lifted my head, and every single word in my brain fled. I just stood there, gulping air. And then finally shut my jaw.

"Dad?" I managed, frozen like a raccoon in the headlights.

He stuck his hands awkwardly in his pockets and shifted uncomfortably. Cleared his throat. And just stood there. "Um. . .hey."

"Hey."

I let the corner of my veil drop. Speechless. And felt my lips curve into a smile at our ridiculous attempts at communication. Just like. . . well, old times.

"Tanzania's sorry she couldn't be here." He gestured clumsily, scratching the back of his neck and fidgeting with the keys in his pocket. "But. . .yeah."

He looked so old now, compared to the young, smooth face I knew from years ago. Flashing eyes that once sparked with anger, mouth that belted out songs and shouts. Head turned away from me as he left, suitcase in hand.

Now those lips wore parentheses of lines from frowns and smiles, and gray streaked his thick, dark hair. He'd softened, and the lines around his eyes made him seem gentler somehow. We stood nearly eye to eye; he was not as tall as I remembered.

Two other kids besides Ashley and I called him "Dad." Begged him to watch their softball games. Laughed with him over dinner.

I was no longer the youngest sibling; I was the second of four. The thought boggled me, made my throat go dry.

"You came," I finally managed, finding my voice.

"Well, he asked if he could marry you, and nobody's ever. . . I mean. . . Shiloh, I. . ."

He blinked faster, and I felt my throat closing up. Tears running over, spilling onto the makeup Trinity had applied so perfectly. I looked away in embarrassment—crying over a dad whose face and name I barely knew.

I groped around for a tissue, and one pressed itself into my hand. I looked up into Adam's face, heavy with emotion.

"Mr. Jacobs." He extended a hand and shook Dad's. And he passed the other arm around me, his warm fingers brushing the bare skin of

316

my shoulder. I sponged my eyes, trying not to smear my mascara.

The jingling of Dad's pockets stopped. "Shiloh, I wasn't. . .you know. Around much," he said, voice husky.

I wiped my nose and mumbled something, but Dad's voice—sharp, urgent, almost harsh—stopped me. "No. Listen. You deserved. . ."

He took a heavy breath, catching with emotion, and gently stroked the curve of my cheek. "You're so beautiful. You look like your mom when you—" He broke off, turning away. "I should have been there. For you."

Yeah, well, you weren't.

But instead of spouting all the hateful things I'd once wanted to, instead I saw myself in slow motion, wrapping my arms around my father's neck. And he awkwardly patted my back.

Around us people laughed, talked. Candles flickered. Glass and crystal sparkled and plates clinked. But for me I noticed only the spicy, unfamiliar scent of Dad's cologne, like a stranger's, and my cheek pressed against his hair.

I knew once Dad let me go, he would walk away and check stock updates on his cell phone, too emotional to talk. He would wave good-bye at the door as Adam and I sped away, and the familiar old silence would return.

A call here and there, both of us trying to recover two missing decades, long after our lives had forked. Years we could never bring back, no matter how hard we tried. Besides, what could he promise me now anyway? To chat like best friends? To gush and visit and fill the house with our laughter?

No. We both knew better than that.

But when I missed him, when I wondered what it felt like to have a father who loved me, I would remember this moment.

"I'm sorry," he whispered, raising his head.

I patted his shoulder as he pulled away. "I know."

Not *I forgive you*, although I did. Not *I love you*, although in some measure I did, too.

Just an acknowledgment of what I knew as truth, and what I hoped could someday—by some miracle—be a little something more.

Dad stepped back and wiped his face. He straightened his shoulders and reached for Adam's hand. Squeezed it hard. "Take care of her, my man." He affected a light tone.

"Don't worry." Adam smiled down at me, hand circling protectively around my bandaged waist. "I'm glad you came, too. I wanted to meet you."

Dad patted my head, trying awkwardly not to mess up my hair. He seemed like he wanted to say more, but did not. And he disappeared into the crowd.

—∞—

It took a trip to the bathroom to recover my nerves, running a dry tissue under my eyes and brushing on fresh mascara. My reflection in the mirror glowed back, pink-cheeked, the veil falling over my bare arms as I dried my hands.

Adam was waiting for me outside the bathroom door.

He kissed my forehead, brushing back my wayward strands of hair. "You okay?"

"Sure." I squeezed his hand and let out a pent-up breath. "You know something? Ashley wired the bridesmaids' dress money to Becky's account. And she sent us tickets to Japan." My voice wobbled as I remembered Japanese crows. The ringing hum of Tokyo cicadas. "Wade's working at Delta now, so he gets some freebies. They were going to use them for a vacation."

Adam's face transformed from surprise to joy. "Well, wonders never cease. Ashley's not all bad then."

"Not entirely. Let's say. . .three-fourths."

"Four-fifths. Maybe a little more."

I laughed. "Ray Floyd wasn't the only one with identity mix-ups, huh? Ashley did surprise me, I have to admit. And so did Dad."

We were almost to the door, tingling with excitement, when Adam suddenly turned to me in the empty hall. "You never told me your middle name," he said. "Remember, Shiloh. No secrets."

No wonder he wanted to know, after the fiasco with Ray and Amanda and their middle names.

I faced him, considering. "Will you make me another bonsai?"

Adam crossed his arms, a smile at the corner of his lips. "Deal."

"All right." I let out my breath. "Papillon, okay?"

His eyes sparkled. "French for 'butterfly.' I like it. It's perfect for you." He took my hand, and I could hear everyone rushing around outside to meet us. Distant footsteps and laughter echoed through the hallway. And when I looked up, I saw Adam's lips. Warm and full, just like when he kissed me in front of the church. Pressing gently against mine and drawing me in for more.

"Not so fast." I pulled him back, jerking my gaze reluctantly from his lips to his eyes. "You haven't told me your middle name. Remember? No secrets."

A look of pure fear crossed his face. "It. . .it starts with a *J*."

"I know. Bible name?"

He nodded miserably.

"I thought so. Jehoshaphat? Jabez?" I pursed my lips. "Jezebel?"

"Shiloh!" He looked annoyed. "Jezebel's the evil queen who got eaten by dogs."

"Well, tell me then." I tapped my slippered foot impatiently.

"Okay." Adam took a breath. "Jedidiah."

"What? You're kidding!" I doubled over in laughter despite my tender abdomen.

"Come on, Shiloh!" he ordered, face flushing. "No more secrets, and no weird middle names for our children. I promise."

"Deal!" I took his hand. Just before he leaned down and kissed me. *Really* kissed me. Long enough, suffice it to say, that people outside began to murmur about where we were.

And then he pulled me, laughing, toward the bright double doors.

About the Author

Jennifer Rogers Spinola, Virginia/South Carolina native and graduate of Gardner-Webb University in North Carolina, now lives in South Dakota with her husband, Athos, and their son, Ethan, after nearly eight years spent in the capital city of Brasilia, Brazil. Jennifer and Athos met while she was serving as a missionary in Sapporo, Japan. Find out more about Jenny at www.jenniferrogersspinola.com.